MW01322421

Clyde

David Helwig

B&B
Bunim & Bannigan, Ltd.
New York & Charlottetown
www.bunimandbannigan.com

Manufactured in the United States
Design by Matthew MacKay

Helwig, David, 1938 –
Clyde
Summary: a successful Canadian investor and political consultant, very much representative of the post WWII generation, threatened by betrayal by his oldest friend, reviews his life.

Library of Congress Control Number 2013940038
ISBN-13: 978-1-933480-36-7 (trade hardcover)

First edition 2013

Bunim & Bannigan, Ltd.
30 Jericho Executive Plaza, Suite 500 W, Jericho, NY 11753
P.O. Box 636, Charlottetown, PE., C1A 7L3, Canada

www.bunimandbannigan.com

Also by David Helwig

Poetry

Figures in a Landscape
The Sign of the Gunman
The Best Name of Silence
Atlantic Crossings
A Book of the Hours
The Rain Falls Like Rain
Catchpenny Poems
The Hundred Old Names
The Beloved
A Random Gospel
The Year One
This Human Day
Telling Stories
The Sway of Otherwise
Seawrack

Non-Fiction

A Book about Billie
The Child of Someone
Living Here
The Names of Things

Translations

Last Stories of Anton Chekhov
About Love

Fiction

The Streets of Summer
The Day Before Tomorrow
The Glass Knight
Jennifer
The King's Evil
A Sound Like Laughter
It Is Always Summer
A Postcard from Rome
The Only Son
The Bishop
Old Wars
Of Desire
Blueberry Cliffs
Just Say the Words
Close to the Fire
The Time of Her Life
The Stand-In
Duet
Saltsea
Coming Through
Smuggling Donkeys
Mystery Stories
Killing McGee
Simon Says

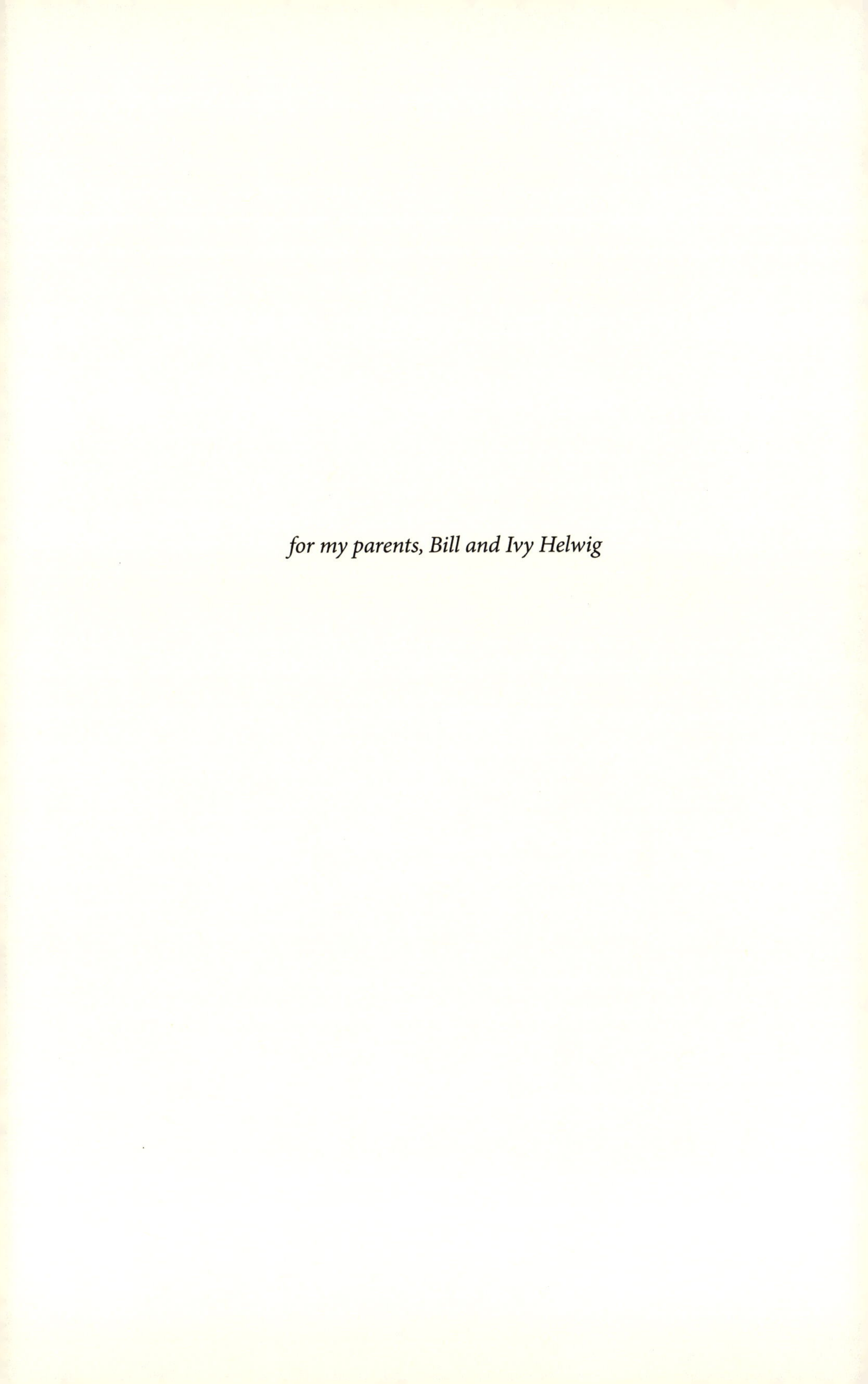

for my parents, Bill and Ivy Helwig

Clyde

David Helwig

1 | Danny

So Danny was dead. No more to watch the slight balding figure limp through the rooms of that little house in Ottawa's Lower Town, a pink flamingo on the front lawn, in winter the top of the plastic head showing above the snow. The note Danny had left him was folded up in his briefcase in the back seat of the car.

This morning, when Clyde arrived at work and found a message on his office answering machine, he thought he understood what it was about, and he set off for Danny's house ready for an argument. As he drove through downtown Ottawa, along Wellington Street past the Parliament Buildings, he noticed a lineup of limousines. Some foreign politician paying a formal visit to the prime minister? If so it was Clyde's business to know about it. He'd check later. The traffic was heavy, but he found a parking place. He entered the silent house, moved down the hall, found Danny in the living room, grey and still, beside him a scribbled sheet.

How it ended: *You could of fixed it Clyde, what we said about the house. But you wouldn't. I said what I'd do – I wrote down every single thing she told me and sent it to that Tom McKay. You should of fixed it about the house.*

"Oh Danny," he said, "you are such a pain in the ass."

Danny lay silent on the leather recliner, a blanket pulled up over him, everything withdrawn from the thin, sick face, the skin greyed and slack, a plastic container of pills and a bottle of whisky beside the chair. Pills, whisky, sleep. Clyde surprised himself, the tears in his eyes as he looked at the slight body, the bald head fallen to one side, the mouth slightly open.

Clyde had made the necessary phone calls, the required decisions, and now he was driving away from Danny's house, past the Parliament buildings, all the formal chambers and small rooms where men and women attended to the business of the country. Past the offices of the newspaper that published Tom McKay's column. Running away: the only thing to do. He would spend a day or so at his cabin in the woods, his place of escape. Stare at himself in the little shaving mirror and decide what came next.

Near Carleton Place he turned off the highway. Passing through a small town he stopped to get gas, have some lunch. Across the road from the restaurant stood a memorial built after the First World War. Wreaths, shiny and new, placed there on November 11, a few days before. When he was twelve years old Clyde attended a Remembrance Day service in the hope that he might evoke the presence of his vanished father. Wreaths, prayers, a hymn, the trumpeter played The Last Post. No matter how he had tried, Clyde could not find the man who had joined the army when Clyde was a year and a half old. His father had died in 1942 in the Dieppe raid.

Maybe his father had been a hero. Sergeant Clifford Bryanton, age twenty-five, his body torn by machine gun fire. Clyde had dreamed about his father in battle and once, from just beyond a room where Clyde was sitting alone, he'd heard a man's voice speak his name. Clyde half-believed that it was his father's voice reaching out to him. When he looked through the doorway, there was, of course, no-one. Lacking a father, Clyde had let other men lead him through life: Francis, the Senator, even Danny in those early days after they'd first moved to the town that was to be their new home.

Clyde was ten years old when they met. He had wakened that spring morning in 1948 on a folding cot in the bare basement of his Uncle Bob's house in the east end of Toronto. His mother was calling down to him that it was time to get up. As he lay there he thought of the empty apartment just off Queen Street. No longer their home. Yesterday a moving truck had loaded up their furniture, left the rooms bare. Today his uncle Bob was to drive them from Toronto to Brockton, the historic town where his mother was going to work for Palmer Eustes, her second cousin, who had a law office there. Clyde ate a bowl a cereal, and they set off, Bob's prewar Chev taking them down to the shore of Lake Ontario then west for an hour on the Queen Elizabeth Way, crossing over the Burlington bridge and turning east along the south side of the lake. In his pocket Clyde had a little map his mother had drawn to show him where they were going. As they drove over the Burlington bridge, his uncle pointed out the steel plants across Hamilton harbour. When they reached the Welland Canal they had to wait in a line of cars at the lift bridge for a freighter to pass through on its way to Lake Erie and the upper lakes. They drove past orchards, cherry trees blossoming. It was a new world.

In their new house on a quiet side street of the small town of Brockton, under a canopy of leaves, they waited for the moving van. Finally it arrived, the two movers setting down the furniture where Clyde's mother told them. Soon they were gone, and then his Uncle Bob said goodbye, and only a few minutes after that, Danny O'Connell knocked on the door, a skinny kid with squinty eyes, smiling, talking too much, calling Clyde's mother Missus and offering to help, reporting that he lived around the corner in the little house above the creek, and how there was no water in the creek except for a month in the spring. Oh that's just Danny, the next door neighbour said, when she dropped in and his mother mentioned their visitor. He'll be living with you if you let him. Danny was four years older than Clyde, and that first summer Clyde's mother paid Danny a little money to be around the house when she was at work. Clyde thought maybe at ten he was old enough to look after himself, and the next summer he insisted, but that first year in Brockton he followed Danny around, went to the patch of woods just outside the little town where the Two Mile creek met the great lake, and Danny told him that in the spring they'd go there with his brother and spear suckers. Some days they stood around outside the drugstore or went to the beach to swim. Danny's bathing suit was a hand-me-down from his brother and it was too big for him. Harold Ratner shouted at him one day, "Hey Danny, your dick's hanging out," and it was. Another day at the beach, Harold used a stick to pick up one of the shimmering white French safes that floated in the water. He waved it at Danny. "Hey Danny, want to suck on this?" Other days Clyde and Danny hung around in the backyard reading Clyde's comic books. Next door, Mrs Benning would be busy in her rose garden. Sometimes in the evening you could smell the sweetness of the blooms.

Now and then they went to Danny's house, if his father wasn't drinking that day. Even when he was sober, the old man had a nasty mouth, called them two little fruits, and Danny would wiggle his ass at him. His father had one leg cut off, and when he couldn't catch Danny, he'd take a vicious cut at him with his crutch. Then Danny would get quiet and sulky. Once or twice Clyde left the house and set off home on his own, but Danny always caught up with him before he reached the corner.

Danny knew everyone in Brockton, and they made jokes with him. Sunday nights they had a community singsong at the park, and when Helmut Regehr, a Mennonite boy who had a nice baritone voice, was going on the stage to sing 'Oh Danny Boy,' Mac Campbell, the master of ceremonies made a little joke about the song being dedicated to Danny O'Connell.

There were two loose women in town, a soldier's wife and a minister's daughter, and Danny had accounts of how various boys kept watch on them, hoping for the sight of something scandalous.

A couple of blocks away from Danny's place was the Murder House, and Danny showed him that too, led him up close to look in the windows of the tilted frame cottage where Stick Murdoch had shot his best friend and then himself with a twelve gauge shotgun a couple of winters before. The Murder House was close by every time you went up town, the empty windows watching.

Danny was always turning up. In the winter Clyde got chicken pox, and one night, his fever so high he was delirious, he tried to get out of bed and fainted. His mother was terrified when she heard him crash to the floor, and when she got him back into bed, she lay on top of the blankets and cuddled against him. When Clyde woke in the morning, she was still there, fast asleep beside him, so quiet and unmoving that for a moment he thought she was dead. Then there was a loud banging at the door and his mother woke with a start, said something to herself that Clyde couldn't hear, and as she got up, tightened the belt of her dressing gown. The door opened, and Clyde heard Danny chattering, offering to help, asking if he could get her something from the store. He wanted to visit Clyde, but his mother said No, he'd just catch the chicken pox, but she let him go to the store for a loaf of bread.

"Danny's never going to grow up," Mrs Millard at Wignall's Dairy said one day that first summer when he was giggling and carrying on. "I don't think so."

Danny winked at Clyde.

"Two scoops for us, Pixie," he said in his funny way. "Two big brownboy poopie scoops of chocolate for us."

"Don't you talk like that, Danny O'Connell," she said. "And it's Mrs

Millard to you."

"Now you be nice, Pixie," he said, "or me and Clyde will take our business to the drug store. We can get ice cream there just as good as here."

"I'll take your business out behind the shed and I'll tan it till it's hot."

"You don't better touch my business, Pixie, or I'll tell Father Marcotte."

"No skin off my nose."

"Skin off your woo-woo-woo, Pixie."

Danny giggled again. Clyde didn't much like being with Danny when he was like this, but he was paying for the ice cream out of the money he got for keeping an eye on Clyde. Sometimes Clyde couldn't make out whether he liked Danny or not. Once when he was peeing, he saw Danny looking in the window, and Danny ran in the back door shouting, "I seen your weenie," and Clyde couldn't think of anything to say except tell him not to be so stupid, but Danny just giggled. Danny was always asking Clyde's mother to let them go on the Moonlight Cruise on the steamer that travelled back and forth across the lake to Toronto every day in the summertime. He told Clyde that they could spy on all the lovers. Clyde knew his mother was never going to agree to that.

In the fall Danny quit school, where he was in Grade 8 and spent most of his time getting beaten up, and his brother got him a job working for Father Marcotte at the rectory and around the church. They got him permission to leave school because his help was needed at home.

His last day at school the Ryan boys went after him again. They called it Danny-Hunting. When they saw Danny on the street, they jumped off the bus from the high school, caught up with him at the park and dragged him screaming into the public washroom where Butch Ryan held him down on the floor while Cappy Ryan, his crazy older brother, pissed all over him. Clyde heard Danny screaming, but he knew he couldn't do anything. Danny got his revenge, of course, all those years later.

By the next summer, Clyde had friends from school, Jim Bennett, Frank Friesen – though Frank lived way out in Irishtown – and sometimes Lyall Ratner, the doctor's son, Harold Ratner's younger brother. Clyde had convinced his mother he didn't need anyone to look after him. It was that summer when he and Jim Bennett started hanging around the golf club where Lyall already had a junior membership –

finding balls that were lost down the bank or in the water and selling them to golfers. You weren't supposed to sell them on the course, but Sim Secord, the pro, usually looked the other way. Clyde first encountered Francis Finster when he sold him a brand new Spalding Dot he'd picked out of the river.

"Where'd you find that one?" Francis said. His wet staring eyes were fixed on Clyde, who just shrugged. It was safer to say nothing, just hold out the ball in your hand.

"How much?"

"Quarter."

"You're quite the salesman," Francis said, as he gave him what he'd asked for. Clyde put the quarter in his pocket with his two dimes. Nearly half a dollar. Money in his pocket; he'd never had that much before.

Danny was around the house all the time the first years in Brockton. Saturday mornings he'd come over, and Clyde's mother would pay him a quarter to help with the cleaning. Danny did all the dusting and mopping, and Clyde's mother put on a pair of slacks and knelt down on a rubber mat to scrub the kitchen floor. When they were all finished, they'd have a cup of tea, and later on Clyde and Danny would go to the matinee and see the Bowery Boys or the Three Stooges or sometimes a western. Danny didn't carry on and giggle as much on those Saturday mornings. His own mother was a small, fierce, silent woman, and he got along better with Clyde's. Once, after he'd hung around all Sunday afternoon, Clyde said to his mother, "I think Danny has a crush on you."

"No," his mother said. "It's just that I understand him."

Clyde remembered an afternoon when he went by the law office on the main street of town to see his mother. Clyde wanted to talk her into going to the Chinese restaurant for supper. He expected her to be alone in the office, as she usually was at the end of the day. Palmer Eustes, the lawyer she worked for, had his main office in Canalville, the small industrial city half an hour away, and he only spent one day a week in Brockton, sometimes just half a day. Clyde's mother kept the office open and, as the years went by, learned quite a bit about the practice of law; people were apt to say that she knew as much as Palmer Eustes himself, but mostly it was her job to arrange appointments for Thursdays, Palmer's day in Brockton. She would take notes on what it was people wanted. Now and then, if the matter seemed important, she would call the Canalville office and arrange for a special appointment. She was usually alone, maybe typing something, if Clyde came in after school, so he was surprised to find Danny there, talking to his mother in a serious way, not giggling. He stopped talking after he noticed Clyde coming in. Just having a little visit, he said. He was up town doing some shopping for Father Marcotte, and the Father was going to teach him to drive next year so he could get a real job. And that happened. Danny handled the delivery truck for the grocery store, though he was never a very good driver. Clyde wondered if that was all of what Danny had been saying to his mother or if there was something more.

Something about Danny made Hazel Bryanton feel an enduring affection toward him, though her sharp eyes must have noticed his failings. Clyde remembered the evening he came back from a Rotary Club trip to the national capital for the high school students with the highest marks in Canadian History. They had been given dinner in the Parliamentary Dining Room by the local member. In the dim dining-room he saw a face he recognized from the golf course. Senator Lawton. The Senator noticed him looking and winked.

Back home the next evening, the porch light was off. There didn't seem to be any bulb in the fixture.

"What's wrong with the porch light?" he said almost before his mother had a chance to ask him about the trip.

"Oh the bulb seemed to be burned out, and I asked Danny if he could change it, but he said it broke off and I'd better get an electrician."

"Why did you ask Danny to do it?"

"Well you weren't here."

"Danny O'Connell doesn't have the brains to scratch his ass when it itches."

"Don't be coarse and don't be cruel."

Clyde was angry, in part, because he knew he should be able to fix the light, but he wasn't perfectly sure how. He'd never learned these things. The next day he found what he thought must be the main switch for the house and turned off the power, then climbed a step ladder and with a pair of pliers he'd bought the previous year, managed to twist the broken piece of bulb out of the socket and replace it. When he turned the power back on, he was half afraid that the light still wouldn't work or that there would be sparks flying out, but it was OK. He was pleased with that.

His mother had probably asked Danny to fix it, he decided, because she was lonely with Clyde away, and it was an excuse to have some company. He told her that if she needed help again, she should call the Harknesses and Fred would come over.

"I can't be asking Fred Harkness for help all the time," she said.

"Well then wait till I get home," Clyde said, though he thought that was a bit of a joke even as he said it. He wasn't much of a handyman, though he was trying to learn.

Danny had maintained his loyalty to Hazel Bryanton over the years. When she was in the Canalville hospital for a hip replacement, Clyde walked into the room one afternoon, astonished to find Danny with her, a little old man he was now, the face brown, wrinkled, simian. He was sitting by the bedside, holding her hand, though when he saw Clyde, he put the hand carefully down on the covers and stood, as if ready to leave, as if, somehow, he shouldn't be there. They hadn't met since their shouting match in an Ottawa parking lot.

Clyde told him to sit back down, but Danny said it was almost time for his bus.

"Danny came all the way from Ottawa," his mother said, "just to see me."

"Well, I had to, Hazel. You know that," Danny said. "Who was ever in my life such a good friend to me? There's some put on a show, Hazel, but you were the true blue. You remember what I promised. Soon as I get back to Ottawa, I'm going straight to Notre Dame to light a candle for you. You'll know right away when I do it. You'll feel it in your heart. A candle to the Holy Mother."

So far as Clyde knew, the woman hadn't darkened the door of a church in fifty years, but she thanked Danny with apparent sincerity. Clyde walked to the front door of the hospital, Danny limping along beside him. Clyde offered to let him stay over.

"I'll sleep good on the bus. In the old days I seen me sleep six, eight hours in one of those seats. But you stay right here with her, Clydie," he said. "Long as ever she needs you, you stay with her. She was that good to the both of us, wasn't she?" He paused, took thought. "When you get back to Ottawa we'll settle it, about the house."

Clyde shook his hand and the little old man limped crookedly down the steps.

Oh, Danny, Danny, he said to himself, or to Danny's ghost, as he finished the club sandwich he'd ordered and walked to the cash to pay. Outside the restaurant Clyde stood in the street and looked toward the monument, the bronze figure of a soldier, and imagined it was his father, high and cold and untouchable.

2 | Dorrie

Clyde turned left off the pavement and along a dirt road up a steep hill, moving between tall trees, over rock outcroppings, the car bouncing in the deep ruts, then he turned left again, parked on the little plateau behind his cabin. He unlocked the place, searched through all the rooms. He hadn't been here for a month, but there was no damage by vandals or animals. He pulled out kindling and firewood from the cache left underneath the building to keep dry, lit a fire in the Franklin stove. Gordie Peters, the neighbour who drained the pipes for him hadn't been round yet, so he had running water. A window looked out over the lake, in front of it a table and chair. The rooms had a bare, unfinished look. Nobody came here, you'd say. His apartment in the city had some good pieces of furniture that Noreen, his ex-wife, had found, paintings on the walls that Jane Mattingly had convinced him to buy.

He dropped his briefcase on the couch. A telephone sat on top of a bookcase beside a cigar box full of photographs that he planned to frame and hang someday. The box itself and the oldest photos came from his uncle. A snapshot of Clyde's father as a boy. His parents' wedding picture. Men and women he couldn't identify in places he'd never been. What he'd put in there himself: Noreen in a black leotard, dramatically lit. A few pictures of Noreen with their son Clifford. Clyde's favourite was a snapshot of Noreen and Clifford standing by a ship canal, a laker in the background. One day Clyde would open the box, study the pictures, decide which to frame. But when he came to the little cabin the organized, life-shaping part of him went into hiding, solitude evoking memories without resolving them.

Westward behind the bare trees the sun was approaching the horizon. The sky reflected in the lake at the foot of the hill was dark blue.

Clyde picked up the phone. He left a message for Perry, his business partner, on the office machine, said he was taking a couple of days off. They'd been partners for years now and covered for each other when necessary. Clyde called his mother, who was silent as he told her the news about Danny, then said, as he knew she would, that she wanted to attend the funeral. All this dying, she said. Clyde would book her a flight to Ottawa. All this dying, all these endings; it was the day of Marion Lawton's funeral a year before that he and Danny stood in a parking lot shouting at each other. That evening Clyde had gone round to Jane's apartment, and that conversation hadn't gone much better. You didn't get to arrange your goodbyes. He glanced at the front of the *Globe and Mail* that he'd brought with him, flipped through a few pages. Bill Clinton was backing off on his promise to fast track trade negotiations. Clyde hoped somebody in the office was reading the American papers and keeping up with all that. The mayor of Toronto, chipper little Mel Lastman, had declared the city Open for Business. Clyde was reminded that he should call the *Citizen* and insert an obituary. Maybe Danny's friends, whoever they were, would see it.

Restless, unable to settle down to read or make dinner, he took one of the clubs from the bag in the trunk of his car, found a plastic whiffle ball, and drove it back and forth across the flat space above the cabin. It was familiar and relaxing to swing the club, the muscles recalling a lifetime of movement, slowly up, then pivoting forward, the weight of the body informing the swing, moving from the right foot to the left. Set, swing, follow through: the muscles remembered. As a kid he had spent half his life at the golf course. Cleaning clubs in the pro-shop, or one of the better players might hire him to go out to the practice fairway and shag balls. Now and then someone wanted a caddy. In later years he worked inside the clubhouse. Clyde learned not to stare at the women in their pleated skirts or bermuda shorts standing on the first tee as he brought them their clubs. Now and then Sim Secord would send him out carrying a stick with a nail in the end to pick up the pieces of newspaper and candy wrappers that had accumulated in the little ditch between the first fairway and the street that ran for a block beside it. That's what he was doing the day he saw Dorrie Stead riding past on her bicycle. She was wearing shorts, and her pale bare legs moved up and down as she pumped the pedals. He hadn't seen her since they picked fruit together earlier in the summer. When he waved, she waved back, and he thought she was going to stop, but then she looked away and kept peddling.

Those years of growing up in Brockton: Danny's death brought it all back. Clyde put away the golf club. As the November day grew dark, he made himself a meal of sorts, then sat in front of the Franklin stove, feeling the warmth of the fire consuming the chunks of beech and maple he fed into it. He could hear rain against the window. Not quite a storm, but persistent drops striking the glass. Was it a long time ago or a short time ago, the day he'd been remembering? It was a lifetime ago, you might say that, but what was a lifetime, really? Was it fifty years ago or just yesterday that he'd met Danny, sold Francis that golf ball? Millions were born and died all over the world every day. In Ireland, Manchuria, Bangladesh. They had lives to remember, as Clyde did. Aging men went back to what it was like when they were young: he couldn't stop thinking about the day that Dorrie Stead showed him her breasts.

Brockton was surrounded by orchards. Clyde had been picking cherries for a week on Willi Siebert's farm, climbing up and down the long ladders among the boughs weighted with fruit, the last of the sour cherries for three days, then the dark sweet ones that had to be carefully picked with the stems on, not like the sours that were torn off without stems and sent to the cannery. He met Dorrie the day he started work. She'd begun picking the week before. They ate a few sweet cherries now and then as they picked, their lips reddened with the sugary fruit, but with the thousands around you, heavy and shining, hours spent lifting them down, carrying the basket down the ladder and setting it beside the others already picked, you no longer wanted to eat them. He'd met Danny delivering groceries to the Billings house a week or so before, and Danny had told him that Willi Siebert was looking for pickers. The work was hard, and it paid poorly unless you were fast and experienced; Clyde was leaving the job next week. He had talked to Sim Secord and lined up some hours in the pro shop at the golf course.

Dorrie was a year older than he was, and well-developed, as his mother might have said – he was sure he'd heard the phrase from her – and as Dorrie lifted her arms among the branches to take hold of a branch, to grip in her short fingers a cluster of dark shining cherries, pull it free, Clyde could study the way her breasts lifted, sank again as her hands lowered the cherries into the basket. At noon, he would follow her to the edge of the orchard and they would talk while they ate their sandwiches. Dorrie always had peanut butter. From the field behind them they would hear the rough crow of a cock pheasant.

He was innocent in those days, but also he wasn't. Well-developed, he said to her once. He was standing on the ground where he'd set a full basket, and he watched her on the ladder above him. My mother would say you were well-developed. She told him he wasn't supposed to be saying things like that, but he believed she wasn't really displeased, and as the week went on, he teased her a little, gently, like the slow quiet touches you'd give a nervous beast. How pretty, said he'd like to see them.

The way Dorrie walked, how she held herself, shoulders back to push out her breasts, a certain kind of swing, made you think she liked being looked at. Her older sister, who was nineteen, had already married. If Clyde thought about that, being married, what it meant, it excited him. Some quality about both of them, Dorrie and her sister, dark eyebrows, not fat but not thin either, pretty, silent, was almost frightening. Somehow, he believed, these girls had a mysterious understanding of what it was all about, what went on between men and women. Clyde knew that Dorrie liked him well enough; they had worked side by side all week, talked, eaten lunch together. This was his last day before leaving for the new job. When they went to the fruit barn at the end of the day to pick up their pay for the week – not much, neither of them was fast enough – there were two men, travelling pickers, sitting on a low wagon smoking. One of them had crossed eyes. They were looking at Dorrie. The one with the crossed eyes turned to Clyde and asked if she was his sister. Clyde shook his head. The man made an ugly gesture at her and winked.

"Hey, big-ones, you want to shack up with us?" he said.

Dorrie ignored him, and he called her stuck-up. Clyde knew it was unfair, that there was something he should say, but he didn't know exactly what it was. He and Dorrie took their money from Willi Siebert's wife, and walked away between two rows of cherry trees toward the dirt road that led to the edge of town.

"I won't be here next week," he said.

"I know," Dorrie said. "I know that." He couldn't interpret the look on her face, something stubborn, defiant maybe.

Just before the end of the orchard, Dorrie stepped into the space between two cherry trees and started to unbutton her blouse. She took it off and stood with it in her hand, and he could see the curve of the soft flesh at the top of the brassiere, which was made of a shiny material and looked faded, as if it had been washed too many times.

"Show me," he said. He was whispering, though he didn't mean to. He had a hard-on, and he could hear himself breathing. Dorrie dropped the blouse to the ground and in a moment she was standing with her brassiere in her hand and Clyde was staring at her breasts, like two soft animals with dim pink snouts, and he was moving toward her, to explore them, but she shook her head, not to touch her, turned away and quickly dressed herself, and they resumed their walk into town, silent most of the way. Clyde wanted to see her breasts again, to feel how soft they were.

Then the next week he'd be at the golf course, and later in the summer she would ride past on her bike and almost decide to stop, but not quite, and after that they wouldn't meet again until school in the fall, and then always with other people. Clyde wondered about calling her, but he never did. He didn't exactly want a girlfriend, going out regularly, quarreling. He couldn't say what he wanted in any way that made sense. He wanted Dorrie's breasts, to touch them. He imagined her drowning in the river and he would save her and she was naked and then what would happen. Once or twice he talked to her on the street. Once Danny came by in the delivery truck, stopped, rolled down the window. "Got a girlfriend, Clydie?" he said. "No," Clyde shouted, "you're still my best girl, Danny." The look on Dorrie's face.

Then a few months later she was quitting school and she got married to Jack Lamoure. Clyde and Jack Lamoure had once got into a fight on the school bus, though it hadn't amounted to much. After that Clyde saw her at a distance now and then, pushing a baby carriage. She and Jack moved into Canalville, where Jack had a job, and it was years before he saw her again. Clyde thought, looking back now after a lifetime, that you could say the young man he was then didn't know that he'd ever see those beautiful breasts again, or you could suspect that he did know.

The next time he saw Dorrie, years later, was at the little house in Canalville where she and her husband lived. By then Clyde had an apartment in Canalville, where he was working for Finster's Credit Bureau. He'd recognized Jack Lamoure's name on one of the collection forms that Louise, the office secretary, had put on his desk. Usually he'd phone, tell the debtor what was owned and demand a payment. If they'd bought something that could be repossessed warn them about that. If someone in the family had a salary, he'd threaten to garnishee. You had to make them feel bad. He didn't usually go round until he thought his presence might shake loose a little cash.

Collection wasn't his favourite part of the business. When he left school and accepted a job with Francis at the credit bureau, the man had given him the Lesson on Deadbeats.

"To work in this business, Clyde, you have to understand how things are. Lots of people are not like you and me. Those people are cheaters and loafers and deadbeats. They'll lie to you, they'll tell you how bad things are, try to make you sorry for them. Don't believe that, Clyde. These people went out and bought things. They think they can get something for nothing by not paying their bills. I forgot, they'll say. Things are bad right now, they'll say. What you have to remember is that they went out and they bought this stuff. Nobody made them do that. Nobody took them by the hand and led them to the store and said if you buy this you'll never have to pay for it. If you or I went to the store, Clyde, we'd know that we had to pay for what we'd bought. Probably we'd save up until we could afford it – I never let my wife buy on time – but the deadbeats don't do that. They go out and buy it first and then they just don't pay. If they get away with this, the whole economic basis of our society is going down the hole in the backhouse. It's trust, you see, all based on trust. I say to you that if you come to work for me, I'll give you so many dollars. At the end of your first week I don't say, Clyde, I've had a tough week, you'll have to wait a bit for your money. I promise you the pay, I give you the pay. If I decide I can't afford to pay you, I give you notice and you find something else. I don't keep you here, week after week, whining about my inability to put the dollars in your pretty little hand. Right Clyde? You see how it is. Trust. Sure we have contracts, lawyers, all that malarkey, but really it's trust. A man's as good as his word. Except the deadbeat isn't. So that's why we're here, Clyde, you and I, and we have to be on the job. You got a debt, you pay it. We're here to make sure that happens, so the next time somebody is selling a car, a lawn set, some golf clubs, and the buyer says I'll make the payments, there can be trust. A deadbeat is a deadbeat, Clyde. A crying deadbeat is still a deadbeat. A deadbeat who lifts his fist to you is still a deadbeat. And that part of our business is about just one small thing, to get some money. Sure there's the other part, credit ratings, helping to arrange a loan now and then. But making collections, we are greasing the wheels of the shining chariot of commerce, and it's got to be done."

Every few months Francis would go through the lesson, just in case

Clyde had forgotten.

The place Clyde drove to that afternoon was a small bungalow, not far from the downtown, no car in the drive; Jack was at work, or maybe they'd had the car repossessed. Clyde parked a couple of houses away, a habit he couldn't explain, just part of his routine, and he walked back, up the path, knocked. It was necessary, it was part of the job; as Francis liked to tell him, every time someone gets away with it, the whole system slows down. He knocked on the door, and Dorrie opened it. She was wearing jeans and a red blouse hanging loose over them, and she held a little girl on her hip, the child with a thumb in her mouth, looking half asleep.

"Clyde." She didn't sound surprised.

"I have to talk to you."

A look, not clear what she was thinking, then she lifted her eyebrows a little.

"Come in. Just let me put Janice down for her nap."

He entered the small front room, saw the sofa on which the payments were due, an old stuffed chair with a blanket over the seat as if the stuffing might be coming loose. A rocking chair that was still painted dark green from the days when it sat on someone's porch. A TV. The hardwood floor was bare, and there were a couple of stains on it. The front window had drapes of some cheap fabric. There was no curtain on the small side window. The only picture on the walls was one from a wedding, not Dorrie's, her sister's, but Dorrie was in it, being a bridesmaid, the dress tight over her breasts. He heard her voice from beyond the room, saying something to the little girl. He sat down on the sofa. It would be easier if they were sitting down.

There was a smell to the house, not unpleasant, but unfamiliar, something to do with the children maybe. As he sat there waiting, he was trying to remember the formula for compound interest, but right then it wouldn't come to him. Dorrie came back into the room, and he tried to look at her without remembering too much.

"It's been a while," he said.

Dorrie nodded. He wished she'd sit down. As if she knew what he wanted, she went to the rocker and sat in it.

"I work for the credit bureau, Dorrie."

"Oh hell."

"I didn't want to phone. I thought it was better to come round."

"There's no money."

"We've got to figure something out. Is Jack at work?"

"He lost his job. I don't know where he is. He can't sit around the house all day. Sometimes he finds someone who'll buy him a drink. Allie's at school. He's six now. He's the one I got pregnant with in high school. I guess you know that whole story. Everybody does. So that accounts for everybody. Now what?"

"Dorrie..."

"What?"

"You haven't been making the payments on the sofa."

"Didn't stop you from sitting on it. Comfortable isn't it? Pulls out into a bed if you have company, but we never have any company."

"How did Jack lose his job?"

"He was drinking. Once too often and got into a fight with the foreman. Can't blame him really. Went out with me a couple of times and then I was in trouble and now he's stuck with all this. He wanted to go somewhere, have adventures."

Clyde sat there, staring at the floor, a little ball of hair by the leg of the upholstered chair. He didn't know what to say next. He'd heard this kind of story before. They'll try to make you feel sorry for them, Francis said. It's all part of the game; they've got to accept their responsibilities.

"I knew he was going to lose his job," Dorrie said, "and I went out and bought it before he did. I just wanted something decent."

"It wouldn't take too much," he said. "As long as the payments were regular."

He thought of one of his uncles who sold insurance during the depression. He went to the houses, collected ten cents, twenty-five cents a week. He didn't think Francis would be satisfied with quarters.

"Couldn't your parents help out? Or his?"

"What do you think we're living on?" she said.

"Is Jack looking for work?"

"I guess so. This is kind of a small place. Word gets around."

"I can imagine."

"I'd get a job" she said, "if I could find anything. Jack wouldn't like it, but he can't really say much. I could leave the kids at my sister's part of the time or leave them with Jack at night. I used to look in the paper when we could afford to buy the paper."

"If I don't get some money, they can repossess it."

"Who'd want it? We've had it for six months. Janice peed on it once."

"You still want it?"

"Of course I want it. I bought it didn't I?"

"I can stall for a few days maybe. I don't know. If you were working... maybe we can think of something."

"Maybe *we* can," she said, sarcastic.

She was looking at him now, and he met her eyes, looked at the shape of her breasts under the loose red blouse, the red lips. He had the crazy impulse to ask her to show him her breasts again. To make them both laugh.

"Why do you do this job, Clyde? It's a job for jerks."

"It's not always this bad."

"You mean it's usually strangers."

"Some people just forget. You got to chase them, but they can pay."

All part of the Lesson on Deadbeats.

"I don't have it. My mother gives me money for rent. I get the family allowance. There's a few dollars left from when Jack was working. Maybe he'll find something."

"I meet people downtown," he said "There's jobs you could do."

In the bedroom the little girl was started to cry. She could tell that her mother was upset, that something was wrong.

"I better go," he said. "But I've got to tell them something."

She was still looking at him.

"Otherwise... ?"

"I guess they'll repossess it.

"Let them."

"That's right," he said. "You've got a chair. Two chairs, in fact."

She almost smiled.

"I'm glad Jack wasn't here. He hates you."

"Why?"

"He said you once had a fight."

"Kids fight," he said.

He nodded and walked to the door. On his way to the car, he took deep breaths. He started the car, to get away somewhere, drove a few miles out in the country, parked, stared at the long rows of grape vines, drove back, went to the office and made jokes with Francis and Louise.

That afternoon, Francis came into his small office while Clyde was on the phone, stood there listening. Clyde didn't like it when Francis did that, but he'd never said so, and in fact he suspected that Francis did it on purpose. There was a small mirror on the wall, and Francis looked in it, flattened an imaginary stray hair back to the grey slicked surface with his fingers, smiled at himself. Clyde was threatening to garnishee a man's wages, hoping the threat would pry some money out of him, and he didn't enjoy having someone listening, but Francis stood there until the conversation was over. Clyde thought he was going to say something about Dorrie's account.

"So many bad people out there," he said. "Not to pay what they owe." He looked in the mirror again. "I'm leaving early today. Things to do. You and Louise are being left in charge. Think you can handle that?"

"We'll manage" Clyde said. He always hoped that Francis might get the idea that he was annoyed at the way he stood and listened while Clyde was on the phone, but he knew it would make no difference. Francis enjoyed it, making him uncomfortable. It was part of the deal, Francis was the teacher and Clyde was the pupil. Clyde was learning, watching and saying nothing.

Francis went out the back door, and Clyde made a note of his phone call on the form in front of him. Made a couple more calls. People made promises. One swore at him. It was almost time to close for the day when Louise appeared at the office door. She had a small brown package in her hand.

"We have to drop this off for a client," she said. She stood looking at him. "Later on. You can have your dinner first."

"Where does it go?"

Louise gave him instructions about what he was to do with the package. Dark roads, empty cars. A big mystery of some sort.

"Are you sure about this?" Clyde said.

"You and I just follow our instructions, Clyde. You know what they say, the customer's always right."

She put the package on Clyde's desk.

"Maybe you better lock it in the drawer," she said.

She gave Clyde a cheerful smile.

"I'll leave you to close up," she said.

Clyde slid the package across the desk into the drawer, locked it. He knew what it must be – a pile of bills wrapped in brown paper and tightly sealed with tape. Clyde sat at his desk, stared at a spot on the wall where there was a small black mark. It had been on that wall since Clyde started work here. Once he had suggested to Francis that they get the office painted, but Francis dismissed it as a waste of money. Clyde was still angry about Francis listening to his phone call, but he reminded himself that Francis had been good to him. He'd wondered whether he might approach him about Dorrie Lamoure's debt, ask him what could be done, but he knew better. What can be done is she can pay what she owes. He could hear Francis saying it. It wasn't Clyde's problem. They got themselves into it.

Clyde locked all the doors, set the alarm and went down to the Jubilee. He went there most nights for dinner, ordered the daily special from Audrey, the waitress who usually did the afternoon and evening shift. He would sit with a copy of the local paper in front of him, and he and Audrey would discuss the headlines, what the Canalville mayor and council were doing, what the police had broken up, gambling last week, sex the week before, who'd been in court, the threat of a late winter storm. Audrey's brother was a plumber, and he was installing pipes and fixtures in many of the houses in the new Hillview subdivision. He had told Audrey that the mayor had his fingers in everything up there. Clyde had in fact run credit checks on a few people who were buying houses there; he knew who was making the decisions, and it certainly wasn't either the mayor or Audrey's brother, but he let her tell him what she thought she knew and agreed with it all.

As he ate his slice of raisin pie with vanilla ice cream and drank a second cup of coffee, he looked out the window. Out there men and women were making babies, borrowing money to buy houses, living their lives. Not dark yet, but the March evening was closing in. Six weeks from now he'd be able to play golf again. After a while he was almost the only one left in the restaurant, and Audrey came and sat down opposite him.

"Bad feet," she said. "I got to work shorter hours. Tell them to hire somebody else to do nights.

"I thought it was quiet in the evenings."

"Busy enough. And when the Toronto bus comes in, and the one from Buffalo."

"So they'll be hiring someone else."

"Maybe. Short hours. Now my kids are gone, I'm gonna rent out a room in my place, get a few dollars and don't have to destroy my feet any worse."

"I know someone who might be interested."

Dorrie had been a waitress one summer in a restaurant in Brockton when they were still in school. He remembered the way she looked at him, as if she expected him to fix it all.

When Clyde got back to the office, he opened the drawer and looked at the small package. He didn't touch it until he had put on a pair of gloves, and then he put it inside a large envelope. Francis had taught him to be sparing of his trust, and he now included Louise and Francis among those he treated with suspicion. He wondered how much Louise knew about this delivery. The customer is always right. Whatever the money was for, wherever it was going, it was out of bounds, and he didn't want his fingerprints on the package. He wondered how much money it was, how hard it would be to open it, take a little off the top, put it against Dorrie's account. Was there a word for what he felt about her, why he wanted to help? Clyde unlocked the back door, then reset the alarm, locked it again and took the package out to his car. Wondered if anyone might be watching him from the other side of the parking lot. It was a cold, quiet night. He set the package on the front seat and drove out of Canalville and several miles along a country road toward Brockton until he came to the First Concession, then turned and followed it to Railway Street. The narrow road beside the tracks was deserted. His headlights caught the bare branches of the fruit trees on both sides. He saw a car parked at the edge of the road and pulled up behind it, observed, as his headlights shone through the back window, that it was empty. He turned off the engine. The car was a recent model Ford and there was a rag hung over the license plate. A very careful man, whoever it was. Easy enough to lift it off, that piece of cloth, memorize the number, but maybe someone was out in the dark, watching.

Clyde sat still for a moment, waiting. For what? It was a cloudy night, and he could see nothing but the lights of a farmhouse beyond the trees of a peach orchard. He put on his gloves, took the package from the envelope and got out of the car. A little wind, the air raw, and a dog barked once at the farmhouse. Clyde was shivering a little as he walked to the car in front of him, and he stood still for a moment before he opened the passenger door, expecting something, a voice, gunfire, footsteps. When the door was open, he put down the small package on the passenger seat, as he'd been told to do, then walked back to his car and drove away, watching at the edge of the beam of the headlights for a figure to come out of the ditch, move toward the car. He saw no-one.

At the next crossroads he considered stopping, turning and going back, driving past to have a look, see who it was, but he decided he was better not to know. He drove toward Brockton and his mother's house – he'd decided he might as well drop in while he was nearby. On the way into the town, he stopped at a phone booth.

"It's Clyde," he said, when Dorrie answered the phone. "It's not much, but I might have come up with something."

"Oh," she said, "OK. Can I call you tomorrow?"

He told her where to call. Probably they were sitting in the small front room, watching television together. He remembered the sound of her voice on the phone, the way she breathed. At his mother's house, he tapped on the door and walked in. Just after he'd rented an apartment in Canalville, she'd made a down payment on this little house and moved out of the one they'd been renting. Clyde never felt quite at home here. She was sitting at a card table with Millie and Fred Harkness, a cribbage board on the table beside her as she looked up, for the first second staring at him as if she couldn't remember who he was. A Frank Sinatra record was playing on the hi-fi he'd bought her for Christmas.

"I was down this way," he said, "so I thought I'd look in."

"Out breaking a few legs, were you?" Fred Harkness said.

He'd made the same joke before.

"Got to get the money somehow," Clyde said.

He walked over to the card table, put his hand on his mother's thin shoulder and kissed her on the forehead. He could smell her makeup.

"Who's winning," he said.

"I am, of course," his mother said. "I'll make some tea when we've played this hand."

"No," he said. "You already got lots of company. You go ahead and win your game. I'll come over on the weekend."

His mother argued a little, but not much. She liked her card game. Clyde told Fred Harkness to let him know if he needed any legs broken, and left. Clyde went back out to his car. He wasn't ready to go home yet. He remembered Dorrie's voice on the phone. He decided to have a drink on the way back at a bar he'd often passed, just across the canal. Do a little thinking. *Jelly's*, the place was called. Strange name.

As he opened the heavy front door, it was so dark inside he could hardly see, almost the only light coming from a large tank in the middle of the room where tropical fish swam dreamily among the plants and castles. The hidden underwater world revealed behind glass, the submarine universe.

Beyond the lighted fish tank, the tables in the restaurant section appeared to be empty, but a skinny bartender appeared, out of nowhere, and made a gesture toward Clyde, who stood uncertainly near the door.

The gesture was neither friendly nor unfriendly, something that might have had meaning in an obscure sign language invented by a jungle tribe on some other continent. A jungle where those odd fish swam in warm rivers. Clyde walked up to the bar, sat on a stool.

"Slow night," he said. The bartender shrugged. Maybe he was a deaf-mute.

After a few seconds he spoke.

"What can I get you?"

Clyde ordered a rye and ginger. As he was waiting he saw a small flame in the darkness at the far side of the room. A woman sitting alone at a table: the flame was the lighter she was using to light her cigarette. She was dressed up, something with a low neck showing the top of her breasts. Waiting for a customer, perhaps, though it didn't seem a very promising place to wait. Clyde looked away from her, back to the bar, and realized that there was a second tank of fish at the end of the bar. He stared into the water, where small black fish hung perfectly still, then flickered forward.

"Your fish?" he said to the bartender.

"Not me. Jelly likes them. It was me I'd get some of those piranhas. You know, you fall into the Amazon, you're a skeleton in five minutes. Fierce little bastards. That's what I'd have. Saw them in an aquarium once. I put a finger up against the glass, and the fish goes right for it. Jelly likes these. He says they're relaxing. They give people something to talk about."

The phone behind the bar rang. He answered, waved the receiver to the woman in the corner of the room. She talked quietly into it, then went back to her table, picked up a coat from one of the chairs and walked to the door. To catch a cab, meet someone, do her job. As Clyde sipped his drink, these things were happening, the money he'd dropped off was being counted, the woman was meeting her customer, Dorrie was watching TV, or maybe she and Jack were busy together in the marital bed. He sipped his drink. The bartender stared into the darkness. Clyde decided he liked this place, the darkness, the quiet. He wondered if it was busier on the weekends, or earlier in the evening. He might come here again. He ordered another drink.

The next morning Dorrie called him at the office, and he told her about the job at the Jubilee, that if she wanted, he'd talk to them, say she was coming. He explained what Audrey had told him. She called him again at home that night.

"It looks like I got the job," she said.

"What you have to do," he said, "is take a couple of dollars a week round to Ralph Sherman at Elite Furniture. He's the owner. I'll fix it that they know you're coming. A couple of dollars a week. It'll get them off your back."

"How long?"

"They'll work it out, let you know."

She was quiet on the other end of the line.

"I know when you finally have a bit of cash in your hand, it's hard, but if you don't there'll be no end of trouble."

"Thanks. About the job."

That afternoon Clyde walked down the street to Elite Furniture. He'd already taken the precaution of going through the file and removing the card with Jack Lamoure's name on it, and while Louise was at lunch, he'd found her copy of the current collection form and put it away in his briefcase with the file card. The bag was locked in the trunk of his car. When he got home he'd burn them.

Elite Furniture was on a side street, a small place, not very successful. Ralph Sherman, who ran it, was a poor cousin to the Shermans who ran a department store on the main street. Short, worried, his hair going. His wife worked in the store, better at sales than her husband. Clyde found Ralph in a small office at the back.

"I've got a collection file, Lamoure, a sofa."

"You're going to tell me we have to repossess, and it's already ruined."

"No, better than that. The husband's a drunk, but the wife's got a job. Starting next week. It will be slow Ralph, a dollar here and there, but what are you going to do? Just like you said, they've had the sofa for six months and they've got kids. You can't get your money out of it that way. This way, bit by bit you'll get at least your cost. Take a baseball bat to them, there's still no more money. She'll bring in a couple of dollars a week. If she doesn't, let me know."

"They shouldn't have bought it."

"That's right, but they did, and you sold it to them."

"She said on the credit form her husband was working."

"I guess he was. Now he's not."

"They'll pay something?"

Clyde took out his wallet and handed him a ten dollar bill.

"I got that. Don't ask me how. That's a start. It'll be smaller from now on, but she's going to be working, so they'll bring in a little. Two dollars a week. You work out how long it takes to get what you paid, then let it go. You're not out of pocket. That's the best I can do. During the depression my uncle used to collect for insurance policies, a dime a week."

"What about your percentage?"

"The money comes straight to you. You should be paying us, but it's a small account, hardly worth the trouble. It'll be OK with Francis. I'll fix that. You can do me one sometime."

"You sure?"

"Take the two bucks a week, give her a closing date, I never have to hear about it again."

"What are these people, your cousins?"

"I went to school with the guy. I'm doing you a favour Ralph. I looked at the sofa. It's not worth repossessing. There's no salary to garnishee. She said she might be able to get work, so I offered them this deal. I know I should be taking a percentage off the top. I'd feel like my uncle collecting dimes. Get stiffed for more money, and we'll gladly take our cut."

"All right."

Clyde put out his hand and they shook. He wasn't sure why he was doing this. What the hell, it was pennies. It was a test Clyde was giving himself. See if he had the nerve. A small thing, but he was glad he'd done it. It was something he was learning about himself, that he had nerve. Maybe it was all he had.

The next week Dorrie started at the Jubilee, and in the evenings, now and then, not too often, he'd go into the restaurant, they'd talk about this and that, he'd eat something, overtip. She was the one told him about Danny.

"I hear your friend Danny O'Connell's going to jail," she said. She was standing close to him, speaking quietly. That voice.

"I didn't hear that. Why? What happened?"

"The cops raided the Fruit Farm."

"What's the Fruit Farm?"

"That club for queers up at Niagara Falls."

"I never heard of it."

"Jack says everybody knew. Danny was one of the ones they arrested. He got four years."

"For what?"

"For what they do, queers. Gross indecency."

That's just Danny, he remembered the neighbour saying. That's just Danny. Too late to do anything for him now, poor little fruit.

"That bothers you," she was saying.

"There's no harm in him," he said. "They could just leave him alone."

She was looking at him, but there was someone at the cash waiting to pay. Clyde left some money on the table and walked out. He wondered about phoning his mother, to tell her, but then he realized she'd already know. Danny would have told her.

It was the next Saturday night Dorrie came to his apartment. They'd never talked about it, but probably they both knew it would happen sometime. He was watching *Gunsmoke* on television, drinking a beer, when he heard the knock on the door.

How much of what happened after that did he remember now, after all these years, how much was a fanciful impression of what was long gone by? The act had been performed millions of times in the earth's history; thousands were at it every second of the day, somewhere. The sweet animal hunger went on, and what could be said about that young man and woman, in haste to commit adultery together in a small room in a small Canadian city while his old-fashioned wind-up alarm clock ticked off the seconds beside them. They were young that night, in the grip of the urgency of youth, and there were things he thought he could remember, how she looked, kissing the breasts he had looked at once in an orchard, her body still youthful and yet a little bruised by childbirth, the struggle of her life, unhappiness, or was that how he wished to see her, or wished to remember her, the sense of her surrender, her abandon, wet, crying out, the weight of flesh, the tangled hair? Did she, if she was still alive tonight, remember any such things? She was perhaps divorced and remarried, settled, contented among grandchildren, a little heavier now – you could tell she'd put on weight – a little trouble with her teeth, and unable to remember Clyde and the time she passed in his apartment.

What he did clearly remember, among all the fragmentary images of how they were together, was that she turned to him, late, and said, "I don't want to go," and what he chose not to say. If she stayed with him all night, Clyde believed, she was his, and his too the fate of her angry abandoned husband, her children, the difficulties of divorce, remarriage. All those things were there with them in the bed as they lay close together, still naked and wet, and he wasn't that brave, didn't tell her to stay, he hadn't the daring for her children, the fights and rage – he didn't have the nerve for that. Instead he offered to drive her home. No, she said, he couldn't do that, but she accepted a ride to her sister's house on the edge of the city, where her children were asleep and safe. Maybe she'd stay the night there.

Not long after that night, Jack Lamoure got a job at one of the steel plants in Hamilton, and they moved there, an hour's drive away, a different world. Paid off the sofa, he supposed, as he heard no more about it. Maybe she stayed the rest of her life with Jack; ill-assorted couples did lie together in a bed full of broken glass for years until the pain began to seem a destiny that could never have been avoided. Or maybe Jack stopped drinking, and they rubbed along happily enough, got older, lived a life.

3 | Francis

Morning, the November air cold, and Clyde, rising from bed in his little cabin in the woods, dressed quickly. It was a bright day for November, a little breeze, and he stood by the tall evergreens beside the cabin, stared across the lake. The water rippled against the pile of rocks that served as a dock. The canoe lay overturned and chained to a tree. Nothing to do here, but he was in no hurry to go back to Ottawa. The letter Danny had sent to Tom McKay at the newspaper was somewhere in the mail. Soon, today or tomorrow, it would arrive and whisper its secrets. Clyde might as well stay at the cabin for now. When he had to deal with all the consequences, he would.

Consequences: sometimes you wondered if you could have made one or two different choices, gone farther in school, become something with a good name, made it all different.

"Are you planning to go to university?" Francis had said to him one day in the pro shop, and Clyde told him he wasn't. Cost too much money, and he didn't see that he needed it. He didn't want to be a doctor or a teacher.

Clyde had been alone in the pro shop when Francis came in. It was his second summer working at the golf course, and Sim Secord was out on the practice fairway giving a lesson. Francis bought golf balls, and Clyde had change on the counter before he'd taken the bill out of his wallet. Francis noticed that and asked Clyde if he always did it. Clyde admitted that he did, couldn't help it.

"Good at math are you?" Francis said.

"Can hardly call it that," Clyde said. "Making change for a five dollar bill."

Francis was staring at him with those wet-looking, slightly protuberant eyes. He had an ungainly body, not fat, but he had no waist, heavy hips, and a way of looking at people as if he was thinking all the things he shouldn't. As if he knew what Clyde and some girl had done last night. When he asked about university and Clyde answered, he said nothing more, just stared, as if he might be adding things up in his head.

"What's your father do?"

Clyde hated saying that his father was killed in the war. It made him sound like a suck, but it was true, and there was nothing else to say.

"Your mother hasn't remarried."

Francis had no business asking about that, but Clyde knew that Francis would never worry about what was his business and what wasn't. If he wanted to know, he just asked. Clyde shook his head, and Francis nodded and went out to meet his friends on the first tee. One of them was Senator Lawton, the man who'd recognized him in the parliamentary restaurant. He had a membership but didn't come to play all that often. Sim said he had memberships at two or three courses in the district, though he wasn't a regular player at any of them. It was all business, or maybe politics, or both. Sim had told Clyde that the Senator was a party bagman. Clyde wasn't altogether sure what that was, didn't ask, not wanting to look stupid, would figure it out later. The Senator asked if there were any caddies available, and when Clyde said No, nobody was around that day, the man rented a cart for his big bag of clubs. On the tee Francis had his driver out and was warming up. He had a short choppy awkward swing, but he hit the ball straight, though never very long. The foursome teed off and walked away down the fairway, and Clyde began to search among the golf carts for the one Betty Saward would need in half an hour.

He thought about the girl last night, what they'd done. She was his first, and he felt different about the world today, a little more knowing. A party in someone's garage, and she came into his arms to dance in a way that made him think she'd give him anything. He hardly knew her, a thin, flat-chested little thing who held herself tight against him, and after a minute he led her out the back door of the garage and down the road. They stopped to kiss and fondle each other. He had a safe in his wallet, and when he asked her she agreed, and they went into a little grove of trees. His first time, not hers, though she seemed younger than he was.

Now was he supposed to phone her, go out every weekend, waiting to find places to do it again? He felt the way he had about calling Dorrie after the week they spent picking cherries. He didn't want a girlfriend, someone who owned him. Maybe there was something wrong with him, but when he thought of trying to find her phone number, calling her, that girl, it made him feel trapped and sick.

He located Betty Saward's golf cart in a back corner, picked it up and carried it through the others, unfolded the handle and pulled it out to the open patch of gravel outside the door where she'd pick it up. Lyall Ratner waved to him from the tee where he stood with his father and two other men. The doctor's son would win the junior championship that year. The previous winner was too old to compete as a junior any more. Clyde watched Lyall take a practice swing, a long soft arc that would lay the ball down somewhere well out toward the first green. Clyde planned to buy a junior membership the next summer. Sim lent him clubs and let him go out without paying green fees now and then, but he always felt uncomfortable, as if someone would tell him he had no right to be playing. Next year. This year what he earned was going to help pay for the car his mother was buying. It was understood that they would share the cost and share the use of it. Clyde would be the first of his friends to have a car. His mother wouldn't often need it in the evening. She wanted to be able to drive to the supermarkets in Canalville, and to go places on the weekend, but if he was going to a dance at the school, the car would be his; maybe he could drive his friends over to Buffalo if they went again.

The week before they'd gone to a black nightclub called The Zanzibar. A late night disk jockey who called himself The Hound Dog broadcast from there, rhythm and blues music. You walked in the door and everyone around you was black, and on the little bandstand at the front a group of three men were playing. All the black men and women in the club ignored you, three skinny white boys from Canada, the waiter brought the beer, weak American beer that was like drinking water, nobody was unfriendly, just paid no attention to these tourists, and you tried to be cool and easy and get drunk and move with the music, but being here among all these others, a different sound to the voices, a different look to how people stood or sat, Clyde was suddenly struck by how many secrets there would be in life, a whole secret story waited for him, all the things that could happen. It was the awareness of that secret story that gave him the courage to ask that girl last night – Helena her name was – if she wanted to go into the darkness of the trees and spread her legs for him, and it was part of the secret that she did.

His secrets, all those old stories: yes, that was the beginning of it all, Francis asking questions every time he saw him, wanting to know all about Clyde, as if he had some important purpose for learning these things, Clyde taking that girl into the trees, not phoning back, scared of some trap waiting for him if he gave in and did what was required in order to be inside her again.

That summer he started to work in the clubhouse as well as the pro-shop. Sammy Kupric, who managed it, asked him if he wanted to do some work in there, and they made a deal with Sim, the hours he was to spend in the pro-shop and when he'd go to the clubhouse. Every morning he came in and first thing, put on the Silex so Sammy could have his coffee when he woke, then cleaned up the showers and the locker room, swept up the cigarette butts, picked up coffee cups, glasses, old newspapers, then splashed water and disinfectant around the toilets and sinks and urinals, mopped the concrete floors. He'd unlock the back door and leave it open to get a little air in the place. If there had been a tournament the day before, the locker room would be a mess, spilled drinks, sometimes a broken glass. Once he'd found a five dollar bill under a pile of towels.

He'd pile the dirty dishes in the sink. If there was time later on he might wash them. Now and then an early golfer would come in and ask for a cup of coffee. Clyde wasn't really supposed to be serving – something to do with the liquor laws, in fact he probably wasn't supposed to be working in the clubhouse at all – but there wouldn't be any liquor inspector around at this hour, and if Sammy hadn't arrived downstairs, Clyde would serve the coffee.

When Sammy came down, he didn't talk, just sat at the table with a cigarette and a cup of coffee, his face pale and puffy. Later in the morning Clyde would go out to the pro-shop and fill in for Sim while he drove round on the tractor and checked the greens or gave a couple of lessons. Sim would play nine holes every day or so, maybe with someone on the club executive, give them a few free pointers. In the evenings Clyde would play nine holes. Sometimes Jim Bennettt came down and met him, or sometimes he'd hook up with local people who played after work. Now and then he played with Lyall Ratner. Clyde's game was improving, but he wasn't as good as Lyall, who was quietly triumphant at the end of every hole, though at the end of nine he said something flattering about Clyde's game. The two of them were going into Grade 13 next year, and that evening on the tee of the seventh hole, Lyall asked Clyde where he was going to university. Clyde said he wasn't, and when Lyall asked where he was going to work, he just shrugged. There would be something, he was sure of it. Not here in Brockton; there were no decent jobs here. He wondered sometimes if he wanted to get a job on the line in the auto-parts factory in Canalville, or at Union Steel. Something would come up. He could move away to one of the bigger cities, Hamilton, or even Toronto.

One afternoon when Clyde and Sim were both in the pro-shop, Francis came across from the clubhouse with the Senator and looked in from the doorway.

"What do you think, Sim, can you spare Clyde to caddy for the Senator?"

Sim knew the right answer to that, and Clyde went out to the first tee, where Francis introduced him to the older man. A big head and neck, like a bull or a buffalo, but his expression was pleasant, someone who was accustomed to having a good time. He gave Clyde the keys to his big Lincoln, which was parked nearby, and Clyde fetched the clubs in their mahogany leather bag and carried them to the first tee, took out the driver, a ball and tee from the pocket at the side of the bag.

"You play this course a lot, Clyde?"

"When I can."

"So you'll give me good advice."

"I'll try."

Like Francis, the Senator had a short sharp swing, and he was inclined to slice the ball; he put his first drive into a sand trap.

"What do you think, Clyde? How do I get out of that? Just pitch it out with an iron?"

"The sand in the trap is pretty hard," Clyde said. "You could probably pick it off the top with a three wood."

The Senator tried it, and it worked. His second shot was near the green.

"Great shot," Clyde said.

"You're a clever boy," he said, "just like Francis told me."

On the sixth hole, the Senator said he was a little tired. "I'll let Clyde drive for me," he said.

There was nothing to do but agree, and Clyde stood on the tee, trying to get used to the unfamiliar club, but he swung easily and the ball flew long and straight.

"Maybe I'll have Clyde drive for me on the next hole," Francis said.

"No you won't. He's my caddy."

As they went round the course, Clyde often had the feeling that most of what Francis and the Senator said had nothing to do with what they were really talking about. He couldn't have explained. Sly remarks from Francis about the riding association and the provincial election. The Senator would answer with generalities that appeared to mean nothing, yet you felt there were unspoken words hidden behind them. When they bickered about penalty strokes, it seemed to mean something else. At the end of the round, the Senator paid him, too much, and went with Francis into the club house for a drink. Clyde went to the pro shop. He knew Sim had to give a lesson at four o'clock.

"You're moving in important circles there, my boy," Sim said.

Clyde just laughed. He knew just about how important a caddy was. As he began shifting clubs, setting some of them aside to be washed, he saw Lyall Ratner coming along the gravel path with Shirley Ledoux. Clyde wasn't quite sure of the relationship between them – Lyall had been going out with some other girl during the school year – but they played together all the time. Shirley was wearing a pleated skirt that swung with the movement of her hips as she walked. Clyde liked to watch her move. She waved to him as she strode up to the tee. Clyde wondered what she and Lyall did when they weren't on the course.

Clyde made good money that summer and his golf game improved steadily. It was a cold Saturday afternoon in September when Francis spoke to him. Clyde just came in on weekends now, and he was passing through the locker room on his way to make an arrangement with Sammy about hours he'd work the next day. Francis was sitting naked on a towel on one of the benches, his flesh as white as the layer of fat on a pork roast before it was cooked, his straight gray hair mussed because he hadn't combed it after his shower. His private parts hung over the edge of the bench where he sat.

"Clyde," he said, "sit down with me for a minute."

Clyde sat on the bench on the other side, looked at him, looked away. The eyes watched him steadily.

"Last year of school," he said.

Clyde nodded. He'd asked Clyde about school before, what courses he was taking. Francis ran his hand over his belly, gave his dark pubic hair a little scratch, flipped his penis into a more comfortable position.

"Then what?" Francis said.

"I'll get a job."

"No university."

Clyde shook his head. He knew Francis wasn't saying what he was thinking.

"School of hard knocks, that's how most of us came up. There's worse ways."

"I'll find something."

"You know what I do?"

"Finster's Credit Bureau. In Canalville."

"At the end of the year, come and see me. We can probably work something out. You're a smart boy. Quiet but smart. I can use somebody like that. A fellow quit on me last week, talked too much anyway, not really reliable. What I think about you is that you're reliable. Sharp, but you don't try to show it off. And you're a good-looking boy; that never hurts. Makes a lot of things easier." Francis picked up a clean towel, stood, began to dry his hair.

"OK," Clyde said. "I'll get in touch." He was flattered by what Francis said, by his interest, and he knew some of what he said was true, was aware of his own quickness, and while he felt grateful to Francis, warmed by the praise, he was also studying the man's use of compliments, careful attention, flattery. These were tools in the handling of men and women, and they worked. Part of the trick was keeping close to the truth. Sincerity, of a sort.

Now a lifetime later, hidden away in his hilltop cabin, Clyde watched the low sun of the November day crossing the sky. He settled down in the rocking chair with a book in his hand. He had never been exactly sure why he'd bought the cabin. He'd done it not long before everything with Jane Mattingly ended: some instinct. As if he knew a day like this would arrive when he wanted to be alone to wait, to think things out. He turned the pages of the book, a pictorial history of the Dieppe raid he'd bought a couple of years before. A lot of the photographs came from German military archives, pictures taken on the beach after the raid, one body fallen on top of another as if in an act of love, in another photo dozens of dead bodies laid on the ground in rows, the dead Canadians who were left behind, another photograph of a captured soldier with his hands raised, watchful, uncertain. When he was young Clyde had invented stories about his father, that he was captured alive but had amnesia, couldn't remember the family he had left behind, how as the years passed, his memory would start to come back to him, and one day there would be a knock on the door, and Clyde would see a face like his own staring at him. Even now he studied the rows of anonymous bodies as if, with sufficient concentration, he might make out which of these dead men had fathered him.

Maybe if his father had come back, he would have proved to be a brutal stupid man and Clyde would have learned to hate him. Or a drunk like Danny's old man, one-legged, coarse and bitter. A couple of his friends had fathers they liked, more hadn't. Clyde had lived his life having none.

A few months after he started work at the credit bureau, when he was still finding his way around, learning how to collect the information for a credit rating, how to effect a garnishment, making a few of the easier phone calls demanding payments, Francis had invited him to dinner at his house and as they sat in the dining room, at the large mahogany table under a light fixture constructed of curving shapes in creamy translucent glass, Francis carving thin slices from the leg of lamb, Madge Finster asked him questions, what church he attended, where his mother's and father's families came from, whether he was interested in politics. She was a large woman with a cast in one eye that was exaggerated by her glasses, and Clyde answered her politely, fearful at first that he was in over his head, that he didn't know why this woman was cross-examining him, a little as if he'd asked for her daughter's hand in marriage. She and Francis had a daughter, younger than Clyde, but she was away at school. Clyde had met her once or twice during the summer, an improbably pretty young girl, given her two plain parents.

Madge Finster asked if he had a regular girl-friend, and Clyde replied that he didn't. He knew that it was expected that he would, that he would date someone and before long marry, but he made do with masturbation and an occasional adventure, an American girl he met at a wiener roast in the summer who was only in the district for a week and who wrote to him after she went home, or he got together now and then with Helena, the girl who had been his first – she worked in a fabric store now and seemed not to like him all that much, for which he didn't blame her – but she proved willing to lie down with him from time to time, once hurriedly in an empty cottage where they found themselves after a bunch of friends had gone in swimming. Jim Bennett had a regular girl friend, and though he was still available for golf most evenings, Clyde suspected that it wouldn't be long till he was married.

That kind of blundering into stability was exactly what he didn't want. It was assumed that everyone had to be part of a couple, but his mother managed beautifully on her own. If she was lonely, she never said so.

When Clyde remembered that dinner with Francis and his wife, he had some idea that he had been desperately nervous about it, afraid that some catastrophe would occur, but he spilled nothing, ate the dinner, the dessert of blanc-mange with tinned fruit, drank his tea, managed the required utensils in a way that suggested he'd been well brought-up, as he had, he supposed.

"What is your greatest interest?" Madge Finster said. Behind her the lace curtains, the headlights of a car passing by.

"Clyde's greatest interest is money," Francis said.

"Surely not, Francis," she said. "And let the young man answer for himself."

"I'm not sure that I know what's my greatest interest." Clyde was, of course, at the age when he often thought that his greatest interest was sex, though he found the problem of how to get it regularly insoluble. "I like to see how things work," he said.

"You mean machinery?"

"No. The world, the way things happen."

"I told you it was money," Francis said.

"Is that how things happen?" Clyde asked, innocently enough, perhaps.

"Mostly."

"I'm not sure."

"You're more of an idealist than Francis," the woman said. "Yes, I can see that."

Clyde didn't think that was true either, but he didn't say so. He didn't think it was true that evening, and he didn't think it was true nearly half a century later as he recalled the dinner, the way Francis watched him, listened to his answers searching for his weaknesses. You're a clever boy, my pet, he would say. Later Clyde knew something of what was concealed behind that ironic tone, but mostly he believed that beyond a man's secrets were more secrets, and at the bottom, things the man himself didn't know, insect appetites and forgotten crimes and perhaps much more.

Some crimes stayed secret, some were found out. When Dorrie told Clyde about the trouble Danny had got into, that he was going to jail, he had mentioned it to his mother, who already knew the whole story. It turned out that Danny had gone to her for help, and she had arranged for him to see Palmer Eustes who stood up in court with him when he pleaded guilty – Palmer said there was really no choice – and asked for a light sentence. Didn't get it, as it turned out. The judge was a pillar of the community who didn't want to encourage queers in their dirty ways, and Danny was sentenced to four years in the penitentiary.

"They should just leave him alone," Clyde said. What he'd said to Dorrie.

"He was such a sweet little boy," his mother said. "The judge said he had to make him an example. I thought that was a very hard way to look at it."

His mother arranged through Palmer Eustes that she could have permission to write to Danny in jail, and she did, and Danny wrote back to her, long letters that didn't tell her much, she said. Then he got out of the penitentiary and vanished until a night years later when Clyde met up with him in Toronto.

Time had passed, and more time: Francis was gone, the Senator and his wife Marion, and now Danny. He could never have guessed in those days that Danny would go on being part of his life until they both began to grow old. When Clyde found the body in the recliner, he had stared at it, as if he could learn to comprehend death. You never could. So he picked up the phone, did what was needed. Clyde had always done what was required, he paid his debts, one way or another, though he was aware that recently he'd lost something, some energy, some desperation. Maybe he was no longer sure what was owed, and where.

The Lesson on Deadbeats.

"They should bring back debtor's prison," Francis liked to say. "Uncivilized is it? Well it's not civilized to stiff an honest man for his money. Says it in the Bible. *If any will not work, neither shall he eat.*" Clyde was about to go out the door and accost a man who was behind on the payments on his second mortgage. He'd driven by the house once or twice. They had a good car, a Cadillac, the kids had bicycles, the yard was carefully landscaped, lawn, hedge, foundation planting, but Clyde knew it was all floated on debt, and if they didn't make the payments on the second mortgage, they would start to sink. Francis had a little company that lent money for second mortgages, and he'd encouraged Clyde to borrow from the bank to invest in it. The difference in the interest rates was significant, and on paper it was a good deal. Clyde knew, by now, that all business was done on borrowed money. If you took out a loan, you built up your credit rating so you could get more. Who owned the houses and cars? No one really. The bank held the money of depositors and lent it to the Ford dealer and then also lent money to you to buy from the Ford dealer. Neither a borrower nor a lender be, something his old grandmother once said when he was visiting, but nobody believed that any more. Money grew when it was in circulation, by its own internal dynamic, so that the faster it moved, the more there was. At the edge of Canalville more and more subdivisions were going up in those days, all bought on borrowed money. The builder borrowed, the buyer borrowed, and now and then Clyde had to go out and remind people that they weren't obeying the rules of the game. He'd decided against asking for a loan from the bank in order to see the money lent out at a higher rate for second mortgages, but he was negotiating with a builder to buy one of the first houses in a new subdivision, with a pretty good chance that when the subdivision was finished he could sell it at a profit. Maybe live in it for six months, plant a couple of trees, then put it on the market. Unless you get married first, the builder said, but Clyde had no plans.

"Tell them we can put them in jail," Francis said as Clyde walked out the door. "They probably don't know any better."

At her desk, Louise smiled. She appeared to enjoy that kind of talk from Francis.

Clyde had made an appointment to see the man at his home late Friday afternoon. He was a salesman, and Clyde suspected that he'd have the best chance of collecting if he made the whole approach very respectable and business-like. They both knew what the appointment was about, and Clyde walked away with a cheque. He suspected that it was kited, but the man said he was owed a lot of commissions, so maybe he'd get to the bank first thing Monday to cover it. If it bounced he was in trouble. Clyde delivered the cheque to the office, and drove out to *Jelly's* for dinner. It was Friday night. He was playing golf in the morning. The food at *Jelly's* was decent enough, the prices reasonable. Jelly Wendorf had the reputation of being involved in crime of various sorts, with connections across the American border in Buffalo, and Clyde suspected the restaurant was used to conceal transactions that couldn't be made public, but even if crime subsidized his dinner, he had no objection to eating it.

He'd met Jelly once or twice and become almost friendly with Maria, the prostitute who worked from the table in the back corner. Call-girl was the phrase she used to describe her work, and most of it was in fact done by answering calls that came in to the bar. If there was trouble, Clyde supposed, it was the bartender who'd be charged, but he suspected that there wouldn't be any trouble. When he'd mentioned the restaurant to Francis, the older man had warned him off, said that it was a place to avoid, though he gave no reason, and Clyde wasn't too worried. He wondered about bringing his mother to *Jelly's* for dinner on some special occasion, her birthday perhaps, whether she'd find it an adventure. She was a puzzle to him, in some ways; he couldn't be sure how she was going to react to things, but he decided to find someplace else to take her on her birthday.

Maria, the call girl, had an interesting face, a long nose and flat lips, big bright eyes, not pretty, but you noticed her. When she talked, she held your attention. Once or twice she said she'd take Clyde upstairs for free when she had a slow night, but he was still waiting. The corner table where she usually sat was empty tonight. There were three tables of people in the restaurant, and the lights were a little brighter, but still his eyes were drawn to the haunted brightness of the fish-tanks. Hypnotic, the queer secret world of the fish. The wide pale body of one of them hanging still, just a little movement at the end of the fins, the eyes wide, looking into the darkness of the world beyond the tank. Pull it out, and it would drown in air.

Maria never did turn up that night. Absent the next couple of times he went in, the corner table empty. The fish showed no concern. Finally Clyde asked Tommy, the regular bartender, where she was, and Tommy only said she took off, went away somewhere. When Clyde asked where she'd gone, Tommy claimed he had no idea. She was just gone. Girls were like that. Clyde wondered whether she'd found someone, wanted to start a new life. The day after that conversation with Tommy, a body floated up in Lake Ontario, near the mouth of the canal, the body of a woman, naked, and Clyde, when he heard the news, was sure he knew who it would be. But the police investigated and it seemed it wasn't Maria. They checked the dental work, and it was some runaway girl from Hamilton; an out-of-date picture of her appeared in the paper, her hair pulled back in barrettes, a wide smile. There was no evidence of how she got into the canal. Maria's departure remained a mystery.

That year there was an election early in the summer. The Senator was president of the riding association and Francis, who was treasurer, volunteered Clyde for various jobs, driving the local member to meetings, delivering posters to constituency workers. One evening Clyde went to the constituency office with a box of pamphlets he'd picked up from the printer. They had rented space above a dress store on the main street. Large photographs of the candidate's face – an unnatural smile on the serious features – filled the windows. Clyde climbed the worn wooden stairs to a large bare room, the floor made of tongue and groove pine that had never been painted, patterns on the walls where they had darkened unevenly over the years. The room was empty, but a radio was playing a tear-jerking song called "Patches" about a forbidden romance with a girl from shanty-town. He'd heard it before on his car radio, the tale sentimental and ridiculous, but the wailing tune made you want to wail along.

On the wall was a huge map of the city divided with red lines to indicate the different polls, down by the lakeshore, along the canal, each section with a large red label showing the poll number. He put his box down on a long table with straight chairs around it, walked to the front window and looked down to the street. Across the road, he could see into the brightly-lit coffee shop where two girls sat at the front table, both smoking. One of them laughed and butted her cigarette in the ashtray on the table. He could imagine the smoky taste of her mouth.

"Can I help you?" a woman's voice said.

He turned back. A tall thin woman of middle age stood by the desk where the small radio was giving out its mawkish tune. She was glaring at him as if he might be a thief.

"I brought the pamphlets," he said, indicating the box on the table.

"They have to be put in the envelopes," she said, "the first five hundred."

"I could help with that."

He introduced himself, and she said she was pleased to meet him but didn't tell him her name. The two of them sat in silence sliding pamphlets into pre-addressed envelopes. No-one else appeared. The phone rang once, and the woman delivered a few brusque sentences. Clyde rose to leave, she thanked him, and he went back down the dusty stairs. He wondered if he should report the stale emptiness of the constituency office to Francis, but he concluded that Francis either knew or didn't care.

It was a couple of days later that Francis took him out to play golf with the Senator for the first time, left Louise to take care of the office and drove the two of them out to a course in the countryside that Clyde had never played before. Clyde wondered if this outing was some kind of reward for the work he'd been doing in the election. The Senator was waiting for them in the pro shop, sitting in a wooden armchair with leather upholstery, looking out the wide windows and across miles of farmland toward the lake. He turned as Clyde took out his wallet to pay the green fees.

"It's taken care of," he said, as if Clyde should have known that already. He pushed himself out of the chair, reached out and shook hands with Francis, then with Clyde. His clubs, the heavy leather bag fastened in a cart, were sitting on the first tee.

"You played this course, Clyde?"

Clyde shook his head.

"Lots of woods. Gives an advantage to a straight ball hitter like Francis."

"Always an advantage to hit the ball straight," Francis said.

"You sound like a preacher, Francis."

Clyde stood on the tee, swinging his driver to loosen up.

"Clyde has a very stylish swing," he said. "Like to watch it. You hit first, Clyde."

It was a long first hole, and Clyde took a few seconds to make sure he knew where the green was, beyond a slight dogleg to the right, then hit the ball, a drive that ran a bit long for the dogleg. But playable. The Senator was watching him as he moved away from the tee and was nodding his head slowly up and down, like some great slow beast. Francis drove, dead straight but a little short of the dogleg. He'd have some trouble knowing where to put his next shot. The Senator drove, and they walked away on the trimmed green grass.

Clyde was hitting the ball well today. It was after the fourth hole that Francis turned to the Senator and said, "I think Clyde's giving us a little extra help, so we don't get beaten too badly."

"What do you mean by that?"

"The last two holes he's missed putts that I think he could have sunk. Being polite to the old men."

The Senator was looking at Clyde, his eyes hard, his lips tight together.

"Is that true Clyde?"

Clyde met his eyes, tried to calculate how he should respond.

"I didn't try too hard."

The Senator was silent, and Clyde could see his shoulders rising as he took two or three breaths.

"Don't do it again. If I come out here with a good golfer, I want to see him play the best game he has in him. There may be assholes who'd be flattered to let you give them a few strokes, but I'm not one of them." Clyde was aware that Francis was watching him as he listened to all this. That look of adding up a column of figures in his head. "And the same applies to everything else. If you're smart enough to beat me, do it. Trample me into the ground. I don't think you will, because I don't think you can, but I don't take any kind of charity. So put the goddam ball in the hole every chance you get."

He turned and walked away, pulling the golf cart behind him. Clyde looked at Francis, who was smiling a little.

"Always something to learn Clyde," he said.

Clyde walked up to the tee and hit his longest drive of the day, watched the ball soar and drop.

"It's a beautiful thing, Clyde," the Senator was saying, "the way you play the game. My wife Marion claims to hate this game, but I don't think she would if she saw you play it." Self-conscious after all that, Clyde missed the green with his iron shot, but he scraped out a par. By the end of eighteen holes he was six shots ahead of Francis, seven up on the Senator.

After the game, they had a drink with the Senator, who stayed behind at the table when they left to drive into Canalville. The election was only two weeks away, and it was going to be close. By now Clyde knew well enough what a bagman was, and he assumed that the Senator was meeting a supporter to put the arm on him for more money for a last minute series of newspaper ads. Some of the ridings were starting to use commercials on TV, but there was no local station yet.

"He has a lot to offer," Francis said out of the silence as they drove.

"So do I," Clyde said, the words unplanned, impelled in part by the anger that simmered in him.

Francis was silent for a while then he spoke again.

"Hard to know just what to do, isn't it? You were trying to be nice to us, and you get called to account. Feel as if there's no right way."

"I'll manage," Clyde said.

"Yes, my darling, you will."

When he got back to town, Clyde drove out to the house he was buying. He had a spirit level with him, and he checked every wall and floor, examined every piece of trim, looked at the plumbing in the basement, made a list of things that had to be corrected before he'd take possession from the builder. The rest of the houses were still incomplete, and he'd decided to move into this one for a few months, maybe until the spring when the whole subdivision would be done, people living in the houses. Then he'd put his up for sale. The price would have gone up, he was pretty sure. If he could arrange the financing, he'd put a down payment on a second one. The builder was overextended, and Clyde knew he could get a good price if he was willing to have them do the exterior this year, close it in and do most of the interior work in the spring. The danger was that the builder would get in so deep, the house would never get finished, but Clyde's instinct told him it would be OK.

In the election, their candidate won, though with a reduced majority. Clyde was invited to the victory party, but he didn't go. He wasn't a member of their party, or any party. He was a worker. He was a young guy on the make.

4 | Lyall

Lyall Ratner had gone away, attended university, and come back with a wife. Clyde met them on the main street of the town one day when he parked near the liquor store after spending a Saturday morning with his mother, driving into Canalville with her to shop for groceries at the new supermarket in the mall. There was a red Triumph angle-parked at the curb, the top down, a pretty dark-haired young woman in the driver's seat, and just as Clyde arrived, Lyall came out of the store and introduced his new wife. She reached out to shake Clyde's hand, then reversed the little red car quickly into the wide street, changed gears and was gone. After that, they met now and then at parties. Cathy Ratner had thick dark hair, the perfect body of a cheerleader, a slight edge to everything she said, maybe just a bit too quick. Her attitude to Clyde always suggested something between condescension and hostility, but she caught his attention whenever she was around. Clyde liked to observe her when she wasn't noticing him, trying to read the movements of her hands, active hands always cutting the air in some kind of gesture. She and Lyall apparently had a busy social life, but Clyde was not one of those invited to the white frame house on a quiet street near the Presbyterian church.

It had been Doctor Ratner's hope that one of his sons would join him in the practice, but neither did. Harold moved away to the west and was seldom heard from. When Lyall started university, there was still talk that he would go into medicine, but he came back with some kind of degree in nothing much and became a partner in Bateson's Office Supply in the city, partners with an older man, Donald Bateson, who was planning to retire when Lyall was ready to buy out his share.

His father, Clyde supposed, had set him up in the partnership, but the work there didn't keep Lyall from playing a lot of golf and hanging around the course afterward, making jokes about not telling his wife where he was. Cathy Ratner didn't play. She drove him to the course in her jaunty red car, then drove away.

Lyall and Clyde had played against each other for the junior championship the summer before Lyall left for university. The two of them had met in the semi-final round, their last year as juniors, match play on a hot August afternoon. Lyall had been relaxed, sure he was going to win – he had a lower handicap – but at the end of thirteen holes Clyde was one hole up. Match play suited him. A bad hole could be forgotten. The only one that mattered was the one you were playing. On the seventh hole he'd shanked a drive, lost the ball over the bank, picked up two penalty strokes, but he won the eighth with an exceptional drive, a good iron shot and a long putt. It went that way, back and forth. Somehow word had got back to the clubhouse that Lyall didn't have the championship in his pocket, that Clyde was giving him a run for his money, and a few people met them on the green of the sixteenth hole. Clyde was still up by one, and Lyall had gone silent. Sim Secord walked across the fairway toward them. If there was any question of refereeing the end of the match, it would be up to him. He waved, but spoke to neither of them. Jim Bennett had walked across two fairways to meet them, and now he was caddying for Clyde, a gesture of support. Standing waiting for them at the next tee, the dark moustache and slicked-back hair immediately identifiable, was Lyall's father. Lyall didn't look especially happy to see him. They talked quietly, then Doctor Ratner came over to Clyde.

"You're giving my boy a workout here," he said. "Good for you."

Knowing that he was being watched, Clyde was tightening up, and he hit a mediocre drive, followed it with a three wood not much better. He was short of the green. Lyall had driven long, and now he lined up an iron shot which lifted in a high arc and dropped perfectly, ran toward the pin and just beyond. It was pretty certain he had this hole, and the match would come down to three or four shots on the eighteenth.

That match must have meant a lot to Lyall: it was something he remembered. At the end-of-the-season party at the golf club the year after Lyall came back to town with his new wife, Clyde found himself, after dinner, standing a few steps away from Cathy Ratner. Her dark green dress was tight at the waist, showed off the shape of her breasts and hips. What did a woman think, he wondered, when she put on a dress like that and looked in the mirror? Thought of how men observing her would feel, was that it? Or something else. Cathy was looking toward him, and he went to her while she watching him coolly, adding him up, putting him in his place. Always like that, since she'd arrived. Might have been the doctor's wife, but she wasn't, and Clyde heard rumours about Lyall's business.

"Clyde," she said, "Clyde, Clyde," extending the vowel in a way that was perhaps mocking, sounded a little like one of the American tourists who showed up on summer afternoons. He met her brown eyes, saw the brightness in them, didn't know what was in her mind. Do you think there's something missing in your husband? he wanted to say, I've always thought that. Medicine wasn't something that would ever have interested Clyde, but he knew it was a failure for Lyall not to have gone into his father's practice. Maybe Cathy was what he'd chosen instead, the prettiest girl in the class.

"So you were the runner-up," she said, as if she'd been reading his thoughts. He often thought people were reading his thoughts. "You were the runner-up and Lyall was the champion."

Lyall had cared enough about that to tell her the story.

"No, I wasn't exactly the runner-up. We played in the semi-final round."

"And you lost."

"I did. On the eighteenth green."

"Is that a good way to lose?"

"Good as any."

"And now you're some kind of messenger boy for a loan-shark."

"If a man said that, it's possible I'd hit him."

"You wouldn't hit me, Clyde."

"No, Mrs Ratner, I wouldn't. No matter what you said. You see what a gentleman I am."

He turned and walked away. He'd given her enough amusement for the night. There was a phone on the bar, and Clyde went to it and dialed. He and Helena still went to bed together sometimes; he didn't know why she put up with him, but she did. Well, he knew one reason why. But tonight she turned him down. She had company.

"Maybe you better not call again, Clyde," she said. "I'm engaged to be married."

Clyde left the club, drove to *Jelly's*, planning to get a little drunk, think about the prettiest girl in the class and how Lyall had won her. Willing to marry, that was part of it, and now what was Lyall to do with her? Clyde had seen them arguing once, in a low voices, out on the terrace. Cathy drove off in the red Triumph, the wheels spitting gravel from the parking lot. Maybe when she had children she'd lose that edginess.

Jelly was sitting at the corner table in the restaurant, and when he saw Clyde walk up to the bar, he waved him over.

"Will you sit here with me, Clyde? I'm all by myself tonight."

"You're always good company, Jelly."

"You out on the course today?"

"Nine holes."

"Play well?"

"A few good shots."

"They tell me you work for Senator Lawton, Clyde."

"No," Clyde said. "You know where I work."

"I heard you did stuff for him."

There were a couple of things, credit investigations that went beyond the usual bounds, but no one had been told about it. Once or twice Clyde had thought the Senator was about to say something serious to him. He'd been wondering if one day the Senator would make him a proposal. It was as if Jelly had heard the still unspoken words.

"You got the wrong man. I just go around chasing bad debts."

"You're the heavy."

Clyde laughed. "Not me, Jelly."

"So who's the heavy."

"The judge. We have real problems, we go to court."

"I got Paulie over there," Jelly said, indicating a short stocky man at a table in the corner. "Maybe we should call him The Judge. He'd like that."

The bartender came over and Clyde ordered a drink. Even while he was talking to Jelly, he was remembering Cathy Ratner, the sharp tongue, the brown eyes. To her he was a guy who was the runner-up. And now Helena was engaged.

"You got a girl, someone regular, "Jelly said, someone reading his mind again.

"No, Jelly, I sometimes wish I did. One of my girls just told me she got engaged."

"So no more nookie for you."

"I guess not."

"You liked that Maria."

"We used to talk sometimes."

"Crazy girl."

"You never hear from her."

"Not one word."

"You think she might have got into some kind of trouble?"

"Not my business."

The drink came. Clyde tasted it, swallowed, drank again, prayed to the booze to make something happen.

"But you know Senator Lawton. You could talk to him."

"Jelly, you want to talk to him, you can find him in the phone book."

"Clyde, you're on familiar terms with the man. You're in politics with those people."

"He and Francis are friends. I've played golf with him a couple of times. That's all."

Jelly nodded, but Clyde knew he didn't believe him. Clyde finished his drink, waved for another, stared into the green depths of the fish tank at a tiny flickering creature skimming between the weeds. After the next drink he drove home.

His mother too could read his mind. One night he was playing rummy with her at the kitchen table, and while they played, he was thinking about Lyall and Cathy Ratner. He'd driven past the Ratners' house on the way to his mother's after dropping in at a farm on the edge of town to get a basket of pears for her. A light was burning in one of the upstairs rooms of the Ratner house, and Clyde was thinking about Cathy Ratner, what she might be doing. His mother looked up from her cards.

"I know you have girlfriends, Clyde," she said," but do you ever think about marriage?"

"Do *you* ever think about marriage?" he said.

"Don't be silly, I'm an old woman now."

"Did you ever think about it? After…"

"There never was anybody came along to make me think about it. You and I seemed to manage just fine."

"I guess we did."

"Anyway you're changing the subject."

"I guess nobody's come along to make me think about marriage either."

She took a card, discarded the eight of clubs. Clyde picked it up and laid down three eights.

"I should have known," she said, reached out to take a card from the pack. "I got a letter from Danny," she said, "from that place he's in. He says he'll be getting out soon."

"Is he coming back here?"

"He says he doesn't ever want to come back."

Clyde knew that he should have made the drive up to the prison in Kingston to visit Danny, or taken his mother to visit, but he never did. You kept busy. You went on with things.

It was one night during a snowstorm that winter that Clyde finally got the call he'd been anticipating from the Senator, asking him to come to his business office after work the next day, to talk to him. When he did, the Senator asked a lot of questions to which he must already have known the answers. Then he talked about how another election must come soon, given the closely balanced numbers in the House of Commons, the amount of ill-will between Diefenbaker and Pearson. Finally he asked, straight out, if Clyde liked the work, chasing deadbeats for Francis, and Clyde said he was getting a little tired of it. Maybe, the Senator said, he could offer him something better.

So Clyde moved on. Downtown. Francis must have been prepared for it. He and the Senator were friends, or maybe colleagues, or maybe partners sometimes, Clyde was never sure, even years later. They were both secretive men, and there was no saying just what was between them. But they had separate businesses.

"We always recognized Clyde was too smart for us, didn't we Louise?" Francis said on the day Clyde was cleaning out his desk. Louise made a sound of agreement. "Too smart for us. Always knew from the day he started making his private deals with people like Ralph Sherman." Clyde didn't respond. Typical of Francis to know and to save up the information until maybe he could make some use of it, even if only to make Clyde uncomfortable for a minute. He took Clyde out for dinner that evening at a nice place, flattered him, even thanked him for his work, something he'd never done before. He tried to give the impression that he and the Senator had planned this new job for Clyde for a while, hard to know how much truth there was in his insinuations. It was obvious that only a fool would have turned down the Senator's offer.

Clyde's job for the Senator had no exact name, Assistant, he said, if he had to say something. Gate-keeper, they said later on. Fixer. Each day Clyde went into a private office – pebbled glass door, a steel safe in the corner, one small window, a beaten up desk – two floors above the County Finance storefront on the main street of Canalville, and Clyde read the mail, answered it in the Senator's name. He was a fast typist, and whether he was writing letters on his own or constructing a reply on the basis of notes from the Senator, he produced neat work with clean carbon copies. He kept the files in good order; they'd been a mess when he came. Some letters he signed in the Senator's name, others he held for him to sign.

The letters that arrived were an odd mixture. One he always remembered was hand-written in a very small, tight script, and was addressed to Captain James Lawton.

Dear Captain L, It is some time back now but we all remember, isnt it remarkable how the years pass by. We never know how we'll end up, you where you are, me here. Sickness comes to us all, my wife last year, now me the next, but keep the chin up, thats the best advice. You were a good one, you know that and I do, and we have our memories us old ones. It was a muddy sort of a time for us, you know just as I know it. best regards from one of your men, Archibald (Archie) McLean.

He showed it to the Senator.

"I didn't know how to answer this one."

The Senator read it over.

"He's trying to ask for money, but he can't quite bring himself to do it. Send him a postal money order for two hundred dollars," the Senator said.

"You knew him in the First War?"

"He may be the one who saved my life. There were two Archies, and I always got them confused."

So Clyde sent the money.

Once a week Clyde and the Senator met with the Manager of County Finance and were given an outline of the company's recent dealings. Clyde drove the Senator to other meetings, and later on would sometimes go on his behalf when the Senator was in Ottawa. The election the Senator had anticipated was held in April, and Clyde was kept busy all over the constituency, setting up chairs for meetings, delivering copy to the printers, proof-reading, delivering finished work, calling canvassers. Their candidate won the election once again, though it was even closer than the one before; still quite a few voters stuck with a man who'd represented them for ten years.

There was a small Christmas party at County Finance every year, mostly businessmen from the downtown area, and the first time Clyde put in an appearance, he met Lyall and his wife there.

"You're getting to be important, Clyde," Lyall said to him. "Playing with the big guys."

"Still a messenger boy," Clyde said.

"Your friend is so modest, Lyall," Cathy Ratner said. "Men are such shy creatures." Who was she mocking? Maybe all three of them, couldn't take anything seriously. She had her arm linked with Lyall's, a glass in her other hand, ice water it appeared to be. A blue cashmere sweater draped itself softly over the shape of her breasts. Dainty, was that the word for her? Petite was what they'd say in the magazines.

"Just what *is* it you do, Clyde?"

"Run errands, just what I said." She made some gesture with her lips, a gesture of what – disbelief? Ridicule? He turned to Lyall. "How's business?" he said, though in fact he already knew that business in the office supply store was not wonderful. They'd expanded into larger pieces of office furniture and some hi-fi sets, but the money they owed, some of it borrowed from County Finance, wasn't getting paid off, at least none of the balance, though they hadn't defaulted on the interest. Clyde watched the other man.

"It's a good thing we moved into the office furniture," he said, "and the sound systems. There's a rumour that *Grand and Toy* is coming to town, a store out in the new mall. If they do, that's rough competition for the smaller stuff. They buy in bulk so it's hard to beat them on pencils and paper."

It was while he was half-listening to Lyall going on about the movement of business from downtown Canalville to the new mall that Clyde had an idea. Between the big new mall and the old stores downtown, he thought, there might be room for something. Two or three storefronts, with parking. Worth considering. Lyall persisted with his self-deluding, self-congratulatory spiel. Clyde was aware that Cathy had her eyes on him, as if she guessed that he might know more than he was letting on.

"Money, money, money," she said.

"You know how to spend it," Lyall said, laughed.

Then she was no longer watching Clyde. Her eyes were somewhere else.

"We haven't played golf for a long time," Clyde said.

"Yes, we should have a game some time."

"Match play."

Lyall laughed.

"What does that mean?" Cathy said. She was looking at Clyde again, her eyes clear, hard, focussed.

"Cutthroat competition," he said. "Just like the club junior championship."

"So Lyall could beat you again."

"Probably."

She shook her head, not clear quite what it meant, turned and walked away. Clyde watched, turned back. Skirts were getting shorter, and he liked the shape of her legs.

"Time for me to go," he said.

"We'll have that game," Lyall said.

Clyde didn't let go of the thought that had come to him while he was listening to Lyall's chatter. Later that winter, just after the Senator got back from three weeks in Ottawa where the Senate was in session, Clyde drove him the hour and a half from Canalville to a meeting in Toronto in an old brownstone office building downtown. While the meeting was going on, he walked around the big city streets nearby and looked at some of the new construction, a complete city block torn up where a new office tower was being built, traffic still going by on all sides, trucks full of earth and stone pulling out of the site. New office towers, new indoor malls, and beyond the city, miles of new suburbs: Toronto was growing, money making more money. An hour later, as Clyde flipped through the *Globe and Mail*, waiting in the reception room for the Senator to finish his meeting, he decided that he would bring up the idea he'd had at the Christmas party, and as they drove back to Canalville along the Queen Elizabeth Way, he spoke about it.

"You mean a new mall?" the Senator said.

"No," Clyde said. "I don't think there's enough business in the district for that, not yet. Something smaller, but more than one store."

"A strip mall they call them," the Senator said.

"Something like that."

"What do you think the most important thing is, Clyde, about the malls?"

"You mean the parking?"

"This strip mall of yours have parking?"

"Enough that if you're driving by, you can be pretty sure of finding a place."

"But you wouldn't have a department store."

"No. Not enough room."

"So what would you have?"

"I thought maybe a liquor store. You've got more people drinking these days, respectable people, a drink before dinner."

The Senator laughed.

"You might need some influence to get a liquor store."

Clyde looked over at him.

"You've got influence," he said.

"So whose project is this, yours or mine?"

"Maybe both."

"Have you got the property picked out for this joint project."

"Not yet."

"Let me know when you do."

"I will."

As Clyde made his way along the streets of Canalville in the next few months he saw a couple of lots for sale that initially looked promising, but nothing that was quite right. He kept looking. It was one day when he was coming back from checking out a property in a neighbourhood down near the lake that he ran into Lyall on the main street and they arranged to play golf the next day. That night Clyde was sitting in Jelly's, at the corner table, drinking. The restaurant was busy; it often was now. Maybe word was getting out that it was good and the prices were reasonable.

"The Senator," Jelly said.

"Yes, I work for him."

"You admit it now."

"Now it's true.

"You're such a careful boy, Clyde. I see why a smart man like that hires you. You're so careful."

Clyde supposed it was true, though he didn't much like being told that. You want somebody to pussy-foot, get Clyde. Clyde the prudent. Clyde the vigilant. So he noticed things, remembered. Was he only such a little prick?

"You do things for him."

"Some things."

"You could deliver something."

"I don't know."

He wasn't sure yet, about a lot of things. The Senator trusted him, he supposed, to open his mail, overhear what was said in his office, and while driving him back from a meeting of some board of directors being told what happened, but Clyde didn't make the mistake of thinking he was important. The man wanted someone to talk to; his daughters weren't interested in his dealings, had husbands, families, one married to an Anglican minister in Ottawa, one to a teacher in a private school near Toronto, so he paid Clyde to listen when he talked. It helped him think, he always said. And gradually he took Clyde more seriously.

"You'll take it to him."

"What?"

"We'll go outside. You got your car?"

"I'm not sure about this, Jelly. You don't mess around with this man."

"The exact thing. You don't mess around. He'll know I understand."

"Jelly, do you know him, the Senator?

"I shook his hand once. I looked at him. People talk, mostly what they don't know, but I can put it all together."

"I could ask him to call you."

"Come out to the car." He stood up from the table, waved off the bartender who was coming toward them. As they went out the door, a line of cars drove by, the headlights blinding them; then a break in traffic, and there was only the dim light from a sign that hung over the door. He followed Jelly across the lot to a long dark Lincoln, watched him open the trunk and take out a paper bag. He passed it to Clyde.

"Take a look."

He couldn't see much in the dim parking lot, only that it was money, a pile of it.

"Five yards," Jelly said. "You give it to him. It's like a deposit, what the lawyers call it, a retainer. I ask for nothing, just to know he's maybe there to say a word for me someday. Just that he knows who I am."

Clyde stood there in the middle of the dark parking lot, uncertain what to do.

"I'll put the money in my trunk, Jelly. I'll mention it. Maybe he'll tell me to give it back to you. Maybe not. That's the best I can do. All I can promise is to mention it."

"Don't bring it back. He doesn't keep it, you do. It's gone."

"No, Jelly. I can do nothing for you to earn this kind of money. It's his or it's yours."

"Talk to him. It's what I said, a retainer."

Clyde went to his own car, put the money in the trunk behind the little tool kit he kept there, and drove home. Sitting in front of the TV set with a beer he tried to watch a late movie. It was *The Hustler*, with Paul Newman and Jackie Gleason. He'd seen it before, but this time he couldn't pay attention, drank the beer and went to bed, where he slept badly. In the morning he went to the office, typed a couple of letters, made a phone call to arrange an appointment in Hamilton the next day. He talked with Ted Perkins, the manager of County Finance. Donald Bateson had made a payment on the balance of the store's loan. Somehow he hadn't yet retired after all; Lyall hadn't taken over. Probably they were surviving on the older man's savings.

Clyde set off for the golf course. There was no sign of Lyall, but Clyde went into the club house, changed out of his suit then waited on the putting green, getting edgy and annoyed. Lyall arrived fifteen minutes late, gave him a breezy wave as he went in to change. Clyde was one of those unimportant people who could be kept waiting. Lyall never suspected just how much Clyde knew about his business. There was a lot Lyall didn't know, and by the time he appeared, ready to play, Clyde was tempted to tell him some of it.

They waited their turn, stood on the first tee, a breeze bringing the smell of weed and fish from the river where it entered the great lake.

"Strangest thing," Clyde said as he swung his club back and forth a few times. "I find myself with five thousand dollars in cash locked in the trunk of my car."

"How come?" Lyall said. He looked confused, interested.

"Long story," Clyde said.

"You're a strange one, Clyde."

"Not very."

Clyde swung the club back and forth.

"So what are we going to play for?" Lyall said.

"You want to bet on the game?"

"Make it a little more exciting."

"Match play isn't good enough?"

"We could give it a bit of an edge."

Clyde looked at him, then bent and found a tee in the pocket of his golf bag. "What do you want to play for?"

"How about your five thousand dollars? That would make a hit, if I brought that home to dinner. Buy baby some brand new shoes."

Was he blaming his wife for his problems with money, that kind of man?

"What would you put up?" Clyde said

"You'd really put up the five grand? Are you serious?"

"I don't know. Am I?"

"You'd play for five thousand dollars?"

"You wanted a bet."

Lyall was assuming that he'd win, easily, that the money was already in his hand. Clyde could sense how much he wanted it. He could smell Lyall's hunger, like some kind of stinking sweat. He felt the breeze on his bare arms, clenched his hands on his club.

"But you'd have to put up something," Clyde said. "If I put up the five."

"My car?" He was laughing. He still didn't believe this was real.

"I've already got a car."

"You're serious aren't you?"

Clyde could feel something in him growing hard and shiny, as if his nerves had all turned to steel.

"You want the bet?"

"Five thousand dollars against what?"

"What have you got?"

"What have I got? A business, a nice little house, a car, a wife, all the usual."

Clyde took a breath. Something was going to happen here.

"Your wife," he said.

Lyall's face was already a little flushed, and now he stared at Clyde, his eyes wide. Clyde was aware of an older couple, both in bright, baggy, Bermuda shorts putting on the practice green, waiting for the young men to shoot.

"You want me to bet my wife?"

"She's very attractive."

Lyall was laughing. Trying to laugh.

"You're out of your mind," he said. "What kind of people do you hang around with."

Serious people, Clyde wanted to say, but he only shrugged.

"Forget it," he said. "We don't even need to keep score."

"You want my wife, is that what you're telling me?"

"Let it go," Clyde said.

"You think she's interested in you."

"No."

"Then what the hell?"

"Let's play golf."

"You think she'd be willing?"

"I doubt it. After all, she's got you."

"That's right."

"So shall we forget the bet?"

Lyall was staring at him.

"I'll just keep the five thousand in my trunk."

"You were joking, right?"

"Take it that way if you like. No bet. We'll just play the game."

"What make you think she'd be available?" Lyall said. He was still laughing a little, but the laughter wasn't convincing.

"I'd have to ask her."

"Ask what?"

"If she was interested in… passing some time with me."

"You think she'd do that."

"Probably not."

"You think she's got the hots for you."

"I don't think she even likes me."

"Then what the hell are you talking about?"

"You're the one who wanted to bet. I've got five thousand, I asked what you have, you said your wife."

"You'd really make that bet?"

"Yes."

"You don't think she even likes you."

"Let it go, Lyall. Call the whole thing a joke."

"You can't find a woman of your own, is that it? It's worth five thousand dollars to you."

"Put it that way if you like. Let's tee off."

Lyall put the tee into the ground. He turned around and looked at Clyde again.

"Are you crazy?" he said.

"Probably. I just mentioned the money in my trunk, and one thing led to another. You wanted to bet. You think you can take the money from me. Maybe you're right."

Lyall swung, and there was a soft snick as the head of the driver hit the ball and lifted it into the air where it sailed high, a dot against the blue sky, dropped to the grass and rolled forward. A perfect drive.

"You can't beat me," he said. "You're offering to give away five thousand dollars.

"I'll take my chances."

"Match play," he said as he put the driver away in his leather bag. "When I win you'll hand me the five thousand dollars cash."

Clyde pressed the sharp end of the wooden tee into the earth.

"In a brown paper bag," he said. "And if I should just by any chance happen to beat you, you'll take a long hike, and I'll drop round for a conversation with your beautiful wife."

"But I'm a better golfer," Lyall said. "Always was."

Clyde swung the club. The ball ended up perhaps ten yards short of the place where Lyall's was lying. He picked up his clubs, and the two of them hiked down the fairway. Clyde was thinking about how he'd replace the five thousand dollars if he lost, and it would be possible, though he'd feel the loss. He put the thought out of his mind as he came up to where he could see his ball against the green of the fairway. Lyall's ball was a little ahead and to the left. The pin was to the left of the green, so Clyde had a little better angle on it. He looked in his bag; the old problem, to ease up on a six or push a seven. He took out the higher numbered club. If he was going to play seriously, there was no point being cautious now. The ball lay, a little awkwardly, behind a small clump of grass. Nothing to be done. He set up, took a long look at the green, put his head down and swung, the ball caught sharply on the back surface, and he watched it loft toward the green. It had been a dry summer, and though the greens were watered regularly, he expected them to be fast, but when his ball landed, the backspin grabbed and it rolled slowly forward, past the pin, a little to the right. Not a bad putt from there. Lyall was standing by his ball, an iron in his hand, and as Clyde's ball landed and rolled, he made a soft noise in his throat. Clyde waited for him to play. He was tempted to laugh when he thought about the bet they'd made. Clyde, Clyde, Clyde, he said to himself, in the drawling way Cathy Ratner had said it. For some reason he imagined her back at their house, in the tub, surrounded by bubble bath, a picture from an ad in a magazine, and that made him laugh too. Lyall swung the club. It was a good shot, but coming in from the left he had tried to cut it too fine, and after the ball hit, it ran a short distance and just into the longer grass of the verge. A hard putt from there.

When Clyde reached the green, he took out the flag and laid it carefully on the green out of their way. Lyall took out his putter, walked to where his ball lay. There was a slight downhill slope to the hole. He walked halfway, went back to the ball and bent over it; he needed a firm tap to get free of the longer grass, but he gave it a bit too much, and it ran past the hole by more than three feet. He swore under his breath. Clyde stepped up to his ball. He was putting across the roll of the green and tried to judge how much to allow for that. Once more he summoned up the ridiculous picture of Cathy Ratner in that bubble bath advertisement, laughed to himself and tapped the ball. The stroke of the putter was a little hard, and if he missed the hole, it would roll on, but the line was right and the ball dropped. Lyall picked up his ball, no need to play it out. Clyde was one up.

They walked back to the next tee, a three par over the moat and the hill into the green beside the old fort.

"You're serious," Lyall said, "about this bet."

He looked like a kid caught stealing from a store. Squirming, wanting to be let off.

"Never more serious," Clyde said. "Can't change the rules now, can we?

Lyall was silent as they tied the next three holes, both playing even par except for matched bogies on the long fourth, though Clyde came within an inch or two of dropping a very long putt and going ahead by two, but on the fifth, his drive tailed off at the end in a late slice and dropped behind a group of trees. The shot left him with a couple of choices, to try to run the ball out between the trunks, or to lift it over. Both shots were dangerous. A straight line from the ball to the green took him very close to one of the trunks. So he tried to go over, but the rising ball caught a small branch that changed its trajectory and slowed it so it dropped short of the green. Lyall's iron shot sat safely on the green, an easy two putt. Clyde made a desperate attempt to run his approach right to the pin, but the hole was lost.

"Back to the beginning," Lyall said, as they stood on the sixth tee.

"One way to look at it," Clyde said. He looked above them where a single gull was soaring on the breeze off the water, adjusting its wings to turn. A couple of people in bathing suits were heading across the seventh fairway to the beach below, a foursome holding their shots until the swimmers were past. Out on the lake, the shape of a freighter. Later in the day he'd talk to the Senator about the money that Jelly was offering. Clyde was almost sure the Senator wouldn't take it, but he would make the offer. Perhaps it was a mistake to let Jelly give him the money. Clyde the Bagman. He still remembered the little parcel of cash he'd dropped off in an empty car years before, though he'd never learned what that was all about. He knew he'd find out sooner or later. He knew such things.

They tied the next three holes, though Clyde found himself in a little trouble on the eighth, behind a tree once again, but this time a high iron shot carried safely past. On the ninth hole, a long three par, Lyall went ahead with a very straight tee shot and a good putt. Not so pale now, he was congratulating himself on that last hole as they came back to the clubhouse. It was a nine hole course, so for a full eighteen they played it twice, sometimes from different tees the second time round.

"So you want to show me this money that's in your trunk, Clyde?" he said as they drank a bottle of pop and waited to tee off.

"You want to show me your wife?"

"That's not very funny," Lyall said.

"Wasn't meant to be."

"Just keep your mouth shut about her."

"You started the conversation."

Lyall went up to the tee, took an angry swipe at the grass with his club. He swung the club hard, as if he was determined to drive the ball all the way to the green by main force, and it sliced right and ended up in the long grass at the edge of the river bank. Clyde tried to think of the bubble bath, to laugh about it as he walked to the tee, but the laughter was gone now, and there was a kind of darkness in his head. He breathed deeply, studied the ball, it seemed to grow larger, every dimple of the white surface a deep cavity. Out of the corner of his eye, he could make out Sim Secord, who seemed to be watching. He blinked, gathered his concentration, managed a smooth easy swing. Not a long drive, but well-placed.

It took Lyall two shots to get from the rough to the green, and Clyde took the hole easily, so they were even again. What was he going to say to Cathy Ratner if he won? He couldn't imagine, and he reminded himself he was a long way from winning. As they walked to the eleventh tee, Clyde could see Lyall's lips moving, though he was saying nothing aloud. For the first time now, Lyall saw that this was real, he'd actually made the bet, and no one was going to tell him that all was forgiven, that like a nightmare, it would vanish when he woke. Maybe it would do him some good to understand the cost of his words. Clyde knew that losing to him was one of the worst things that Lyall could endure. Clyde was a messenger, a debt-collector, who came to beautiful Brockton in the same years as the DPs from Europe and like them wasn't to be taken altogether seriously.

From just off the next green, Clyde sank his approach shot for a birdie, surprised even himself as the ball curved and dropped. Lyall slammed his putter against the earth. they didn't speak now, nothing to be said. Once again on the next tee, Clyde felt a kind of darkness closing in around him, the ball grotesquely enlarged, tamed the feeling. He swung. He was one up, and there were seven holes to play. Lyall had begun to hit wild shots, was in the rough again, but was saved by a lucky bounce. Five holes to go. Four. Clyde was still one up. The sixteenth hole was usually played as a dogleg around a set of sand traps and a little hollow of rough ground leading down to the lake. The light breeze was behind them, and Clyde decided that he'd take the chance of driving straight, right over the traps. It left an easier shot to the green, one where you could see where you were shooting, instead of going down the dogleg and hitting blind. He teed the ball a bit high, thinking that if he got it well up in the air, the breeze would help it along. Took a deep breath, released it, and the club head moved in a long smooth arc, the ball lifted, but he couldn't tell if he was going to make it over the traps. He saw a bounce where the ground fell away, but was unable to see where the ball had settled.

Lyall was looking at him, as he walked back to where the bag of clubs lay. They both knew that this could be the end of it, and Lyall stood with his driver in his hand for a long moment before he walked up to the tee. He swung, and there was a heavy sound to the crack as the club met the ball. It flew straight, the same direction as Clyde's shot, but lower. It wouldn't make it, Clyde thought, not enough lift, but there was a chance that Clyde too would find his ball in the rough or in one of the traps.

His first guess was right. Lyall's ball was dug into a small hole in one of the traps, and his own landed beyond and rolled toward the green, though it had bounced to the left at a surprising angle, but his approach shot to the pin was clear. Lyall dropped his bag of clubs, walked into the trap with an iron in his hand, studied the ball. As he was lining up, a woman in a black bathing suit, with a towel around her shoulders came up the path that followed a hollow in the ground toward the beach. There were two children with her. The black bathing suit made her thighs look whiter, heavier. Lyall looked toward her angrily, his lips moving, no sound. He swung the club, and the ball lifted and hopped into the next trap.

Lyall pounded his club and mouthed an obscenity at the woman, looked at Clyde as if he was about to claim some kind of foul, a chance to play the hole again. Clyde met his look, waited for him to speak, but Lyall said nothing, went to the second trap and swung. The ball lifted free of the trap, but stopped short of the green. Clyde lined up his shot. He could win the round with this shot; Lyall had two more holes to get back even, but the way they were playing it wasn't likely. Approach shots were deceptive, looked easy, but you could get yourself in a lot of trouble. He lined up, swung and the ball landed just short of the green, ran toward the pin. He would be two up at the end of the hole. He watched the woman's fat white thighs rubbing together as she and the children crossed the course. Clyde won the hole, and they moved to the seventeenth tee, and as they stood there, he was aware that he could still blow it. What he needed was to play automatically, shot by shot, drive, long iron to the green, though in fact his iron stopped a little short, Lyall, tight now, had missed the green to the right. There was an airless concentration around them as they putted, Lyall short from the far edge, Clyde misjudging the angle of the slope and running long. Then Lyall missed his second putt, only six feet, but it curled around the cup and stayed on the grass. Clyde was tempted to miss his on purpose. All he needed on this hole was a tie, and Lyall was already picking up his clubs, but he concentrated, and the ball dropped. It was over. By the time he'd put the flag in the hole, Lyall was a hundred feet away, walking fast across the fairway past the tee for the last hole and along the edge of the ditch by the first fairway. When Clyde got back to the clubhouse, Lyall's car was gone. Would he drive home and tell Cathy the story? Hard to say. A bet was a funny thing. Nobody enforced the rules, but at some time in your life, when you were eight or ten or twelve, you came to realize that it was a matter of the deepest honour, though maybe you couldn't have said what honour was. You gave your word, which meant you had locked yourself in. It was a trap for pride; to back down meant humiliation. Lyall could drive home, tell his wife the story, and when Clyde arrived the two of them could tell him to hit the road, the whole thing was a childish game. For some reason, Clyde didn't think Lyall would do that. He wasn't clear-headed enough to know the price and how to pay it. It was what he would think of tomorrow.

As he climbed out of the shower, Clyde looked down at his naked body. Clyde, Clyde, Clyde, he said to himself again, dressed and got in his car. When he got to the house Clyde parked by the side of the road, his wheels on the grass, no curb on the old streets here in Brockton, only a low ditch to carry off rainwater. There was no car parked in the driveway; perhaps she wasn't home. It was a while since he'd seen the red Triumph. He opened the gate that led to the low white house, small gables indicating the upstairs bedrooms. It was an old house with mullioned windows, the clapboard painted white, the trim a dark green. He pressed the round button beside the door and waited.

Then she was standing in the doorway, in pale brown slacks and a off-white top, sandals on her feet. She looked only a little surprised to see him.

"Clyde," she said, saying his name the way she liked to do, a way that always sounded mocking, perhaps was. The dark hair was pulled back behind her ears, and the brown eyes were watchful, bright. Clyde wasn't sure what to say, said nothing.

"Well, come in," she said, stood back.

He entered the house, aware of how close he was to her as he passed, not touching. He felt that he might be able to smell her skin or feel the heat of her body.

"You've never been here before," she said.

He didn't say it was because he'd never been invited, wasn't on their list of people to see.

"It's a nice old house," he said.

"I'm sure you know what it's like with old houses," she said. "Always something needing attention. But it's nice to have a few gentle ghosts for company on the cloudy days."

He looked at her, the dark hair, pale clothes, trying to interpret what she said. Just making conversation, he supposed. A social skill. The living room, where they were standing, was painted white and seemed a little bare, one or two small prints on the wall, not very much furniture. Perhaps it was stylish, this bareness, whiteness. It focussed attention on the woman who was standing opposite him, who sat down and indicated a chair to him.

"You have ghosts?" he said.

"I like to think so. The nineteenth century gentlewomen of Brockton reminding us of our manners."

Clyde could see the sunlight shining through the leaves of an old tree outside the window of the dining room that adjoined the room where they sat.

"We must invite you round for dinner sometime, Clyde. If you'd be willing to come. Would you?"

She was handling him, condescending a little as always. She crossed her legs, and he was aware of the shape of her thighs, one poised on the other. He saw that she was smiling at him, as if his presence there was some kind of a joke the two of them shared. Maybe it was. Maybe she knew already the reason he'd come.

"I thought you were playing golf with Lyall today."

"We already played."

"And what was the outcome of the big match, Clyde?"

"I won."

"I thought Lyall was a better player. I thought you were the runner-up."

"Well, today I won."

"On the eighteenth green?"

"The seventeenth."

Her breathing was noticeable, slow deep inhalations, as if she'd just run up a flight of stairs. No doubt it made her nervous, having him come to the door of the house like this. Her face was a little flushed, the eyes bright. As if she'd been running. He wondered what she'd been doing when he came to the door.

"So you won, Clyde."

"Yes, I did."

"And where's Lyall, off sulking somewhere, sent you to tell me the news?"

"Something like that I guess."

"He's not a good loser. He certainly does not like to lose. But I'm sure you know that. You've known him since you were little boys."

"Him and his brother."

"I've never met Harold. What's he like?"

"He's an unkind person," Clyde said and was surprised at the words after they were out, not that they weren't true, but he'd never articulated the thought before.

"I'm sure that you, on the other hand, are a very kind person."

"And you," Clyde said, "are the prettiest girl in the class. Lyall brought home the prettiest girl in the class."

"Is there sarcasm in that, Clyde?"

"Not about you," he said, and he was looking at her, in her pale loose top that caressed her shape, the dark green sandals on her feet, the bare toes which were to him, at that moment, a scandalous, improper nakedness.

"Where is Lyall?" she said, suddenly serious. "Why isn't he here?"

Clyde looked at her, the lips that were not smiling, soft pink flesh, and her tongue licked nervously, vanished. He listened for some noise outside the room, something to assure him that the world was still there, but he heard nothing except his own breath exhaling.

"We had a bet on the match," Clyde said. "He lost."

"He can't afford to lose," she said, and maybe there was a hint of impatience. Whether or not Lyall told her about his money problems, she knew. And she didn't like it. Sat here in the beautiful house with her gentle ghosts, helpless, waiting for Lyall to fix things. Clyde felt sorry for her.

"Nobody can afford to lose," Clyde said, "when you think about it. There are so many things we depend on."

"I don't know what you're talking about," she said.

Clyde just shrugged.

"How much?" she said.

"Well it all started when I told Lyall I happened to have five thousand dollars in cash in the trunk of my car."

"He lost five thousand dollars?" she said, and now he could see she was frightened.

"No."

"I don't understand."

"I bet the five thousand dollars cash."

"What did Lyall bet?"

"You."

He watched her face, the way the expression changed as she tried to take it in, confusion, shock, some kind if embarrassment perhaps. She grew flushed, stared at him.

"What do you mean?" she said, quietly now.

"He thought he was going to win. He wanted the five thousand dollars."

"Where is he? Where is he now?"

"I don't know."

"You're lying," she said. "He wouldn't do that."

"He thought he was going to win."

"Why didn't he?"

"It's a game. I play it quite well. Sometimes you win. Sometimes you lose. He thought he'd come home with the five thousand dollars, and you'd be pleased. 'Buy baby some brand new shoes,' he said. But golf is a difficult game. A bad bounce, a couple of tricky putts. I was playing well. The idea of winning appealed to me."

She stood up, but aware that he was watching her, she sat back down again.

"And I'm supposed to…"

"Only if you happened to want to."

"Why would I want to?"

"I don't know. Curiosity. Anger."

"Anger?"

"He did make the bet. He offered you."

"He wouldn't do that."

"He did it."

"I only have your word for that."

"Do you think I'd be here if it wasn't true? That I'd make it all up and come to your door. I have some nerve, but I don't have the nerve for that."

"You're here."

"And the story I told you is true."

"And I'm supposed to get into bed with you because you won me in a golf game."

"Let's just say that you're free to do it, if the idea appealed to you. For this one afternoon you've been given a holiday from your promises."

"You've got to be crazy to think I'd do that. You think I can't resist you, that I'm just waiting for you to ask?"

"Actually I've always thought you didn't much like me."

"You're right. I think you're a jerk."

"I wasn't so hungry for a little cash that I bet my wife."

"You don't have a wife."

"Do you think it's the kind of thing I'd do?"

She looked at him now, for the first time, as if she saw someone there. Their eyes met, and then she looked away.

"You never need money that badly," she said.

"What do you know about it?" he said. "Whether I need money or I don't. I've been quite aware of your condescension, Mrs Lyall Ratner, and I've never thought I deserved it. I won that golf game because I win things, Lyall lost because he loses things. I know my limits. He doesn't.

All I bet was money, more money than I could afford, but I could have managed, and it would have been worth the loss to watch him squirm every time I won a hole. It was worth it to watch him make the bet, because he was so confident and because he couldn't think about what came next. You know that, don't you, Mrs Ratner, that your husband's not too good about seeing what comes next. That's why he didn't end up in medical school. He's a weakling, your Lyall, and he got so excited about a few dollars that he bet his wife. I don't really think you'll have me in your bed, that you'll even rise above your glib contempt to wonder about it, but at least the next time you meet me at a party, you won't look down your nose at me. You're the prettiest girl in the class, Mrs Ratner, there's no doubt about that, but what else?"

The phone was ringing. She got up and went to the table by the front door to answer it.

"Oh hi, honey," she said. The afternoon sunlight was bright as if shone through the white glass curtain on the door, illuminating her face, which was flaming red, her eyes wet. She listened for a moment.

"No," she said, blandly, "there's nobody here."

Waited.

"OK," she said, "See you at six."

Clyde was a little surprised when she told Lyall there was no-one here, but then he thought that there was nothing else she could say. His anger was gone now, the desire to be cruel to her, and he felt some kind of sympathy for her, the situation she was in. He could stand up and leave, set her free. She came back into the room, sat down in the chair and looked toward him as if she expected more hard words.

"So you hate the both of us," she said.

"Resentment," he said, "is a better word. Probably unfair, to resent you. I suppose it happens to beautiful women. They have some kind of power over us, and men start to be angry about it. Men get wound up about things, at least I do, and then you find you reached someplace you never expected to be. Like here."

"He called to see if you were here."

"Did he say that, 'Is Clyde there?'"

"He said, 'Is anybody there?'"

"Hoping I'd chickened out."

"Doesn't know you very well, does he?

"If I'd waited another hour, I might have."

"I doubt it. You like winning."

"What would he have done if you'd told him the truth?"
"I wouldn't dare find out."
They sat there is silence. Now he could hear a bird calling in a tree somewhere outside the house.
"Who was the one to suggest it, the bet?"
"I mentioned the money. He said did I want to play for it."
"Who mentioned me?"
"I guess I did."
"Why?"
"Because I wanted you."
"You wanted to fuck the prettiest girl in the class."
"You."
"To get even. For my contempt."
"I was willing to take it as a provocation."
"I treat you the way I do because you make me angry. So pleased with yourself in your quiet little way."
"We are what we are."
"Do you have a girl-friend?"
"No. Not really."
"Why not?"
"Afraid to be tied down maybe."
Again they sat in silence. She was watching him. She pushed the hair back from her face with both hands.
"You are a son-of-a-bitch, aren't you Clyde?"
Once again there was an edge to her look, something bright and defiant.
"If you say so."
She was looking at him, intently. You could say she wasn't sure whether he was a human being or another of her ghosts, as if she was trying to see into his brain. Her face was bare, a little inhuman almost, as if she had removed a layer of makeup, of social pretence.
"A hard, cruel, cunning son-of-a-bitch. To make that bet."
"Lyall made the bet."
"My poor dim Lyall."
"If you say so," he repeated.
"Five thousand dollars."
"It's only money."
"And it's what I'm worth to him."
"It's what I had."

Again she was studying him.

"Shall we go upstairs?" she said.

"Yes."

She stood up and he followed her as she climbed the stairs, turned to her left and led him into a bedroom with sloping ceilings. The bed was covered with a white cretonne spread, and she pulled it back, threw it on the floor at the end. She turned and glanced at him as he stood by the door, looked away and began to undress, quickly, then turned to him again, defiant, and his eye was drawn to the thick bush of dark pubic hair, flagrant, astonishing, the round breasts with their dark nipples. As she pulled back the pale blue sheet and climbed into bed, he was taking off his clothes and, as he moved across the room caught a glimpse of himself in the mirror of a dressing table. For a moment he thought he heard a voice somewhere in the house, a woman's voice speaking to him. The naked woman beneath him didn't say a word.

It was months later that Clyde picked up a novel, a best-seller that someone had left behind in the office and, glancing through it, found scenes where the author tried to say what it was like, a man and a woman together, and as Clyde read the unconvincing description, the overstated empty words, he thought back to that afternoon. You couldn't say in words what it was like: the two of you in some kind of nowhere together, and time didn't exist.

Other things were going on in the streets of Brockton. A few doors away, a fifteen-year old boy was pushing a hand lawnmower over the lawn at his parents' house, the curved metal blades chattering against the steel plate at the bottom. Down by the river, a clergyman was studying the beach where, the next Sunday, he would bring a group of young people to be baptised by immersion in the water of the river. He would bend them backward, holding them firmly, duck them under and bring them up, newly born. The clergyman liked to come here first, to see it all in his mind, plan where they'd enter the water, just where he'd stand, how they would come to him.

While the two bodies in the old house grew damp with sweat, up on the main street of town, in the butcher shop, one of the butchers, a short, heavy man, took the chilled carcass of a lamb out of the walk-in cooler and carried it to the back doorway. There were iron hooks on each side, and he hooked the shanks of the back legs on them so that the carcass hung splayed in the doorway, and then he raised the cleaver in both hands, brought it down sharply on the cold flesh and began to sever the carcass into two sides of meat, the sharp cleaver striking through the spine, splitting it, all the way down the long back and neck. When he was done, he carried the sides of meat to the butcher block and cut them into front and back quarters, cut, chopped, sawed them into pieces of a size for cooking.

You couldn't describe what the man and woman were doing. You only knew that they were apart from the events around them, the sheltered backyard where a young wife went out to sun-bathe behind a wooden fence, wearing, for the first time, her daring new bikini, nervous, though she knew no-one could observe her on the back patio, lying down to feel the sun on her skin, but before long, self-conscious, standing up and returning to the house. You couldn't measure out the time of it. On another quiet street, another housewife filled a pie shell with bright red cherries, sugar, flour, a little cinnamon, and when she had put on the pastry top, she set it in the hot oven, adjusted a little mechanical timer that began to tick, would ring when it was time to take out the pie. At the boatslip by the river, two boys sat on a rickety wooden dock, lines in the water, watching the sunfish that swam past their worms, refusing to bite. They waited, watched the fish dart away if they moved the line.

Perhaps, as he was putting the lawnmower away after finishing the last corner, as he was looking for the light rake, the boy a few houses away thought he heard voices nearby, singing. The butcher laid out the pieces of lamb in the refrigerated counter. The clergyman was breathing heavily as he climbed up the hill from the beach; at the top, when he stopped to catch his breath, he looked up through the trees to the brightness of the blue sky. The boys on the rickety dock pulled their lines from the water and set off for home.

Even afterward, the woman didn't speak to Clyde, not one word, and he found nothing that could be said aloud, but when he'd climbed from the bed, he turned toward her where she lay on the pale blue sheets, slack, splendid, watching him as he dressed, and he found himself saying, "You could call me, if you ever wanted to." She didn't answer.

Clyde drove to Canalville, to his apartment, stood in the shower, then dressed. Later he called the Senator. The Senator told him to come round to his house, and when he got there they sat on the screened porch looking past a rose garden and over a wide lawn to the low stone fence that separated the property from the neighbour's.

"Did you promise the man something, Clyde?"

"What I'm doing right now, that I'd tell you about it."

"How much money?"

"Five thousand dollars, he said. I haven't counted it."

"He's some kind of criminal."

"There are rumours. I don't know anything definite. There used to be a prostitute working out of his restaurant. That could have been just the bar-tender, with a little freelance operation."

"She's not there now."

"Disappeared. Nobody seems to know where she is."

The Senator's massive head was leaning forward, as if he hadn't quite enough strength to hold it up. He didn't turn to Clyde or look toward him.

"That body in the lake."

"Yeah, that's what I thought, but it was someone else. So the police said. A runaway from Hamilton."

On the lawn a robin cocked its head, listening, then pecked the earth, flew away. Clyde remembered Cathy Ratner lying on the bed watching him dress, arms raised above her head, her body slack. He took a deep breath.

"And if I turn down the money?" the Senator said.

"He told me I should keep it."

"Will you do that?"

"What do you think?"

"I think it would be foolish. What can you do for the man to earn five thousand dollars?"

"That's exactly what I said to him."

The Senator lifted his head now, sniffed.

"I can smell those roses from here," he said. "Marion does a lovely job with the garden. She has help, of course, though she's surprisingly strong for an old woman, but she does the important things. She's trying to produce a new rose. The Marion Lawton rose it will be called if she succeeds."

Clyde said nothing. He was distracted by the memory of the sunlight coming through the curtains of the bedroom. He wondered what she would tell Lyall. Nothing. By now she would have washed the sheets, showered, dressed herself in something pretty, a bright cotton dress, started to make dinner for her husband. They would lie to each other about the episode, and it would disappear.

"When are you starting to meet with people about our project?" the

Senator said.

"Friday," Clyde said.

"And you'll give the gentleman back his money," the Senator said.

Clyde made a sound to indicate his agreement.

"You could tell him," the old man said, "that it's too much for a gift and not enough for a bribe." He was silent for a moment. "No," he said, "don't tell him that. Just be polite. I know you will. Would you like to stay for dinner?"

"Not tonight, Senator, but thank you."

"A woman?"

"In a manner of speaking."

"You're full of mysteries, Clyde."

"No," Clyde said, "I don't think so."

Clyde drove to *Jelly's* and ordered dinner. When the man came in later on, he would return the money, say they were flattered by the offer, thought well of him, but neither he nor the Senator could accept.

Clyde wondered if Cathy might call him, or if there might be some response from Lyall, but there was silence. A month later, Clyde heard someone in the clubhouse remarking that Lyall wasn't playing much golf this year, and certainly Clyde never saw him at the course. Clyde himself played less that year, every hole haunted by the strokes of his game with Lyall. Whenever he drove to Brockton to visit his mother, he was aware of Cathy Ratner in that house a few blocks away. He spent too much time wondering about her, what she was doing, whether she hated him, or whether she expected him to come back to her door. During the act he was no one, her eyes were closed, but what was in her eyes as she lay on the bed and watched him dress? He was not to know.

He thought he saw her once, later that summer, but it was on the edge of a town an hour's drive away, near Hamilton, and it made no sense that she would be there. A ghost, like the ghosts in her house. He had an appointment to talk to Jake Everard at his large construction yard a mile or so outside the town. He wasn't looking forward to the interview. Clyde parked outside the tall wooden fence that Sunday morning and was met at the gate by an old man whose torso was bent forward, as if his spine had locked into that position, who had come from a shack by the entrance, a heavy cane in his right hand. Clyde explained why he was there, and the old man pointed out to him a little house at the end of the yard, a tiny bungalow that had been moved from some other site and set up on concrete blocks. Trucks, loaders, huge earth-moving equipment, it was all parked in neat rows along the road beside him as he walked, something military about the muted power of the big machines, the way they were set in lines, an army awaiting the order to move. As Clyde got closer to the bungalow, he saw a black dog lying in the shade underneath, the dog with its head on its paws watching him come closer, looking at Clyde as if counting his steps, waiting for the moment to attack. It was a big dog, but when Clyde was a few steps away and the dog rose to its feet, he saw that it was chained to one of the blocks, though with enough loose chain for the dog to travel ten or fifteen yards.

The door of the little bungalow opened, and a man appeared, walked down the steps to meet Clyde, not a big man, but heavy through the shoulders and chest, the face clean shaven, a sharp nose, the mouth set in a frown.

"Come in," he said, put his hand out to shake, a big hand, but the handshake was perfunctory, the grip loose. He didn't bother showing off his strength. They went up the set of wooden steps which was leaning against the sill in front of the door, not attached. Inside, a desk in the corner of the one room, on it a black telephone, a bottle of rye. Against the back wall, a cot with a mattress, sheets, a pillow. The door to a small bathroom stood open, and on a table near it, a hotplate, with a kettle and a teapot. On one of the walls was a big map of the whole district, various notes on it in pencil, beside it a calendar from an equipment company, an old fashioned drawing of a long-legged girl is a short skirt.

"You want a drink?"

Best to say yes, Clyde thought, and the man poured him half a tumbler of rye, the same for himself, though Clyde noticed that as he settled himself behind the desk he didn't drink any of it. He motioned Clyde to sit in the straight chair in front of the desk.

"Why doesn't he come himself, instead of sending a messenger boy?"

Clyde looked at the man.

"This is what he wanted," Clyde said.

"You do everything he wants."

"That's what I'm paid for, just like the men who work for you."

Clyde took a sip of the rye. It didn't appeal to him at ten in the morning, but it gave him a few seconds when he didn't need to say anything.

"So you want something from me. Or you wouldn't be here."

"No, I wouldn't say that. We're offering something to you."

"You bet."

Clyde looked at the man. He could get thrown out of here on his ass, or the man might pick up the phone and cause no end of trouble.

"We heard you took a beating on the dock at Wood River."

"Who told you that?"

"Word gets around."

"You think you're gonna lend me money? Pay off my debts."

"No."

"What?"

"Save you money, maybe. So what happened at Wood River doesn't happen again."

"I bid too low and got fucked, that's what happened at Wood River."

Clyde looked at him, met the grim grey eyes. Was he such an angry man or was it just his way of keeping on top of the situation?

"Somebody asked us to act as... negotiators you could call it... to try to make an arrangement."

Jake Everard took his first swallow from the glass of rye, belched quietly behind his hand.

"You want to rig the bids."

Clyde picked up the glass of rye, drank, burning his mouth and throat, needed it now, and needed the time. It had gone too fast. He hadn't had much breakfast, and he felt as if the rye was going straight to his head. He put it back down on the table. He wondered if he should be quoting what the Senator said about jobs put out to tender. It was supposed to be the most efficient way, he said, save the customer money by fair competition, but in practice that didn't happen, too many personal feelings, too many impulsive mistakes. Statistically it all evened out, but only approaching infinity. "Which of us lives at infinity?" the Senator rumbled in his froggy voice. Clyde didn't think Jake Everard would have the patience for that kind of talk, so he said nothing, waited, what seemed safest. Either he threw him out now or he was ready to listen to the details. The silence extended itself a long time. Jake drank again. Clyde waited.

"Why does he send a kid to do this?"

Clyde shrugged his shoulders. "I'm what he's got."

"If you weren't talking to me, what would you be doing?"

"Sleeping. Playing golf."

"I always thought that looked like a stupid game."

"It does unless you're playing it."

"Bang, bang, bang," he said, making a chopping motion with his two hands. "But I guess that's life, one way or another. I bang around with big machines."

Clyde nodded.

"So what's in it for the old man?"

"Somebody's got to take the completion bonds."

"What percentage extra?"

Clyde was impressed with the speed at which Jake Everard had seen it all, laid out as clearly as the townships on that map on the wall.

"Maybe a quarter, a half. We think of this as a long term investment. If it all works out, you can plan your schedules better, save money that way, not get screwed if you come in way too low."

"And if I don't agree?"

"You'll be left out in the cold. The others will play without you. That's the best that will happen."

"What kind of jobs, government, private?"

"See what we can work out."

Jake took another large swallow of the rye.

"I didn't get your name," the man said, "when you called. Just who sent you."

"Clyde."

"Drink up, Clyde. You still got time for a few holes this afternoon. I told my kid I'd take him fishing."

Clyde didn't drink all of what was in his glass, but walking back out to the gate, the earth was a little unsteady beneath his feet, and the sun blinded him. He was frightened by what he had just done. He shivered a little in spite of the hot sun. It was at that moment he thought he saw Cathy Ratner, the little red car passing the gate, the dark hair of the woman driving, and he walked faster, and then he was watching the old man bent forward in the doorway of his shack, leaning on the cane, moving slowly, awkwardly, out of the dark shade into the brightness to open the gate. Clyde drove half a mile down the road, saw a little park with a ball diamond, a few kids playing a pickup game. He pulled into the parking lot, put his head back and closed his eyes, picturing the red sports car, wondering if he'd imagined it.

The next year Lyall let his membership in the golf club lapse, joined another club, farther away, or so Clyde heard. Though he knew where the Ratners lived, often drove to his mother's house only a quarter mile away, the two of them managed to disappear from his life. Lyall and

Donald Bateson were still in debt to County Finance, but they kept up their payments. Once, years later, Clyde saw Lyall and Cathy, with kids, across the parking lot at a mall in the city. He turned the other way.

5 | Noreen

The first time Clyde saw Noreen, she was pushing a wheelbarrow, wearing shorts and a man's shirt, her feet bare and stained with earth. It was at the Senator's house a few miles from Canalville and just at the edge of the escarpment, overlooking the flat farmland toward the lake. Clyde had come to discuss the cost of newspaper advertising for their candidate in the November federal election. As Clyde parked his car, a tall young woman appeared from behind the garage manipulating a wheelbarrow loaded with manure. Long, bare, elegant legs. He had no idea who she was, but when she set down the handles and waved to him, he was happy to wave back. As he reached the door of the house, Marion Lawton was coming out.

"Did you meet Noreen?"

"We waved to each other."

"Will you drive her to Toronto?"

"When?"

Marion looked at the tiny silver watch on her wrist.

"Twenty minutes after one," she said decisively, as if all this was part of a maneuver that required precise timing.

"Sure," Clyde said, not sure what else to say. The best way to deal with Marion was not to ask questions. She had her own ways, and no one else, not even the Senator, ever understood perfectly what was behind her decisions.

"Tell Jessie to make you sandwiches for the trip," she said, and she walked away.

Clyde went into the house and found the Senator in his den. The room was panelled in dark mahogany, the shelves full of books, in the centre of the room stood a wide desk with a leather top that was generally kept clear of paper. The Senator was sitting in an armchair with a book in his hand.

"Reading some new stuff about Dieppe," he said. "Terrible mess."

"So they say."

"Do you read about it?"

"I have. Sometimes I don't want to."

"I was in Ottawa. At first they claimed it was a great success. But Churchill wanted a failure and that's what he got."

The Senator put down the book. Clyde gave him the advertising budget. Charles Upton, the local member, had decided to retire, and Barton Dred, the new candidate, who was a car dealer and one of the directors of County Finance, wasn't as well known. The budget for newspaper advertising was substantial. The Senator advised Clyde to make sure that the paper's publisher knew that they were putting a lot of money in his pocket so he'd press the news people to give them adequate space. They talked about the local radio station, and whether it was worthwhile to buy some time. The Senator owned a small interest in the station, but that didn't mean he'd waste the local committee's money there.

"What about the contract for that fisheries place?" the Senator said.

"The bids are due to go in tomorrow."

"It's all worked out?"

Clyde explained that Jake Everard's was the low one. As part of the deal, Jake had contracted to buy gravel from one of the other bidders and agreed not to bid at all on a runway for a new airport a few miles away. County Finance was to hold completion bonds on both jobs. The parties to the arrangement had never talked to each other. Everything was negotiated through Clyde, nothing on paper. Clyde outlined all this to the Senator, who was sitting with his head hung forward, the way he always sat when he was listening and concentrating. At the end he nodded.

"Should be good for everyone," he said. "In the long run, more of the work will be done better and just as cheaply. No more damned auction sales." Clyde wasn't sure whether he believed all that, but what did he believe? Not much.

"You ever go to an auction sale, Clyde?"

Clyde admitted he hadn't.

"Marion used to collect antiques, before we had more furniture than we knew what to do with. We'd go to sales now and then. Craziest thing you've ever seen. Some piece of junk gets bid up and a good thing goes for five dollars. Makes no sense. You see that girl in the yard?"

"Yes."

"Calls Marion her aunt. Marion's sister's husband's niece, if you want to put it precisely."

"Marion says I'm to drive her to Toronto."

"Tell her no if you don't want to. We'll find somebody."

"I'm happy enough to do it."

"Do you suppose Marion has a mind to be matchmaking?"

"I wondered."

"You'd better watch out. Marion gets what she wants."

"I have that impression."

"Strong girl. Dances ballet and what not."

"Marion says I'm to order up sandwiches from Jessie."

"Marion could run the world if they'd let her." He picked up his book. "The girl's from Ottawa," he said. "Her father's a government engineer."

Perhaps it was a warning. Now and then he wondered if a day would come when he didn't have to keep secrets. He knew his way around the house, and he found Jessie in the kitchen. She wasn't a full time cook, but she did some baking and prepared dinner most nights, and Marion was left free to pursue perfection in her garden. Clyde mentioned the sandwiches.

"We have orders to leave at precisely twenty after one," he said.

"She should have stayed in the army," Jessie said.

"What?"

"She was one of those CWACs, during the war. Some kind of an officer."

"I didn't know that."

Clyde went out the back door of the kitchen and walked round toward his car, looked at his watch. It was quarter to one. He saw Noreen spreading the manure from her wheelbarrow in one of the rose gardens. He walked across the grass toward her.

"Have you been given your orders?" he said.

"Yes," she said, "Marion has me organized."

She wiped a hand over her sweaty face, leaving a dirty streak. She had a long straight nose and a high forehead, a look that might have been called aristocratic if you liked her, or if you weren't sure, you might think they were the features of a bird of prey. Those shapely legs, hair the colour of caramel pulled into a pony tail. The bare feet looked used and tough. She was smiling at him.

"I'll be finished this in five minutes," she said, "and then I'll take a shower and pack my bag and meet you at your car."

"Right."

Clyde went to the car and sat in the driver's seat waiting, reading through the *Toronto Star*. The Senator encouraged him to feel at home in the big house, but he didn't want to sit inside waiting for the girl. He didn't expect her to be right on time, but she was, her hair wet and hanging loose, a small suitcase in her hand as she came out the door with Marion. She kissed the older woman on the cheek, took the bag of sandwiches from her and walked down the steps. Clyde liked the way she moved. He opened the trunk, and they put the suitcase inside.

"You travel light," he said.

"You bet I do," she said.

They waved to Marion, and Clyde drove away from the house.

"Marion says we're supposed to get married," she said.

"Why not?"

"So you better tell me all about yourself."

"My name's Clyde," he said.

"And... "

"Now it's your turn."

She laughed, and they kept laughing for most of the trip. Clyde was amazed at how easy it all was. Noreen was about to begin her last year of university and was the choreographer for a college show, on her way to Toronto today for a meeting with the show's writers and director.

"So where are you staying?" he said as they were driving into Toronto across the bridge over the Humber river.

"Wherever you get us a room," she said.

"Are you serious?"

"If we're going to get married, we better get to know each other."

He glanced across. She was smiling.

"Don't you think I might be a couple of years too old for you?" he said.

"We'll give you an audition."

That night, in the small hours of the morning, the two of them, naked, not perfectly sober, stood in front of the mirror in the hotel room he'd rented while she tried to teach him the first steps of ballet. They were both giggling.

"Clyde," she said, "you can't do ballet with an erection."

"I can't help it."

"Oh well," she said, and led the way back to bed.

He'd assumed she was on the pill, but it emerged, as the night went on, that she wasn't.

"I'm going to get knocked up," she said, "and then you'll have to marry me."

They didn't wait to find out, but went to get a marriage license the next morning. It pleased Clyde not to think about it, just to act – he was old enough not to be careful for once – and as they wandered down the street together, he realized that he was tired of being alone, and he thought he'd never laughed so much in his life.

Within a few days, they were married and had moved into the house in a new development at the edge of Canalville where he'd been living alone. Noreen quit school, though she travelled down for the first weeks of September to choreograph the show. Clyde was kept busy by the election campaign, renting halls for local meetings in various parts of the riding, trying to organize newspaper stories and photographs, driving the candidate out to shake hands at factory gates. His rule of thumb was to check everything three times so there could be no embarrassing disasters. The national party was sending someone from an advertising agency in Toronto, and Clyde wanted the man to find nothing left for him to do, that Clyde had done it all. At the end of the day, Clyde and Noreen met in bed, where he took those toughened dancer's feet in his hands and spread them apart.

She probably did get pregnant that first night in Toronto. Certainly she was carrying Clifford a month later when Marion and the Senator gave a reception for them. It was a rainy afternoon late in September, and Clyde listened as his educated wife explained to him what the pathetic fallacy was, the two of them under an umbrella at the side of the old brick house, drops of rain splashing into a puddle in the driveway, the tall elm at the end of the yard high and dark, the leaves still green. The rose gardens were full of petals knocked from the blooms by the heavy rain, though by now it was easing a bit. Today there was something fierce about her, the shining bird-of-prey look as she prepared to meet up with all those who came to congratulate them.

They entered the house. Other cars began to arrive and once guests had gathered, their coats taken away by local women who'd been hired for the afternoon for just such tasks, the Senator called them into the big front room and there were a few toasts, Noreen's brother, John, a little older than she was, his voice shaking with nerves as he spoke, Jim Bennett, and finally the Senator as host, who congratulated his wife on her matchmaking abilities and managed to suggest, though he never quite spoke the words, that in offering his best wishes to the couple he was representing the Queen, the Prime Minister, and the entire federal cabinet.

A great number of the men and women present that afternoon were Noreen's family and friends. The clan, as she said, among them Marion's sister Florence who was married to the brother of Eleanor Simmons, Noreen's mother. Then there was a younger uncle and some cousins. Among the local guests were his mother, guarded by the Harknesses, Francis and his wife, Jim Bennett and his, even Frank Freisen, though Clyde hadn't seen much of him in recent years. The Senator had invited Barton Dred, the election candidate they were working for, and John Martin Cameron, another member of the board of directors of County Finance. At the last minute Clyde had invited Perry Devoe, the Toronto advertising man who was working on the campaign. The rooms were full of the sound of slightly raised voices as people spoke in the forceful way they use when speaking to strangers. He walked up to Noreen as she chatted with a very tall red-headed man.

"This is Alex," she said. "He thought he was going to marry me until you came along."

Clyde smiled and shook the man's hand. By now he knew Noreen well enough to know that when you were most convinced she was dramatizing, she was usually telling the whole truth. The common impulse to elide difficulties, tell white lies, be pleasant, wasn't one she shared. Once, as they lay naked side by side, breathing slowly after making love, she kissed him on the cheek and said, "I tell everything, and you tell nothing, is that correct, Joe the Silent?"

"Couldn't really say," he answered, and it made her laugh. Her directness was always a shock to him, but he loved it.

"I'm going to take Alex out on the dance floor," she said, "and we'll cling together as if we were saying goodbye to something young and sweet and always to be regretted."

As she was walking past Clyde to get to the dance floor, the back of her hand brushed against his penis.

Clyde found his mother in the Senator's den, alone with the man, who was leaning back against his desk, his thick hair a little rumpled as if he'd been out in the rain and rubbed it dry.

"You're mother's very well-informed, Clyde," he said. "She's been quizzing me about the new bill reforming the Senate. She thought I was going to have to retire at seventy-five. I explained to her that they're stuck with me for life. It's just the new appointments that have to retire at seventy-five. And I stumped her on the sentence from Cicero that's painted on the wall of the Senate chamber. She couldn't quote it. Though that was an unfair question. You know that one Clyde?"

Clyde shook his head. The Senator's voice was more resonant than usual, a little insistent. Nervousness in the face of this crowd and the whisky he'd taken to dull the nervousness.

"*It is the duty of the nobles to oppose the fickleness of the multitude.*"

He looked at Hazel Bryanton and smiled.

"Nobles," he said. "Didn't know you were in such high-flown company, did you?"

"Oh I think I had some idea," she said. "And the fickle multitude is all of us poor folk who are being encouraged to vote for Mr Dred."

"Your mother should not have been wasted working for that dim Palmer Eustes," he said to Clyde.

"Palmer has been very good to me. He took me on when I was a poor widow with no qualifications."

"Yes, I suppose he's a kind man. But he's boring."

"Not one of the nobles," she said, and Clyde wondered if she'd gone a bit too far, but the Senator laughed. John Martin Cameron, short, upright, his white hair shining, stood at the door as if waiting to speak to the Senator. The Senator turned, took in his presence, didn't look especially pleased to see him.

"Dance with your mother, Clyde," he said.

"Would you like to?" Clyde said.

"It's an occasion," she said. "I suppose we should."

The rugs had been taken up in the large room that overlooked the front lawn, and a woman in a bright blue dress sat at a piano half hidden behind a large bouquet of white peonies. She was playing 'Moon River ' And just as she'd said, Noreen was clinging to Alex and staring into his eyes. Clyde was jealous. Was this the pain he'd always tried to avoid? All this was unfamiliar, and now nothing was safe. Anything might happen between Clyde and this woman who was carrying his child, and there was no limit to the suffering that might ensue. Nearby two small children, Noreen's cousins, were trying to dance together, stiff as puppets. He put out his arms and was astonished to learn for the first time, at something close to thirty years old, that his mother was a wonderful dancer, smooth and elegant and light on her feet, much better than he could ever be. Why had he never known?

"He's a sly man, the Senator," she said as she moved across the floor, "But not without charm."

"Where did you learn to dance so well?" he said.

"Just by going out on the dance floor with Halsey Riggler, and then with your father. Clifford was an excellent dancer."

The young man who died on that beach, had once been a wonderful dancer.

At the end of 'Moon River', Noreen's father came to them and suggested he ought to dance with the mother of the groom. Clyde walked over to one of the tall windows and looked out. There were raindrops on the glass and beyond, a grey haze, but through it you could see the farmland below the escarpment, the neat rows of trees, peaches, cherries, here and there the long lines of grapes tied to wires were strung between wooden posts. The land of the old lakebed, deep fertile alluvial soil, lay flat all the way to Brockton a few miles away, but today the farmland vanished in the rain and cloud.

Marion Lawton was standing beside him.

"Studying the lay of the land, Clyde?"

"All those miles of alluvial soil," he said.

"The lake that used to be."

"That's a nice way to put it."

"I'll save that for my memoirs," she said. It was a phrase he'd heard from her before.

"When are you going to start these memoirs, Marion?"

"Once I'm no good for anything else. But I'm making notes."

He turned and looked at her, the firm, handsome face, deep wrinkles at the eyes and around the mouth.

"Shall we dance?" he said, and they did, but awkwardly, and as Marion saw Eileen Simmons passing, she called out to her that she should dance with Clyde, and the two of them made the attempt. The woman, he could tell, was trying to like him, and he took that as a kindness.

An hour later, Clyde, who was beginning to feel a little drunk, found himself in conversation with Noreen's father and wishing that he wasn't either drunk or having the conversation. He was glad when Noreen came by and rescued him.

"She says you're a sharp operator," Alan Simmons said.

"Daddy, I didn't say that, and stop being resentful. I proposed to Clyde and he accepted, and that's the way it is."

"Did she propose to you?" the man said. Like Noreen he was tall, long legged.

"I can't quite remember. I think it was Marion proposed it to both of us, and we knew better than to disagree."

"Marion's a busy-body," he said. "Says and does things she shouldn't. Always did."

"I'm very grateful to her," Clyde said. "I've never been so happy."

Noreen looked at him, perhaps surprised by the declaration.

"She's a wonderful girl." Fathers were expected to say that, but perhaps he meant it. He sounded sincere, almost desperately so. An engineer and civil servant now compelled to watch his daughter go off with some buccaneer. Clyde thought he would never please them, felt as if he had gone into debt to this clan of hostile strangers.

"Yes," Noreen said. "I am a wonderful girl. Now that we've established that, Daddy, you better come and dance with me. I saw Clyde dancing with his mother a while ago, and they were very smooth."

Noreen led her father away. Clyde saw Perry Devoe standing in the door way watching him. Perry was a small but athletic-looking man with curly hair. At first, when he'd been sent from the agency, he and Clyde were edgy with each other, until one day when Clyde was putting away some posters in the trunk of his car and Perry noticed the golf clubs.

"You play golf," he said. It was the first time since he arrived that he'd sounded as if Clyde was a human being, not some dimwit in need of instruction. "Let's take the afternoon off and play." Clyde knew there would be a pile of phone messages waiting in the constituency office and more in the Senator's office at County Finance, a contract to examine, but he agreed, and once out on the course, he and Perry discovered they liked each other, though some of their kidding was a bit rough-edged. Clyde was the better player, but Perry had a long swing, slow back, fast forward, that moved the ball where he wanted it to go. Sometimes he talked to the ball, giving it instructions, and at one point in the game he changed balls because he insisted the one he was using wasn't listening to him anymore. They laughed a lot that afternoon, and by the end of the game were prepared to work together.

Now Perry moved slowly down the hall toward him as if planning each footstep. He'd had quite a bit to drink.

"She's quite something," he said, "that girl you married."

"I think so."

"A thoroughbred filly."

Clyde had no answer to that.

"You going to be happy with her?"

"I hope so."

"Maybe I should get married. What do you think, Clyde?"

"I never give advice, Perry. Not even about golf."

"Have you asked yet if we can change his name?"

"I don't think he'll go for it."

"But I told you Clyde, it's awful hard to get people to vote for a man named Dred."

"It's a name you remember."

"It's *dredful.*"

"Not one of your better ones, Perry."

Noreen came out of the front room, looked around her and vanished again.

"I'm going to leave before I'm too drunk to drive," Perry said.

"You're pretty drunk now."

"I won't tell anybody."

He smiled at Clyde and walked down the hall to the front door. Clyde made his way back to the kitchen. Jessie Pritchard, who'd created all the little meat tarts and sandwiches and cookies, was sitting on a straight chair with her feet up on another. Alice Fevers, one the local women who were helping out, stood filling a plate with cookies from a large metal cookie sheet. A wind had come up, and the rain was blowing against the kitchen windows. The hill of the escarpment rose not far behind; all you could see through the windows was a blur of green leaves.

"Thank you, Jessie," Clyde said. "The food was wonderful. I ate a lot of those little tarts."

"I thought maybe I'd shown a heavy hand with the cloves."

"Wonderful."

Clyde went to the window, but even standing close he couldn't see much more.

"Not much of a day," he said.

"Makes people happier to be in here at a party," Alice Fevers said. She was about to go out the kitchen door, when it opened. It was Elaine Haverman, the Senator's younger daughter. who'd come from Ottawa as her mother's assistant for the party. He husband, the clergyman, had stayed home with the children.

"Oh, hello Clyde," she said.

It was always a little awkward with the Senator's daughters. They were never quite sure whether to treat him as an equal or as a cat's paw who lived by his wits and wasn't to be trusted.

"I came to thank Jessie for the food," he said.

"I just wanted to find a chair."

"I'm glad you could come today. The Senator said you might not make it."

"Probably hoping I wouldn't. He still thinks of me as a moody teenager shouting at him and poking around the attic looking for family secrets."

"Find any?"

"You always do."

"Think so?"

"Of course."

Clyde remembered how he had gone through the papers in his mother's desk, looking for secrets, wanting to know how things were.

"That's the nature of family life," the woman was saying to him. "Knowing only half the truth."

"I suppose you're right," Clyde said, though he had no idea. "I'm going to find my wife."

Clyde followed Alice Fevers, who had completed her tray of cookies, out the door. There was laughter and applause from the front room. To get there he made his way through the crowd of people in the dining room who were arguing about the new Canadian flag, someone orating fiercely in its favour – Clyde quite liked it himself – and when he arrived in the front room, he found the woman behind the peonies producing a surprisingly convincing version of one of the new Beatles songs while Noreen was doing the twist with one of her girl cousins, who couldn't quite keep up but was trying valiantly. It astonished him to realize that this nimble and pliant dancer, all swaying shoulders and hips, was his wife and was at this moment pregnant with his child. He looked to see if red-headed Alex was watching her, but he had vanished to whatever other world he inhabited.

"She's very beautiful," a voice said, and for a moment he thought it was his own, that he'd spoken his thoughts aloud, but then he realized that it was his mother who was standing beside him. He looked down at her, and she met his eyes. He didn't look away. It was a moment of the kind of intimacy that was rare between them, however closely they'd lived over the years they were alone together.

"I'm glad you decided to settle." She glanced toward Noreen dancing. "She is a very striking young woman, Clyde."

Her voice suggested affection and wonder, and yet, years later, when he and Noreen were no longer together, Clyde believed that his mother had foreseen it all that day, as the two of them stood there and watched his new wife dancing. It made no particular sense to think that, but he did.

"We'll go soon," she said. "I'm having dinner with the Harknesses, and Jim and his wife are coming, though I suppose I've eaten just about all I need this afternoon."

Clyde went off to find her coat and by the time he came back with it the dancers were back to old standards. 'Moonlight in Vermont.' Noreen saw him helping his mother with her coat and came to them.

"You're abandoning us, Hazel," she said.

"You two will do fine."

The Harknesses had got their coats and after Noreen had hugged his mother, the lot of them made their way out. Noreen turned to him.

"Do you think he's here too, somehow, your father?"

"No," Clyde said. "He's dead. I never knew him."

"But she did."

"She told me he was a good dancer."

They were silent. She put her arm around his waist.

"Pretty good party," she said.

Clyde saw the Senator watching them from the end of the hall. His hair was still rumpled. He was talking to Harry Gregory, a tall, bald man who was another of the shareholders in the finance company.

It was starting to get dark when the last of the guests left, and Noreen and Clyde said their thanks to Marion and the Senator. Marion was sitting in the big armchair in the Senator's den with a pencil and a pad of paper, writing down numbers.

"Are you working out your income tax?" the Senator said. "It's a little early."

"Of course not," Marion said. "Somebody told me about a new

mathematical system for bridge, and I thought I'd try it. I'm not impressed so far."

"But you have no cards," Noreen said.

"They're in my head," Marion said and went back to her figuring.

Instead of going straight back to their house in Canalville, Clyde and Noreen drove down the river road toward Brockton, stopped the car at the old Oak Grove, got out and clinging together under the umbrella, wandered in the darkness under the ancient trees, toward the river, their feet getting soaked by the wet grass. There was a line of light in the west, the clouds above it heaped and grey.

"Test question," she said, "what is the pathetic fallacy?"

"The mistaken suggestion that these trees and that rain and those dark clouds have anything in common with the feelings of this man and woman with wet feet who are soon going home to bed."

"And if they did?"

"They would be horny as hell."

"Right. One hundred marks to you Mr Clyde Bryanton. You win."

"And what's my prize?

"Me and a baby."

"That's a big prize."

"We'll get even bigger as the months go on."

And they did. Once the college show she was working on was finished, Noreen started a dance class for young children in a rented space near the city bus terminal, and even when she was hugely pregnant, she went on showing the little ones all the positions and where they led.

At first the physical intimacy of marriage was a shock to Clyde, finding drawer space for Noreen's clothes, her laundry accumulating in the bedroom closet mixed with his own, two kinds of shampoo in the bathroom, tubes of makeup on the counter, and he might walk into the bedroom and find her naked, bent over her swollen abdomen, going up and down her legs with a little electric razor. She held strange opinions, and they had arguments. Dirty dishes piled up, and now and then one got dropped or thrown. It was all an astonishment to a man who had lived alone for years. He would wake in the night confused about who it was in bed with him, once thinking it was Helena, once that it was his mother, and he would lie there putting his thoughts in order, Noreen, it was Noreen, and they were married, she was with child, and he would move toward her, her skin hot to the touch, and she might mumble a little, and draw him inside her.

Things were more settled after the November election, which Barton Dred lost, though only by a thousand or so votes, and went back to his car dealership to wait for next time. Clyde was trying to rent out a couple of stores left empty on the main street of Canalville when the tenants decided to move to the expanding mall, and in one case, he suggested to the Senator they rebuild one of them, splitting the main floor in two and putting an apartment upstairs. The Senator agreed, and Clyde found a builder who'd do it for a reasonable price. Most of the work was interior and could be done in the cold weather. Clyde went by every day to check on the job, aware as he watched it progress that this was a footnote to the city's history, Canalville's old main street of wide storefronts and established businesses changing into something smaller, less assured. This was his world, where there was no more illusion of stability. The old days were gone.

Clyde had understood the principle that everything must change, but until now he'd been too young to understand its full force, the unrelenting way time altered the world. Perhaps he should have foreseen it all, that in spite of good intentions his marriage would prove to be less than permanent, that many years later he would no longer be certain what Noreen was up to. But he didn't.

For now they were learning to live together, waiting for their child to be born. One Saturday in the spring they had driven down to his mother's house for a short visit. Late in the afternoon Noreen was restless, unable to sit comfortably, and she wanted to go for a walk, so they all made their way down to the water, the park by the Brockton public beach, and they stood on top of the hill, the American fort opposite on the other side of the river. On the way, Noreen admired the renovations of some of the old houses that were changing the face of the town.

"No fishermen anymore," his mother said, as they looked over the water.

"Why not?" Noreen asked her.

"The fish are gone."

When Clyde was a boy, every weekend, a cluster of small boats anchored on the sandbar just outside the river mouth, fishing for pickerel, but the fish had disappeared and so had the fishermen. A few years later, it would become clear that further upstream, lethal industrial chemicals had for years been leaking into the river after being dumped in a disused canal, and Brockton began to get its drinking water elsewhere.

"The fish are gone," Noreen said, and they looked over the glittering blue surface. Far out a freighter was making its way across the lake, eastward from the canal.

That evening, driving home by a roundabout route, entering Canalville on a road he wasn't familiar with and while they were stopped at a traffic light, he noticed a For Sale sign on a house diagonally across the corner from the service station and immediately knew that this might be the place for his strip mall. Both roads were busy and on weekdays were full of people going back and forth to work. Beside the car, as he waited for the light to turn green, was an orchard that was being torn up to make way for a new subdivision, the fruit trees ripped out and pushed into piles of brush by a bulldozer. Everything was changing here; the city was expanding in a new direction. If he bought the house on the corner, which was on a large lot, and one or two of the houses beside it, there would be room for a row of three or four stores, and cars could enter the parking lot from both adjoining roads. He wanted to tell Noreen what he was thinking, but it was all too tentative and was moving too fast in his mind – he'd have to check on the price of that house, maybe go to the registry office and discover who owned the houses beside it, work out how much money he'd have to raise, whether he wanted to approach the Senator. His own money was heavily tied up. Probably it was still zoned residential or maybe farm and residential; he wasn't even sure where the city boundaries were out in this neighbourhood. This land might be in one of the rural townships. He wondered if a liquor store was possible. There wasn't one anywhere nearby.

"What are you thinking about?" Noreen said.

"Work," he said.

"Well, stop," she said, "think about me."

"All right."

So he did, recalled how he had looked at her in the bedroom this morning, the great round belly, the stretched skin smooth and a little transparent, he could see the veins, the navel extruded, her swollen breasts, tall legs looking thin beneath the gravid torso, almost as if they couldn't support the weight, though of course they could. He could see the belly change shape slightly as the baby moved inside it, and then she would put on a dark gold dressing gown and move down the hall, huge and slow.

"Now what are you thinking about?"

"Your big belly.

"Are we nearly home? I have to pee again."

"We're nearly home."

"Are you ever going to stop being Joe the Silent?"

"I don't know."

In spare minutes over the next few days he ran to the registry office, visited a couple of real estate agents. It all appeared to be possible. Dangerous but possible. Lying in bed he went over his plans. Until the night Noreen shook him awake.

"Time to go."

"You're going to have this baby?"

"I believe I am."

He turned on the light beside the bed. He was trying to shake off the last blur of sleep, struggling to his feet, not sure exactly what he was supposed to do first.

"The postman said it was going to be a boy," she said.

"The postman?"

"I met him coming down the street the other day. He said it must be a boy, the way I was carrying it."

"Are you ready to go?" There was a small suitcase by the front door that he'd insisted she prepare a week before. She laughed at him, but she did it.

"I'm leaking."

"Take a towel to sit on. Let's go."

He waited at the hospital, though they tried to send him home, drank coffee, paced, tried to read a magazine, did calculations in a little notebook, and before morning they told him he had a son. A nurse led him to a room where he found Noreen, looking flushed, almost feverish after her labour, and she showed him the tiny breathing creature that was his child, then he went out into the darkness, drove back to the house and went back to bed, alone.

He slept a little, woke to the silence of the empty house, the only noise the rattle of the refrigerator. He lay in bed for a few moments remembering that he had a wife and a son. After breakfast he walked to a real estate office and signed an offer on the corner house which would be the beginning of his strip mall.

All his cash was tied up in three houses being built in the subdivision where they were living, so he'd have to get a mortgage and raise cash for a down payment. In fact he had barely enough cash for the deposit and wrote a cheque for the lowest amount that would make his offer convincing.

His offer demanded a response within 24 hours and a closing in two weeks. He wanted to get on with it, but it meant he had to raise a chunk of cash in a hurry. He could have talked to the Senator, but he wanted to start this on his own. He'd go to the Senator after he had the first piece of property tied up. So where to get the money?

"I'm a father," he said to Francis, when the two of them were sitting in his small office at the credit bureau. The blank eyes stared at him, giving nothing away.

"That was quick," Francis said.

Clyde just nodded.

"You were never a patient boy, Clyde. Do anything for a piece of ass."

He assumed Francis, for his own good reasons, was trying to make him angry. Maybe he still felt resentful that Clyde had left his job. You never knew with Francis; often there appeared to be a kind of free-floating malice in what he said or a pleasure in expressing what you thought he wouldn't dare to say.

"OK, Francis, now that you've congratulated me, let's get down to business."

"What kind of business?"

"I want to borrow some money."

Francis stared at him with those eyes that looked like the eyes of a blind man, unblinking, without expression.

"Wait a minute," he said. "Tell me again. I don't get it."

"Me. Borrow money. From you. They call it business."

"I call it horseshit, Clyde. You work for a money factory. If you're coming to me, there's something wrong."

"No. This is just the way I want to do it."

"Tell me the whole story."

"No. If you don't want to make the loan, say so, I'll go somewhere else."

"Secrets, Clyde, you're always keeping secrets."

"Joe the Silent."

"Who's that?"

"What Noreen calls me."

"Keeping secrets from your wife. You want to stay married to her, you better tell her what you're doing. I'm sure she's a wonderful piece of ass but wives expect to be more."

"It's you I'm not telling, Francis, and you're not my wife."

"No, my darling, I'm not."

The two of them sat there, watching each other, like old enemies. Clyde was tempted to mention the money drop out in the country all those years ago, just to stir things up, but wisdom prevailed, and he kept his mouth shut.

"What I need is short term."

"Until?"

"I'm putting my house on the market, pull my equity out of that."

"You must be in real trouble Clyde, that you can't go to the Senator."

"All wrong Francis. And I'll talk to the Senator when I'm ready."

"You do too many things without telling him, he's going to be angry."

"He doesn't own me, Francis."

"Don't be so sure."

"He doesn't."

"He's not a man to trifle with."

"I know that."

"You think you do."

I'd get a friendlier reception, Clyde thought, if I went to Jelly Wendorf, even if he wanted ten percent a week. Clyde wouldn't need the money for long. He stood up.

"I'm going to the hospital to visit my wife and son, Francis. I'm sorry we couldn't do business."

Francis watched him, fish-eyed, blank.

"Sit down, Clyde," he said.

Clyde met his eyes.

"I am not in any kind of trouble, Francis, and I won't eat shit in order to borrow a few dollars I need to put something together."

"So proud, Clyde, you're so proud."

"I have to be. I'm a father now."

"How much to you want, and for how long?"

Clyde named a figure.

"Until I sell the house, that's all."

"Why not just wait for the money?"

"I have my reasons."

"You don't want to make a conditional offer."

Clyde looked at him. Francis raised his eyebrows.

"Nobody ever said you were stupid, Francis."

"What did they say?"

"They said you were an asshole."

"Don't be coarse Clyde. I like to think we're gentlemen here."

"I'm sure we are."

They made an agreement on the interest rate, too high, and Francis wrote out a cheque. Clyde deposited it in his business account at a downtown bank on his way to the hospital. He talked to the manager, made a mortgage application. When he sold his house, his equity in it would pay the debt to Francis with enough cash left to make an offer for one of the neighbouring properties if one suddenly came on the market.

His mind was racing as the small elevator in the hospital took him upward to the maternity ward. When he walked into Noreen's room, she was holding the baby to her swollen breast, the little face pressed into her flesh, eyes closed, the mouth moving. Clyde felt almost faint for a moment, as if he was looking inside a human body at the hot bloody workings of life. Noreen had her hair pulled back, and she was pale, her face concentrated on her work. He walked over to the bed, and she put up her face for him to kiss. He sat down in the chair in the corner of the room and watched until the baby fell asleep and she lifted it away from her breast.

"He has to keep working at it," she said. "To make the milk come in."

"So tiny and already he has a job."

"He sucks, and I make milk. We all have our duties."

"What about mine?" he said.

"You look after us."

"I'm trying to," he said. Noreen was holding the tiny creature on her shoulder, rubbing her fingers over its back.

"Do you want to hold him?"

Clyde took the baby, carefully, carefully, one hand under the head, the tiny creature warm in his hands. He sat down in the chair with the child against his chest. He found he was rocking back and forth, some animal instinct teaching him to do it. They sat like that for a few minutes until the nurse came to take the baby back to its nursery. Noreen slid down on the pillows and pulled a cover over her.

"All right, Joe the Silent," she said. "What are you up to?"

"Aren't you going to tell me all about what it's like to give birth?"

"It's hard work and it hurts like hell, but then they hand you the baby, and you can't think of what to say, so you cry a little."

"What do you want to call him?"

"After your father."

"Clifford?"

"We can give the name a second chance."

"Okay," he said.

"Now tell me what you're up to. You're all wound up about something, and it's not just this baby."

She was so acute. Or he was so obvious, distracted even at the great moments.

"Well," he said, "we're going to sell the house."

"My god, why? Where will we live? We have a baby."

So he explained it all, quickly, that they'd move to the house on the corner while he got hold of the properties on both sides. Once it was all put together, they'd find a lot and start building a new place for themselves.

Noreen listened. When he got to the end, she stared at him for a long time. Then she nodded.

"I've always thought I'd like to build a house," she said.

"We'll get the best contractor in the district."

"No," she said. "I mean with my own hands."

"Really?"

"I wanted to take shop class in school, but girls couldn't."

"Probably you shouldn't start by building a whole house."

"You mean I should make one of those little wooden shelves like the boys in Grade 9."

"Something like that."

"I'm going to go out and buy tools with some of that wedding present money my parents gave us. Is that OK?"

"If that's what you want. Sounds crazy to me."

"Selling our house sounds crazy to me."

"Yeah."

"I'm going to sleep now," she said.

He bent and kissed her.

Clyde checked with the real estate agent from a payphone in the hospital lobby. The retired couple who lived in the house were prepared to accept his offer, but they were worried about the closing date, only two weeks after acceptance, and they weren't ready to move so soon. Clyde said he was willing to add a clause agreeing to rent the house back to them for three months, and he arranged to meet the agent that night to set a price and sign the agreement to put his own house on the market. He was pretty sure it would sell quickly.

So he'd have a baby and no home for it. If necessary maybe they could bunk in with his mother for a month or so. It would be crowded in the little house, but they'd manage somehow. It was a gamble, but he was going to win. He had to.

When he got to his office, there was a message for him to call Jake Everard. Any other day he might have driven an hour to his construction yard to avoid talking to him on the phone, but he picked up the receiver and dialed. It took the deep-voiced woman who answered the phone a while to find him. When he came on the line Jake explained he'd got a call from the regional manager who was accepting tenders for the airport to ask why he wasn't tendering.

"It's just too bad you're so busy," Clyde said.

"That's what I told him."

"Then he has his answer."

"I don't like all this," Jake said.

"Just part of doing business," Clyde said. He was going through a routine, didn't particularly like it himself; he'd set up what was required of him. It was part of the job. So long as no one found out.

"Hey," he said, "we just had a baby. I've got a son."

"Congratulations," Jake said. "Same to your wife. It's nice having a kid, makes it all worthwhile."

"Thanks, Jake," Clyde said.

On the desk there was a letter asking the Senator to be Chairman of a fund-raising campaign for a new university building, give money – that was understood though unstated – and put the arm on others. Clyde couldn't answer for the Senator, but at first he didn't pick up the phone to call, uneasy at the thought of the deal he was trying to make, starting on his own. He suspected that the Senator would hear uneasiness in his voice, know that he was concealing something, but he decided that he'd better tell him about the birth of his son, and that event would be the explanation of any strangeness.

Two days later, he drove to the train to pick up Noreen's sister, Martha, who was arriving to help out for a week or so. She was older than Noreen, shorter, heavier, less outgoing, and Clyde found conversation with her difficult. When they got back to the house, she saw the For Sale sign in front of it and expressed surprise.

"Yes," Clyde said, "we're moving."

In bed that night, Noreen told him that Martha was convinced they were on the point of bankruptcy and was prepared to send her father to seize Noreen and the baby and take them away to safety.

"And what did you say?" Clyde said.

"I said we were just fine, and that you knew exactly what you were doing. See what a loyal little wife I am."

"Damn good thing."

The baby started to cry. Clyde went to the crib and fetched the screaming little thing, and Noreen exposed a heavy breast with a reddened, tender-looking nipple, and offered it. He fed a little and slept.

"Now what?" Clyde said.

"I guess I'll change him and put him back."

"Is that what the book says?"

Noreen was looking at him, a strange smile on her face.

"Oh Clyde," she said, "are we going to be any good at this? Aren't you supposed to know without looking in a book."

"We've never done this before."

"And I never had little brothers and sisters. I was the baby."

They managed, though it was never easy. Their house sold quickly and for a good price, but as a result they had to move in with Clyde's mother for six weeks while they waited for the place on the corner to be vacated. The baby woke two or three times every night, and the two of them would tiptoe around, whispering, trying not to wake Clyde's mother, who slept only a few feet away. Clyde counted the days till they could leave.

But in two months, they were in the house he'd bought, which was spacious but awkwardly arranged, the walls covered with dim wallpapers, the wood stained dark colours. Noreen wanted to paint, but Clyde wasn't convinced they should bother renovating a house that was going to be torn down. The debt to Francis was paid, and the rest of Clyde's equity from the sale was invested in a T-bill.

Clyde had spoken to the Senator as soon as his purchase of the house on the corner had closed, the old man staring at him with a look that wasn't too friendly, then looking away.

"I asked you before, Clyde, is this your deal or ours?"

"I could maybe do it alone, Senator, but it would be hard."

"You think with me it will be easy?"

"No, but easier."

"Why didn't you tell me at the beginning?"

"I thought there was no point coming to you with something hypothetical. Now I've got the corner house, it's all possible."

The Senator stared at him for a few seconds.

"We haven't played golf for a while, Clyde."

"I guess we've both been busy.

"Noreen want to come out with us?"

"I'll ask her."

Noreen had never showed any interest in learning the game, but said she'd come along and caddy, so they made the arrangement with the Senator, dropped Clifford off at his grandmother's one Sunday morning, and met up at the course. Noreen had been working out at a portable barre she kept in the basement, and her body was slender again after the pregnancy, and today she was wearing one of the new miniskirts with bare legs and on her feet openwork leather sandals, and while the tailored white blouse she'd chosen was of almost virginal respectability, her breasts were big with milk.

"Motherhood suits you," the Senator said, staring a little when he first saw her.

"But skirts like that should be illegal."

"The newest thing, Senator."

"This club does have some kind of dress code, you know."

"Are you being stuffy?" Noreen said.

"I suppose I am, Noreen, but I'm an old man and I have the right."

"Well just concentrate on the game, and you'll hardly notice me at all. I'll be a good little woman, quiet as a mouse."

Clyde was aware that Sim Secord was standing at the door of the pro shop admiring Noreen's long bare legs. Noreen, excited to be back out in the world, and full of devilment, claimed that she was going to carry both bags of clubs, and while Clyde knew she might be strong enough to do it, he said she should take the Senator's while he'd carry his own.

"I'll get a cart," the Senator said. "I can't have some young girl carrying my clubs."

"Of course you can," Noreen said. "What else are young girls good for?"

The Senator just stared, but she stood her ground, and he gave in and let her carry the heavy bag. Clyde recalled being paid to carry it a few years before. It struck Clyde that the Senator was unexpectedly upset by Noreen's challenge to his habits. He was looking tired these days, but once they were out on the course, Noreen kept him cheerful, and it was a perfect summer afternoon. At the end of the game, they both shook hands with the Senator as Noreen lifted his clubs into the trunk of his car. As they got into their own car, Noreen looked across at him.

"You're a good golfer," she said. "It made me horny watching you whipping those balls down the fairway."

He looked across at her.

"Everything you do makes me feel that way," he said.

"Drive us out in the country," she said. "Clifford can wait a few more minutes for his tit."

Clyde drove quickly to the edge of town and along a deserted concession road.

"Turn in there," she said, pointing to a lane that went past a big willow with low-hanging branches. She was already pulling up the short skirt and taking off her underwear.

As they drove out of the lane a few minutes later, Clyde saw a woman in a print housedress watching them from the far end, wondered how long she'd been there. They picked up Clifford and drove home.

In the next few weeks, Noreen, lively and sociable with strangers, got to know the neighbours on both sides of their new house. Both were couples with grown children who might or might not want to sell, ready to move on now their children were gone, or wanting to hang on to the place where their lives were rooted. Clyde waved to them when they were in the yard, but he hadn't yet broached the idea of buying, and he thought it might be better done through a real estate agent. Traffic at the corner was getting heavier, trucks going to the construction sites of the new subdivision, and Noreen said one of the women had complained to her about it. Should she have offered to buy their house? Noreen asked. He didn't know the answer to that. He didn't know the answer to lots of things, and there were nights when he lay awake, too much awareness tickling his brain.

The Senator grumbled a little about being left out at the beginning of the project, but he didn't appear to be seriously annoyed. County Finance would back the purchase of the other properties.

Once they were settled into the new house, Noreen went out and bought her carpentry tools, as she'd planned, and a book about how to do woodwork. Clyde came home one day and heard the screech of a power saw, then nails being hammered. He found that she was repairing the wobbly back porch. The work was maybe a little crude, but it was effective. A month later she went back to teaching her dance class. Sometimes she'd take Clifford with her in a carry cot which she'd stow in a corner of the room, and by now his sleeping habits were a little more stable. Clyde arrived there one afternoon to drive home with her, walked in just as a group of little girls ran off the floor and began to change their shoes and pull jeans over their tights, chattering like a flock of starlings. Noreen's hair was done up in a bun, and she wore a loose red smock over her leotard. As she saw him, she picked up an astonishing wide brimmed black hat from the top of a table, put it on and spread her arms.

"Look what I found," she said.

"Very stylish," Clyde said.

A man with a tweed jacket was standing near him, waiting for one of the little girls.

"That's a remarkable hat," he said. "My daughter worships your wife, you know."

So do I, Clyde wanted to say, but the words didn't come out. The man's face was familiar, and when Clyde put out his hand to introduce himself, he recognized the name he was given. Alec Murtch. He was a member of the city council. Clyde's new property, he'd discovered, was within the city boundaries of Canalville, though not by much.

I have a little zoning problem. He didn't say that, not that day, but six months later, he found himself in the man's law office explaining the situation. He had a development contract drawn up with County Finance representing the Senator's interest, and one of the neighbouring properties was in their hands, with an option on the other, at a price that was beyond the current market, but if the zoning application failed, the option would be dropped at comparatively little expense.

"It's an interesting idea, what you're proposing," Alec Murtch said, "and it would probably be a convenience to the neighbourhood. You're going to get flak about traffic when you bring it to council, and you should probably discuss it with the city engineer first, get him to agree that the entrances and exits you have planned won't cause accidents. I can't represent you, of course. You could get another lawyer, or you could represent yourself."

"Isn't that dangerous?"

"Maybe. Some of the wackos on council, you never know what's going to set them off. Sometimes they'll take against a lawyer. I hate to admit it, but often as not it's a matter of personalities. People think it's all money, the rich get what they want, but it's not that simple. Crazier than you'd ever think. Councillors can decide whatever pleases them about these things. Talk to the city engineer. Get letters from some of the people in the new subdivision, saying that stores nearby would be a great thing. Maybe you should talk to the mayor."

The mayor had been on the other side in the last federal election, and Clyde was afraid that was going to prove a problem. To his surprise the man turned up on Sunday afternoon when Clyde and Noreen were sitting in the backyard. Clyde was wearing shorts and a t-shirt, and Noreen was covered with paint from working on Clifford's room that morning.

The mayor introduced himself. If he'd taken the trouble to come round, Clyde thought, he must be interested in the project.

"Alec Murtch there, he was telling me about your big idea, and I thought I'd drop by, take the lay of the land"

Noreen got up from her chair.

"I'll just leave you men to your business," she said. Playing the obedient little woman again, annoyed perhaps at being interrupted on Sunday afternoon.

"Alec spoke highly of you, Miz Bryanton," he mayor said. "Said you teach dancing to his little girl."

Noreen did a deep balletic curtsey and skipped up the back stairs. Clyde explained his plan, thinking that was what was expected, showed the mayor the shape of the three properties, and they walked out to the street to look around and see how the entrances would affect traffic. No worse than the service station across the street was the line that Clyde used.

The mayor listened, looked around him

"This has been quite a spell of weather, hasn't it," he said.

Clyde made a noise, agreeing.

"The little fella well?"

"Yes, fine."

The man appeared to have lost interest in the whole thing. Clyde waited for him to speak.

"So what do you think?" Clyde said finally a little desperate for a response. The mayor looked down the street, nodded.

"We'll have to see. Thanks for letting me know about it," he said, putting out his hand. Clyde shook it.

"Say goodbye to your wife. Thanks for your time. I'm parked around the corner here," he said and walked away, disappeared behind a large tree. Clyde found Noreen upstairs in their bedroom feeding the baby.

"What the hell was that all about?" he said.

"What?"

"He didn't say a bloody thing, just walked away."

"Don't ask me," she said. "I'm only a girl."

"I told him all about it, and he says nothing, just walked away."

"Maybe you said the wrong thing."

"Thanks for your support."

The baby pulled his mouth away from the breast, twitched a little, as if he was distracted by the voices.

"I told him what we want to do," Clyde said. "He didn't say a word. What the hell was he here for?" Clyde said.

"Calm down," Noreen said.

"I can't," he said and left the room.

He took his golf clubs out of the trunk of the car and hammered a little plastic ball back and forth from one end of the yard to the other. When Noreen appeared on the back porch, the one she'd worked so diligently to repair, carrying the baby, he stared at them, his wife and child, as if he couldn't think who these people were, and Noreen held his eyes until he looked away.

"Maybe you should go out and play golf," she said.

"Give me the baby and change your clothes," he said, "and we'll all go for a drive."

They drove down by the canal, got out of the car and stared up toward the next lock. It was full and a boat had entered from above; now the water poured out, the lower gates opened, and the long freighter slid out of the lock, and under the pilot's expert control, moved along the narrow channel between the stone walls, the long iron vessel sliding slowly past them, one or two merchant seamen standing at the edge of the deck. Noreen waved, and one of them waved back.

"Don't you think there's something sexy about it?"

"What, waving at sailors?"

"The way that ship slides up the canal."

He laughed.

"How did I ever manage without you?" he said.

"I don't want to know," she said.

The council meeting to consider the zoning change was two weeks later. He got a call from Alec Murtch a couple of days before, suggesting that if, as he assumed, the Senator was involved in the deal, he should be in the little public gallery for the meeting.

"If the wackos think you're keeping him a secret," he said, "they're more likely to get their backs up."

Clyde went to the meeting in his best suit, white shirt, sober tie, uneasy with the knowledge that the personal whims of ten men, their prejudices, preferences, old resentments, were going to control his future. He understood why politicians were offered bribes. It was an attempt to give yourself a little edge against this terrible uncertainty as you tried to convince a group of strangers to support your vision of what should be done. They knew you planned to profit by their decision, and they resented that. Clyde was afraid that if he was pressed too hard, he'd lose his temper. He was on edge all the time now. He drove the Senator to the meeting, but they didn't sit together. Clyde was in the front row, in case he was called to answer questions, the Senator sat at the back hunched in his chair. One or two of the councillors nodded to him as he sat down.

Clyde waited through the first part of the meeting, and then the zoning change came up for discussion. It was going well, the mayor studiously neutral, Alec Murtch asking well-phrased objective questions, bringing up the question of traffic. Clyde had talked to the city engineer who had been careful not to commit himself, but who had, at least, not pronounced against the idea. When Clyde was asked to comment on the traffic problems, he repeated his line about the service station; what he planned would have no worse effect. He'd taken the time to phone Jim Bennett's brother who was on the police force and couldn't find anything much in their records about traffic accidents at that corner. Some of the councillors were watching Clyde as he spoke, and he wondered what they were thinking. He tried to be bland and reassuring. He sat back down, and the mayor directed the matter back to the council.

One of the councillors got to his feet. Bill Morden.

"What I want to know, your worship," he said to the mayor, "is why this isn't on the agenda?"

"It is," the mayor said.

"I don't see it," he said, shaking his papers.

Morden, an angular man with sharp handsome features, leaned forward aggressively as he spoke. He'd been on the council for years, and he appeared to be enraged, or prepared to be enraged, at just about everything, an unfocussed fury, almost a hint of dementia about it. No doubt his anger helped to convince those in his ward, who were poor, that he shared their feeling of deprivation and resentment. The other councillor from the ward, Ben West, was a very quiet, sensible man, and the two of them continued to be elected year after year, rage and calm, the two faces of the streets that sent them. Ben West took the papers out of his colleague's hands and pointed to something.

"It should be on the other page," Morden said, "not on the back like that. We don't want any secrets here."

"Well it's there, councillor," the mayor said calmly, "and we often print stuff on the back of the page, so let's move on."

"We don't want stuff hidden away on the backs of pages."

"Move on, councillor."

"Have they talked to the neighbours?"

"I believe a notice of the request for a zoning change was sent to all taxpayers with property within the required distances. Is that right?" He looked toward the city manager, who nodded. "And I believe we had one reply, which is attached to your agenda. It concerned the question of traffic, and that's been brought up."

"We don't want them slipping it through before we have a chance to look at it."

"Nobody's slipping anything anywhere. We're discussing it right now."

"Needs a good hard look."

"This is your chance."

"What I think is we should postpone the whole thing to the next meeting."

Clyde felt a weight in his chest. If they postponed the decision, somebody was sure to find more objections, or more reasons for postponement, and they'd put it off again and again until it was all impossible. Bill Morden stared fiercely at the mayor, or perhaps at the wall behind him, the precise focus of his intensity unclear. That someone he didn't know planned to profit by the zoning change was enough to make him irritable and negative. Some instinct developed during his years on the council told him that postponement was his best chance to destroy something he didn't like when he had nothing concrete to argue against it.

"Why do you want to postpone it?" the mayor said.

"I don't want it rushed through."

"Nobody's rushing it through, councillor. It's in its place on the agenda, the neighbours have been notified. I don't see there's any reason not to vote on it. You can make a motion to table if you think you can find anyone to second it. Otherwise I'm bringing it to a vote."

Bill Morden looked around for encouragement. The other councillors avoided his look, remained concentrated on their papers, except Ben West, who wasn't as afraid of Morden's incoherent rage, looked toward him and made a thumbs-down gesture.

"I think it should be tabled," Morden said, but he sat down. The mayor brought the rezoning to a vote, and it passed, two councillors voting against it, not Bill Morden, inexplicably, though he insisted on a recorded abstention. He was fighting in some altogether different war.

After the vote was over, Clyde dared, for the first time, to look across the little public gallery at the Senator who gave the slightest of nods, and Clyde got up to leave. Once outside, where a chilly breeze was blowing, he waited for the Senator, who came along a couple of minutes later, making his way slowly down the steps to the street, holding the metal rail. Men grow old and die, Clyde thought, no matter how clever they've been.

"You've done it," the Senator said when he came down the last step to the pavement. "Congratulations."

"One more step forward," Clyde said, not wanting to let on how excited he was. When he got home he'd tell Noreen, and they'd find a way to celebrate. He led the Senator to the car, drove out in the country and dropped him off at the front door of his house.

"We'll have you over for dinner," he said.

A few days later, they did, Clifford left at home with a baby sitter, Clyde feeling a sense of holiday as they drove away from the house. Noreen was silent, unreadable, and his couple of attempts to draw her out failed. Now she had a child she'd begun studying the newspapers, grew distressed over Vietnam, the state of the world. The dinner didn't go well, laborious at first, the Senator tired and morose, though Clyde could see he was trying to stir himself. He toasted Clyde's success with the new venture, but Clyde understood that the old man couldn't feel more than a limited enthusiasm for something invented and largely controlled by someone younger. It was one of those nights when Marion delivered herself of random thoughts that flew in and out of the conversation like little birds, perching and then vanishing, but Jessie Pritchard had prepared a good meal, roast beef and Yorkshire pudding, a fancy chocolate cake for dessert. As they sat over their coffee, Clyde and the Senator got talking about the council.

"Morden's a starving dog, sniffing around for carrion, doesn't know if it's there or not, just knows he'd got to keep on sniffing, but if he once catches a whiff of something good, he'll dig all night, though the chances are some bigger dog will grab it away from him. No brain, just that raging empty gut."

"People keep voting for him."

"He's a rough old hound, but he's their own."

"I often wonder what people think when they're voting."

"Most people don't know what they think. But they'll follow someone who does. They want someone to lead them."

"Like LBJ," Noreen said quietly. She was increasingly and irrationally preoccupied, it seemed to Clyde, with the American war in Vietnam, as if it might come here and threaten her son. She spent one afternoon a week at a church hall counselling draft dodgers and deserters on how to stay in Canada. In his father's war, deserters were shot.

"I'm not sure," the Senator said, "that he knows what he thinks, that man. Wants one thing, then another."

"He wants to bomb Cambodia, that's what he wants this week." It was deliberately provocative. Clyde wished she'd let it go, but what the hell, he thought, he was happy enough about her impulsiveness when she decided to spend the night with him hours after they'd met.

"If you're going to make war," the Senator said, "you have to make war."

He too was speaking very quietly, and when Clyde looked toward him, he saw that there was a slight twitch beside one of his eyes. He'd never seen it before. The lines in his cheeks looked darker and deeper.

"Bomb anything that moves," Noreen said. "Is that war?"

"It is exactly the nature of war."

"In defence of what?"

"The way we do things, and against an alien ideology."

"Against people who think they'd like to run their own country."

"And every other country around would be the next thing."

"The domino theory."

"All those people have to do is stay north of the 17th parallel."

"The Vietnamese never accepted that border. In fair elections Ho Chi Minh would have become the elected leader of the whole country."

"Hypothetical history is easy to write. But the world is real and the war is real, and it's Johnson's business to win it."

"The only way he can win it is to obliterate the whole country, and he seems to be on the way to doing that."

"He'll do what he has to."

The Senator's voice had grown quieter still, Noreen's had an unnaturally deep and hoarse quality.

"I don't think we need to talk about this," Clyde said.

"Why not, Clyde?" Noreen said.

"Because you're never going to agree, and there's no point in it."

"The point is to say what I think."

"You can think it without needing to say it tonight sitting at this table."

"Just be sweet and girlish, is that it?"

"That's not what I said."

"So what do you think, Clyde?" the Senator said. He was trying to draw Clyde into the argument, and Clyde didn't know why. Noreen was staring at him, her eyes shining.

"I think it's not our war, and I'm damn glad of it," Clyde said.

"So we can turn our backs and feel virtuous," Noreen said.

"Put it that way if you like. We're observers, a small country without too much power, and that's a lucky thing."

"So we let the Americans do our dirty work for us, keeping the lesser breeds in order."

"You can put it that way."

"They drop napalm on Vietnamese women and children, and we just smile and go back to manufacturing their planes."

"We all know," the Senator said, "that the world would be a better place if it was run by a bunch of bra-burning feminists."

"I'm not sure that any feminist has ever burned a bra," Noreen said, "it's just one of those folktales that give men another chance to be distracted from what matters by the idea of bare bouncing tits."

""I had very beautiful ones when I was young," Marion said. "James was quite taken with them. It was part of my power over him."

There was a pause, which was perhaps what she intended.

"That's enough of that, Marion," the Senator said.

"Don't try to shush me, James, or I'll tell them even more shocking things than that about you."

"'Whatever is, is right'" Noreen said, obviously quoting something, though Clyde couldn't see the point of it. One of those leaps of thought he didn't follow.

"Who said that?" he said.

"A poet."

"I might have known," the Senator said, in a different tone now, as if ready to make peace, "that we'd end up with poetry."

"Oh Rose, thou art sick," Marion said.

"The invisible worm," Noreen continued, and Marion went on and completed the little poem.

"That flies in the night
In the howling storm
Hath found of thy bed
Of crimson joy
And his dark secret love
Shall thy life destroy."

Clyde had never heard those cold words. The Senator picked up his wine glass and drained it. He held out the bottle to Noreen.

"A little more," she said, "I don't have to drive."

The Senator poured her half a glass of dark red wine.

"Did you mean everything you said?" Noreen asked him.

"Every word."

"So did I," she said, and they let it go at that. Clyde tried to work out what hour of the day it was in Vietnam, morning, he thought, and a mother was holding a child and washing it with water from a small bowl, and far off in the jungle a Vietcong guerrilla was curled up in an underground bunker, trying to sleep after a night spent moving toward the site of a planned attack. There was a noise of birds, and far off, a helicopter.

They set off home a few minutes later. Noreen was very quiet in the car as they drove through the silent streets. When he came back from driving the baby-sitter home, the house was dark, and he stumbled in the front hall. Everything was quiet, as if the rooms were empty, as if Noreen had taken Clifford from his bed and vanished into the night. He went up the stairs. It was dark in the bedroom, but he could see a pale shape lying on the bed.

"Come and get me, Joe," a voice said. Clyde took off his clothes and joined her there in the timeless, urgent place that men and women went to.

That timeless, urgent place. Clyde remembered sitting alone in his office at County Finance one morning a few years later, not long before they moved to Ottawa, the phone ringing.

"It's Cathy Ratner," a voice said when he answered, and for a brief moment he didn't know who that was. Then he did.

"Cathy," he said.

"You remember me now?"

"I remember you."

"You once said to me was that I could call you sometime."

"I guess I did."

"Well I'm calling you. I want you to come here."

"I'm married, Cathy."

"So am I. I always was."

He didn't know what to say. After all these years.

"You owe this to me, Clyde."

"Do I?"

"Didn't you offer? You said I could call."

"That was a long time ago."

"Don't be a shit, Clyde."

Her voice was hard.

"Come this afternoon," she said."You know where I live."

She hung up. Clyde was shaking, though he didn't know exactly why, because he wanted her or because he didn't. He had always intended to remain faithful to Noreen. He remembered how Cathy looked as she stood naked in that sunny bedroom, the pale skin, the hair. He wondered if he did owe her something. Whatever the reason, he found himself driving to Brockton, parking his car outside her house early that afternoon, unsure what he would do when the door opened, a chill inside him, though it was a warm spring day; the shaking that had begun when he answered the phone had retreated, but never quite gone away.

He knocked, and she opened the door quickly, as if she'd been watching for him. She didn't speak, just gestured for him to come in. She was different. Something wrong. The pallor beneath her makeup, the hair, her clothes looked too big for her, though as always, she was tidy, well groomed.

She was staring at him, bruised hollows under her eyes. He stared back.

"I guess you hadn't heard."

"I haven't heard anything," he said.

She led him into the living room, pointed to a chair. It was different now, blue walls, dark blue and brown furniture, an abstract painting in black and white hanging over the mantel. In the dining room, he could see a set of Barbie dolls sitting on the table.

"The kids are at school. Lyall's picking them up to take them to a birthday party. So they won't be arriving, looking for mummy. Why don't you say something, Clyde? Oh I know why. There's nothing to say, is there? I'm sick, and I look awful. I always liked looking pretty. You've got the luck, you might as well enjoy it, but I don't have that any more. I don't even have my own tits any more, these are falsies. Yes, they are, and yes, of course it's cancer, and I've had chemotherapy and they make promises but I think pretty soon I'm going to die. Poor bloody kids eh? I'm not a bad mother, really, but they'll have to do without. Oh Lyall will marry again, I guess, he's not the kind to be alone. Why don't you tell me to shut up, Clyde, or to get to the point? Why don't you say something?"

"Nothing to say."

"I want you to fuck me, Clyde. You offered. I could call you, you said, and we both knew what that meant. Well I called, and I know it's not what you were planning, and I don't care if you're married. She's not dying of cancer, is she? Lyall can't do it. I don't know whether because he's scared or it's sympathy or disgust, all three probably, but he can't get it up, and I thought maybe you could. You're heartless. Or maybe it's not that, but I thought of you. I want something nice to think about in the dark of night. I'm tired of do-it-yourself."

Clyde was shivering, and as if to warm himself, he got up from the chair, went to her and put his arms around her. She clung to him. She was so small, shorter than Noreen, thinner than she once was, and he could feel some cold pressure against his chest from whatever kind of prosthesis she was wearing.

"Sometimes, Clyde, I hated you more than any human being in the world. Why would that be? You never did anything I didn't let you do. But there's something about you, that you never learned the rules or some damned thing like that."

"Let's go upstairs," he said. He didn't want to hear the things she had to say.

As they made their way to the bedroom, he noticed the two children's rooms, the toys piled around the bathtub.

"How old are they?" he said.

"Wrong question."

They were in the bedroom, and she began to take off her clothes. He obediently followed her lead, trying not to look but not to avoid looking. Her thighs were thinner, a different kind of pallor. The thick bush of pubic hair was gone, just a thin dusting of darkness. On her chest, two curving scars, a tangle of sewn flesh where her round perfect breasts had been. The two of them got into bed, and he drew her toward him.

"You're shivering," she said.

He didn't speak, kissed her mouth, and was relieved when the blood began to stir. He could do what was required, though it seemed as if the thin, anguished body beneath him was something he could break, as if he was too big, too heavy, too strong, but her response was intense, an edge of hysteria to it, and he extended himself, dutiful, cold. He couldn't help it if he damaged her. It went on, and she sang out in desperation or rage, and once again, as years before, he was standing by the bed dressing himself as she watched, though this time she had drawn the covers over her.

"I can't come back," he said.

"I got what I wanted."

He walked over to the bed, looked down at the grey, weary face that smiled up at him. "I'm truly sorry, Cathy," he said, "for what's happening to you."

"Of course you are," she said. Then he turned away and left the house, drove the few blocks to the golf club where he had a shower, and then he drove home. He remembered that Lyall would be on his way to the school to pick up the children and take them to a birthday party. Lyall's wife was dying. At a corner, a block and a half from his own house, Clyde pulled over, stopped the car. From where he sat, he could see past the stud frame of a ranch style bungalow under construction, next door to it his wife Noreen and his son Clifford in front of their own house, Noreen sitting on the steps, wearing shorts, her arms clasped around her knees, Clifford doing some kind of gymnastics on the grass, and as he looked at them like this, secretly, from a distance, they were nameless, beautiful strangers, as mysterious as a tribe on a far island, or aliens dropped from a spaceship. He stared at them, trying to remember that they were his own, that he had made promises. It was a long time before he was able to start the car and go to them.

Things happened and were unspoken. The past was a map of secrets. And the years passed, and Danny was dead and Clyde was almost sixty looking out the window of his cabin over the bright surface of a deep lake in the rocky hills of the Shield, the sun beginning to vanish behind the trees on the far shore. He had thought he should open the box of photos, read them like Tarot cards, but he couldn't do it. Earlier he'd called the funeral home, then the church.

"Yes, I think we know Danny O'Connell here," the priest had said. "Little fellow with a limp. What did he die of?"

Clyde caught himself as he was about to speak, remembering that suicide was considered a sin. They might refuse to perform the funeral.

"Cancer," he said. It was not the first lie he'd ever told. Besides if Danny had waited just a few months his cancer would have finished him.

"So much of that," the priest said, and Clyde had agreed.

6 | Perry

"Do you speak any French?" Perry said.

"Not really," Clyde said. "Do you?"

"A little. We'd have to have someone who's bilingual."

"And what would we call ourselves?"

"DB Consultants."

"Doesn't tell much."

"Consultant is becoming the magic word, Clyde. Nothing can be done without consulting a consultant. We will be the arbiters of efficiency, the voice of objectivity. We provide the highest level of expertise. We define the problem. We get the data, we analyse it, we consider and reconsider. We put it into well-chosen words. We offer meaty conclusions, and at a price that makes our importance undeniable. The more expensive the consultant, the higher the quality of his truth."

Perry was lying on the long sofa in his Toronto apartment, holding a glass of red wine as he delivered this speech. He and Clyde had eaten an excellent dinner at Three Small Rooms, the new restaurant at the Windsor Arms, then walked along Bloor Street and up Bedford Road to the apartment. They had got through a bottle of wine with dinner, but when they got to the apartment, Perry insisted on opening another. Clyde sat in a stuffed chair, upholstered with the same dark brown corduroy as the couch, his own wine on the glass-topped coffee table in front of him. He had his legs thrown over the side of the chair, and his head leaning against the back so he could look out the wide glass windows of the apartment over the lights of the city.

"So we'll be very expensive."

"We will be the Rolls Royce of consultants, The Waterford crystal of consultants. The Yves St Laurent of consultants."

"I'm not sure that we'll get any business."

"Of course we will. I know people. You know people. After all these election campaigns, we have connections."

"What if the wrong party wins?"

"We are above party. Have you ever joined a political party?"

"No, but I've worked for one."

"You're an expert, not a mere political hack. *Moi, la même chose.* I will call myself *M. Même Chose.*»

"You always start speaking French when you're drunk."

"An overflow of high spirits."

"I think if you work for one party, you'll never get work from the others."

"There are municipal governments, provincial governments, even companies that want the view from Parliament Hill. Everything has turned around in the last few years. 1967, 1968, that was the hinge, in Canada anyway. Look how the campaigns have changed since the one where you and I met up."

Clyde got up from the chair and went to the window. Not far away was Varsity Stadium and beyond, the low buildings of the university campus. To his left, he saw the high towers of hotels and offices, the new T-D Centre designed by Mies van der Rohe bright and glittering against the night. Below two figures walked along the sidewalk, the bodies foreshortened by his angle of vision. Funny little people of the world. He wasn't altogether sober himself. He saw lights crossing the sky, a plane on its journey. Beyond the city was the lake and in Canalville, on the far side, his wife and son waiting for him. Soon he would catch a bus and be taken home to them.

"You see all that bright country?" Perry said. "It can be ours."

"Ottawa, you said."

"Not a metropolis, but it's the national capital, where government resides, and more and more, my friend, government is the country's biggest business. Bilingualism alone is becoming an empire. When he first got elected in 1968 Trudeau started bringing *les québecois* to Ottawa, and the French are by tradition *dirigiste*. They have the example of the church, which controlled all things with a steady hand, and while they have pitched out the *curé*, they still have his habits. And you know what the polls say. This current election is going to be close, and your friendly neighbourhood social democrat is going to have the balance of power. More *dirigisme*. But there are still many who think that the government can't even pick its own nose. The solution? Consultants. We stand to one side and observe and see the truth, write it up in a little report, assessing *pro* and *contra*, and justifying the expenditure of public monies in such and such a good cause, and everyone is happy."

Perry had phoned Clyde the previous weekend and told him he must come to Toronto and talk, that he had plans for their future. Since the first election campaign when they'd worked together, the two of them frequently met up to play golf or have dinner. The previous summer Perry had brought Irene, his girlfriend, down for a week in Brockton. They went to plays at the Festival, drove around the miles of orchards.

Although it was only a month from the coming election, Clyde had made time for a day in Toronto. By now they had two cars, but Noreen's needed work on the transmission, so Clyde had left his car with her and come to Toronto on the bus, enjoying the odd detachment of the trip down the highway, seeing the subdivisions, the small factories beside the Queen Elizabeth Way, but having, for the duration of the ride, no attachment to any of it. It was like watching a movie of the world, and now the later scenes of the movie were taking place in the brightly lit buildings he observed from the wide apartment window. On the balcony was a small barbecue. Perry said he and Irene made hamburgers out there during the hot weather. They planned to get married sometime after the election and were buying and renovating a house in Cabbagetown; the neighbourhood was beginning to come up in the world after its decades as a slum.

Over dinner, Perry had explained his bright idea – that he and Clyde should move to Ottawa and open a private company to advise various government departments. Clyde was sceptical, but he'd developed a good deal of respect for Perry's intuition.

"The Senator is not going to live forever," Perry was saying.

"True," Clyde said. There was no doubt the old man was weakening.

"You are not going to inherit his little empire."

"Probably not."

"What will you do?"

"I'm building my own little empire."

"Two strip malls and a cherry orchard, soon to be a subdivision."

"Something like that."

"The Senator has a financial interest in these things."

"The strip malls, yes."

"What happens to it all when he dies?"

"A good question."

It was one Clyde had asked himself. Now and then he had wondered if he might be able to take over County Finance. It was closely held, and the other shareholders allowed the Senator to run it without much interference. When he was gone, why shouldn't Clyde be in control?

"You're smart, Clyde. You've done well for yourself, but is Canalville where you want to spend your life, a small Ontario city with a small Ontario future? Cut and run. Go national. Sell out, put the money in blue chips and go for the brass ring."

"In Ottawa?"

"I said brass, not gold. But it's the national capital. Look at how fast Campeau is building houses, and he can't keep up with the market. Money follows power, as some great philosopher ought to have said."

"I'll think about it, Perry."

"You be the silent partner, if you like. I want your money. Office rent, a good secretary. I'll work for peanuts."

"What about your house in Cabbagetown?"

"I can sell it at a profit anytime."

"Have you told Irene about all this?"

"I want you lined up first. We'd be perfect together. I do the tap dance, you follow up with the charts and the figures."

Clyde turned and looked back at his friend, who had one of his legs thrown over the back of the couch, the glass of wine balanced on his chest as he stared at the ceiling.

"I'll think about it."

"We both have to finish with this election first. I can't get enough people for all the errands that need to be done. Call me when it's over."

Clyde picked up his glass of wine."Done," he said and got up to leave.

Once outside, Clyde walked down to Bloor Street, flagged a cab and directed the driver to the bus terminal. He was a few minutes early, and he walked past the ticket counters to the back stairs and down to the toilet. He noticed a man standing at the washroom door, back half-turned, and when Clyde moved away from the urinal, the same slight figure was standing in front of one of the sinks, studying himself in the mirror. The face was familiar.

"Danny!" he said.

"Oh my God, look what the cat dragged in. Hello, Clydie."

"What are you doing here?"

"Blowjobs."

"What?"

"I'm doing blowjobs. I don't suppose... No, it wouldn't be your style."

"You don't mean it."

"I know it's not exactly high class, Clydie, picking up men in the bus terminal shithouse, but it's a living."

"You're kidding me."

"Could be, Clydie, but it's actually true."

"Why?"

"Well, when I was getting out of the joint that first time they said what are you going to do, and I said I thought I'd go into brain surgery, but that didn't really work out."

A stranger came in, a short heavy man in a worn three-piece suit, stared at the two of them for a moment as if unsure what to do next.

"Let's go across the road and have a drink," Clyde said.

"Aren't you going to miss your bus?"

"There's another one."

Danny looked at the stranger and winked.

"Isn't he a sweetheart? He's going to take me out for a drink."

Still looking confused, the man stood up at the urinal, and unzipped. Clyde started toward the stairs and Danny followed along.

"Why are you limping, Danny? What's wrong with you?"

"My leg got broken and didn't heal right."

They made their way up the stairs, past men and women who sat in the emptiness of dead time between arrival and departure.

"Did that happen in jail, the broken leg?" Clyde said as they went out the door to the pavement, a streetcar in front of them slowing to stop at the corner of Dundas. He studied the faces in the lighted car.

"No. It was after that. Someone threw me out a window."

"Seriously, Danny."

"S'true. Clydie. I was partying with these two guys, and we were pretty stoned, and one of them thought it would be fun to throw me out the window. It was only one floor, but the way I landed I guess I broke my leg, hurt like hell at first. I was lying there shouting, but I wasn't wearing any clothes except my shirt, and the guys decided they weren't finished with me, so they took me back in, and they had a whole lot of pills and when I complained about my leg, they just gave me more pills, and, you know, it went on like that, and by the time I got to the hospital, they said they'd have to break it all over again, so I just left. Don't you tell Hazel that story, Clydie. Don't you tell Hazel about any of this."

By now they'd crossed the road and were walking into the beverage room at the Ford Hotel. It was a dim, noisy place, at least half the men there already drunk. One or two waved to Danny as he passed. They found an empty table in the back corner.

The waiter took their order without saying a word.

"I won't tell her, Danny. But is it really true, you make your living giving blowjobs in the bus terminal?"

"Well not always in the bus terminal. It's been a bad week, and I have to pay my rent tomorrow. You know how it is, someone's on his way out of town and wants a little thrill before he goes back to North Bay, and there I am, his little thrill."

Clyde took out his wallet, handed Danny five twenty dollar bills.

"Is that enough for your rent?"

"Thank you, Clyde. That will do nicely. Are you rich?"

"I'm not poor."

"Tell me all about you, Clydie. Are you married?"

"Yes."

"Did you marry Dorrie Stead? I always thought you might."

"She was already married, Danny."

"That can be fixed."

Dorrie Stead. Danny had been gone a long time.

"And Hazel, she's OK?"

"Fine. Just fine."

"You have any babies?"

"A son. Clifford."

"Won't they be waiting for you back at home? Your wife. What's her name?"

"Noreen. Like I said, there's another bus."

"There's always another bus. That's what I tell myself when I've got the rag on."

Clyde looked across the table at him, the hair thinning, mouth pulled a little to one sight, eyes more squinted than ever.

"They shouldn't have done that to you, Danny."

"What?"

"Sent you to jail."

"Well, thank you, Clyde, for your wishes. The joint wasn't too bad, not once I got used to it. My second beef, Tony Drummond, he was my old man there, and he looked after me pretty good. If anybody messed with me, they were in big trouble. Hey, remember Cappy Ryan? He came in on some kind of beef, assault with a deadly weapon or something, and I told Tony about Cappy and Butch and how they went after me, Danny-Hunting, and Cappy pissing on me, and Tony and two other guys got Cappy in the showers one day. His face was swollen up for a week."

"So you got even."

"I certainly did. You still working for that Francis Finster?"

"No."

"I always figured they let him go because he was such a big-shot."

"What's that mean?"

"At the Fruit Farm, when the cops raided it."

"Francis was there?"

"Of course. He was always there."

"Are you sure?"

"Clydie when someone has his little sausage up my bum, I usually know who it is. Well maybe not always, in the dark sometimes, but yes, your friend Francis was there, and then the cops were there, and then Francis wasn't there. Like I say, I guess he was too important. I heard Francis had something on just about everybody."

Clyde might have put it all together years before, when Dorrie told him about the raid – why he'd been sent out on the country roads with a package of bills. Francis had picked the right cop and been allowed to slip out the back door. The money was a bribe, or just a thank you. Clyde drank from his glass of beer.

"So you went back to jail."

"Only one other time."

"Same thing?"

"Well it's sort of legal now, but you're not supposed to do it in public, and sometimes the police come to the baths, but what happened was I was hitchhiking and there was a little misunderstanding, I thought he was just being shy, and I tried to help, but then I got charged with assault. The cop who arrested me was very nice about it, said there was nothing he could do because the guy was really fucked up."

"Oh Danny."

"So you think I should go back to my original plan and go into brain surgery?"

"Something like that."

"If you say so, Clydie, I'll call the medical school tomorrow."

"Glad to hear it."

"Tell me about Hazel."

"She's getting towards retirement age, but she's in no hurry. She and Palmer figure they'll just go on. He might close up his bigger office in Canalville, keep the little one in Brockton."

"I got nothing good to say about that man. Tony said if I had a decent lawyer that first time, I'd got probation or something."

"I think maybe Palmer's better on real estate."

"Hey, remember the burning-glass, Clydie?"

"No."

"Sure you do."

"I don't."

"You had this glass in a drawer in your house and we took it outside one day in the summer, and you knew how to do it from your uncle, took a little piece of paper and all, and you held the glass so all the sun came shining in on the paper, and first it started to smoke, and then it burned."

"The magnifying glass. I remember."

"I just thought of that the other day. That was when I knew you must be about the smartest little kid around. Cause you knew how to start a fire with a burning-glass."

"You got your brother to take us out fishing that day."

"Down at the spiles, and you kept getting your line all tangled, and Terry got mad."

"He got mad easy, didn't he?"

"When I got arrested he smacked me around. I said, 'Thanks Terry, that's really a big help,' and he smacked me again."

Clyde lifted the glass of beer. He'd begun to sober up from all the wine with dinner, but the beer was making him drunk again. A woman with short shorts and heavy eye makeup looked in the door of the room and waved one of the men over to where she was standing, launched into some kind of story.

"You could come down and stay if you wanted, visit my mother."

"Your wife doesn't want some little fag hanging around the house."

"It would be OK with her."

"I can't go back there, Clydie. Not till I'm rich and famous, with a big pink car like Liberace or somebody."

"So what are you going to do?"

"I manage, Clyde, I manage."

"You still got your driver's license?"

"No, I don't think so. I mean I don't exactly have the pink Cadillac yet."

"Can you get a license? Somebody lend you a car?"

"There's a guy, a bartender up at *Skippers*, he's kind of a half-assed friend, if I don't ask too much. He takes messages for me, stuff like that. Maybe he'd help."

Clyde took a business card out of his wallet, wrote Perry's name and phone number on the back.

"This guy's a friend of mine. We're maybe going into business together. I'll call him tomorrow. He's got a lot of jobs for the election, deliveries, pickups. He can probably give you some work, for a month or so anyway. Call him tomorrow and tell him that you're going to get your license. He might have something while you're waiting, stuffing envelopes or some damn thing. He can't get enough volunteers."

"You're a sweetheart, Clydie, trying to look after me."

"You used to look after me."

"You could call it that."

Danny was staring him, as if it would help him understand all the changes.

"You still play golf with those guys around town, Jim Bennett, Lyall Ratner?"

"Jim Bennett, now and then."

"Noreen eh? That's your wife's name."

"Yep."

"She nice?"

"Sure. She teaches ballet to little kids."

"Oh Clydie, would she teach me?"

"Sure."

"When I'm rich and famous I'll hire her for ballet and tap. The world's first crippled tap dancer."

"I don't think she teaches tap."

"Ballet is good enough. I met one of the boys from the ballet school one night at *Skippers*. Oh Clydie, he was so beautiful. But I didn't ever see him dance."

Danny was rubbing the side of his face with one finger, a habit

Clyde remembered from their boyhood.

"I suppose you better go now, eh Clydie? Hung around long enough with your faggy old friend."

Clyde looked at his watch.

"I got a while," he said. "There's an hour between buses."

But somehow they had run out of things to say. Conversation grew more of an effort. Clyde talked about his mother's new friend, Peggy Wilberforce, who was a widow and lived just around the corner, but Danny didn't seem to have much interest in this woman he'd never met.

"I'd like to see Hazel again," he said, "but I'd have to be doing something a little nicer. And don't you tell her none of this. You ran into me, and I was fine, you can tell her that."

They sipped the beer, tried to find things to say, and before long they had said goodbye on the street, and Clyde was staring at the lights of the traffic from inside the bus window. When he got home, Noreen woke for a moment, cuddled up against him, mumbled that he smelled of cigarettes and fell back asleep.

He called Perry the next morning and tried to explain who Danny was and why he should hire him to run errands.

"Is he smart?" Perry said.

"Not especially."

"Is he a good driver?"

"No."

"But I should hire him."

"Yes."

"I guess if we're going to be partners, I have to learn to co-operate without asking questions."

"You already asked questions."

"I'll find him a job."

Late that afternoon, Clyde was sitting on a wooden chair in a tiny storefront office for one of the Canalville constituency's more distant polls. He sat with the poll chairman, a handsome slender man, who gave the impression of being constructed of bones too thin for their length so he appeared fragile, a house of glass. They were going over the records of the volunteers who had been going street to street, and trying to work out where the candidate could most profitably spend a morning knocking on doors.

"We need an area where there's some support," Clyde said. "I don't want him getting completely discouraged. We've got television coming to a soccer game his son's playing that afternoon."

They were going over the map when a phone call came in. A teenaged volunteer answered and waved to Clyde.

"For you, Mr Bryanton," she said

It was the Senator looking for Clyde, asked him to drop round to his house that night. Clyde agreed, though it meant he wouldn't be home until after Clifford was in bed.

It was a cold starry night when he got out of his car at the Senator's house. Marion met him at the door and led him into the Senator's den, darker than ever tonight, with only one green-shaded light at the corner of the desk. A decanter of whisky stood on a silver tray, with two tumblers and a glass pitcher of water. Marion left him there with the old man, who rose slowly from the chair behind the desk where he was sitting with one or two pieces of paper laid out in front of him, a few sentences written in his thick forceful strokes, his black fountain pen lying to one side. He reached for the decanter. Each of them took the whisky and water the Senator prepared and Clyde sat in one of the upholstered upright chairs.

"I'm drawing up a new will," the Senator said. "I'd like you to be the executor, if you're willing." Clyde was moved and flattered by the offer.

"Yes," he said, "of course."

The Senator took his fountain pen and ticked off the first of the sentences written on the piece of paper in front of him. He went on to his next point, a large bequest to the university for which he'd been raising money over the last few years.

"They've offered to make me chancellor in return for the money I've already raised and this bequest. Ten years ago I would have laughed at such a proposal, buying a position of honour – not that I didn't understand that all positions of honour are bought – but I would have thought myself in no need of it, but now I'm on my last legs, I grab whatever I can get. Chancellor Lawton has a pleasant ring to it, and I get to confer degrees on all those pretty and hard-working young people."

The Senator went on. There were bequests to his daughters, his grandchildren, and Marion was left a life interest in the bulk of the estate, with a division between the Senator's daughters and the university on Marion's death. Bill Romanuck had drawn up the will, the Senator's Toronto lawyer having retired and suggested Bill, who had once been one of his juniors. He would prepare a final version for signing in the next week. The will did not stipulate how County Finance would be handled, but as executor Clyde would, at least initially, control a substantial block of shares.

"Of course by the time all this comes about," the Senator said, "I'll be dead and won't give a hoot, but making these arrangements gives me a certain grim pleasure."

The Senator marked off another of the notes he'd made on his sheet of paper. The fingers were thick, the skin dark with deep wrinkles at each knuckle. Firm powerful hands, and they were giving Clyde his blessing, or so it seemed. As the executor of the will he would have a good deal of power.

"The next thing. There's going to a certain amount of publicity when the university board of governors appoints me as chancellor, and of course they want some kind of little biography. When I was thinking of that, I decided that I'd like to have something that you can hand out to newspapers and such-like after my death. Might as well have them saying what I want as what they decide they know on their own."

"You're not planning to die soon, are you?"

"I'm not planning to die at all, but it will happen. Sooner rather than later, I expect. Marion tells me that I no longer walk, I amble. Do you have a notebook?"

"Not with me."

The Senator took a couple of sheets of paper from his desk drawer and passed them to Clyde who folded them in half to take notes.

"I didn't learn shorthand," he said.

"I speak slowly."

Clyde took a pen from his jacket pocket.

"I was born in Burnsville, October 11, 1893. A hell of a long time ago isn't it? Another century. Some of this is in *Who's Who*, but we might as well go through it all. My father was a farmer's son but became a merchant in a small way." He gave his parents' full names, and Clyde wrote them down. "I attended the local schools, played a good deal of lacrosse, a little baseball, and in 1912, I went to work for Malcolm Ford as an office boy in his insurance brokerage. It was through his influence that when I enlisted I received a commission, and after serving in England and France – won a DSC, though I'm not sure I deserved it – and being promoted to Captain, I returned to Canada in 1919, and the next year I married Malcolm Ford's daughter Elizabeth."

Clyde looked up from his notes. The Senator met his eyes. The flesh of his face looked heavier tonight. By the dim light of the one lamp, the hollow under his eyes was darker, deeper.

"She died in 1926."

He was silent for a moment.

"Have you got all that?"

"Yes."

The Senator didn't go on. Clyde waited, wondered if he was supposed to ask, did.

"What did she die of?"

Diphtheria. Why did that word come into his mind? A story about someone, one of his mother's uncles.

"She was drowned," the Senator said. "We were travelling in northern Ontario. It may have been suicide. Don't write any of that down."

Clyde couldn't bring himself to look up. He thought he might be hearing voices beyond the door, he couldn't make out the words, but they were talking about death. Marion was in another room of the big house. She must know more of the story, how it had come about, or maybe it was all over before she met the clever, ambitious young widower she was to marry.

"In 1927 I married Marion Murchison, and we had two children, Anne, born in 1928 and Elaine born in 1934. I ran the Ford insurance brokerage during all those years, and founded County Finance in 1945."

The voice went on, the volunteer work during the Second War, the appointment to the Senate, and Clyde dutifully wrote it down, notable events, service clubs, boards of two charities. The man was reciting his own obituary. They had gone over some border into another reality, the formal words, the ceremonies of survival.

The Senator finished his recitation and was silent.

"May sound odd to you, Clyde, young as you are," he said after a moment, very quietly, "but there is a certain pleasure in summing it up, as if all of it made some sense. Not that it does. *We're here because we're here because we're here...* and so on *ad infinitum*. You probably know that old song. The men sang it going up to the trenches."

The whisky went to his lips.

"Type up two versions, a shorter one for the university, and the longer one to keep in your files. I'm coming in to the office tomorrow. I'll have a look at them. I'm sure you know what's wanted."

"I think so," Clyde said and got to his feet.

"Thank you, Clyde," the Senator said. "Did you hear from those polling people?"

"Tomorrow. I should have it when you come in."

"I used to think I could talk to my barber, and find out all I needed to know about public opinion, but now we spend a fortune on these self-styled experts."

"Political science."

"Politics will become a science when sex becomes a science."

"They seem to have that in mind too." Clyde picked up his jacket from the chair.

"You're very reliable, aren't you Clyde?"

It might be a compliment or an insult. Clyde could think of no answer, said goodnight and left the room as the Senator reached for the decanter. Outside he saw hundreds of stars in the clear sky. As he drove home, he thought of the Senator's first wife, a young woman in a long pale dress wandering down a moonlit road under the trees of the great boreal forest, sinking into a deep northern lake.

Clyde hadn't been home since breakfast that morning. As he walked into the house, he heard the scream of Noreen's power saw from the basement. On one wall of the unfinished space, she had her barre and enough room to do her dance exercises. On the other side of the basement, her workbench, tools, the little table-saw she'd recently bought. He opened the door to the basement, walked down the steps. She turned off the saw, lifted the piece of wood she'd been cutting, noticed him standing there.

"Hi, Joe," she said.

He waved and sat down on the steps. She was wearing jeans, a t-shirt, and her hair was pulled up under a white painter's cap with *Pratt and Lambert* written on the front.

"I'm nearly finished for tonight." She carried her piece of wood to the workbench, took a sanding block and began to rub it along the newly cut edge.

"What are you working on?" he said

"It's for Clifford's room, drawers at one end, open shelves at the other."

"Amazing woman."

"You could get us both a beer," she said.

He turned and went upstairs, got two bottles of Black Horse from the refrigerator and snapped off the caps.

"You want this down there?" he shouted from the top of the stairway.

"I'll come up."

He could hear the sound of a broom as she swept the basement floor. She kept her work space tidy. Clyde had never quite believed what she'd said about carpentry, wanting tools, but he found the whole thing intriguing. Something oddly sexual about her cutting, shaping, gluing these pieces of wood. When she came up the stairs, the cap off, her hair hanging loose, he was sitting in one of the living room chairs, had left her beer on the little table beside the other one.

"Why don't you take off your clothes," he said.

She went to the front window, pulled the drapes and did. Picked up the beer and drank.

"Naked woman with a beer bottle," she said.

He made a noise.

"To bed, Joe the Silent, to bed."

The election, when it took place a couple of weeks later, was very close, but Barton Dred won by a hundred and eight votes. His opponent's committee threatened a recount, but there was no hope in it. Clyde had taken a chance when the results started to come in and he thought they might win, of setting a few people to work decorating the committee room with balloons and streamers. If the results turned around and he had to concede, they could shove them in a back room, but when the results were close to final and the cameras from the television station arrived, the room was full of balloons, and they got some good shots of the candidate's teen-aged children batting them in the air.

The next day was Halloween. Clyde had decided he was going to take things easy, slept late, then went to the office and opened a pile of mail, sorted it into three files for response, from immediate to eventual. He had the first architect's drawings for the small apartment building he was putting up at the corner of the new subdivision, and he was a little uncertain about the design, but he decided to come back to the drawings in a couple of days, clear-headed. He had a week before he had to go to the bank and make the line of credit final. He'd probably need more money from the bank in the spring. He wasn't working with County Finance on this development. He wanted independence, and they were heavily invested in two new office buildings. Clyde had argued against that investment, but the Senator had over-ruled him, convinced that he could arrange government leases on enough of the space to make the buildings profitable.

In the afternoon, Clyde met Clifford at his school then drove to

Brockton to pick up his mother. She was coming to their house to help give out candy to the neighbourhood children, and afterward to have a late dinner with them.

"What time can I put on my costume, Dad?"

"Six o'clock maybe."

"Did Mom get my sword painted silver?"

"Yup."

Clifford had decided he wanted to be a pirate, and Noreen had contrived a small sword out of scraps from her workshop. With that, an eyepatch, a red bandana round his head, a black scarf around his waist and a black mask, he'd make a convincing enough small privateer. Clyde drove to Brockton and parked outside the law office. His mother walked from her house to the office except in the worst weather. She came out and got in the back of the car.

"I'm going to put on my costume at six o'clock," Clifford told her, the moment she opened the door.

"I'll be there to watch."

"Let's go to the park," Clyde said. "I brought the soccer ball."

They left the car and walked to the park where Clyde remembered playing kick-catch-and-run in the fall afternoons. The field was empty, and he set down the soccer ball and kicked it, Clifford off in pursuit, the little legs running fiercely. He kicked it, and it went off at an angle. It rolled past Clyde and toward his mother. She gave it a small tidy blow with outside of her foot and it rolled toward Clifford.

"Good kick, Grandma Hazel," Clifford said, gave a mighty swing of his leg, just missed the ball as it rolled past him. He fell dramatically to the ground. Clyde seized him under the arms, gave him a great swing through the air and put him back on his feet. The boy raced after the ball, which lay a few feet beyond him. He kicked it further down the field.

"I'll beat you to the ball," Clyde said, and the two of them started to run. On the street at the end of the park, Clyde saw two girls in costume, one a witch in black, the other a bride in white. Everyone was someone else. When they reached the ball, Clifford gave it another kick and it went down the little hill at the end of the football field, resting in the patch of weeds that grew there.

"Who has to go get it?" Clyde said.

"You do."

"Why?"

"You just do."

He picked up the boy and hugged him, as he wriggled to escape.

"You have to go get it," Clyde said.

"Why?"

"You just do."

"You're stalling," Clifford said. It was a sentence he'd heard often enough when he found excuses not to go up to bed. Clyde laughed and went down the hill, picked up the ball and threw it back to the field. Beyond him the afternoon sun caught the huge bare trees at an angle, outlining each branch with golden light. For a moment Clyde was among the dead, watching all this with the detachment of the vanished, his son running and shouting, his mother standing perfectly still, her hands in the pockets of her tweed jacket.

"You won the election," his mother said as they drove along the Stone Road toward Canalville a few minutes later.

"Not me."

"Your man won."

"Yes, barely."

"Don't you feel that you won as well? You're part of it all."

"I do my job."

"It's only that?"

"I can't take sides as enthusiastically as most of them. I never played on teams. Golf was my game, and you play that against yourself. I figure I'm like the team trainer who packs the bus, makes sure they have the right sticks and skates. Or I'm the guy the sells the tickets at the arena."

"You don't believe in politics."

"We need some kind of system. It's not a bad one, what we've got. Sometimes I think it's a bit like inventing a steam engine to pick peaches, but it could be worse."

"You think people know what they're voting for?"

"More likely they know what they're voting against. Some of them are still on the team their father was on and will never change. Some of them can't remember who's running. Some of them refuse to vote because they think all politicians are crooks."

"Are they?"

"About the same as everybody else. There's always a little give and take. Mostly take, so some people would say."

"Don't you think that's cynical?"

"No."

"You sound like your father. I always thought he was cynical, but if he was, why did he join the army?"

"I wouldn't know."

"I never did."

Clyde was silent, could think of nothing to say. He wanted his mother to tell him more, but he didn't know the right questions to ask.

"Dad," Clifford said.

"What?"

"Do you think any other kids will be pirates?"

"Most of them don't have a mother who'll make them a silver sword."

When they reached the house, Noreen had just got back from her ballet class and was putting candy out in a bowl in the front hall. She had cut out a jack-o-lantern that morning while Clyde was still in bed, and she'd set it up on a table in the front window, but she hadn't yet lit the candle.

His mother began peeling vegetables for dinner, set them in water on the stove. Noreen had put a chicken in to roast.

The phone rang, Perry calling to congratulate him. His candidate too had squeaked in by a few votes.

"Your friend Danny says it's the first time he ever won anything."

"Probably is. Was he any help?"

"He tries hard. Cheerful. That's always good."

"Now we're both winners, maybe we should move on this new thing."

"I'll talk to you."

Noreen was getting Clifford into his costume. She had put some kind of fake jewels on the handle of the sword, now tied the scarf around his waist and put the sword through it.

"Don't be swinging it around," she said.

"Only if I'm attacked."

"Were you talking about Danny?" his mother said.

"I think he did OK." He'd given his mother a censored version of his conversation with Danny and explained that he'd got him work with Perry's election headquarters. He had the impression that she had seen through his evasions about what Danny had been up to, but she was pleased they'd found him a job.

Noreen pulled out a large paper shopping bag with handles.

"OK, pirate," she said, "that's for the swag."

"What's swag?"

"Your loot. The stuff you get."

"I'll get lots of swag," he said. "Are you coming with me?

"Joe can take you."

"His name's Clyde."

"That's why I call him Joe."

The house next door to them was dark, but the one beyond had a pumpkin on the edge of the porch, and two little children, a ghost in a white sheet, and a tiny person in a rabbit suit were coming down the stairs. Clyde stood on the walk while Clifford climbed the steps and knocked.

"Trick or treat," he said firmly when a woman with heavy glasses and a dish towel in her hand came to the door. "I'm a pirate."

"Come in, Pirate," she said, "and we'll find you a candy bar."

All along the crescent Clyde could see small groups, little children going back and forth to the doors, one or two parents standing hunched against the cold, guarding them. In the windows the fiery eyes of the pumpkin faces. Before long, the little ones would head home, and the older children would appear in small gangs, without parents, and later a few hulking teenagers with a half-hearted bit of costume, and after that the streets would be quiet except for the delinquencies of soaped windows, an egg thrown at a doorway. Clyde remembered once in his teens, a gang of boys had discovered an old farm wagon, pulled it up to the main street of Brockton and left it on the steps of the town hall, a bale of hay burning on the back of it.

"I got a bunch of candy at that house," Clifford said as he came down the walk.

"You going to be able to eat it all?"

"Probably I can. If you let me stay up late."

"We can save some for tomorrow."

Clyde reached down and took his son's hand, and they went on for two more blocks. By then the boy was beginning to look a bit tired, his bandana fallen to one side, and it was getting cold.

"What do you think, my friend? Time to go home."

"OK, Joe," he said and looked up to see what response he'd get.

"You too?"

"Can you carry my swag?"

They made their way back to the house, and Clifford settled down to eat his candy while Noreen made a salad, and his mother greeted the children at the door.

"Cold out there," she said.

"Winter's coming."

And soon enough it did. They got the footings poured for his apartment building, but the rest of the construction would wait till spring. Clyde had sold a few of the lots in the subdivision, though the sewers weren't in yet, but he still had too much money tied up, interest to be paid. In January pipes froze and burst in one of his stores. The tenants had been turning off the heat at night to economize on electricity, but they were convinced that the frozen pipes were Clyde's responsibility. Clyde threatened to cancel their lease, they threatened to go to court, and finally they agreed to split the cost of repairs. All of it made Perry's proposition more appealing.

By summer, though he was still on the run, things were a little easier. In August, he and Perry met on a golf course near Ottawa with Tom McKay, a journalist who had spent years in Ottawa as a political reporter, and now had a weekly column. Perry had met him through the member of parliament recently elected for his constituency, an old pol who'd been retired then resurrected himself. He'd known Tom McKay back when he first started covering the Hill, and Perry had met up with them and some other political friends in a bar, announced their new venture, and learned that one of the man's passions, outside of politics, was golf. Perry had talked up Clyde's skill at the game, and managed to contrive this afternoon's outing during Clyde's next trip to Ottawa.

Now he was in the capital city for a few days to try to find a property where they could set up an office, and they were set up to play on a local course. Clyde wasn't quite sure of the script for this golf game, whether he was supposed to win or lose. He'd have to wait and see how good a player McKay was. Perry would tip him a wink; he was in charge of this encounter. They met on the first tee at two o'clock, and Clyde had the impression that McKay was already drunk, his face pink and shining, but that might be a permanent condition. He had big hands, Clyde noticed as they were introduced, and he took hold of his golf club as if he planned to choke it instead of swinging it. A young woman, maybe seventeen or eighteen, was putting on the practice green behind the first tee, and Tom McKay gestured toward her.

"How'd you like to have her pull your cart?"

"Very tasty," Perry said.

"She could try a few strokes with my putter any day."

Perry laughed dutifully, Clyde smiled.

"I'm like the Minotaur, every now and then you have to feed me the flesh of a virgin. OK. Let's play golf."

He teed up his ball, took a practice swing and then delivered a vicious hammering blow that landed the ball well out the fairway. Clyde nodded to Perry to go next, and Perry's drive left him a little behind the other man. Clyde teed his ball, lined it up, and without any practice swing sent it sailing over the green fairway, the ball growing smaller in the air, dropping and running out of sight down the gentle slope. McKay looked toward him.

"Perry warned me about you," he said.

"A long way to go yet," Clyde said and picked up the bag of clubs. As he walked up the fairway, the soft grass under his feet, a few clouds in the sky, he felt completely at home. He remembered what he'd said to his mother about team sports. It was true that you played golf against yourself, even on a day like this when he was trying to impress a stranger, get his attention, his help. To play well, you had to collaborate with the earth and the wind, the way the slope ran, the texture of the grass.

That was how to play the game with this man he didn't much like but apparently needed. Let the course tell him what to do. He did that, and he was having a good day. Tom McKay played well, putted aggressively and with some success, muscled the ball around the course, but Clyde was three or four strokes ahead.

"You got one of those fucking elegant swings, don't you, Clyde," he said on the fifteenth tee.

"It gets the job done."

"I guess you're one of those elegant kind of guys." A fair bit of hostility in that, Clyde thought.

"You and I are slash and burn players," Perry said to the man, "just hammer the ball like Jack Nicklaus." Trying to take the edge off it, hoping for some kind of distraction. "Clyde plays to the layout of the course."

"Piss-elegant," the man said as he walked up to the tee.

Clyde looked toward Perry who made a small gesture with his mouth. Desperation? They were supposed to get this man on their side, and now Clyde had annoyed him. McKay was teeing off first though Clyde had won the previous hole. Was he supposed to make an issue of it? He remembered the Senator, many years before, warning him never to play below his level, but he thought something else was expected of him here. Tom McKay smashed his ball down the fairway, kicked away the broken tee. Clyde prepared to shoot, opened the club face just a little as he set up, let his hands move through fast, his shoulder drop, and the ball sliced into the trees at the edge of the fairway. He waited for a response.

"You just elegantly fucked that one, didn't you?"

"Happens sometimes," Clyde said. He looked toward Perry, who was coming up to take his turn, but Perry wouldn't meet his eyes.

Clyde's ball was lost in the trees, and he dropped another, took a two stroke penalty. By the end of the hole he was only one stroke ahead. He wondered if that was close enough, or if he was supposed to lose. The next hole was a short three par over a water hazard, and they all landed on the green.

"You used to do some speech-writing, didn't you?" Perry was saying to the red-faced man as they tramped up a small slope to where the three balls lay.

"Ten years ago," he said. "Before I had the column. Are you planning to do speeches?"

"Why not? I've done it before."

"What do *you* do, Piss-Elegant?"

"He's the best political manager in the country," Perry said, quick off the mark

"That true?" McKay said to Clyde.

"Maybe the second best," Clyde said, "on a rainy day."

"What the hell does that mean?"

"It means I'm pretty good."

Clyde's putt was the furthest away, but he went for it, too angry to be politic, didn't quite have the roll figured and it slid past the hole. They ended up with two putts apiece. The next hole, the seventeenth, was a very long four par. He wasn't sure what Perry wanted him to do now, whether he was supposed to lose the game.

"Do you suppose that little cutie is waiting for us on the putting green?" McKay said. "I've been thinking about that all the way round. Fresh young pussy."

Clyde wondered if this was all a performance, the tough-guy journalist, the whole thing meant to keep everyone at a distance. The eyes in that raw-looking face were small and cold. When his turn at the tee came, Clyde looked at the gentle slope of the fairway, its slight declivities, the green on a hill nearly four hundred yards away. He let it all sink in, breathed, swung, listened to the perfect click. It was, almost certainly, his longest drive of the day. If he decided he had to throw away strokes, he'd do it on the iron, play into the sand trap. Tom McKay pulled his drive a little to the left of the fairway so Clyde and Perry found themselves walking together.

"That was a hell of a drive," Perry said.

"Felt good. What am I supposed to do? Let him win."

"Tie maybe."

"He won't notice me doing it?"

"He won't care."

Perry put his iron into the sand trap at the edge of the green, didn't have to fake the difficulty of getting it out. By the end of the hole, he was tied with the older man. Deliberately missed a putt to let him go one ahead on the eighteenth. As they hiked in to the clubhouse, Clyde saw that the same young woman on the practice green. He couldn't believe she was there again. Tom McKay noticed her too.

"She must be waiting for me," he said. As they went past, he left his cart at the edge of the practice green and walked over to her. Clyde kept walking, didn't hear what he said, but as he looked back over his shoulder, he could see her, standing up straight, the putter in her left hand, carefully mouthing two words. Then she walked away. McKay caught up to him and Perry at the clubhouse porch.

"Gotta keep trying," he said. They all shook hands before going off to their cars.

"That was a pretty good game," he said to Clyde. "You pushed me. I've been thinking about doing a column on the new generation of guys coming to Ottawa. It's not a bad idea."

"We'd be pleased to be mentioned."

"You're goddam right you'd be pleased."

He nodded and walked away, pulling his cart. Clyde didn't speak until they'd put away their clubs and were driving off in Perry's car. "Is he a complete shit," he said, "or did I miss something?"

"I think it's a performance."

"And he spends all his spare time helping the orphans in Biafra."

As they drove back to his hotel Clyde, charged with frustration, could see the Ottawa River in the distance between the trees, a wide powerful current. It used to be filled with rafts of timber coming down from the north, sweeping past the city, the high gothic towers, the landscape of power.

How much magical wisdom would it have required for Clyde to predict on that August afternoon that the surly and arrogant Tom McKay would become his sworn enemy? But that was all still to come. The moment a few years later when he walked into *Mamma Teresa's* on a winter night, and the two of them, Tom and pretty Jane Mattingly, were sitting there. And then. And then. Danny's letter must by now be in Tom McKay's big ungentle hands, telling whatever Danny had picked up of Marion Lawton's secrets, what she knew of the Senator's life, of Clyde's. Marion was a clever and prudent woman, but the old sometimes grew careless.

It was the evening after that golf game when Noreen called Clyde at the hotel in Ottawa with the news that the Senator was in the hospital after a minor stroke. Marion was even more than usually distracted, and since she didn't drive, there were constant calls to Noreen, who had the bright idea of hiring Danny as a kind of chauffeur and companion. At first Clyde laughed at the suggestion – after all she'd never met Danny, only heard Clyde's stories – but she was convinced she was right.

"You know what a batty old things, she is" Noreen said. "The stranger he is, the better."

Clyde got from Perry the telephone number where Danny sometimes picked up messages, arranged to meet him on the way through Toronto.

"What do you think, Danny?" he said, as the two of them sat in a doughnut shop on Church Street. Danny knew many of those who went by, waved to each one.

"Clydie, I have my friends here in the city. People know me."

"And you pay your rent in the bus terminal shithouse."

"That was a bad week."

"It's up to you, Danny. It's a job. It would put money in your pocket."

"So tell me about this old lady I'm supposed to look after. She's not dirty is she? Some of those old people, I've met them in rooming houses, they smell."

"We're not looking for a nurse, Danny. She needs a driver, maybe someone to run errands, maybe do some gardening. She's very smart, but she didn't bother to keep up her driver's license, she has a little arthritis, and now her husband's had a stroke."

"Would she like me, Clyde?"

"We'll give it six weeks, find out. At worst you come back to the city with a few dollars in your pocket."

Danny waved at a two men who went by, young, shiny clean, both with neatly trimmed moustaches, the gay uniform.

"OK, let's try it. When do we start?"

"How about right now? I'll take you wherever you're living and pick up your stuff."

"I don't have much. One little shopping bag is about it."

"Why don't we go to Eaton's and buy you some new clothes for the job."

"Whose treat?"

"Mine, Danny. If it all works out, you can pay me back."

"Do I get a chauffeur's uniform with a cute hat like an airline pilot."

"Not quite what I was thinking."

"Remember old Mrs Kropfeld, when we were kids, how she'd bring her chauffeur over from Buffalo, New York for the summer. He had a cute uniform."

"If you get along with Marion and take the job full time, you could ask her for a uniform. If all your stuff goes in a plastic bag, you probably need new pants and a couple of shirts."

"They have some cute underwear at Eaton's."

"Let's go."

Danny was looking at him, a strained look on his face, the mouth tight.

"I said I'd never go back, Clydie, until I was driving a big pink Cadillac."

"The Senator is a powerful man, Danny. You work for him, people will treat you with respect."

Danny turned the coffee cup in front on him, first in one direction, then in the other.

"Does Hazel know about this?"

"Not yet. You want to phone and ask her what she thinks?"

"She'd just tell me to do whatever you say. Hazel thinks the sun shines out of your asshole."

"Is she wrong?"

"I never looked, not really."

"So?"

"Let's go buy my outfit."

Clyde drove Danny to his rooming house, and true to his word, he came out with a large paper shopping bag containing all his possessions. Downtown, Clyde parked the car, gave Danny some money and sent him off to shop, bought himself a newspaper and sat in the car reading it as he waited. Tom McKay's column was about changes at the Department of External Affairs since the last election. Clyde wondered if Perry's efforts would get them some kind of mention.

The Senator would probably recover from this stroke, and he might have years to live. Or he might not. Clyde might be able to gain control of County Finance after his death, if it came soon. Or not. He could try to persuade the Senator to sell him some of his holdings – questionable perhaps when the old man was weak and ill – or he could rely on his power as executor. If he couldn't get control, he'd move on.

Danny opened the back door of the car and threw the bags with his purchases on the back seat.

"Once they saw the money they were very polite. Everything I tried on, they said it looked wonderful. I told them I had a new job and I had to dress the part. They said what was the new job, and I said I was going to be a houseboy. I don't really know what that is but I thought it sounded nice. Maybe I should have said I was going to be a valet. Remember *The Shadow* on the radio, Lamont Cranston and his Filipino valet, Cato."

"We used to listen to that."

"I always wondered what a Filipino valet looked like."

"Short."

"Did you ever wonder, Clydie, when we used to read your comic books if Batman and Robin were, you know, a couple?"

"I don't think so."

"Everybody says so now. I think I knew. You know how I always wanted a Batman poster on my wall. I used to think about what a big one he must have."

Clyde wondered what Noreen would make of Danny. He was tempted to give Danny advice about dealing with her, with Marion, with the Senator, but he knew that was foolish. It would work out or it wouldn't. Part of the way home, he pulled off the highway and told Danny to drive. Even taking back roads, it was an adventure, but they survived.

Clifford was sitting on the front steps when they pulled into the driveway, and he ran into the house to tell his mother they were home. Noreen came down the steps, and as Clyde introduced Danny, she threw her arms around him and hugged him.

"Ooo," Danny said, as he drew away. "Nice ones on you, Noreen."

"You're damned right."

"Treats for Clydie."

Danny turned to Clifford, who was standing watching all this and held out his hand. Clifford shook it.

"I'm your daddy's funny old friend," he said, "and I've got a new job down here."

"You're going to drive the car for Aunt Marion," the boy said. Noreen had explained it all.

"Do you suppose I could call her Aunt Marion?" Danny said to Noreen.

"Try it," Noreen said, laughing. "She'll let you know soon enough if she doesn't like it."

"And you're going to teach me ballet," Danny said, as he limped over to the car to get his two bags of clothes.

Danny went off to have a shower and put on his new clothes, and then they drove out to the Senator's house. Noreen, planning ahead, had bought Danny a road map of the district, but he was convinced he'd never find his way from the Senator's house back into Canalville. Clyde made him a simpler sketch in the corner of the map.

When they arrived at the house, Marion was in the garden, wearing a gardening apron and a straw hat.

"Is that her?" Danny said.

Clyde led the way across the lawn and introduced the two of them. Marion stared at Danny, unsmiling, curious.

"What do you know about roses?" she said.

"Well… ," said Danny, waiting, hoping inspiration would strike, "they smell nice."

"That's a start," Marion said.

Clyde left him, with the understanding that Marion would show him around, find the car keys, act as navigator on a trip to the hospital, and Clyde would go off to make arrangements for an apartment where Danny could stay. When he came back that evening to pick him up and show him the apartment, there had been no disasters.

"I was just quiet as a mouse," Danny said as they drove away. "Did what I was told. Do you suppose I have to remember the names of all those roses, Clydie?"

"I doubt it."

"She seemed to think I would."

Clyde was back and forth a lot for the first few days, but Danny settled in, and when the Senator came home from the hospital, he found it was convenient to have someone on hand to run errands.

"Never had any use for those people myself, but it seems foolish to put a man in jail for it," the Senator said one day. "He doesn't molest children does he?"

"I don't think so."

"He's not much of a driver."

"He gets you there."

"You're right, he does. Marion seems to like him."

"My mother always did."

"Well then he must be all right."

A week or so later Clyde went to see Francis. As he waited for Francis to finish talking on the phone, Clyde noticed a slim young man in tight bell-bottoms going into the back office that had once been his own.

"How's the Senator?" Francis said as they sat down in his office.

"He's home, seems OK. Remember Danny O'Connell?"

"Don't think I ever knew him," Francis said, his blank eyes as empty as always.

"Old friend of mine," Clyde said. "We hired him as a driver, helper, what-have-you. Someone for Marion to order around."

"Is he living there?"

"Not now. We're trying it out for a few weeks. If it works out, there's a room off the kitchen he could have."

"The Senator going to get better?"

"For now. He's not going to live forever. That's why I'm here."

It was a terrible thing to be planning already for the man's death, but it had to be done.

"You can't have your old job back, my pet. I admit you were better than some of the ones I've hired, but Conrad, this new boy, is sharp as a tack."

"It wasn't really the job I came about."

"No, it wouldn't be. You need to borrow money again?"

"Not that either."

"What?"

"You want to buy an apartment building?"

"What are you up to now?"

"Nothing, really, but I have too much money sunk into property."

"Safe as houses," Francis said.

"So I hear."

"What do you have up your sleeve now?"

"Nothing definite yet."

"Oh Clyde, you and your secrets."

"I'm not the only one with secrets, Francis." He let that hang in the air for a moment. Then turned the corner. "Who knows where all *your* money is? Nobody."

Francis was watching him, his eyes unblinking.

"You were a little pisser selling golf balls."

"Now I'm selling an apartment building. The place is full, all the tenants on lease, you could remortgage it and get out some cash."

"I don't need cash," Francis said.

"It's a good piece of property, Francis. You could do a lot worse."

"Why is it I never believe you're telling me the whole truth Clyde?"

"I learned from the master."

"Why don't you just advertise the building?"

"I'm not that desperate."

"Spill the beans, Clyde. What are you up to?"

Clyde studied the man. His high shoulders were beginning to have a permanent hunch.

"Think about it, Francis. There's no catch."

"That big office building that your people are putting up. If the Senator dies before it's finished, there won't be any government leases going in there."

"You're not the only one worrying about that."

"If I keep my money in my pocket, I might pick that up at a good price."

"Better you than me."

"You don't like office buildings?"

"I like my apartment building better."

"Then why do you want to sell."

"I have some ideas. If I wait till I'm under pressure to sell, I'm going to get screwed. Right now I don't need to sell it, but I would, for a good offer."

"Try your old friend Gerald Wendorf."

"Jelly? Why?"

"Don't ask questions, Clyde."

They watched each other, friends, enemies, the same way it always was. The eyes staring down at the boy with the golf ball in his hand.

"OK, Francis," Clyde said, getting up.

"Say hello to your old friend, Danny was it? Maybe I remember him after all."

Clyde nodded at him, left the office. The new boy, Conrad, was watching him from the end of the short hallway. Clyde looked at him for a moment, turned and went out.

He walked the couple of blocks to the storage loft above an old store where Noreen taught her dance class. Seven little girls and one boy were following her brisk commands. A record of rhythmic piano music pounded away in the background. Not anything Clyde recognized, but he had grown familiar with the dance terms he heard. *First position. Second, fourth. Plié, demi-plié, battement. Porte de bras.* Noreen was wearing a black leotard, and now and then she would illustrate a movement, her long elegant body shaping itself to the conventional gesture. Her hair was pulled back and pinned in a tight bun. Fierce, beautiful. He watched for a few minutes till the class was over.

"Let's get Clifford and go to the drive-in," he said. "I'm buying."

"Joe," she said, "you are a good-time-Charlie."

One of the little girls, a chubby red-head with a jacket pulled on over the leotard ran over to hug her.

That night, after Clifford was in bed, Clyde drove down to the restaurant to see if Jelly was there. It had been a while. A new man stood behind the bar, and in the corner, where Maria once waited for calls, there was a tall, heavy-set woman with dramatic eye makeup. A couple was eating dinner at one of the tables. Business went on. The tanks of fish had been removed, and without them the place was darker, less interesting, just another restaurant and bar. Clyde had read in the paper that one of Jelly's places, up near Fort Erie, had lost its liquor license for serving after hours.

He asked for Jelly, and the bartender said he was upstairs. Clyde gave his name, said he was here on business and settled down at one of the tables with a rye and water. The woman at the corner table looked toward him, and he waved. In a few minutes Jelly appeared in the doorway from the kitchen.

"Long time," he said, as he shook hands.

"I got a wife to keep me home nights."

"Still a good-looking girl. I saw her downtown one day. She remembered me."

"She remembers things."

"I heard the Senator's sick."

"He's home now."

"You got some little faggot driving him around."

"Danny," Clyde said, "he's an old friend from when I was a kid."

How did Jelly know about Danny? Next thing he'd be telling Clyde why he was here.

"The fish are gone," Clyde said.

"I got tired of them. I looked at them one day and thought I didn't want to be staring at a bunch of stupid fish."

"Things change."

"Ronnie said you got business with me."

"You probably know I own a little apartment building up on the Unger road."

"I heard that. Maybe you told me. You worked hard, getting these properties developed. You're still a young guy."

"I want my equity out of it."

"What's that got to do with me?"

"Francis Finster, you know, at the credit bureau. Where I used to work. I was talking to him about selling it, and he suggested I talk to you."

Jelly was looking at him intently, the eyes, more and more hooded by drooping eyelids as he got older, were fixed and hard.

"Tell him to mind his own business."

"I thought he must know something."

"He knows nothing about me, that creepy faggot."

"You know some things about him."

Jelly looked away, snorted, looked back.

"You remember the Fruit Farm where they all used to do their number till it got busted."

"I heard about it."

"Who the hell do you think owned it?"

"Why?"

"Good money in it. Live and let live, I figured. Nobody else will rent to them at any price, or if they rent to them and find out, they're gonna give them the boot. Jelly, they said, rent us a place, so I did. The money was good. I had a guy, kind of a caretaker, and he let me know who's there. Just in case. It's all legal now, they can bum-fuck who they like."

"So why did Francis send me to you?"

"I don't hardly know the man, but I think he's a little crazy. Maybe likes to do things just to see what will happen."

"Secrets," Clyde said, "he likes secrets."

"His life's one big secret, so he wants secrets about everybody."

"So he sent me here just to stir things up."

The phone rang, the bartender answered, wrote down an address and gave it to the woman sitting in the corner who went out the front door.

"I'll drink up and go," Clyde said.

"No hurry. Long time ago, that you first came in here. You were a kid."

"I guess so."

"You looked like you were going to shit yourself when I gave you that bag of money."

"Why'd you do that?"

"Curious. I heard rumours that maybe the old guy was a little bent, and I wanted to see if I could get a piece of it."

"'Tell him it's too much for a gift and not enough for a bribe.' That's what he said, then he changed his mind and told me not to say that, just give it back."

"And you wouldn't keep it for yourself."

"I told you. It was too much. You would have owned me."

"This apartment building, the places all rented?"

"Yes. It's a good investment. You could remortgage, get some money out of it, still carry the place. I want out of it."

"The old man's going to die."

"We're all going to die."

"The only way I'd be interested is if I'm going to pay you cash money. We put through the sale for one dollar and further consideration."

Clyde was silent. He could imagine Francis watching him, smiling.

"I can think about it," Clyde said.

"You got nerve, Clyde, or you wouldn't own these places, but maybe not enough for this kind of an arrangement."

"I'll think."

"You want another rye?"

Clyde shook his head. Jelly waved to the bartender and indicated Clyde's glass.

"What the hell," he said. "Have one on me. Your last visit to the old place."

"Is it?"

"I'd say so."

"I miss the fish."

"You liked them cause it was the first place you went to drink, when you were a kid."

"You had liquor license trouble at that place near Fort Erie."

"We'll get it fixed."

Clyde finished up his new drink, shook Jelly's hand, and left. When he got home, Noreen, who was sitting on the couch reading a book, her long bare legs only half covered by a dressing gown, told him Francis had phoned, left a number. Clyde called him back.

"So did you talk to him?" Francis said.

"No," Clyde said. "I decided not to."

"Then where were you?"

"You're not my mother, Francis. I don't have to explain every time I go out of the house."

"He turned it down."

"What the fuck did you call for, Francis?"

"What a temper, Clyde."

"You want to buy the place after all, but you won't say so."

"I'll take a look at it."

"When?"

"Tomorrow."

They arranged a time. Clyde hung up the phone, went into the living room and looked at Noreen who was concentrating on her book. He went and sat down beside her, reached out and slid the dressing gown open so he could look at her.

"You know what's nice about women?" he said.

"No idea."

He bent and kissed her.

"The way they look. The way they feel. The way they smell. And then there's the carpentry."

"Yes," she said, "there's the carpentry."

It took a month of haggling, but he and Francis made a deal for the apartment. He suspected that Francis was planning to resell it at a profit and maybe take back a second mortgage on part of the purchase price, but Clyde did well on it. Money in a T-bill. The Senator appeared to be recovering, but every time Clyde thought he'd worked himself up to ask the about buying some of the Senator's shares, he failed to say the words. He didn't want to hear him say no. Clyde began to travel back and forth to Ottawa. At the price of that humiliating golf game, they got a mention in Tom McKay's column, and that led to a couple of useful connections. Perry hired Yvette, a pretty French-speaking young woman, as executive assistant; she had some experience in commercial translation. Clyde was living in two worlds. He'd find himself in a meeting at the finance company and thinking about a proposal he and Perry were writing for the Solicitor-General. Or driving to Ottawa, he'd wonder if he should be trying to contact Public Works on the Senator's behalf about leases for the new office building.

Danny was still driving Marion, doing odd jobs in the house and garden, running errands.

"That's me, Clydie," he said one day, "the messenger boy."

"I thought you were the chauffeur."

"That too."

"You're a factotum."

"A fuck-toadem? Don't call names, Clyde. I do not fuck toads."

"Fac-totum. It means someone who looks after everything."

They were on the way to Brockton to pay a visit to Clyde's mother. Danny could have borrowed the Senator's car and gone on his own, but he wanted Clyde to go with him this first time. It was a Sunday afternoon, and Clyde was due in Ottawa by noon Monday.

His mother met them at the door, put out her hand to shake Danny's.

"So here you are home after all your adventures," she said.

"But you moved, Hazel. I went away, and you moved."

"This is all mine Danny. I own this house, bought it with my own money."

"I bet Clydie helped."

"You bet wrong. This little cottage is all mine."

They sat down, and to Clyde's astonishment, his mother appeared with a bottle of sherry on a tray.

"Where did you get the sherry?" he said.

"I went to the liquor store and bought it. I called Peggy and said I was having a special guest and what would she recommend, and she recommended I serve sherry with cheese and biscuits. Myself I had more in mind a fatted calf, but I wasn't sure where you purchase one."

"Fatted calf?" Clyde said.

"From the bible," his mother said. "The parable of the prodigal son.

I suppose I should have sent you to Sunday school so you learned these things."

She went to the kitchen and came back with a plate of cheese.

"So Peggy is your new friend, Hazel?" Danny said.

"You must meet her, Danny. She's very lively. We're planning a trip to Florida." It was the first time Clyde had heard of this. He was pleased. A move to Ottawa seemed more and more likely, and he'd been worried that his mother might feel abandoned.

"Now this limping, Danny," his mother was saying. "There must be something the doctors can do."

"Oh you'll soon get used to seeing me like this."

"Clyde wouldn't tell me what happened."

"It was just a little accident, and I didn't look after it like I should."

"The doctors can do wonderful things, Danny."

"You know about my new job, Hazel?"

"You're changing the subject, Danny."

"Yes I am."

Clyde drank his glass of sweet sherry, as much of it as he could. His mother and Danny chattered on, then Danny announced it was time to go.

"But I'll be back, you know that, Hazel."

"Come anytime."

A day later, Clyde was in Ottawa sitting in the bar of the Lord Elgin with Perry. It was a clear bright day, and as he drove through the rocks and hills of eastern Ontario on into the flat land of the Ottawa Valley, Clyde had been thinking that this might someday be home. The trees were bright red and yellow, the colours reflected in the calm water of the lakes.

"I got a call from Irene, a couple of days ago," he said to Perry.

"What in hell was Irene calling you about?"

"She said she wanted to know what was going on."

"Going on with you?"

"Perry, this is none of my business. I don't want to know about it. But she called me. I didn't know what to say."

"I've got involved, I guess that would be the word, with Yvette."

"I thought you and Irene were getting married."

"Well it just didn't happen. I hired Yvette, and then, well you can guess."

"I thought maybe that was it."

"Did you tell Irene what you thought?"

"No."

"Joe the Silent."

"Where did you get that?"

"I asked Noreen why she called you Joe."

Clyde took a drink from the glass on the table in front of him. "Are we ready for this meeting?" he said.

The next morning, they had an appointment with two civil servants about the development of a new policy on land acquisition for national parks. Perry had found two retired park supervisors and put them both on a small retainer to hold themselves available for a future contract, and Clyde had written a paper on tax valuations and commercial valuations of various kinds of land.

"I'm not sure whether we want this job," Clyde said.

"Of course we want it."

"It could be a hornet's nest."

"Clyde, we don't set policy. We don't have to take the flak. We make our report and walk away."

"And if the report causes a mess, we don't get any more work."

"All you have to do is stop sleeping. You can manage that. Two jobs is easy if you don't sleep. Six months we'll have it all sorted out. I cobble together a bunch of stuff, and you turn your famous powers of analysis to the whole thing."

"Maybe."

"I had another chat with the guy from the Treasury Board."

"Another retired civil servant?"

"I decided to wait until we know we have the job," Perry said. "I don't really like him, but once we have something under way, we can make him a proposition."

At the meeting the next day, the two civil servants sat, one behind a desk, one at the side with a clipboard, and both worked at being probing and sharp. Halfway through the meeting, Clyde realized that both sides were faking it. Everyone was in favour of parks. Taxes paid for parks. Nobody was in favour of taxes. So how did you get new parks while maintaining the illusion that nobody was going to have to pay for them.

"What do you think?" Perry asked him, when they were back out on the street. It was a grey day, a chill wind blowing off the river and tumbling an empty coffee cup over the pavement. Last week, the Senator, when he heard Clyde was going to Ottawa again, asked him if he could handle both his jobs at the same time. Clyde was on the point of saying he'd abandon the Ottawa venture if the Senator would sell him some of his shares, but once again he didn't speak. He owed the man too much already, maybe that was it, and knew too little, even now, of what was in his mind.

"If we get the job," Clyde said to Perry, "maybe Noreen and I will come up for a weekend to celebrate, and we can get started."

They got the job. To formulate a new acquisition policy. Clyde and Noreen drove up on Friday. His mother was leaving work a bit early and picking Clifford up after school, taking him to her house for the weekend. She'd drive him back to school on Monday morning, and they'd arrive early Monday afternoon. Perry had signed contracts with the two retired civil servants, and they spent Saturday morning with them. Perry would amass information from provincial and U.S. Parks departments. He had hired a lawyer who was half Cree to draft a preamble on the issue of land claims.

Noreen had spent the morning with her family, but late Saturday afternoon, she and Clyde went for a drive outside Ottawa for a break from all the meetings. Since Clyde's last trip, Perry had officially broken off with Irene, and he was spending the weekend in Yvette's apartment so that Clyde and Noreen could use the rooms upstairs from the office. They drove down back roads and stopped beside a lake, the water all grey and silver ripples under the clouds that were blowing in from the west. The two of them stood on the rock a few feet above the shore. The trees were bare now, the earth brown with the dead leaves, and on the far side of the lake a little flock of ducks paddled in front of a high bluff covered with tall spruces.

"You glad about this job, Joe?" Noreen said.

"Wish I knew."

"Not a bad place, this part of the country. Where I grew up."

Clyde took a deep breath. Sunlight penetrated the clouds and a patch of brightness lit up the lake.

"You never know what's going to happen," he said.

"I thought you always knew. That you made it happen."

Clyde stared at the water that grew darker as the sun went behind a cloud. Below that leaden surface fish swam, invisible. She was right. He could make things happen.

"Penny for your thoughts," she said.

"They could issue new shares."

"Whatever that means."

He turned and put his arms around her, and they kissed. Back in Ottawa, they met Perry and Yvette for dinner. They were all a little giddy and laughed at jokes that weren't awfully funny. Perry and Yvette were busy being in love, couldn't keep their hands off each other, and Perry kept ordering more wine, which Clyde obediently drank until his mood changed, and he couldn't laugh any more. Perry sketched out plans for the future of their partnership, but Clyde still wasn't sure it had one. If he could talk the Senator into issuing new shares for him, that might be the future.

"A toast," Perry was saying, "to DB Consultants and all that sail in her."

Clyde lifted his glass, and as he did so, he was aware that Noreen was watching him. She smiled, and she drank too.

One evening just after the Christmas holidays, he drove from his office in Canalville to the Senator's house with some documents for him to sign. He could have called and got Danny to pick them up, but he brought them himself. When they were signed, the Senator offered him a whisky, but he refused, sat in the chair that faced the old man's desk, forming the words. The Senator poured himself a drink from the decanter. Clyde noticed that there was a tremor in his hand.

"I have some cash on hand," Clyde said, "and I wondered about investing it in County Finance. If you were willing to create new shares."

The Senator poured water into his drink, put down the pitcher, settled back in his chair and stared into the glass as if the energy of his look would cause the two liquids to blend.

"It's been how many years, Clyde?"

"More than ten."

"You've been invaluable."

Clyde waited for him to say it. Yes.

"I can't do it alone," he said. "I don't have an absolute majority of the shares, though as you know I have the largest holding. I'd have to consult with the other directors. There's always some resistance to issuing new shares. Leave it with me. It might be best to wait until a regular directors' meeting. I'll do what I can Clyde."

"Thank you," Clyde said. He left the old man with his whisky, went down the hall and out the front door of the house. Outside it was a cold night, the millions of stars bright above him, bodies moving through space light years away.

7 | Noreen

Clyde drove to the church early. When he left the house, Noreen was still getting dressed; she was coming to meet him in her own car. He parked half a block away and walked along the street under the empty trees. The clouds sailed by on the great current of the late fall wind. The man was gone. A car drove past, turned, the living about their business. In front of the cathedral the hearse of the funeral directors was already parked, two men standing nearby. The men in dark suits. He'd once played golf with one of them, shook his hand.

"Everything's OK?" he said. They nodded, opened the back of the hearse to take out the casket and wheel it inside. Clyde entered the church. On a table beside the door was a box containing the printed order of service, on the back the short biography of the Senator which Clyde had written. One of the secretaries from the office was coming to hand these out. Clyde went down the side aisle and into the vestry. The rector of the Anglican cathedral, with whom Clyde had made the arrangements, a soft-spoken, smiling man, was talking to Bob Haverman, the clergyman married to the Senator's daughter, here to bury his father-in-law.

"Everything's OK?" Clyde asked again. The two men nodded.

It was all in the hands of the professionals, Clyde reflected. Probably there was no need for him to be here early, but that was what he did, double-checked things, prevented emergencies. When he opened the door into the nave, the two men in dark suits were wheeling the wooden box that contained the Senator into its place at the head of the centre aisle. The man was gone, but the physical remnants lay there in their dark ship as the first of the witnesses entering the church door, two old men, one with a cane, both with medals pinned to their jackets, bronze and silver trophies of the war they must have shared with the Senator. He had won a medal. Clyde knew nothing about the circumstances, mud, gunfire, men dying. James Lawton had survived that war, come back and built a life, held power in his hands. He had shown force and vanished when his hour came.

More men and women were appearing, taking their seats, one or two kneeling to pray. Some of them had lived under the man's power, in small ways or large. Clyde went back down the side aisle, outside, saw Danny, wearing a shirt and tie under his suede jacket, standing at the corner. He came over when he saw Clyde.

"Marion's coming with her daughters. She said for me to bring the other car just in case. I parked round the corner."

"I'm waiting for Noreen."

Danny went into the church, stopping just inside the door to genuflect toward the altar and cross himself. A large well-dressed man that Clyde had met at the Christmas parties saw him, put out his hand. The occasion demanded such forms. They were all gathered at the dim edge of the world in a place of silence and perhaps fear. The great waters waited for the man to be sent to them.

Noreen, tall and striking in a dark coat and high heels walked up to the door. She took his hand as they went up the aisle and took seats. The Senator's will had specified that there be no music at his funeral, and the church was full of tiny sounds, feet moving, whispered words. Two men in military uniform, representatives of the Senator's old regiment, walked stiffly down the aisle and took seats. One of them knelt and closed his eyes. The other sat upright.

Clyde could hear the breathing of those around him, like a rippling of tiny waves. Marion, accompanied by her daughters, one son-in-law, a couple of grandchildren, took her place in the front row. A man, unknown to Clyde, wearing a black cape and carrying a walking stick, entered a pew across the aisle. John Martin Cooper, who would deliver the eulogy, seated himself nearby. Francis and his wife took positions a little to his right. Clyde nodded to them. Barton Dred, his wife, and three other men in dark suits, sat together just behind him. Faces Clyde recognized from pictures in the newspaper. A quiet scuffling while the last arrivals took their places, the church almost full now, and from the back, Bob Haverman's ringing voice speaking the opening sentences.

"We brought nothing into this world," he was saying, "and it is certain we can carry nothing out. The Lord gave, and the Lord hath taken away; blessed be the name of the Lord," and the two clergymen, preceded by a boy carrying a cross, made their way forward to the chancel. They read, spoke, prayed. Without any pause for music, the service sped by, an arrangement of old-fashioned words, as good as any, Clyde thought, to see him off. He was moved, but only in a detached way, with a sense of passing generations, of inevitability. He owed the Senator a good deal, but there was always a certain distance.

A couple of weeks ago, while the Senator was in the hospital, the end coming closer, Clyde had been sitting in his office reading through the local newspaper when his eye fell on a familiar name, an obituary notice. A choking sob had shaken him, grief or guilt or only some terrible recognition of finality. The prettiest girl in the class. It was six months ago he had touched her dying body. He went out for a very long walk.

John Martin Cooper was making his way to the lectern where a brass eagle's open wings held the large Bible. A short stiff man with white hair. Tomorrow Clyde would be summoned to a meeting with him and the other surviving directors. The new shares had not been issued. The Senator had been increasingly unwell in the preceding months, and neither he nor Clyde had mentioned the matter again after Clyde's first request. Clyde wondered if he had been foolish not to press the issue. John Martin Cooper spoke briskly, in a clear voice. The Senator was an upright man, a man of his word – that appeared to be the text. Clyde looked at Noreen sitting beside him, a dark blue dress, navy coat, her hair clean and shining, combed out long. Her eyes were closed.

Then it was over, and the two men in uniform led the pallbearers as the coffin sailed down the long nave out into the dark November day, to the black car that would carry him off, and he would vanish, as men vanished, into nowhere, into no-one-knew-where. The child is born, comes to manhood, lives his life.

"Man that is born of woman hath but a short time to live," Bob Haverman said at the side of the open grave, "he fleeth as it were a shadow, and never continueth in one stay."

When it was done with, he and Noreen sat in the car.

"Will you take me home, Joe?" she said. "I'm not going to Marion's."

"Do you have a class?"

"No."

"So?"

"If Marion asks, tell her I'm having a mood."

"Are you?"

"Maybe."

He started the car, couldn't say anything.

"Don't be crabby with me," she said.

"Why not?"

"There's no point. I'm not going to change my mind."

"OK."

"What's going to happen?" she said.

"What do you mean?"

"County Finance. Who's going to be the new boss? You?"

"We'll see. There's a meeting tomorrow."

"I wouldn't be worth much as the boss's wife."

"I'm not too worried."

They drove in silence, and at the house she reached over and gave him a quick kiss on the cheek.

"Let the dead bury the dead," she said. "Somebody said that."

She opened the car door and was gone before he could speak.

At Marion's house, men and women stood around, uncertain what to say, how to behave. The Senator wasn't there to tell them. Not that he did, in words, but when he was present in the house, everything appeared to have a purpose, a meaning. In the front room, John Martin Cooper was talking intently to Marion, who looked as if she wasn't paying attention, and when Danny passed by with a plate of sandwiches, she waved him over and began to talk to him. Cooper, a little annoyed, walked away. The Senator's two daughters scuttled back and forth to the kitchen, organizing food, and Clyde elected himself bartender for the first half hour until everyone who wanted a drink had at least one. He wondered what Noreen was doing right then.

Elaine Haverman came up to him, a glass of wine in her hand.

"I wanted to say, Clyde, that it was a wonderful idea of yours to hire Danny. I know he's had his problems and I admit that at first I had my doubts, but mother's taken to him. Someone to talk to. I think she'd be lost without him."

"Actually it was Noreen who first suggested it.

"Tell Noreen she's a genius. Where is she? I saw her at the church."

"She had to teach a dance class."

"I bet she's a wonderful teacher.

"I think so."

Clyde assumed she was, but of course he had no idea.

"And you knew Danny when you were kids."

"That's right. He and my mother were always great pals."

"He's a funny duck, isn't he?"

"I guess so."

"Well I'm glad he's around here. It means I'm not leaving her on her own in this big house."

Elaine turned away and Clyde got himself another drink, wandered into the hall, looked into the Senator's den, vacant chair, empty desk, waited for the voice to instruct him, heard nothing. He wished Noreen were here with him, and he left as soon as he felt he could, said goodbye to Marion, waved goodbye to John Martin Cooper, knowing they'd meet in the morning.

When he got home, he heard music from the basement, Leonard Cohen singing 'The Sisters of Mercy'. Clyde could gauge Noreen's moods by the kind of music she chose. Leonard Cohen was for the bleak silence when nothing else could reach her. Clyde felt a certain jealousy of the beautiful sexy Jew with his flat coaxing voice. He went downstairs where Noreen was working out at the barre, her face pale and sweating, legs lifting and falling in rhythm with the music.

"Clifford home?" he said.

"He called from Roger's house to say could he stay for dinner."

"You want some scrambled eggs?"

"Sure, but wait a few minutes and I'll finish here and wash up."

Clyde sat down with a book about Sir Francis Drake that he'd picked up in Ottawa the last time he was there. A strange mixture of violence and piety those Elizabethan sailors. Drake's cousin Hawkins had killed a man with one blow. Drake beheaded a man who'd been his close friend. Slaughter and then prayers on deck with no bad conscience. Those little sailing ships, always at the mercy of wind and tide, a sudden storm or a drop in the wind, could change the course of battle, perhaps the course of history. He listened to the sound of the shower from upstairs, then it stopped, and in a few minutes Noreen appeared in slacks and a bulky sweater.

"Shall I make eggs?" she said.

"I will." He set down his book and went to the kitchen. Noreen was sitting at the table, one foot up on the chair as she poked at a little bone spur.

"Poor old feet," she said.

"Poor old head," Clyde said and kissed it.

"Just one of those days, Joe."

That night in bed Clyde lay awake for a long time, anxious, excited. The armada was sailing up the channel. The sisters of mercy were mumbling things he couldn't understand, things about his wife. The Senator's body lay in an expensive wooden box in a hole in the ground.

When Clyde entered the boardroom the next morning, just down the hall from the office where he usually worked, the three surviving directors of the company were sitting at one end, John Martin Cooper, Barton Dred – Member of Parliament due at least in part to Clyde's exertions on his behalf – in a dark suit and dark tie as if he must be prepared for another funeral at any moment, and tall bald jovial Harry Gregory. The room, which had bare walls, was furnished with a bleached-oak table, long since out of style, and wooden chairs with armrests that curved down to join the front legs. Marion had pressed the Senator to refurbish the room, put up decent pictures, buy good antique furniture, but he refused. Said he didn't want to encourage more meetings or longer meetings.

John Martin Cooper, who sat at the end of the table, indicated, with a gesture of his long chin, a place for Clyde at the far end. Where the menial sat to be interrogated by his betters. Clyde took the seat. He didn't like the way this was playing out.

A sheet of lined paper lay on the table in front of John Martin, a ball point pen beside it. Half the sheet was covered with writing, which seemed to be numbered points.

"By a vote of the directors, who are also the current shareholders," John Martin Cooper said, "I have been elected as the new managing director of the corporation." Clyde listened, speculated on why the man used all three of his names.

"Who voted the Senator's shares?" Clyde asked.

"If you read the articles of incorporation, you will be aware that first offer of those shares must be made to the other shareholders of the company. We have arranged financing, and all the shares will be purchased by the three of us at book value. The question of voting the shares is moot."

"Not until the sale is completed."

"The articles of incorporation are clear. No-one else can buy the shares, and therefore no-one else can vote them."

"As executor of the Senator's will," Clyde said, "I would be inclined to insist that the shares are effective as voting instruments until the sale is concluded."

Barton Dred looked toward the head of the table.

"Do we have a legal opinion on that?" he said.

"Also, as executor, I believe I should have a right to be assured on behalf of the heirs that the financing of this purchase is sound before anything proceeds," Clyde said.

"The financing will be in the form of a loan from the company," Harry Gregory said with a smile, as if the whole thing pleased him immensely.

"We've passed a motion to the effect." John Martin said, as if that ended discussion.

"So the Senator's money is being used to buy back the Senator's shares."

"Marion will be paid a fair price," Barton Dred was saying, "and surely she has no interest in the management of the company."

Clyde didn't need to ask what his position would be after all this was done. No position at all.

"I think every single element of this arrangement you've made could be questioned in court," he said. He looked toward the three men. Harry Gregory was still beaming with pleasure, the smile creating deep lines in his cheeks. Barton Dred was pursing his lips, and John Martin Cooper's long jaw was thrust forward, his hands held in front of him almost as if in prayer.

There was a long pause.

"Gentlemen," John Martin said. "Would you step out for a moment and let me raise what might be called a personal matter with Mr Bryanton."

Barton Dred and Harry Gregory looked from one to another, uncertain. Clyde looked at the man at the far end of the table, the face grim, a little paler perhaps than usual. Harry Gregory stood up, and Barton Dred followed him to the door. When it was closed behind them, John Martin Cooper picked up the ball point pen, rolled it between his fingers, then spoke quietly.

"I had a call shortly after the Senator's death," he said, "from a man named Jake Everard."

Clyde tried to hold himself perfectly still, not to react. The back of his neck was cold, and he was afraid he might shiver visibly. His adversary let the sentence hang in the air.

"You know the man?"

Clyde said nothing.

"You stand mute, as they used to say."

Clyde thought there was nothing to be gained by speaking, waited.

"I expect you know what he told me, though perhaps it's as well if we don't make any of this explicit. The man made it quite clear who it was that had spoken to him, what had been required and the result. I do not believe that James Lawton, who was a war hero and an upstanding member of the community would have been party to such a scheme unless he had been persuaded to it, even tricked into it, by someone who lacked his scruples. I could guess who that might be. It would please me greatly to call in the authorities, but that would involve the Senator's reputation, Marion's, and that of the company. So I have told Mr Everard that the matter is dead and buried, the arrangement he spoke of is over. I will allow you to walk away scot-free. However I do not expect you to interfere with our recent decisions, which are perfectly fair, and will offer Marion a good deal of money and perfect financial security."

Clyde listened to all this. The story of how he had corrupted an older and better man. He wondered if Cooper believed all of what he was saying or if he only wanted to force Clyde to accede to their plans. If Clyde didn't, the tale would be told to the police. They had Clyde by the balls. If he tried to fight it, he'd lose. Jake Everard was an honest man. He'd never wanted to be part of the Senator's scheme. Any judge, any jury, would believe him. Perhaps he should have worked that out, told the Senator. Who wouldn't have cared. He was proud of his contrivance. No more auction sales.

And the Senator was gone.

"I have two pieces of property which I hold in partnership with County Finance," he said.

"My suggestion is that we have the properties evaluated by an independent professional, and either you buy out our interest or we'll buy out yours at that valuation. We have no desire to cheat you."

"Good of you," Clyde said as he stood up. The man was watching him. Clyde remembered the fight with Jack Lamoure on the school bus years before, the two of them wrestling in the seat, how in the seat behind he saw Bobby Russell watching, cheering on Clyde's adversary, remembered the look of concentrated hatred on that young face. To be hated wasn't altogether a new experience.

"I must," he said, "bring in Bill Romanuck to deal with the probate of the Senator's will. He's the lawyer who drew it up. I intend to express no opinion on the forced sale of his shares or on how the book value is determined. If he should raise the matter on his own, I'll advise him to consult Marion about it. As you know she is by no means a fool. If she raises questions, you'll have to answer them. That's as far as I can go."

"That all makes perfect sense. You can have the rest of the week to clean out your office."

Clyde opened the door. The two men in their dark suits were standing in the narrow hall a few feet away. Clyde smiled pleasantly at them. "We reached an agreement," he said. "A gentlemen's agreement."

He found he was laughing. When he got back to the small office, he picked up the phone and called Perry in Ottawa.

"I just got fucked," he said.

"How was she?"

"Not she. They."

"I don't get it."

"Dig up lots of work," Clyde said. "It's all over down here."

When Clyde got back outside, large white flakes of snow were coming down. He wandered along the street, not seeing what was in front of him. For some reason he was thinking of Jake Everard. He wanted to drive out the country roads stop by his construction yard, find him in the bungalow, sit down with him and say, Look Jake, no hard feelings. I know you're an honest man. They'd drink rye, and shake hands when they parted company. The snow kept falling, big goosefeather flakes tumbling one after another through the dark day. After a while he found his car and drove home, told Noreen as much as he dared of the story.

A month later he was sitting in an armchair in the large living room of a house in Ottawa where Noreen had been raised. It was Christmas, and they were surrounded by her family. Clyde was an outsider, brought here because of the festive season, but he failed to understand the old jokes, was tolerated, though perhaps distrusted. When he and his wife and son left, they would go back to the house a few streets away that he had just bought, and when the Christmas holiday was over, he would go to work in the office of DB Consultants as one of the partners in the business and the winter would be a cold one. Ottawa was always frigid and snowy, the world's coldest capital city, they said, next to Ulan Bator. Might as well be Outer Mongolia, it was so foreign to him.

Against the side wall of the room was a small fireplace with a brick mantlepiece, and a large log burned slowly. Clyde put on another log from the brass scuttle that stood nearby, replaced the firescreen. He looked at the pattern of curving stained glass in the decorative panel above the front window, the dim yellows and greens, divided by lines of lead. The afternoon was growing dark. In front of the window was a narrow seat.

Noreen's father, Alan Simmons, appeared, a dark figure in the unlighted hallway

"Can I get you another drink?" he said

Clyde felt the right answer was No, but he said Yes. "I don't suppose there's anything I can do to help," he said.

"The women have it under control."

After dinner he would phone his mother who was in Florida with Peggy, the two of them having found a cheap last minute flight. Maybe next year she would make the trip from Brockton up to Ottawa. Clyde listened to the shouting from upstairs where Clifford was playing some kind of hockey game with a couple of his cousins, the two uncles supervising. Noreen appeared in the doorway behind her father.

"Are you getting my hubby drunk?" she said.

"Your hubby?"

"I'm trying to be one of the girls, Daddy. Couldn't you tell?"

"I'm surprised Clyde can put up with you, Noreen," Alan Simmons said.

"Clyde adores me," she said.

Her father was watching Clyde who believed this was some kind of trap, but he felt like that about everything today. In dreams you never understood how or why the trap was being laid.

"It's starting to snow," the man said and left the room.

Noreen came to Clyde, bent and kissed him, put her tongue in his mouth.

"Who's drunk?" he said.

A few minutes later, the dinner was served, the children at a small card table set up in one corner of the dining room. The four women appeared from the kitchen with bowls of vegetables as Noreen's father stood at the end of the table to carve the bird. Across the table, Clyde confronted the bright, slightly protruding eyes of Angela Simmons, John's wife. She was staring toward him, perhaps hoping for the support of another stranger here at the family celebration. Clyde smiled, could think of nothing to say to her.

"John and I," she was saying, perhaps more loudly than she intended, trying to be heard over the conversation, "spent Thanksgiving with some friends out in the country, and before they ate they sang the grace, the whole bunch of them, in harmony."

There was a moment of quiet.

"Well, Angela," Noreen's mother was saying, the tone kindly enough, "you're welcome to try, but I don't think you'd get too much harmony out of this lot."

"Or too much religion either," Noreen said.

Clyde looked back across the table at Angela, whose face was fixed in an eager smile. Her thin high forehead was pale, glistening, her hair pulled tightly back in a bun. He noticed that her ears were long, narrow, very fine and transparent, something almost botanical about the inward curves. He couldn't help seeing her with this curious objectivity, just as, perhaps, she was seeing him, the two outsiders observing each other's strangeness. He watched her eyes shifting nervously, trying to find a place to settle.

The winter night closed in.

Afterward everyone volunteered to do dishes, and John Simmons took charge, with his mother acting as supervisor. Clyde took a towel. When they were done, he left the kitchen, found Noreen sitting with a magazine in the dining room, smoking a cigarette she'd taken from John's open package beside her. The smoke rose round her head. As he watched her lift the cigarette to her lips, he was remembering, from a long time ago, his grandmother.

How the old woman sat by the front window of her small house near St Clair Avenue in Toronto, her chair at an angle so she could see whatever passed by on the street, the package of cigarettes and matches and a flat brass ashtray on the little pedestal table beside her, the cigarettes raised slowly to her mouth by the first two fingers of her left hand, which were stained yellow from tobacco. At seven years old Clyde believed that she was waiting there, watching intently, in the belief that her older son, his father, would one day appear on the sidewalk, come up the steps and enter the house. She never expressed any such thing, only said that she liked to see what was going on. Late in the afternoon she might get up from the chair and begin to cook something for his uncle Bob to eat when he got home from his work at the CNR freight warehouse, and when it grew dark, she would draw down the blind. In the evening she smoked at the kitchen table, with the radio on. Clyde remembered once sitting there with her, listening to the Lux Radio

Theatre, the two of them unspeaking.

As a young woman Millie Bryanton had worked for a rich family in a big house at the edge of the Rosedale ravine. When she married, her husband demanded that she leave the job, and she did. That was almost all Clyde knew about his grandmother, that and how she sat quietly smoking, her eyes fixed on the street, though it was a respectable neighbourhood where little out of the ordinary occurred. Men left for work in the morning, women shopped, children went off to school. Yet on that street, when Clyde remembered it, it was always dusk, a slow ingathering of life by the lighted windows, and his grandmother struck a wooden match on the box, lifted the flame to her cigarette.

It felt very late by the time they started home that evening, driving along quiet streets in the falling snow. The new house had a tiny basement, no room for Noreen's workshop. They'd bought it mostly because it was available and empty. When Clyde checked his watch, he saw it wasn't late at all. Clifford was exhausted, falling asleep almost before Clyde said goodnight. He went back downstairs, where Noreen was curled up on the couch, a book in her hand, her eyes closed. She opened them when he entered the room.

"Was it too awful?" she said.

"Not at all," he said. "They're good people."

"Are we?"

"Hard to say."

"Handsome people. Your new sweater's very flattering."

He stroked her hair.

"Hard to believe we're here, isn't it?" he said.

"Starting over."

When they went back to work after the New Year, Clyde and Perry planned a renovation of the little building that contained their office, to put in more working space upstairs, turning the attic into a tiny apartment. With Clyde's capital as security they could borrow at rates not far above prime, and once the offices were ready, they would bring in one of their parks consultants, who had proved to be smart and efficient, on a longer term contract. They were also going to start a small document translation service, which they would use themselves when it was needed, and sell to others.

Every day Clyde scanned the Ottawa papers as well as the *Globe* and *Hansard*, keeping himself up to date. Perry insisted that they must be visible, so most evenings they would stop off at the Chateau Laurier or the Lord Elgin Hotel, or pick up Yvette and Noreen and have dinner at *Mamma Teresa's*. It was in the Lord Elgin bar one late afternoon that they met Barton Dred. Clyde noticed him come in, alone, and made a point of catching his eye and indicating the empty chair at their table. It was obvious that joining them was the last thing he wanted, but no one appeared from the wings to save him, so he was forced to sit down. It had been a long time since he'd met Perry, but he summoned up his name.

"So you're in Ottawa now," he said to Clyde.

"DB Consultants," Clyde said.

"What are you working on?"

Clyde let Perry answer that, studied the man's face, wondering how much John Martin Cooper had told him. He didn't want the story about the bid-rigging spread around the rumour mills of the national capital.

"You left us in a hurry," he said to Clyde.

"I'll be back to do what's needed," Clyde said, "once the Senator's will has gone through probate."

"I had a call," Barton Dred said, "from Bill Romanuck. He was asking about the transfer of the Senator's shares."

"I told your friend Mr Cooper that he might question it."

"But you and John Martin had sorted it out. You'd agreed."

"I allowed it to go forward on the understanding that the lawyer probating the will might raise any questions he thought appropriate."

Barton Dred looked confused. It was clear that Cooper had not explained his hold over Clyde.

"I spoke to John Martin after the call. He said that he'd ask you to speak to Bill Romanuck."

Once you have a man by the balls you don't let go.

"I'll be driving down to Canalville to see Marion and sort out some other business. We'll see what she thinks."

"We don't want Marion deciding, do we?"

"Marion is old and sometimes eccentric, Barton, but if I were you, I wouldn't underrate her abilities."

The MP looked as if was trying to swallow something a little too big for him to get down.

"Still, that's all hours away from here," Perry said cheerfully. "Ottawa is another world."

"And now you two are part of it."

"We're starting a translation service, by the way."

"Really."

"You never know when you might need such a thing."

"Mostly done for us," Barton said.

"You never know, a speech, something from the newspapers. We're always there."

Perry had put on his salesman's hat. It was a useful distraction, and it was going to be essential to them. Clyde's virtues were clarity, conviction, a quick insight into figures, but it was Perry who was going to have to find the work. Barton Dred drank his rye and water quickly and made an excuse to leave.

"Was I undiplomatic?" Clyde said.

"Maybe a little, but Mr Dred is never going to get off the back benches, so it doesn't matter much. What's going on with this will?"

"I can't tell you Perry."

"Smells of fish."

"Very old fish."

The next day Clyde made some calls, arranged to meet with Marion and the lawyer, separately. Two days later, he got into his car and made the trip down. He'd arranged to stay in Brockton with his mother, though he didn't want to have to explain the whole situation. If she guessed something was wrong, he'd simply refuse to explain. She was his mother. She'd have to accept that.

"I'm surprised," Bill Romanuck said to him when the two of them sat in his office overlooking a big parking lot, "that you agreed to the transfer of shares before the will was probated."

Clyde looked at him, the wide cheeks, grey eyes studying him.

"I was subject to pressure, Bill."

"What kind of pressure?"

"I'm not prepared to tell you that. I don't think it's in my best interest to tell you that."

"They have something on you."

"John Martin Cooper was able to persuade me not to take it to court, though I warned him that the will would be going to probate and that you might raise questions."

"And now I have."

Clyde nodded.

"How bad is it, what he has on you?"

"Bad enough."

"Defalcation?"

"No. No such thing. My loyalty to the Senator and to his interests is not in question. Never has been."

"Does Marion know about this?"

"I don't think so. I'm not certain."

"Are you willing to explain to her, if not to me? If she understands the situation, I can take instruction from her as my client. She need not tell me the background, but were she to do so, the information would be privileged."

The two of them sat in silence. Clyde looked at a picture on the wall, four Bartlett prints in a single frame, all scenes from southern Ontario in the pioneer days of the nineteenth century, a log drive, deep snow around a small house.

"I'm going to see Marion this evening. Perhaps I'll talk to you again tomorrow."

Clyde went to a hotel on a busy corner of Canalville's main street, sat in the bar for a while and had a couple of drinks, waved to acquaintances who passed by. Wondered what each one knew or thought he knew about Clyde's move to Ottawa. For old times' sake, he walked down to the his old hang-out, the Jubilee Restaurant, for dinner. Hadn't gone in for a long time. Old Harold was on the cash, still owned the place after all these years. He shook Clyde's hand, and a new waitress brought him a menu. He wasn't hungry, but he ate something.

It was dark and cold as he drove out to Marion's. It was Danny who answered the door.

"Hi, Clydie. Marion's upstairs, but she'll be down in a minute. You want some coffee? I made fresh."

Danny was wearing a white shirt and a dark striped tie, and his thinning hair was combed back and emphasized the round skull-like shape of his forehead.

"You're staring, Clyde. Is there something wrong with how I look."

"Different."

"I'm a changed man."

"I'll have the coffee, if there's lots."

"I keep it fresh in case someone drops in."

"Many who do?"

"Not many."

Clyde went and sat down in the front room, picked up a copy of a gardening magazine, though he couldn't concentrate on the words. Flipped through the pictures of bright perfect gardens. He heard Marion coming downstairs, got up and went to meet her. She put out her hand for him to shake, though she had never done such a thing before. Her hand, though the knuckles were a little thickened by arthritis, was long and elegant. Behind her shoulder he noticed the Senator's office, unchanged, a light on, as if waiting for his arrival. They went into the front room and Danny brought his coffee.

"You want anything, Marion?"

"No thank you, Danny. I might have some chocolate later."

Danny vanished down the hall. Clyde supposed Danny had always possessed a sense of theatre, and now he was playing the trusted family retainer, discreet, thoughtful, not without a certain influence perhaps. Clyde took a sip of coffee, and looked toward the handsome woman who sat upright in her chair, watching him. He'd take his chances, he decided, and tell her everything.

"This goes back some time, Marion," he said. He went through it, step by step, the idea of the bid-rigging, the fact that all the arrangements were made by Clyde. She asked the names of all the companies, and after a moment's hesitation, he told her. Explained Jake Everard's hesitation, his later phone call.

"What was his objection? Did he want a larger share?" she said.

"I think he's an honest man, and it made him uncomfortable."

Marion said nothing, and he went on to his meeting with John Martin Cooper and the issue of the Senator's shares. Set out the situation as clearly as he could, and explained that Bill Romanuck had questioned Clyde's agreement to the transfer of the shares.

"So Cooper holds you responsible for the bid-rigging."

"He believes that I am an unscrupulous and ambitious man and that I led the Senator into it."

"He is a fool isn't he?"

"He's in a position to do me a lot of harm. I could end up in jail."

"What if I was to say that the Senator told me that he had ordered you to set this up?"

"Did he?"

"What does it matter? I would testify in court that he did. I know what he was capable of."

"I believe that would be hearsay evidence and not acceptable, and besides I'm still guilty of doing it."

"Suppose I testified that I heard the Senator order you to do this, and that when you objected he threatened to fire you."

"If you were believed, that might be helpful."

Marion stood up.

"Wait here," she said.

Clyde watched her walk out of the room, her head and shoulders held very straight. He listened to her voice on the telephone. On the way back into the room, she called Danny, asked him to bring her a cup of hot chocolate and more coffee for Clyde.

"He's on his way over," Marion said.

"Bill Romanuck?"

"No, that crook Cooper."

Clyde stared at her, her face drawn tight in anger, the eyes hard. There was no hint of the vagueness which was perhaps something she put on for public show. Danny appeared with the chocolate and the coffee pot, didn't say a word.

"When that man comes, Danny," Marion said to him, "you answer the door and bring him in here. Don't be polite."

Clyde sipped the coffee. He was very frightened. He could end up in a federal penitentiary among Danny's old pals. He didn't look forward to that, or to hearing the testimony that might lead to it, but it was too late. He'd assumed that Marion was calling Bill Romanuck, to get his advice, and he took that as a sensible way to proceed, but to summon John Martin Cooper was dangerous.

They sat without speaking. Clyde thought to mention that he had met her sister Florence at Christmas, but in the circumstances it seemed pointless enough. Marion had picked up her gardening magazine and appeared to be reading it with some attention. Clyde marvelled at her calm. It occurred to him to wonder if her calm state of mind was evidence of some unnatural serenity, if, in fact, she might be a little mad. Certainly the situation they were in went beyond the bounds of anything he had experienced.

At last there was a knock on the front door, and Danny led John Martin Cooper into the room. His eyes took in the fact that Clyde was there, and he tried to not show his shock. Marion ignored him as he took off his coat, looked around for a place to put it, settled for the back of a straight chair.

"I've been informed," Marion said, "of how you've been trying to cheat me."

"I wouldn't," he began, looking toward Clyde, "trust… "

"Be quiet and listen," Marion said.

The man's face flushed, his mouth tightened.

Marion went through the situation with the will, making clear that she had grasped perfectly what she'd been told about it, about the question of the transfer of the Senator's shares. Clyde had explained it clearly, and she had taken it in.

"I understand," she said, "that you have threatened Clyde in order to have him agree to what you have done. I think you should know, that some years ago, sitting in this room with Clyde and the Senator, I heard my husband give Clyde instructions to effect a bid-rigging scheme. Clyde said it was illegal and he preferred not to do it. My husband told him that if he didn't do it, he'd be out of a job. Now we are both aware that Clyde is guilty of a criminal offence, but I believe my testimony would be of some help, and long before such a case ever comes to court, you will find yourself making a legal defence of your actions in trying to cheat a poor widow of her inheritance. I do not believe that a self-righteous prig like you, Cooper, will enjoy the exposure."

Cooper stared at her, looked toward Clyde as he expected something from him. Clyde met his eyes. He couldn't say a word, and wondered what Marion would do if her bluff was called. Perhaps it wasn't a bluff. She would see Clyde go to jail rather than lose the battle over the shares. He realized that was probably true.

"I don't believe you're serious," the man said.

"Perfectly serious."

John Martin Cooper looked at Clyde again, as if he might stop this, order the woman to desist.

"You have two choices," Marion said. "I will show you the telephone in the Senator's office. You can either call the police and report the bid-rigging, in which case you will be the defendant as of tomorrow morning in a very large suit for malfeasance in the matter of my shares, or you can call Mr Romanuck and agree that the ownership of the shares will be properly and legally settled after the will is executed."

"I'm not prepared to make that decision tonight."

Marion stood up and walked toward the man. Clyde thought for a moment she was going to hit him. When she was in front of him, she spoke to him very quietly.

"I did not share my bed with James Lawton for fifty years without finding out a little of how the world works. No doubt a poor widow has disadvantages, but I would not suggest, Mr Cooper, that you try the limits of my determination. You have cards in your hand. With one telephone call, you can bring about a criminal prosecution. You will not be thanked for it, but you can do it. Or you can take the other choice."

She stood there, then smiled, a polite and engaging smile.

"I'll show you the telephone," she said and led the way out of the room. Clyde closed his eyes, tried to keep his breathing even, felt, as never before in his life, a threat of hysteria. That he might begin to scream and be unable to stop. Breathe in, breathe out. He heard John Martin Cooper's voice on the phone, then without looking at him, the man walked into the room, took his coat and left. After the front door closed, Marion appeared in the doorway. She had a bottle of whisky and two glasses in her hands.

"I thought you might need this," she said. "I do."

Clyde nodded.

"He made the sensible decision."

Clyde met her, took the bottle and glasses from her, poured them both a drink and carried Marion's to the chair where she sat. Her hands were shaking as she took the glass.

"What a performance," she said.

"Yes," Clyde said, drank down enough whisky to burn his throat. "Maybe I'll get us some water." The water pitcher still sat in its place on the Senator's desk. Clyde took it to the kitchen and half filled it with water. The door to Danny's room was closed. Clyde carried the water back, added some to Marion's glass, some to his own.

"All I can say is thank you," he said.

"Imagine that silly little man thinking that James would be over-persuaded by you."

"The Senator was a war hero, John Martin said. He wouldn't have done such a thing."

"I wonder if Mr Cooper ever served in war. Perhaps occasionally a nice man becomes a hero, but when you're sending young men out to kill, it's not necessarily the nicest who are good at it." She took another large drink of her whisky. "Do you ever wonder what your life might have been if James hadn't taken you up?"

"Yes, I suppose I do, sometimes."

"If James hadn't taken you up and I hadn't told Noreen she ought to marry you. I know she didn't exactly do it because I said so, but I put the idea in her head."

"It would be another world."

"We can't go back and do it over, can we?"

"Would you want to?"

"We can't. That's all there is to it," she said.

Clyde poured more whisky for them both, filled each glass with water.

"You don't suppose he'll change his mind."

She shook her head.

"It's a long life," she said. He wasn't sure what she meant him to take from that.

Clyde drank, felt the alcohol relaxing him, though he was aware still of a little chill in his bones.

"What did you think of James, secretly, in the dark of night?"

"I don't think I ever stopped being a little afraid of him."

"Yes," she said.

She looked at Clyde, nodded, looked into her glass. Why has she asked him that, he wondered.

"You knew he was married once before."

"He told me when I first drafted the obituary notice."

Marion drank again.

"He killed her, you know." Clyde stared into his drink, unable to lift his eyes. "So he could have me."

Once again he wondered if this woman was perfectly sane. He was unable to respond to her words.

"She was a melancholy, nervous woman, Elizabeth Ford. Neurasthetic was the old word for it. Pale lips, helpless grey eyes. She couldn't satisfy a man with his kind of animal energies. He had married her, one could say, for her father's money, but it was probably not quite that simple. She was the daughter of his mentor, she was available and wished to marry. Her father was unwell, and died not long after the marriage. She could never satisfy James, she wasn't strong enough. Then he got to know me, and I was a healthy, vital young woman, quite his match, and we began to meet, secretly. In those days, of course, it was much more dangerous for me than it was for him. Men sowed their wild oats... well I'm sure you know all that."

Clyde remembered the night the Senator had mentioned his first marriage. Supposed then that it was because it was part of the documentary record, and he didn't want to appear to be concealing it.

"'Get rid of your wife,' I said to him one night when he came to me. He thought he could silence me with caresses as he'd done before, but

I was determined. I held myself back from him. Not that I wanted to. My desire was as strong as his, I would think of him much of the time when he wasn't there, imagine him with me. But I knew the way things were. Someone would see him leaving my door, it would all come out, and the woman who had the legal hold on him would win. I wouldn't let him have me, that night. 'Get rid of your wife,' I said to him again, 'then you can have me all day and all night too.' I held him off, though after he left, I was painfully roused and unsatisfied."

"Why are you telling me all this?" Clyde said.

"I want you to know. I want someone to know. It's not something I can tell my daughters."

Clyde waited.

"He had mining interests up north. There was a new mine they wanted him to invest in. When he went north that summer to see the mines, she went with him. I saw them off at the station. I was friends with them, you see, friends with her. She was pale, frightened I think. Perhaps she knew, but also she didn't like travel, the long train trip, the bad roads once they were there. She looked back at me as they stood on the steps of the train, and I wondered if she knew it all, what I was to him, and the danger she was in. I might have told her not to go, that she looked unwell, that the trip would only make her ill, but I hardened myself and smiled at her, my Judas smile. Well, she never came back."

She looked at Clyde, and then her eyes flickered to the doorway.

"Go away, Danny," she said, "this story is not for you."

When Clyde turned his head, he saw no-one there.

"He came back without her, and I was his prize, a strong eager woman, his equal in desire. She had gone out into the woods alone, he said, in her moody, melancholy way, vanished. Her body wasn't discovered for months, and until then, of course, his visits to me were still a secret. The body was found in a lake, identified by the clothing, brought back and buried. Now he had everything, her father's business, which he'd inherited through her, and a woman who was right for him. We married as soon as it was suitable, a few months later. A man wasn't expected to stay alone forever. It's possible there was gossip, at first, but we lived a very respectable, and at first a very quiet life. I had the sense never to mention her name to him, and she gradually disappeared into the fog that blurs all events of the past."

She took a sip from the glass.

"What should be done about those shares?" she said briskly, as if the story was gone now, vanished, unimportant.

"I'll talk to Bill Romanuck in the morning and tell him the transfer will be nullified. The best thing for you, in the circumstances, is probably for the company to sell itself to one of the larger finance companies, one that has sound management, in exchange for shares in the larger company."

How did he know that, in an instant? Not something he could explain, and yet he was certain he was right.

"The dividends should provide you with a steady income. I'll try to arrange all that. John Martin Cooper may not be pleased, but he'll get good value for his shares. They might offer him a directorship."

"If you and Mr Romanuck agree to it, I expect it will be a sensible thing to do."

Clyde stood up.

"I told my mother I'd be staying there tonight," he said. "I'd better be on my way."

Marion shook his hand.

"Was I right," she said, "that you and Noreen make a good couple?"

"Yes," Clyde said.

"You're both strong people," she said. He supposed she was right.

Outside the air was brisk, a cloudy starless night. He drove the few miles of country roads to his mother's house. The Senator had taken his wife into the woods, to a high stone cliff perhaps, those bare ancient pre-Cambrian rocks, and he had thrown her down into the deep cold water and watched the figure struggle, listened to her hopeless small cries, seen her go down. Marion didn't know that for a certainty, had never heard him confess the act. It was only what she suspected or feared or wished, that he had disposed of one young woman in order to possess another one. Clyde tried to recall the Senator, his speech, the sound of his voice, the way he held himself, to assess the character of the man, to understand whether he was capable of killing a woman he'd eaten with, slept with.

Recently Clyde had been reading a book he'd been given about the slaughter of the Tsar's family by the Bolsheviks. There was always the rumour that one or more of them was still alive, but that was wishfulness. They had been shot down, man, woman and children. Killing was easy once you made the decision. As he thought that, he was driving past the lot where the Murder House had stood when he was a boy. Gunfire and blood. He turned, the wrong way, deliberately, down the street he'd resisted for years, drove past Lyall Ratner's house. It appeared to be uninhabited, and there was a For Sale sign in front of it. He could stop, force a window, walk up the stairs, search for the past in the empty rooms.

Down a few more streets, then back to his mother's small cottage, pulled in behind her car. She came to meet him at the door, her round face smiling, and he was aware of how it had changed with age, the wrinkles at the eyes, the slight pouchiness of the cheeks, and he put his arms around her and hugged her.

"What's wrong, Clyde?" she said. "You seem a little desperate."

"It's a desperate old world," he said. "But we manage, don't we?"

"I hope we do."

Clyde slept badly and after breakfast with his mother he drove into Canalville and found Bill Romanuck's office, told him, at least in outline, the situation, and how he thought they should proceed once the probate was completed. Then he got on the road and drove back to Ottawa. The house was quiet when he walked in that evening. He put down his bags, and went up the stairs where the two small bedrooms huddled under the roof gables. Clifford's was dark, the boy already asleep, but there was a light from the other. Noreen lay under the covers, looking at the pictures in a book of photographs.

"Joe," she said, her voice deep and intense, "Do you ever think that you got it all wrong? That you should have done it all another way?"

She'd read his mind, knew all he'd been wondering about as he drove along the highway. But he couldn't tell her the story unless he told it all, and he couldn't do that. He sat on the bed beside her, and she took his hand.

"I went to have a talk with Nelly Boucek," she said, "my old dance teacher, about whether I could do some teaching for her, and probably I can, but then she took me off to a dance show at the National Arts Centre, in the Studio, a contemporary dance group from Montreal. And there it was, everything I'd never done, never thought, what I should have done all those years when I was teaching ballet to the little girls. These kids work for next to no money, day after day, move by move, inventing each step until it's something… I don't have words." She was moving her hands, as if to communicate to him the shape of the dance. "It's bare and abstract and yet it's so… passionate." Her hands moved again, dancing. "Three of them on that bare stage in blue shirts, one of them with an umbrella, and all so perfect it hurts me to see it. Or on the empty stage with one stepladder. Four of them lying in a square, and the music lifts them up. All in grey and as if they were more naked than anyone could ever be. Oh Joe, why can't I explain? I did ballet when I was a little girl, and once they thought I should have gone to the National Ballet School in Toronto. I liked it, you know, I liked it. It was a way of using myself. OK really. But just OK. I was so stupid. I didn't see. And I missed it all."

She squeezed his hand.

"I don't have the words. I'd like to show you, but I don't think I can."

"Do it now," he said.

"It's too late. I know I'm not in bad shape, but I don't think I could. I'm too careful. I can't give up everything and start over again. I don't know how."

Clyde couldn't find anything to say. He wondered if he was supposed to send her away, drive her out into the cold to discover what she'd missed. He didn't know what he was supposed to say or do.

"I feel as if I'd been sleepwalking," she said. "Or speaking the wrong language, as if I was a foundling, brought up in an alien tribe."

"What are you going to do?" he said.

"I don't know if I can do anything."

"What am I supposed to do?"

"I don't know."

He moved away from her, stood up.

"Where are you going?"

"I want a shower," he said. "I've been in the car for hours."

"Come back, Joe, when you're all clean, and we'll figure out what you're supposed to do."

In the following months, she began to work out with a modern dance class, but it never satisfied the fierce desire that had been awakened in her, and after a while, she gave it up. It might have been a mistake to bring her back to Ottawa. Perhaps the presence of her family stifled her.

"Joe," she said to him one night a few months later as they were going to bed, "what you have in front of you tonight, all hot and available, is a fertile woman. I stopped taking the pill."

The thought of another child shook him for a moment. He was used to Clifford, who was his son, part of their life. Another baby would be an intrusion, but he had to agree that it made some sense that there should be another child, if that was what she wanted. Even so it was months before she got pregnant, and he stopped thinking about the possibility of a new child. He and Perry were busy with half a dozen projects, Noreen was teaching, Clifford had taken up competitive swimming, they had the kind of life that most couples had, driving here and there, constant planning, so when Noreen told him she was pregnant, he was almost surprised. It would mean a larger house, and he began to keep his eyes open for one.

Then one summer day he and Perry were on the golf course. Perry and Yvette hadn't married, but now they were considering it. The week before they'd done eighteen holes with a backbench MP who had a good chance of a cabinet appointment next time round, and Clyde was astonished at Perry's ability to keep the man involved in talk, weaving a conversational fabric out of nothing. Today they were on the sixth hole when Clyde saw a figure cutting across the neighbouring fairway toward them, a tall man with no golf clubs. He recognized Alan Simmons and knew at once that something was wrong. He wouldn't let himself think what it might be, but he dropped his clubs and went to meet the figure striding toward him. He'd left Noreen at the house that morning. Clifford was away for a week at a swimming camp.

"What's wrong?" he said when he met his father-in-law, at the top of a little rise in the green fairway.

"She lost the baby."

"Where is she?"

"They're going to keep her overnight at the hospital."

Noreen had been four months pregnant, and the child wasn't yet very real to Clyde, but as he sat in the chair beside her hospital bed, it became clear that the tiny embryo had been for her already a person, a part of her life, and she couldn't stop crying for its loss. Clyde held her hand, could think of nothing to say.

"I was sure it was a girl," she said, "and I thought I could help her to get it right. Not like me."

Clyde had always assumed, foolishly, that Noreen had got it right, that she was pleased with their life. There were rules he didn't know; the song had verses he'd never learned. Tears were running down Noreen's cheeks. A life had been torn out of her. There was nothing for her to do but weep.

"Oh Joe, I'm so useless."

"Not to me. Not to Clifford."

"He's a boy. He doesn't need me."

"A boy needs his mother," he said, and she tried to smile at his joke.

She wiped her face with a Kleenex.

"Are we rich this week?" she said.

"Yes, we're rich this week."

It was an old joke between them, going back to his early days developing properties when he was always on the hop to keep everything together, rich one week, poor the next.

"If we're rich, I want to buy one of those old houses out in the country. I don't care if it's a ruin. I want to renovate it, move all my tools out there and spend the days working. Can we do that?"

"You want some derelict log cabin?"

"No, one of the limestone places. And you'll come home and find me covered with plaster and sawdust, but I'll do it. I told you I always wanted to build a house. This will be the next best thing."

"I thought you might want another baby."

"Wasn't meant to be, Joe."

"You never know. Let fate take a hand."

"Fate took a hand," she said and started to cry again.

When he left the hospital, Clyde drove an hour north to the camp where Clifford was spending the week. Parents weren't supposed to visit during the weekdays, but when he arrived, Clyde explained the situation to the head counsellor, and they fetched Clifford from the pool where he was swimming laps. Clyde waited by a couple of pine trees at the edge of the dirt track that led in from the main road. Clifford walked toward him, a sweat shirt pulled on over his bathing suit.

"Is something wrong, Dad?"

Words he himself had never spoken. He explained the situation. They hadn't yet told Clifford that Noreen was pregnant.

"Is she OK?" Clifford said.

"She's upset. She wanted this baby."

"I thought she might be pregnant," the boy said.

"You're quick to notice things aren't you?"

"Can she have another baby?"

"I think so. If that's what she wants. She says she wants to buy a house in the country and fix it up."

The boy nodded. Clyde found that he had nothing more to say. He could hear a red squirrel chattering in the pine tree nearby. They'd invaded the animal's territory.

"How's the camp?"

Clifford looked away for a moment before answering.

"The coach is a prick."

Clyde wondered what he was supposed to say in reply to that.

"If you wanted to say I was needed at home I wouldn't mind," Clifford said.

"What's wrong with him?"

"He doesn't like how I do anything. It's like being on the golf course with you, but a lot worse."

He put his arm around the boy's shoulders.

"It's just a few days," he said. Dumb, obvious, you said these things. There was nothing else to say. "I'll see you on the weekend."

"About mum. Am I supposed to talk about it? Not talk about it?"

"Just don't give her a hard time for a while."

The boy gave a little wave and walked away. His body was beginning to change shape, to look like the body of a man. It wouldn't be long until he asked some girl to show him her breasts. There was a breeze in the needles of the pines. He heard a distant voice, singing.

The coach is a prick. Boys becoming men, the ways they found to reach out to the alien adult world. He was Clifford's age, or maybe a year older, when he joined a school rifle club, much against his mother's wishes. She hated the thought of him firing a gun. Once a week, the lower hall at one end of the school was shut off by a huge rolling steel door, and targets were set up at one end, wooden pallets at the other. Most of the men teachers in those days had been in the army during the Second World War, and one of them, a burly man with a thin moustache, had taken charge of the weekly target practice, the .22 rifles brought from a locked cabinet in one of the storerooms, targets set up, the bullets distributed. The rules about handling the guns were rigid. Clyde wasn't a great shot, but he enjoyed the challenge, the slow pressure on the trigger, the sights lined up on the small black circle, the lift of excitement at the crack of the explosion. Once near the end of the year, before the big cadet inspection on the football field – everyone in an itchy khaki uniform distributed by the cadet quartermaster from a stock in the huge dim attic – the rifle club was taken by bus to an army firing range near the lakeshore. At the end of the range, behind the targets, was a hill of earth that had been heaped up to catch the bullets after they passed through the targets, a series of huge numerals at the top indicating the number of the target below, each target raised and lowered on chains. Half the boys worked in the protected alley below the targets, an earth bulwark built up behind them, then a wall of concrete behind and above. After each shot, the boy in control of the target would indicate where the shot had struck by raising a small black and white bull's eye on a stick, up and down to indicate a hit, then the bulls-eye was placed over the bullet hole to indicate its placing. A complete miss was indicated by waving the wooden handle. Then the two groups of cadets changed places, and those who had been scoring at the targets took their places ready to shoot from the top of one of the grassy banks which were constructed in a series of straight lines across the range, one every twenty or thirty yards from the target area to the end of the field. When the order was given, they fired one shot, waited for the indication of where the bullet had struck, fired another. On the outdoor range they used army .303 rifles, and Clyde remembered the impact of the shots against his shoulder. He supposed that his father had gone through this kind of drill in the days after his enlistment. It was unknown whether he had ever fired a shot on that stony beach before the machine guns finished him.

It was late in the winter that Noreen found the house she wanted. That Saturday afternoon Clifford was going to a movie with his grandfather while Clyde and Noreen drove out to meet Perry and Yvette at a new restaurant half an hour from Ottawa in an old stone mill, their tables looking out a window over the river, which ran a dark golden brown between the ledges of ice.

"What I think," Perry was saying as he raised his glass of wine, "is that we could toast the success of DB Consultants. We're a success, aren't we?"

"*Ben sûr,*" Yvette said.

"Haven't gone broke yet," Clyde said.

"The man is so careful," Noreen said. "Does he drive us all crazy?"

"We pay him to be careful," Perry said. "So the rest of us can be flightly."

"True," Noreen said. "I can always be Nonnie-the-Ditz, because I know Joe will fix things."

"None of this is true," Clyde said. "Who is the fastidious carpenter at this table? Right, Noreen. Who always plans ahead so we have three possible jobs lined up? Right, Perry. I just follow along with my little broom and pan picking up the orts and shavings."

"What is *orts*?" Yvette said.

"It's what's left on your plate after you finish eating that quiche."

"That's an ort?" she said, pointing to a piece of pastry on her plate.

"Exactly," he said and plunged the fork into his salade Niçoise.

After lunch they got in their separate cars to drive back to the city. He and Noreen planned to make the weekly trip to a supermarket on the way home. The road he chose was new to both of them.

"Look over there, Joe," Noreen said, a few miles along the road, pointing. "Stop the car."

A hundred yards or so away, surrounded by snow, stood an old house, the pale grey limestone shining in the frosty winter light, one of those classic nineteenth century stone houses, an elliptical fanlight over the door, a panel of mullioned glass squares on each side. Behind the house stood a log barn, the blackened logs chinked with white plaster, a wide opening leading to the dim interior, a drive shed in its day perhaps.

"Let's go and look," she said.

Clyde stopped the car and the two of them got out. No tracks in the snow, no sign that anyone had been near the house over the winter. Out here among the bare fields, the wind blew cold, and while they were wearing winter coats, they hadn't dressed for hiking, but Noreen set off down the lane, her feet sinking into the deep snow, Clyde behind her. She looked around at him and laughed.

"Mark my footsteps, good my page," she sang.

"If you get tired," Clyde said, "we can trade places."

But Noreen plunged on. Clyde could feel snow getting inside his boots as they sank into the drifts. Noreen was still singing the Christmas carol. By now they were about halfway up the drive, when suddenly Noreen caught a foot on something and fell headlong into the snow. She was laughing again.

"You better save me, Joe, or they'll find my bones here in the spring."

When Clyde reached her, he set his feet and gave her a hand, so she could pull herself up. Her cheeks and nose were red with the cold and the effort of walking, her eyes bright.

"Are you frozen?" he said as he brushed the snow from her parka.

"Brought up tough," she said, and pushed off once more through the deep snow.

They struggled on, and as they grew close to the house, Clyde wondered for a second if they would make it back to the car. Yes, of course they would, but it was scary out here, his heart pounding, his face stung by the wind. A few flakes of snow were beginning to fall. Noreen was pushing ahead now that she was near the building, but she stumbled again, her toe catching in the frozen crust, righted herself, stood for a second and pressed on.

She stopped close to a front window, the dark green parka vivid against the luminous grey stone, a jigsaw of large mortared pieces that had stood here for well over a hundred years.

"It's empty," she said. Clyde reached the window, put his face against the glass and looked in. A large room, wainscot with plaster above, wallpaper peeling. Against the wall, a fireplace with a plain wooden mantel. A piece of linoleum covered the centre of the floor, but around it, the wide pine floorboards were visible. It looked as if the house had been deserted for some time or, if not, this room had been disused.

"It's mine," Noreen said. "This is the house I've been looking for."

The snow had drifted against the walls, and to reach the doorway, they had to go around a tall drift. A table stood in the front hall, a kitchen table that didn't belong there, as if, moving out, someone had abandoned it.

"Oh Joe," Noreen said, throwing her arms around him. "Buy me the nice house."

"Better find out if it's for sale."

"It's empty. It must be for sale." She started to fight her way through the snow to the other window, stopped. "I've seen enough. I want it." She started back through the snow toward the car. It was a little easier now they had broken a trail, but by the time they got in the car they were both panting and Clyde's boots were full of snow. He started the engine, then, sitting in the driver's seat he bent his legs round the steering wheel, pulled off the boots and dumped as much snow as he could.

"What do you think?" Noreen said.

"I'll phone around," Clyde said. "See what I can find out."

"I've always been good, haven't I, Joe, living in all your different houses?"

"That's right," he said. "You've never complained."

"I want this one. I'll set up my workshop."

"You'll need help."

"There are good tradesmen around."

The snow was falling more heavily now.

"There's a map in the glove compartment," he said.

Noreen took it out, and Clyde opened it and marked the location. He got his boots back on, banging one knee as he did it, and they drove through the blowing snow, unable to see more than a few feet in any direction. When they reached a crossroad, he noted on the road sign at the junction the name of the country road they'd travelled. By the time they shopped at the supermarket and reached home, it was too late to start phoning about the house, but Clyde promised that by Monday afternoon he'd have found out about it, one way or the other. That night in bed Noreen put her strong arms around him and pulled him tight to her. It still surprised him, how strong she was.

"You're good to the old crazy lady," she said.

"Not crazy. Not crazy at all."

"So you say."

"Where did that Nonnie-the-Ditz come from?"

"They used to call me that, John and my father, when I was fourteen or fifteen. I think I went through puberty in a big hurry so I was out of step with everything, too tall, full of crazy thoughts, didn't know what having tits was all about."

"But you learned."

"I met a nice boy, Eric Lepage, and he taught me."

"What happened to him?"

"He was older. He went away to school. Other things happened. You know how it is."

Clyde wasn't sure he did. Living was opaque and arbitrary. A shining wall of dark glass. You made up your mind and went forward, like a good soldier, but the wall of glass was always there just in front of you.

On Monday he called a real estate agent whose sign he'd seen near the old mill where they'd eaten lunch. The agent knew the house Clyde was referring to, knew it had been empty for years, but he didn't have any idea who owned it. He was able to tell Clyde which registry office would have the record, and by lunchtime, Clyde had driven out there and had the big ledger open in front of him. He found the name of the owner. From the tax rolls, he discovered her address, in Sudbury, and after a few minutes indecisiveness about how to proceed, he went to the real estate agent he'd spoken to and gave him the name and address. The alternative was to contact the owner directly, but he'd decided that a tentative enquiry from an agent was less likely to create panic or unrealistic expectations. He told the agent not to push too hard to begin with, just to see if they could start some kind of negotiation. The house had twenty acres of property with it, and he didn't want to owner to decide that someone was planning a subdivision and inflate the price.

A meeting with a man from a central Ontario tourist association was in Clyde's book for late in the afternoon; the association was considering hiring someone to represent its interests in Ottawa, and by the time the meeting was over, he was late getting home, and Noreen had just left to teach a dance class. Clifford was watching TV.

"Mom says we're moving to the country," he said.

"We're looking at a place."

"I'd have to go to school on a bus."

"I suppose. I did it for five years."

"I didn't know that."

"Have you eaten?"

"Yeah. Mom said to tell you there's some leftover lasagna."

Clyde didn't bother heating it, just put it out on a plate and ate it cold with a beer, watching TV with Clifford until the boy decided that the show was boring and went up to bed. Living in the country, school buses, it was to be a different kind of life, a long drive to work every day. He wondered if they'd like all that.

"Well," Noreen said as she came in the door, "did you buy it?"

"I'm trying," he said.

In fact it was a slow negotiation; the woman in Sudbury who'd inherited the property from her grandmother's estate was convinced that the acreage was worth more than it was. Clyde made an offer, a little low, but not unreasonable, giving her a week or so to think about it. Don't make it seem too important was his instinct, just let her take her time and consider the possibility of that much cash in her pocket. She rejected the offer, he came up a bit, she countered and he met her halfway. All this took a month, but the closing was to be quick, and so long as the title was sound, he told Noreen, she would have the house by the summer. She was planning to offer Clifford an hourly wage to help her out in the early stages of the renovation.

They took possession of the house in May, and Noreen began to move her tools out there and to make arrangements with local tradesmen. An electrician hooked up service to a single outlet at the back door of the house to that they could string an extension for a work light and power tools. Noreen bought a sleeping bag and an air mattress, and spent most of the week there. Clyde would find himself at the house in the city frying sausages for dinner for himself and Clifford. He tried to convince Clifford to start to learn a little basic cooking, what he'd known at that age, but the boy's only domestic skill was ordering pizza.

Clyde worried a little about Noreen alone in that old house, but she was gripped by her vision of what the place could be, and nothing would stand in her way.

After school ended, Clifford began to stay out there, though he objected to the smell of the outhouse they were using until the new well was drilled – the old one had gone dry. Noreen kept Clifford busy fetching and carrying as they emptied out closets, the basement, tore down temporary partitions. She found a small truck for sale on the lot of a local garage and bought it to haul material from the lumberyard and trash to the dump. It was all hard, dirty work, and now and then Clyde would find himself on the long green fairways of the golf course with some politician or civil servant and thinking he should be working with her instead, but she never complained of his absence. She'd found a deserted quarry nearby, and as if the house wasn't enough, she began to haul chunks of limestone to make a back patio and a couple of raised gardens, though so far nothing had materialized except a large heap of rock and a wheelbarrow, bought at an auction, for moving it. As she had predicted he would come home and find her covered with plaster, staggering with exhaustion.

In August, Clyde took a week off and spent it out at the house, mostly clearing out the log building. Some of the old iron and wood was set aside for Noreen to consider later, but they filled the truck with broken furniture, rotted straw, bedding, a baby carriage, window frames with broken glass, steel pipes with faucets still soldered on, a suitcase full of mouldy clothing, a mirror in two pieces, a stained mattress, and a pile out-of-date tall green beer bottles, and Clyde hauled it away. At the local landfill he saw men and women who must be neighbours, and they appeared to know who he was, waved or nodded. Noreen would have been able to call them by name.

On Friday night, they had a small fire burning in the yard, Noreen's wood scrap and some brush that he'd dragged from the far end of the old drive shed, piled there for no apparent reason, the logs underneath damp. The evening had grown dark, and Noreen brought out a couple of rickety kitchen chairs, and the two of them sat side by side staring into the flames and drinking warm beer. Noreen's father had visited during the afternoon and taken Clifford back to town with him. In another two weeks, the water and electricity – including baseboard heating – would be hooked up, and the house would be livable. Noreen had promised Clifford that they would stay in town one more winter.

He'd be changing schools at the end of that year anyway. Though September was still a week away, there was a chill in the air, and it grew dark quickly as they sat there, an occasional mosquito buzzing past, though the worst of them were gone now after a dry summer, and the smoke from the fire kept them off. Clyde looked at the shape of the stone house against the last light in the west, a thin line of blood red, a pale yellow streak above it, and above that the night. He didn't yet feel what Noreen obviously did, that this was their home, the place where the future would occur. That they would settle here. The big downstairs rooms, now stripped of old wallpaper, the plaster beginning to be patched, electrical outlets rewired, the floors repaired where the electricians had cut into them, were fine and bright, the stone fireplaces awaiting burning logs. It would be beautiful, no doubt, and surely he would settle into it. Yet there was a shiver of uncertainty. Noreen was pals with the tradesmen, Sparky McCracken, her electrician, Don Peets, the plumber, full of stories about their jokes and warnings, and she knew the people who lived nearby. Clyde's life was still in Ottawa, though that too, from time to time, presented itself as a charade in which he pretended to know what couldn't be known. The shining wall of dark glass, opaque, taunting, was always there.

He reached out and took Noreen's hand. The last of the light was going. Stars were bright above them.

"It's beautiful here, isn't it, Joe?"

"Yes," he said. It was very quiet, and then he heard footsteps on the drive and a man's figure came out of the darkness and stood on the far side of the fire. A square pleasant face, but the flickering firelight made it look elfin, deep-eyed, the mouth between a smile and a frown.

"Hello Chris," Noreen said.

"I saw the fire," he said. "Stopped to see if everything was all right. Didn't know if you were here. Then when I heard your voices I thought I'd invite you round tomorrow night. My place. Some people are coming. Guitar, fiddle. A few people."

"Where's your place?"

"I thought you knew."

"On the river, you said."

"I guess I figure everybody knows."

He gave instructions.

"Drop in," he said. "Everybody's welcome."

He hadn't moved any closer, and as the fire burned down a bit, his face was darker. He made an odd gesture, closing both eyes slowly, then opening them again, lifted both hands, a wave, a blessing and turned away. Vanished into the darkness. Noreen got up and put a few more pieces of wood on the fire.

"Who was that?" Clyde said.

"Chris Harnett. He came a couple of times with Sparky McCracken. Works for him when he needs a helper. Does some carpentry. Other than that he's a musician. I guess."

"A whole world out here," Clyde said. "People you know and I don't."

"We'll go to that party," she said, "and you can meet some."

When the fire had burned out, they went in the house, put the two air mattresses together and spread the sleeping bags over them. The next afternoon, they drove into town, washed up and found clean clothes, drove back out to Chris Harnett's place. It was a big frame cottage at the end of a lane that curved through thick woodland, the place built only a few feet from the river. The moon was bright on the moving surface of the water. The cottage had no interior walls, a sleeping loft at one end, not much furniture. A lot of people, mostly young, sat in groups on the floor. There was a strong smell of marijuana, and a guitar and violin case stood by the ladder that led to the sleeping loft. Chris Harnett came to meet them, and pointed Clyde to the refrigerator where he could put the beer they'd brought. As Clyde opened two bottles, he saw a young woman a few feet away look toward him, smile as if she might know him then look away. Yes, he thought, we must know each other. In some untold story. He took Noreen a beer. She was talking to Chris Harnett's mother, a sturdy woman in jeans who was explaining that this was an old family property, and that Chris had built himself the cottage a couple of years before. She herself lived in Ottawa, but she spent her summers in the farmhouse at the other end of the drive, the house where she'd been raised.

"I think of settling there, but the winter's too much for me."

Clyde turned his head, and the young woman he'd noticed before was watching him. There might have been an edge of malice in her smile. He was, he supposed, out of place here. All the men at the party had beards or pony-tails or dogs, or all three, evidence that the early hippie communities had survived, preserving their folkways. As Noreen went on with her conversation, he crossed the room to the window. Through it he could make out the silhouette of a pine tree against the moonlight on the water. Otherwise the window reflected the lights of the interior. A figure appeared beside him, reflected in the glass. He turned.

She was blonde, but her eyes were brown, a golden tone to her skin, and she was smiling. A long cotton dress of a yellow printed fabric clung to her and showed the shape of her small breasts, the bump of the nipples. No one wore clothes like that anymore,

"What do you do?" she said.

"We bought the old Finnegan place," he said.

"That's not what I asked you. What do you do?"

"This and that."

"No need to be ashamed of it."

"I'm not." Was he? He wasn't sure why he didn't want to tell this young woman about his work, but he didn't.

"You must work for the government."

"Sometimes."

"What's your sign?"

"I'll leave you to guess that."

"You leave me to guess everything.

"Why not? I'm sure you're good at it."

"You're very mysterious."

"Oh yes."

"Maybe you're a spy."

"That's right. You've guessed it. I'm a spy."

"But who do you spy for?"

"Anyone who'll pay."

"A cynical spy."

"It goes with the trade."

"Spies have all the women they want, don't they?"

"In books and movies. I'm not so sure about real spies."

"Do you have all the women you want?"

"Yes."

"You're a very accomplished liar."

"A spy has to be. It's part of the training."

"I'm sure you're very well trained," she said.

He had the impression that her body was undulating very slightly within the fabric of the dress, and yet he knew it couldn't be true. Maybe he'd been breathing marijuana out of the air. A little group of people on the far side of the room were passing a joint. Noreen was talking to Chris Harnett. He laughed at something she said. He was reaching for his guitar, tuning it, and beside him a man with thick hair and a reddish moustache was tuning a fiddle. The young woman swayed, a slow dance to music that hadn't yet begun to play.

"Now there's going to be music," he said.

She was still smiling at him, perhaps in mockery. She made an odd face and turned away, and the fabric of the yellow dress was tight over her plump hips. Biology said, "You must have that. Take it now."

The guitar played a few chords and the fiddle started up, a slow known tune, then a higher, stranger line, and Chris Harnett looked down at his fingers on the guitar as if to learn the words from them and sang.

The water is wide, I cannot get o'er,
And neither have I wings to fly.
Give me a boat that will carry two,
and both will row, my love and I.

The two figures in the boat, arched, stretching, almost out of sight on the gleaming river. Noreen was standing next to Clyde, her shoulder against his.

"Who's the golden girl?" she said.

"I didn't find out her name."

"That's not very effective flirtation, Joe. Not even finding out her name."

"Was I flirting?"

"I don't know. She certainly was. She looked as if she was ready to crawl into your pocket."

"Didn't notice."

"Big ass on her."

He bumped her with his shoulder.

"Listen to the music," he said. The wailing violin was playing a high counterpoint to the voice, something ancient, almost oriental about the line of music. The voice was a little fogged and reedy. At the end of the song, Noreen led him to a corner where they sat down leaning against the wall. The next thing the two played was a very slow and moody version of 'Carrickfergus', then two upbeat and recent country songs and a Phil Ochs number that Clyde hadn't heard for years. Then they quit, and someone else picked up the guitar and began quietly to pick out chords. Clyde went to the fridge to get them more beer. The golden girl had disappeared. She lay somewhere in the darkness under the trees by the river, the long dress pulled up to her waist. On the far side of the room, Chris Harnett was talking to Noreen. It wasn't just the firelight, Clyde decided, that gave his face that elfin look. He had ancestors of some other species altogether, wood dwellers, creatures of malign magic.

After they'd finished the next beer, they thanked Chris and told him they were leaving. He shook Clyde's hand and bent to kiss Noreen on the cheek, and they followed the headlights down the curving track that led to the road, then home. They made love a little precariously on the air mattresses. When Clyde woke in the morning from a long sinuous dream of searching through an ancient temple surrounded by forest, he found that Noreen was gone, and when he went outside, he found her, in shorts and a sleeveless T-shirt, her long thin arms and legs strung with muscle as she pushed the loaded wheelbarrow over the ground, wheeling chunks of rock from the pile to the far corner of the house.

"What are you doing hauling rock at this hour?" he said.

"Couldn't sleep," she said. "I thought I might as well do something useful."

Clyde went back into the house, poured water out of the bottle they'd brought with them, and plugged the electric kettle into the extension that had been rigged for the power tools. He found a packet of cookies and ate a couple. When he'd made coffee, he carried a cup out to Noreen.

"I'll take you out for lunch," he said, "at the Old Mill."

She nodded her head and lifted another rock.

Noreen stayed out at the old house most days until November. She organized all her dance classes for Friday and Saturday and spent the weekends in Ottawa. By now she'd bought a little furniture, so it was no longer necessary to sleep on the floor. At the end of the school year, they sold the little house in the city and moved.

It was during the summer of the first year they lived out there that Clyde received a call from Elaine Haverman asking him if he would drop round to see her when he had time. What the Senator had requested in his will had been effected by now, and Clyde, along with Bill Romanuck, had advised Marion in the negotiation that had led to the sale of County Finance to a large western Ontario trust company. John Martin Cooper had been given a position on the board of the larger company, and Marion's holdings gave her a substantial income. Western Trust had paid Clyde a finder's fee for putting together the deal.

It was a warm summer evening when he drove to the Glebe to see Elaine. He'd go out to the country afterward or, if he was late, he'd phone Noreen and stay in the little apartment on the top floor of the house where DB Consultants did business.

Elaine met him at the door. She had put on weight. Wearing high heels and a loosely draped skirt, she had a largeness of presence now, was no longer the slightly self-conscious woman he remembered from his first days working for the Senator.

"Thanks for coming, Clyde. It's very kind of you. The family has depended on you a good deal over the years. Mother drops heavy hints about the will and how you fought for her interest."

"The other way round too." He wasn't about to get into all that.

Elaine led him to the living room. There was something a little ecclesiastical about the room, the stained dark wood, maroon upholstery, dark swags of curtain at the edge of each window, two large brass planters, a shelf of old leather-bound books. You expected a voice to begin to intone the liturgy at any moment.

"Would you like a drink? Robert's on the phone with the bishop – his annual checkup, more or less – and that always takes a good deal of time, so I won't wait for him to come and offer you one."

Clyde was about to refuse the offered drink, thinking he would get out more quickly that way, but he changed his mind, and she went to a table in the corner and poured two glasses of sherry from a blown glass decanter. Everything was part of a comfortable clerical establishment. People took on these styles. He thought that Elaine's voice had got slightly louder and richer, as if she too had to be heard from the pulpit.

"It's about mother," she said. "You'll have guessed that. You have influence with her, and with Danny too. He's become quite a part of her life. An odd couple, really, aren't they?"

"Yes, I suppose they are."

"Mother is well over eighty, you know, and I'd like her to move here. We could do more for her, and if anything went wrong we'd be close by. But I haven't had much success in convincing her. I thought I'd try to enlist your help. You have influence. Surely she can't stay in that big old house forever."

"But that's part of the point of having Danny there with her, isn't it?"

"Yes, of course. That's one of the things she said. She won't leave Danny behind."

She took a sip of her sherry, stared at him. The features were softer, more flesh covering the bones, a darkening under the eyes.

"So you think it's hopeless," she said.

"You really want her to come here to Ottawa."

"Yes, I do. I'm sure that my motives are impure, but motives are. Maybe I just want to prove that I'm a better daughter than Anne. Anyway Anne has all those schoolboys to fuss over."

"Well, Elaine, you know your mother well enough to know bullying won't work."

"I do indeed."

"I have one idea. What if you suggested that the Senator's estate buy Danny a little place in Ottawa, give him a life interest with the proviso that it reverts to the estate when he dies. Then he might be willing to come with her. Danny would still work for her, but he'd have a certain independence. She's a generous woman, and I think the idea of doing something for him would appeal to her. And if she moved to a house that was easier to handle, they wouldn't be crowded in there together. She could even move to an apartment if it became necessary."

"Or some kind of facility with care."

Clyde hadn't wanted to say that, but it had been in his mind.

"Would you present the idea to them, Clyde? They both respect you so much. It's the best chance of convincing them. Tell mother she can be here watching her grand-daughters grow up."

"All right," he said. "I'm about due to visit my mother. I'll drop in and see Marion while I'm there."

"I'd be very grateful. I do think Cecily and Margaret would like to have their grandmother close by. Though they're a bit in awe of her."

"We all are," Clyde said. He sipped the dry sherry. Not bad, really, though he'd be willing to wait a few more years before the next glass. They sat in silence for a moment, and from somewhere in the house, he could hear Robert's voice, though he couldn't make out what was being said. It was early enough, he supposed, to drive out to the country, if he left soon.

"Clyde," Elaine said, and it was obvious from the tone that this was a new subject, "do you know anything about my father's first wife?"

"No," Clyde said, "except that she existed."

"Years ago, when I was a girl, I was poking about in the attic and found a wedding picture. I showed it to mother, and she said it was father's first wife, that she had died young, and it was all very sad."

Clyde remained silent.

"You were close to father. I just thought you might know more."

"No," Clyde said, "I don't."

Just as he was finishing the sherry and getting up to go, Robert Haverman appeared at the door of the room.

"Everything as should be with the bishop?" Elaine said.

"All manner of thing shall be well," Robert said and shook Clyde's hand. "You on your way so soon?" he said.

"We're living out in the country now," Clyde said. "It's a bit of a drive home."

"Clyde's had a clever idea," Elaine said to her husband. "I'll tell you about it."

Clyde said his goodbyes and went out into the warm summer evening. A week later, he was in his mother's living room explaining the errand that had brought him there.

"What about you?" he was saying. "Should I be insisting that you move to Ottawa?"

"Marion's older than I am," his mother said. "I'm still working."

It was true. Palmer still attended the law office once a week, and Hazel Bryanton went in every day from 1 till 4, did some typing, answered calls. They were both well past the official retirement age, but there seemed no reason they should quit if they didn't want to.

"You're a wonder," Clyde said.

"Is that a compliment, Clyde, or merely an expression of astonishment?"

"It's both."

"Shall we turn on the Blue Jays game?" she said.

"If you like."

So the two of them sat there and watched baseball, and his mother explained to him the infield fly rule. The next day Clyde drove to Marion's house and presented his idea.

"Would Danny like to have his own house?" she said.

"I'll ask him."

At first Danny appeared a little suspicious, as if Clyde might be trying to trick him. Clyde made clear that it was a way of convincing Marion she could move to Ottawa without abandoning her whole life. She hadn't said no to the suggestion.

"She likes having you work for her."

"Very nice of her I'm sure."

"It's a good job isn't it?"

"And we like things the way they are."

"Wouldn't you like to have your own place?"

"They'd give me a house, just give it to me?"

"It would be yours for life, then go back to the estate."

"Why?"

"Because that's where it came from."

"What if I wanted to leave it to someone?"

"You don't have any children do you?"

"It might surprise you, Clyde, but I do have friends."

Clyde had no answer to that.

"Look," he said, "there's nothing in this for me either way. Elaine wants her mother to move to Ottawa. Someday Marion may have to move into an apartment with nursing care. If you have a place of your own, you can go on working for her, wherever she lives. But you and Marion can talk about it. It's up to you. Why not let them give you a house in Ottawa? You're not going to get one any other way."

"Thanks for your confidence, Clyde."

"Think about it. This is a big place, all those stairs. Marion could have a fall any time."

"Actually she fell last week, but she didn't break anything."

"A place all on one floor would be easier for her."

"OK, Clydie, Marion and I will talk about it."

Clyde got up to leave. Danny was watching him as he pulled on his jacket. "I hear your friend Francis is in the hospital," he said. "Not going to get out is what they say."

Clyde looked back at Danny, suddenly taking in how much he'd changed. The thin face was starting to be wrinkled. The squinting dark little eyes stared. He thought he knew Danny, but as they looked toward each other now, he thought perhaps he didn't know him at all.

"Where do you hear these things?"

"Like I said, Clydie, I have friends."

"I suppose I should go and see him."

"Well that would be up to you, wouldn't it?"

Clyde put out his hand, and Danny shook it half-heartedly.

"Do whatever you want," Clyde said. "But one way or another, things are going to change."

"They always do."

Clyde said goodbye to Marion who was sitting in the front room with a book about roses. On his way to the door he saw that the Senator's den was still unaltered, occupied by memories. Clyde drove into Canalville and left the car in the parking lot of the General Hospital. At the front desk, he was told the number of the room, and he went up in the elevator with two young nursing assistants who were gossiping about one of the orderlies. The hall was bare except for a gurney that stood against the wall. The door of the room was open. Flowers on the table, and a few cards. Clyde stood at the doorway, not sure whether to go in or turn away. A voice spoke from the bed.

"Who's there?" The voice was a little thin, breathless.

"It's me," Clyde said and moved forward. Francis lay on his back, his eyes open. He turned his head.

"What brought you?"

"I heard you were in hospital. Thought I'd drop in, since I was in town."

"I didn't think you came here anymore."

"I had something to discuss with Marion."

Francis paused, as if to gather the energy to speak.

"Danny O'Connell must have told you I was in this place."

Clyde nodded.

"Likes to keep track of everybody, little Danny."

Clyde tried to imagine Danny's life these days, how he and Francis were in touch, but too much was missing, a world he didn't know.

"You been here long?" Clyde said.

"Too long, but I'll be out soon. Feet first."

"I hope not."

"That's the way it's going to be."

"I'm very sorry, Francis, if that's true."

"So you're very sorry," Francis said, paused, took a breath. "You always had a way with the soft words, Clyde. Until the time came to slip in the knife."

"Why do I make you so angry, Francis?"

Francis said nothing for a moment, turned his head away.

"You were such a very pretty boy, Clyde, but so cold. Not just that you weren't our kind, or thought you weren't. A person could never get in touch with you." Another pause, breath. "You have no heart."

Frost rose from the earth though the steel frame of the building, a chill that penetrated Clyde's veins, the heart he didn't have held in its grip.

"That's the one good thing about knowing that you're dying," Francis said. “I can say whatever I want.”

Clyde stared at the face, pale, depleted, the eyes that might have been dead already. He tried to imagine what he could say in response to what he was hearing, but there was nothing.

“Cat got your tongue?”

“Yes.”

“Truth from dying lips. Felt sorry for your wife, you know. Deep down inside you there’s nothing.”

“Deep down inside all of us there’s nothing.”

“Oh yes, you would believe that.”

“What’s deep down inside you Francis?”

There was a silence, one word spoken so softly Clyde wasn’t sure he heard it. Or was it only the sound of breath exhaled. Love, was that what he said? Deep down inside Francis there was love. A dying man, he wanted to believe that. Maybe Clyde had imagined it. It was only the struggle to breathe that caught his ear.

There was a long silence, Francis turned his head again, those strange blind-looking eyes holding Clyde in their gaze.

“Give me little kiss, Clyde, and you can skip the funeral.”

Clyde bent over the bed and met the warm twitching mouth with his own. It was an empty enough gesture, but if that’s what he wanted, it was well enough. He stood up again.

“Goodbye, Francis,” he said and walked from the room, down the hall. The bare walls and long perspective to a far window made him dizzy. At the elevator, the door opened, and Madge Finster stepped out. She had grown fat and moved with difficulty as if her legs had trouble bearing her weight.

“Clyde, how good to see you.”

“I’m just down for the day. I heard Francis was here.”

“Did you see him?”

“Yes.”

“He’ll be so pleased. He often speaks of you, the great old days when the two of you worked together.”

“I’m glad I could be here.”

“He’s very low,” Madge Finster said, “but I try not to lose hope.”

“Of course.”

“I mustn’t keep you,” she said. “You’re an important man these days.”

“No. But I keep busy.”

"So glad," she said as she turned away and went down the hall. "So glad."

Clyde got in his car and drove. If he drove fast enough, his mind would empty and he would be aware of nothing but the speed.

It was nearly a year later when Marion, after another fall, decided to move to Ottawa, and Elaine Haverman asked Clyde is he would help find a place for Danny. Clyde scouted around, and when he had two or three possibilities, Danny came up by bus, and they settled on a small place in the Lower Town, well past the market area, in a district where prices weren't too unreasonable. Like a house in a child's drawing, Clyde always thought. Here is the roof. Here is the window. Here is the door.

So it was purchased and Danny settled in. Danny's house. For life. And it was that convenient arrangement they'd fought over more than once in the last few years, and the pointless resentment that Danny cherished over it, even as he knew he was dying of cancer, prompted his vengeful letter to Tom McKay at the newspaper. Telling him everything, Danny said, though it wasn't clear just what Danny knew. How many of the secrets. Would Clyde find himself reading newspaper headlines about the bid-rigging? That house, which always reminded Clyde of a child's drawing of a house, was where he had been summoned two days before to find Danny under a blanket on his recliner, grey and dead.

Tomorrow Clyde would drive back to Ottawa to get himself ready for the funeral. He had called the newspaper and inserted an obituary. He didn't know Danny's gay friends to notify them, couldn't know how many of them would find out about his death. He'd managed to get hold of Danny's brother on the phone, but the man sounded unwell and uninterested.

Tomorrow he would go back to it all. Clyde got up from the upholstered chair by the window of his cabin, put on a warm coat and went outside. Above him, he could just make out the shapes of bare branches, the sky scattered with stars, that intense brightness that came, they said, from such vast distances. What he was seeing was light from the past, energy sent out across the infinite reaches long ago. Out there in the darkness, all the moments of the past were moving toward his eyes, the days of his childhood, and before that all the years of human history. Light set out from the far stars as Napoleon's army retreated from Moscow, as the men crossed the channel to Dieppe, as a Fenian waited on a dark street for Darcy McGee, as Clyde and Danny ran through the streets of Brockton under the high old trees.

The air was cold . Winter was moving in, another year past, as the planet moved toward the new millenium. Clyde knew I.T. specialists who were making a fortune preparing for the Y2K problem now that the magic date was on the horizon, all those computer programs unprepared, threatening some massive breakdown, the virtual universe threatening to fold into itself and vanish to a point of light like one of those infinitely distant stars. It would happen or it wouldn't. Clyde was too old to be more than functionally literate on the new electronic devices. You could always hire someone.

A little light from the windows of the cabin shone on the rocky hill. He went back inside, sat with the book recounting Drake's circumnavigation of the globe. History was chaos punctuated by successful acts of will, then a vanishing. His mind wandered. Back in Ottawa Perry was drafting a lobbying campaign for a manufacturer's group. Clyde's son Clifford, grown up, qualified as a teacher, was preparing a geography class he was to teach the next day. In the undertaker's workroom, Danny's remains lay waiting, an effigy of the man who once was. Clyde wondered if he should try to contact Noreen, tell her about the funeral. If she'd stayed in the old stone house, she was only a half hour's drive from where he stood now. But so far as he knew, she hadn't been in touch with Danny for years; she would feel no need to see him off. Let the dead bury the dead, she had said to him once.

His life with Noreen had changed after they moved to the country. Especially in winter Clyde often stayed in town, in the tiny apartment upstairs from the office, rather than risk the drive home when he was tired. Clifford had settled in at his new school, though he complained about having to get up early to catch the school bus. Noreen still worked on the house, the garden, turning the log shed into a workshop, never still, striving toward some ideal form that she had in her mind. Clyde moved in and out of the picture.

What he remembered: how one night they were lying in bed in the darkness, side by side but untouching.

"Joe," she said, paused, was silent.

"What?"

"Have you ever... been unfaithful?"

"No," he said, and it was half a second before he realized that it was a lie, but he didn't go back to it, make the correction. The event with Cathy Ratner was unreal, something in another life.

She lay there unspeaking, and he waited.

"I have," she said. "There's someone… "

"Chris," he said.

"Yes," she said. "I couldn't help it."

She told him because she wanted him to know, and then what? To let it go on and tolerate it, to ask her to end it: the options were equally pathetic and impossible. He was starting to shiver. Perhaps he was supposed to ask her how long, how often, what now, but he couldn't. He could not touch her. He could not cry out. He rose from bed and began to dress. He'd known it of course, since that first night, the singing, the ladder to the sleeping loft, known that it was going to happen, was happening, though he'd never allowed the secret knowledge to speak out. Did Clifford know? he wondered, but he couldn't ask. He had to get away, to escape from it all.

"You can have the house," he said as he left the room. "It's all yours anyway."

He manoeuvred the car down the long driveway, drove fast along the highway to the city, tried to stop imagining the things the two of them had done together. Jealousy was the most terrible thing because it removed you from the picture, left only the lovers in their knotted sweetness. You were not there, and you thought you might as well be dead. You wept with self-pity. He went to the little attic apartment above the offices. He would find himself a new place. He would live. The years would pass. Sometimes he would ask himself whether he should have behaved differently that night, talked about it, tried to transcend it, but he had done the only thing he could.

Noreen's family were polite, even kind about it, one or the other calling him now and then, even inviting him round, though the only time he ever went was to pick up Clifford when he was visiting. The only comment on the breakup he ever heard was from John's wife Angela. It was a couple of years later that she phoned him. He couldn't imagine what she wanted when she turned up at his office for the appointment she'd made. He found himself studying her face, across the desk, observing the line of red at the edge of her eyelids, the pale, almost yellow iris, the nostrils wide as if with terror. She had come in the door in a smart green suit with a tight skirt, and her hair was shorter now, fluffed out to cover those strange long ears.

"I probably shouldn't have come to you," she said to him that afternoon, "but you know your way around, or so they tell me, and I've decided that I've got to do something. I'm driving myself crazy, and I need to be involved, do you understand what I mean, to find something real, a serious job. I married too young, I know that, but I can't go back and live it over. So I came to see you, Clyde, to ask for a little help. You're a worldly man. You always reminded me of someone, you know, but I can't ever think who it is. I once found myself thinking I knew you in some other life. I don't suppose you believe in reincarnation, I don't, not really, but there are times when I know things that I shouldn't, and it must come from somewhere. Do you ever feel that?"

"Sometimes I think people can read my mind," Clyde said. Had Angela read his mind at that moment, she would have known that he was speculating on whether she expected him to seduce her, whether, now that he wasn't with Noreen, she thought of him as an available man. It was possible. What she wanted, he thought, was reassurance, of any kind at all. Someone to pay attention to her, to make her life more exciting.

"I didn't tell John I was coming to see you. Poor John, I've worn him out with all my craziness. I told him I was going to look for a job. You think I'm just another hysterical woman, don't you? I can tell the way you're looking at me. Well, I can't help it."

"People get restless," he said. "I can understand that."

"Do you? You don't think I'm completely nuts?"

"No."

He met her eyes. He could take advantage of her need, and some cruel part of him wanted to. He was living alone, he wanted a woman, and she was probably available. What was the source of her desperation? Her husband was a decent enough man, from all Clyde knew. She had two children who did well in school. Perhaps it never made any sense to seek the cause of anything. A person was a fact, inexplicable.

"We don't have any jobs available here," he said.

"Nothing at all?"

"We have all the staff we need."

"I come cheap. I shouldn't say that, should I?"

"I have one idea for you."

"Tell me."

"I know someone who's working on a new recreation centre out in Gloucestor. I met him through the club where Clifford used to swim. I know he needs volunteers, and it's a good cause. I don't think that what you need from a job is money, not mainly that, and volunteer work often leads to real work, if you find it suits you."

She was disappointed.

"I should have known better," she said. "I don't know why I thought you'd help."

He took out a card and on the back of it wrote Marcel Rioux's name and phone number.

"Tell him that I recommended you call," he said.

"I suppose it's all I can expect, isn't it? I don't know why I even came to you."

"This is work that needs to be done," Clyde said. "It's worth a commitment." She wouldn't look at him now; she had come looking for danger and was getting a sermon, was that it?

"I just thought there might be something you needed."

"We've had the same staff for three years," he said.

"What you've got to have in this town is connections, and I don't."

He held out the card.

"I don't know quite what you want," he said. "But this is what I can offer."

She stared at him, her mouth a little open, the eyelids redder.

"I always wondered why Noreen left you," she said. "Now I know. It's because you're a cold fish." She took the card, turned her back and walked out. He had never seen her since. When Clyde asked Marcel Rioux, he said she hadn't phoned him.

8 | Jane

Outside it was a freezing February night, late, the streets empty. Clyde placed himself far enough back from the apartment door that he would be easily visible through the fisheye lens. He heard the chain unfastened, the deadbolt, and the door opened. Pyjamas. Bare white feet. He closed the door behind him. She met his eyes with her own, large, pale blue.

"Hello," he said.

"Hello Clyde."

In the bedroom, she unplugged the telephone.

"Were you expecting me to call?" he said.

"Made that clear enough, didn't I?"

"Tom might have been here with you."

"He doesn't come here very often."

Noreen, in their later years, between dancing, carpentry, hauling stones and earth had grown increasingly to be all lean muscle. Jane was tender flesh, pale and yielding. Feared almost that he might damage her, but when the morning light came upon them, she was in his arms, waking to command him again. Try to devour her, she was untouched.

Jane plugged in the phone to call her office and say she wouldn't be in. When she hung up, the instrument rang, but she unplugged it without answering. Mid-morning the door buzzer sounded, but she ignored it.

Nothing was only accident. He had come upon them last night in *Mamma Teresa's*, the pretty Jane Mattingly in a sweater delphinium blue like her eyes sitting with burly, rough-spoken Tom McKay, the two of them at a corner table, dimly lit, Clyde shivering a little, a refugee from the cold and snow, nodding to them as he passed by on his way to join friends. Later in the evening, less sober, they somehow all ended up at the same table, Tom hostile as always, while Jane turned her eyes quickly toward Clyde each time she laughed, as if they shared a joke, and though they had met only twice, once before with Tom McKay here in *Mamma Teresa's*, once last fall at a government reception, tonight they seemed intimately close, as if both had waited years for this, and as Clyde was leaving the restaurant he checked the phone book to see if he could find her number, stumbled back to his office, and later he phoned. Yes, she said.

Now pale breasts lay against his chest. He got out of bed, they wandered naked through the rooms, and she talked about the pictures on the walls, colourful flat abstracts she had bought for herself. If Clyde had seen them one at a time, he might have called them pointless and unappealing, but staring at a whole wall of them, the colours and shapes gave off rays of energy, a translation of all his bright desires.

It was a couple of months after that February night that they flew to Paris. Clyde had never before left North America. He and Noreen had taken holidays in New York, once in Vancouver, but the night flight over the Atlantic, the bodies curled under blankets for the short passage of darkness between the dinner service and arrival while the cry of jet engines resonated through the plane, was bizarre, fantastic. Jane had lived in France for a year, six months in Aix-en-Provence perfecting her grasp of the language – a preparation for the good civil service job she now held – and then a few months in Paris.

The plane landed in sunlight. Once through customs, Jane led him to the bus that would take them into the centre of Paris. She bought their tickets. During the night, curled up beside him in the narrow aircraft seat, she had become a stranger, strong and firm and in charge of the blundering middle-aged provincial at her side. They rode into the city, disembarked by a tall tower, and Jane summoned a taxi, gave instructions, checked them into the hotel, chatting fluently to the tall slender woman with grey hair, the *patronne*, and up they went in a tiny, open elevator that rose inside an openwork metal frame, and once in the small room under the gables with a view of rooftops, she led him, blunted and dazed, to the bed. And then they were sitting at a round table in a café which looked exactly, ridiculously, like a Parisian café. From where they sat they could observe the busy square in front of the huge baroque church.

"I used to come here with Nick," she said, "and we'd fight."

"Who was Nick?"

"My American boyfriend, who had all this wonderful charm, but then you'd start to notice that he wasn't just cruel by accident. It was a game. He'd try to make me cry, and I'd try not to, but I would. Then we'd make love and it would all start again. I suppose it was exciting, in a way."

She didn't talk like this in Canada, or perhaps he was suffering from amnesia, no idea who she was. She was tearing pieces from her croissant dipping them in her coffee then putting them to her lips, sucked the coffee out of them, swallowed them down. An old woman was limping by with a large fabric bag with handles, a baguette sticking out of it. The small cars drove aggressively past on the narrow thoroughfare.

Clyde read the printed slip the waiter had left on the table. He didn't know much French, but he knew arithmetic. He passed money to the waiter, who dropped coins on the table with an efficiency that only looked insouciant.

Jane led him down narrow streets to the *rue Bonaparte* and toward the river, the chestnuts and plane trees in leaf, the old stone walls and the upstream island perfectly beautiful in the sunlight. Intoxicated after a sleepless night, Clyde focussed his mind on the street signs, names familiar from his desultory reading of history. This was the old world, and the brightness of the sun on the golden stone was at this moment happening only for his pleasure. He stopped Jane, who was leading them along a gravel path under trees, pulled her toward him and kissed her.

"Paris is famous for kissing," he said.

"And I am famous for being kissed."

They walked until they were exhausted, made their way back to the hotel for a nap, Jane falling instantly asleep. Clyde looked at her, astonished. This young pale stranger lay naked on the bed they shared, canted to one side, her face relaxed, empty, her breast crushed against the sheets.

"You are famous for being kissed," he said and put his lips to her shoulder.

They woke to the sound of church bells, voices from the open window, ate dinner in a small crowded restaurant, where the owner, who greeted them at the door and took them to their places, appeared to know at least half the customers.

The next day, passing a small shop that sold antique jewellery, they studied a long necklace of round amber beads.

"Let's go in and get it," he said.

"Oh," she said, "are you going to buy me things?"

"Men buy things for their beautiful young lovers."

The clerk who came to serve them wore a dark suit, white shirt, neatly knotted necktie. Clyde didn't speak, just indicated the amber necklace, and the man, knowing his role, took it out of the window and displayed it to Clyde on the palm of his hand, then turning gave it to Jane to examine. She held it up, turned it toward the light. Each of them was playing a role, and each of them was playing it perfectly.

Clyde reached for his wallet. The man asked Jane a question, as if he knew that she would speak perfect French, and she answered. He took the necklace to the counter and wrapped it, wrote out a bill, the pen moving slowly, deliberately, with a dignity suited to the moment. Back in the narrow street, the sun was reflected in the water that washed down the gutter at the edge of the cobbles. Ahead of them a women in a maroon skirt and black jacket stood and watched as her little dog bent his back and shit on the pavement.

That night in their room, after dinner and a bottle of red wine, Jane unwrapped the necklace and draped it over naked breasts and belly, the amber beads sliding across white skin like liquid gold. He watched as the supple young body offered itself, as if preparing to submit to some darkly criminal desire. His brain shaped the body's portrait, the hollow at the collarbone, the cage of ribs, the hinged framework of the pelvis.

In the night, wakeful, he listened for the noises of the city. He wondered when the metro shut down, imagined an underground city, another life, a maze of tunnels where dreams waited to invade.

Jane took Clyde to the art galleries, the Louvre, the Jeu de Paumes, and he tried to love the pictures she cared about. She was well-informed and articulate. In a café, Clyde observed the two of them in the mirror, a moderately well-preserved man of middle age and his pretty young lover. He saw another couple come in, the same arrangement, old and young, but the man was short, with a round head like a bowling ball, a fringe of hair, heavy red lips, rough complexion. The girl was at least six inches taller, very thin, with dark eyes, fine bones, and when they sat down nearby, she was quick to light a cigarette. The faces weren't quite like any that would be seen in the cities Clyde knew. This was a city with exotic faces, foreign habits, a strange timetable to each day.

Old men with great noses like the one you saw in pictures of de Gaulle. Looking in the mirror he caught the reflection of a man leaving the bar, an archetypal figure, clean shaven, precise features, wire-rimmed glasses, a beret. They were near the Sorbonne, he was a professor perhaps. Suddenly he laughed out loud as he realized that he must buy Clifford a beret like that. He wasn't sure that the boy would ever wear it, but he might.

"What are you laughing at?"

"I decided to buy Clifford a beret."

"Will he like that?"

"He might."

"But you'll like giving it to him."

"Yes."

The next day he was to pick up a rented car in the northern suburbs and drive to Dieppe. Jane suggested that she travel with him, but he told her he'd prefer to go alone. It was something he must do by himself, he said, though as he thought about it, he decided that if Noreen had been with him in Paris, he might have been willing to have her accompany him to the beach where his father had lost his life. They'd been together so many years. Jane announced that she would shop for clothes while he was gone.

Clyde had to drive with great concentration to manoeuvre the small car through the fast traffic on the way out of Paris. A man at the car rental agency who spoke good English had given him instructions, drawn a little map, and after a few miles, it was straightforward highway driving, northwest to Rouen, and then on a more northerly bearing to Dieppe. For two hours he drove past the farmland criss-crossed by hedges and trees, cattle at pasture, stone outbuildings with orange tile roofs, an apple orchard just come into leaf. When he reached Dieppe, he followed the signs to the centre of town, found himself driving along the *rue du 19 août 1942*, which carried him to a wide ramp leading down to one of the beaches where the Canadian soldiers had struggled away from the landing craft, half drowned by their heavy equipment. Depleted after a sleepless night, a bit light-headed, Clyde plodded across the round sea-washed stones of the beach, the stones the British military planners had forgotten or ignored and which ripped the treads off the Canadian tanks as they tried to make their way ashore. In each direction there was a headland, sources of a lethal crossfire. The tide was out, and the rocks on the channel side of the beach were wet. The beach plunged down a steep slope into the little waves. The sun glittered on the water. Further along the shore the tall cliffs gleamed white, a line of bright spring grass at the top. He could see small boats toward the horizon, fishing craft perhaps. A ferry ran from England into the harbour which had always been the centre of the town's economy. He stared down at the rounded stones.

He was here.

There ought to be a form of words. Some religions had a prayer for your dead father. Himself, he had no prayers. He bent and picked up a stone, held the rounded shape in his hand, a rock on which his father's blood might have poured. It felt cold against his palm. He couldn't know where on this beach the young Sergeant Clifford Bryanton had died. All his life long he had met silence when he searched for the man. A strong young body dressed in khaki, a rifle in his hand, sodden from the struggle through the salt water, shaking with fear, anticipation, hearing the noise of failing tanks grinding uselessly into the incline of the steep beach. His father had once been in this place and had died here. Clyde could not find him. He looked out at the sunlight glittering on the little waves. Blinded, helpless, he could focus on nothing. Everything was vanishing. It was an emptiness he could never have imagined, and he heard a voice, but it was a woman's voice, and it was far off and going farther off. Someone was falling.

Clyde was aware of footsteps on the stones. A dark shape bent over him. An old man was studying him, speaking softly.

"*Monsieur,*" he was saying, and then French words that Clyde couldn't quite make out. Clyde realized that he must have fainted, that he had fallen on the stones of the beach. He started to get himself up, searched for words.

"*Va bien,*" he said.

Once again the man was speaking to him in careful sentences, but Clyde could understand little of it. The man was concerned, wishing to help, but they were deaf to each other.

"*Mon père,*" Clyde said and his hand indicated the slope of the stone beach.

"*Vous êtes canadien?*" The man said and Clyde nodded. The man indicated a café not far from the beach, and the two of them walked awkwardly over the stones toward it. *Va bien*, he had said to the man. It goes well. Did it?

The man who had found him on the beach, who had a dry elegant face, spoke to the *patron* as they entered the cafe, and the *patron* turned to Clyde.

"You are better now?" he said in accented English.

"Yes," Clyde said. "I think I'm fine."

"Your father was one of the Canadians."

"Yes."

" *Mort?*" he said as if that could only be asked in French.

He and the old man – Maître Plamondon, a retired notary it appeared after the awkward introductions in two languages – sat at one of the tables and Clyde had a coffee and a sandwich of *saucisson* and fresh butter. Clyde realized that he hadn't eaten yet; when he saw his face in the cafe mirror he was very pale. Perhaps hunger was part of the reason he had fainted. When he was done he took out money to pay, but Maître Plamondon took the bill from the table and held up his hand to indicate Clyde should put his money away.

It was a simple thing, kindness. It was the one defence against the emptiness that was all around them.

Through the proprietor Clyde explained that someone was waiting for him in Paris, thanked the two men, and started back toward the place he'd left the car. But first he turned and walked back down to the beach, picked up one small stone. He would take it to Clifford, who might value it. Clyde glanced once more across the sun-struck landscape where the events had occurred, nearly fifty years ago, August 19, 1942, and prepared himself for the drive back. A few miles along the road, he pulled over, turned off the car and sat still for a long while, staring across a pasture field. It was dark when he arrived back in Paris, and he got lost as he tried to return the car, drove in circles until he saw a familiar intersection, then had difficulty finding the taxi rank that the car rental agent had told him about, and when he found it, waited a long time for a cab to show up and paid the substantial amount to get himself to central Paris and the hotel.

The room was dark as he entered, and for a moment he believed he was in the wrong room, that there was a stranger in the bed.

"Clyde?"

"I'm back."

"Did you have your great experience?" she said.

"No," he said, "but I went there."

The next morning, after she showered, she came into the room wrapped in a towel and tried on her new clothes for him. As he lay there watching her exhibiting the clothes, he thought he might write a letter to Maître Plamondon, though he wasn't sure what he would say, only he felt that addressing himself to that man he might find the words he'd never before been able to articulate.

They spent most of the day walking by the river, holding hands, exploring the Île St Louis, sitting under a plane tree and watching coal barges and the long tourist boats going by. At night they went to a jazz club in a basement a few blocks from the hotel, where a rather studious French guitarist played long intense phrases, was joined by a black clarinetist, and the two of them exchanged licks. Jane and Clyde listened attentively, drank the expensive whisky that was brought to them, and when they left the club made a wrong turn somehow, and found themselves in a maze of narrow streets, going nowhere. Finally they came on the river, picked out the towers of Notre Dame against the dark sky and found their way back to the square in front of Saint Sulpice where two young women were dancing in the space between the church and the fountain, following some imaginary music.

"We could dance too," Jane said.

"In bed. We can dance in bed."

They did, and then drank glasses of the wine they kept in their room. Clyde was a little hungover in the morning, but the indefatigable Jane led him to the Hôtel de Cluny. He knew little about the Middle Ages, and the dim ancient building, stairs upward to rooms full of sculptures and tapestry, downward to the remains of the Roman baths, was full of strangeness, exaggerated by the state of his poisoned brain.

Then it was their last night in Paris. He had packed up his suitcase, the presents in a straw bag he'd bought at a market and would carry on his shoulder, a bottle of Calvados for Perry, two silk scarves for his mother, the beret for Clifford, a couple of shirts for himself. They had eaten at a restaurant nearby which they'd grown to like. In the past few days the neighbourhood where they were staying had grown familiar, a temporary home.

Clyde set the alarm before they climbed into bed and turned to each other. Sometime in the night, he woke, and Jane wasn't there. He spoke, and there was no answer. When he turned on the light, climbed from bed, her suitcase was where she had left it, a couple of shopping bags there as well, but her clothes, set out for morning, were gone. Clyde stood naked, helpless, looked out the small window across the slopes and angles of the rooftops. What if she never came back? Maybe she had met up with Nick, her lover, found that she was addicted to his cruelty and returned to him. Clyde knew nothing about her really. He went into the bathroom, looked at himself in the small mirror. Portrait of an Unknown Man.

As he was about to turn out the light and get back in bed, he heard the sound of the elevator, and a few moments later a key in the lock. Her face, tired, without makeup, was blank and bare.

"What happened?" he said.

"I woke up, and I wanted to see the city in the middle of the night, so I went out and sat in the square for a while, listened to the fountain."

"One last look."

"I guess so."

She spoke quietly, from far away, her eyes cast down, thoughtful. The next morning they flew home.

It was a few days later that Clyde met up with his son. Clifford was still living at Noreen's old stone house in the country but had driven into Ottawa to visit friends. They were sitting in a delicatessen and Clyde pulled the beret out of his briefcase and passed it over.

"Souvenir of Paris," he said.

Clifford gave him a look.

"They wear them," Clyde said. "I saw it with my own eyes. I swear."

Humouring him, Clifford pulled on the hat.

"Makes you look like a different man," Clyde said. Clifford was taking off the beret. Clyde reached into his pocket and took out the stone.

"I went to Dieppe," he said. "I picked this up on the beach."

When Clyde passed the stone across the table Clifford took it in his hand, looked down at it as if trying to solve all the mysteries in the stone. He reached out to pass it back to Clyde.

"It's for you," Clyde said.

"You sure you don't want to keep it."

"I picked it up for you."

Clifford put the stone on the table in front of him.

"I wonder about him," Clifford said.

"So do I."

"You can't remember anything."

"Not a thing. I imagine things, but no, no memories."

Clifford drank from the glass of Coke in front of him.

"So when's the golf course open for the summer?" he said.

"Not long. Have you sent in your university applications yet?"

"No."

"Isn't it time?"

"I'm not sure I want to go."

Clyde took up the cup of coffee, something to do before he answered. He told himself not to get angry. He kept his voice down.

"What's the problem?"

"I've been in school all my life."

"You're young. That's what you do when you're young."

"I don't have to keep on doing it. You didn't."

He looked over at the boy. A couple of red blotches of acne on his face. He looked so young and undefended.

"My mother didn't have a cent to give me. I could probably have done it, working, but in those days you could still get along without. Am I supposed to say I regretted it all my life? No I didn't, not really, but why not go, when I have enough money to help you out?"

"You haven't spent it all on your new girlfriend."

What did you say to that? Nothing.

"Let me tell you what I think," Clyde said. "My generation was about the last one that could get away without a university education. Now it's expected. If you ask me whether all of those kids are getting their money's worth, if what they learn makes all that much difference to what they become, I'd have to say No. But it's expected now for any kind of a decent job that you'll have a degree. Maybe if you're smart enough and tough enough you can make a living without, but why make it hard for yourself? And I haven't spent so much on my new girlfriend that I can't pay your fees and whatever else is necessary."

"Are you rich?" Clifford said. "I've never known."

"Are we rich this week? That's what Noreen used to say. Money comes and goes. I know more or less what I have today. I never count on tomorrow. Anything can happen. Tell you what, the day after you graduate from university, I'll go through my records and tell you how much money I have."

"You really think that offer's going to change my mind."

"Don't be a humourless little snot, Clifford. I just want to reassure you that you'll be warned if I throw away your inheritance getting shagged."

Clifford was silent, taken aback. Clyde had the sense that they were teetering on the edge of something bad.

"I thought you liked school," he said, hoping to make peace.

"Mostly."

"You just want to do something foolhardy for a change."

"Yeah, probably."

"Too bad you quit swimming. I figure you thrashed out half the problems of puberty pounding away at the pool."

"I wasn't good enough to get anywhere."

"Not many of us are."

"You're a pretty good golfer."

"So what's pretty good? You're pretty good at school."

"I'd like to be better than pretty good at something."

"Maybe you will be."

As he looked across the table at his son, the shadow of a beard on his face, the skin still breaking out, he had a glimpse of the longing that was within him, and he regretted how much there was that could never be told to another human being, not even to one who was your own blood. You couldn't say how it had been for you, the danger and shame, the small triumphs.

"Take a year off if you want. Go work in the Arctic or something. There's lots of time."

Clifford picked up the stone that lay on the table on front of him, held it in his hand as if to learn something from it.

"How old was he?" he said.

"Twenty-five."

"I'm eighteen."

"He didn't get much time, did he?"

Clifford stood up from the table, put the stone in his pocket, picked up the beret and gave it an odd look.

"Well, thanks for the hat," he said.

He walked to the door of the delicatessen, broad-shoulders, lean hips, a swimmer's body. He was going off to meet Melanie, his new girlfriend. In the event it was the fact Melanie was committed to going on with her education rather than anything Clyde had said that convinced Clifford to enroll in the University of Toronto. By Christmas he'd begun to find it challenging, showed no signs of regret. He was even swimming again, as an alternate on a university team.

It was a day when Clyde had just returned, slightly dismayed, from being lectured by his dental hygienist, a lecture complete with disgusting photographs of diseased gums, instructions on how and when to floss and the present of a new toothbrush – the whole thing a distasteful sort of welcome to the wonders of aging – that he got a note saying Perry wanted to talk to him. Perry and Yvette had finally married, and she was heavily pregnant, and Clyde anticipated probing questions on how to be a father; but Perry, who was sitting in his antique Quebec rocker in one of the fine wool sweaters he'd been wearing recently, this one pale blue, started another rabbit altogether.

"I think we should expand, old pal," he said, as soon as Clyde had taken a seat in an uncomfortable wooden armchair.

"Why?"

"It's time."

"The gods have spoken, is that it?"

"Who was it said we could make a go of it up here in the National Capital?"

"The young Perry Devoe, I believe it was."

"Well then."

"How are we to go about this expansion?"

"I thought you'd never ask. You've got offices in the building next door, right, space available if we need it."

"Not right now, but they come empty now and then."

"You could raise the rents and hurry things along."

"I could end up with an empty building."

"People always need office space."

"Every time a government department moves on, they leave behind three or four floors of offices. That's happening too often. Soon the rents won't hold up anywhere. I'm lucky to have the place full."

"Clyde, you're a worrier."

"No. I'm careful. I gave away a lot of money in the divorce settlement. I don't want to waste what I've still got."

"That must hurt, giving it away."

"Noreen wasn't unreasonable. Her lawyer was, but we worked it out. But don't tell me how to manage property rentals."

"What I'm telling you is how to make money. You don't mind that do you?"

"Tell me more."

"There's lots of bright young things out there, the universities are turning them out in mobs, and they're ambitious."

"Smarter than middle-aged jerks like you and me."

"Speak for yourself."

"I just saw my dental hygienist. I feel ancient."

"They never used to have dental hygienists."

"And everybody had false teeth."

"I have bad dreams about teeth. I wish you'd never brought it up."

"Go back to telling me about these bright young graduates."

"Energy. That's what they've got. Harness that, you can light up the planet."

"And you know how to harness it."

"What we do is organize the place on a more individual basis. We have a name, a location, terrific service staff with techno-smarts, we're state of the art in everything, and if we aren't we will be tomorrow. So you bring in a brilliant kid, give her an office, key to the washroom, introduce her to the receptionist and tell her to go out and find work. She can bill by the hour like lawyers. We provide the setting for the jewel, and we are suitably rewarded."

"It sounds a bit like Amway."

"C'mon."

"A pyramid scheme, with us on top."

"You want to make money or not? We are on top. And we're here to consult. We'll help them price the job. Show us your draft, show us the figures, we've been around the block, we can help."

"How many of these brilliant kids are we bringing in?"

"Ten maybe."

"You want ten more offices?"

"What's that, one floor of the building?"

"Who pays the rent?"

"It comes off the top of what they invoice."

"Perry, sometimes you make me tired."

"Why would that be?"

"Crazy ideas make me tired."

"It's a new world out there, Clyde. We've got to keep up with it. The other advantage of this is we get people creating connections with all the political parties. We have somebody working for every department, even some foreign governments. An election comes along, the government changes, we're still in the picture."

"And I bet you've already got a list of people you want to hire."

"One or two. There's a kid who's been working as a parliamentary intern. Father's a diplomat. She speaks French, English and German. She's been going out with some guy from the West German embassy."

"Do you by any chance have a personal interest in this young person?"

"Clyde you're the one who eats cuties for breakfast. I'm a happily married man about to be a father. I just want to make a lot of money."

"Buy a house in Toronto," Clyde said. "The real estate market is going crazy."

"Yeah I read. Buy and flip. The motto for the Eighties. You figure it's going to last?"

"For a while maybe."

Perry rocked back and forth a few times. Clyde looked at him as he sat there in the elegant pale blue sweater, dark blue slacks. His hair was thinning a little.

"So can you find us some offices, Clyde?"

"Let me think about all this. I've got one double office where the people who rent it complain about everything. They say there are mice in there. There are no mice in there. I could probably buy out the lease and be better off without them. They're threatening not to pay their rent anyway."

"Can I call Janine? Tell her to volunteer for the German army… I'm sorry that wasn't a good joke."

"What do you mean?"

"I forget about your father."

"So do I most of the time. Let me think over the weekend."

It was Friday afternoon, and as usual Clyde and Jane would meet up in a bar somewhere, drink for a while then go back to her apartment. Or sometimes his. The next day they'd go to the market or hiking out in Gatineau Park. Sometimes they saw each other during the week, but they both worked long hours, so the weekend was their time together. Sitting in a little café on Saturday afternoon, Clyde was talking about Perry's new proposal.

"I told him," he said, "he might make more money speculating in Toronto real estate."

Jane was looking at him, her eyes wide and bright.

"Should we do that?" she said.

"It's a possibility."

The next week Clyde bought out the lease of the querulous tenants, and Perry brought in their first new consultants. A couple of weekends later he and Jane went to Toronto to look at houses.

"What do you think?" she said, as they ate dinner that night.

"I would guess that there's still some life in this real estate boom.

Hard to say how much, but if you don't get too greedy, you could probably make a few dollars. All the other prices – carpenters, plumbers, what-have-you – will be going up at the same time because everyone's buying and renovating. I think you could still make a few bucks."

"Am I the one who's investing?"

"Isn't that what you had in mind?"

"I don't have any money, Clyde."

"What else is a sugardaddy for?"

She didn't want to joke. "Tell me exactly what you're thinking."

"You want to buy a house, I'll front the down payment. You make money, you can pay me when you sell it. If you don't make money, we'll see about it."

"Isn't it dangerous, going into business with your lover?"

"We're not going into business. I'm giving you something."

"And what do I give in return."

"You enjoy yourself making some money. Next time you can do it on your own."

She stared down at the food.

"It doesn't seem very grownup, Clyde, but if I admit the truth, it's probably what I wanted, for you to let me have the money. Maybe I thought we'd do it together, but I don't have any cash, so I don't know how I thought we'd do that."

Clyde waited, ate his dinner.

"Do you suppose it makes me some kind of a whore? To take your money?"

"It's not a word that had ever occurred to me."

They ate without speaking. Clyde finished his food.

"So I'm a whore," she said. "I take money from my lover. I want that house."

"Which one?" he said, though he was pretty sure of the answer

"You know," she said. "The one out near the Danforth."

That night, back in the hotel room, as they undressed for bed, she stood in front of a mirror and looked at herself.

"The pale smooth body of a young harlot," she said.

"We don't get to die pure," he said. "None of us."

"Clyde," she said as she walked toward him, "sometimes you know just the right thing to say."

When the sale closed she travelled to Toronto alone, signed, handed over a certified cheque, met with the contractor and planned the renovations. Jane had a lot of imaginative ideas, and some of them she could afford. While she was there, she bought a futon and had it delivered, and as the renovation proceeded, they would travel down once a month or so, sleep in the house, check on progress. It was costing her a lot to carry the mortgage payments, the amount of the mortgage including most of the cost of the work being done on the house, and now and then she looked frightened about the whole thing.

It was a few months later, about the time the house was almost finished, ready to go back on the market, that Clyde got a message to call a man at the office of the Secretary of State. Where Jane worked. What was that all about? She'd said nothing to prepare him for it. Clyde called, and the man, a fairly senior officer, suggested he come in and talk to him about a new project, and they made an appointment for later that day. Clyde tried to call Jane to find out what this might be about, but he couldn't get hold of her; the receptionist said she was in Montreal for a meeting.

So Clyde attempted to prepare himself for the unknown and set off to the offices of the ministry. Mark Lejeune, the officer he was to meet, was a tall man, more or less completely bald, though he was obviously younger than Clyde. He had a broad smile and an easy manner, acted as if this interview was something both of them had anticipated for a long time.

"Heard good things about you and about DB," he said.

Clyde smiled and nodded and didn't ask where he'd heard these good things.

"You people work in both languages."

"Yes, of course. I could have brought one of our Quebec people if you'd asked."

"No, we'll just have a little informal chat. If this project goes ahead it would come to a committee of our people."

Clyde smiled, didn't ask questions, and after a little more chatter, Mark Lejeune began to explain. Heritage projects were currently divided among a number of ministries, and there had been suggestions that as many as possible should be linked, perhaps brought together in a single ministry. They were looking for research and analysis on how this might be done.

"Everyone wants to protect their own backyard, Clyde. You know what it's like. That's why we need to go outside for this. We need objectivity."

Clyde took out a notebook and began to put down a summary of what Lejeune told him. It would be a substantial piece of work, would perhaps offer a chance to break in some of the new people that Perry wanted to hire, although it would need a gentle touch to start asking questions that might lead to old territory being lost, new territory being won.

It emerged that Mark Lejeune wanted a proposal within a week, that the department's budget allocations were about to be made, and if he was to find the money for this research, he'd have to do it soon or wait for at least a year.

Clyde promised the proposal, and they talked about dates for the work.

"How many proposals are you asking for?" he said.

"If yours is good enough, we'll take it to the committee. Give me a good long list of what you've done for other departments to cover the question of competence. You guys are good, we know that. If we start looking for competing proposals, we'll miss the budget deadline."

Clyde wondered, couldn't help it, how much Jane had to do with this exceptional confidence. Clyde opened his briefcase, packed away his notes and shook hands with the man who was still smiling broadly

Clyde was alone in the elevator when it reached the ground floor, and when he walked out he found himself facing Tom McKay. The wide face, bright pink skin darkening toward a flaming red made him look drunk, though from what Clyde had seen he looked that way at any hour of the day or night. Maybe he was always a little drunk. The hard eyes were watching Clyde, making connections.

"Piss-Elegant," he said, "what are you doing here? She bring you in for a quickie on top of the desk?"

Clyde said nothing.

"No," the man said, "you're hustling work. Your new squeeze lining up jobs for you. Pick the pockets of the government instead of making an honest living."

Clyde began to move away. He knew if he opened his mouth, he'd say the wrong thing. Just keep walking.

"Nothing to say? I'll find out what you were here for," the man said. "And I'll have your nuts, sooner or later. You can count on it."

A heavy woman in a maroon suit was standing at the far side of the lobby overhearing these words, not even pretending not to listen, fascinated. Clyde walked past her, out the door, flagged a cab to drive him back to the office. He called Jane's apartment and asked her to call him when she got back, even if it was late. He was in bed, on the edge of sleep when the call came.

"Of course I recommended you to Mark Lejeune, Clyde. It's something I can do to make up for the money I took from you. Makes me feel less like a high class trick."

"I'm grateful, Janey. It was a nice idea."

"You don't sound grateful. You don't want me to pay you back."

"You'll pay me back when you sell the house."

"And I'll get you jobs if I feel like it."

"You don't think you might get accused of conflict-of-interest?"

"I told Mark I knew you. I arranged to be out of town when he talked to you. I knew he'd be impressed. You've got a hell of a record. When it comes to the committee, I'll just keep my mouth shut."

"Did you tell him you sleep with me?"

"Who I fuck is my own business."

"Did you tell him you owe me money?"

"You're the one who said nobody's pure, Clyde. Why are you giving me all this grief?"

He explained that he'd met Tom McKay on his way out of the building.

"He figured out why I was there, said so."

There was a long silence on the phone.

"God damn journalists," she said finally.

"He's bitter, Janey. You dumped him. He holds a grudge."

"Let him. He was no damn good anyway. I'll talk to Mark and call you tomorrow night." She hung up. When she called the next night, she told him the invitation to bid on the job had been withdrawn.

"Men," she said. "Pissing to mark their territory. And I get pissed on too."

"It was a good try."

"It didn't work. That's all that matters. I figured out a way to make you some money, so I don't feel like a gold-digger, and some guy I went to bed with a couple of times puts his big red nose into it. I can see why all those feminists become nuns or lesbians."

Two days later Tom McKay published a column about the heritage project in the Secretary of State's office. He knew a great deal about it, and his suggestion that other ministries would see it as a raid on their territory was a prophecy that was almost sure to come true once he'd made it. Nothing was said about his confrontation with Clyde, but the way he discussed the plan to use outside consultants, there was a clear implication that the whole project was less than above board.

Clyde spent the weekend with Jane, but it wasn't one of their more pleasant ones. Apart from Tom McKay's interference in her plan, she was annoyed that she was kept poor carrying the mortgage payments on the house.

"I hate it," she said, "having to think twice before I spend money. I saw a painting I wanted, and I can't have it."

"You could put the house on the market. Or rent it."

"Did you really used to spend your whole life like this?"

"Usually I had a lot more than one house to worry about."

"And that's how you became a rich sugar daddy."

She was sitting up in bed, the sunlight from the apartment window catching the tops of her plump little breasts, the undercurve shaded.

"What I have I made developing property."

"And now it's all in the bank."

"It's here and there." Another of the offices in his building was coming empty the next week. Perry had a bright young man all prepared to move in, an economist who'd just finished a *stage* at a conservative think-tank. Clyde never trusted economists. He didn't think they knew anything about money.

Jane decided to rent out the house for a year, and she discovered that the brother of one of her colleagues was looking for accommodation in Toronto for himself and his wife while he held some kind of fellowship at the university. Prices were still rising, and at the end of a year, she would put the house on the market. On the weekend when she went to Toronto to meet her new tenants and arrange a lease, Clyde left her at the hotel and drove another hour or so to pay a visit to his mother. He parked his car in the driveway, went round to the back, tapped on the door and walked in. She was standing at the edge of the breakfast nook talking on the phone, and when she turned toward him, he was shocked to see a large bandage over her nose. She put a hand over it, made a face and finished her conversation.

"What happened?" he said.

"I fell and cut my nose on the edge of one of the electric heaters. They had to put in stitches."

Clyde went and put his arm around her. She felt small, old, easily broken.

"How did you fall?"

"I don't know. It was strange. Just as if someone pushed me. I was standing there and suddenly I went over. The doctor said it might have been some kind of a little stroke. He had a phrase for it."

"Transient Ischemic Attack."

"That's it. How do you know these things, Clyde?"

"I read the newspapers."

"All those medical columns."

"Among other things."

"Where's Jane?"

"Toronto. Renting out her house."

"I suppose you gave her the money for that house."

"I lent her the down payment."

It wouldn't have been true to say his mother didn't like Jane. When she was with her, they got along, but it was clear she disapproved of her, too young, too pretty, something like that. Probably it would have been truer to say she disapproved of Clyde keeping company with such an attractive younger woman. That it was a little vulgar, ordinary, a coarse way to behave and unlikely to end well. Perhaps his interpretation was all wrong. His mother was a complicated and secretive woman.

"Tea?" she said. "Or do you want a drink?"

"Tea," he said. "Shall we go out for dinner?"

"When are you going back?"

"After dinner."

"Don't trust her on her own in the big city."

"That's right."

She was filling the kettle from the kitchen tap.

"When I was in France last year," he said, "I went to Dieppe."

He hadn't mentioned it until now.

"Did you find him?"

"I fainted. There on the beach. I hadn't eaten all day, that was probably the reason. A man came by, a retired lawyer, took me to a café."

She plugged in the kettle and turned and looked at him.

"I suppose I could have remarried," she said, "and given you a father, some decent man, but I didn't want to, though I couldn't tell you why. None of it is very clear now. I thought as I got older I'd understand more, but I don't. I don't seem to remember much about Cliff, little things, packing his lunch in the morning before he left for work. How he whistled when he was sitting on the back steps in the evening. I don't even remember if I loved him. I know I wanted to get married. I thought he was good-looking, and I guess I thought there would be a whole lifetime to learn about loving him."

"I'm glad I went there," he said. "I picked up a stone from the beach and brought it back for Clifford."

"He told me when they came to visit last summer. Do you think he'll stay with that girl?"

"Beyond me to guess. I imagine she has her own ideas."

"Plans to go to graduate school she told me."

"These modern girls."

"If I was doing it over I'd be a lawyer, not a lawyer's office girl."

"People used to say you knew more law than Palmer anyway."

"But I didn't get the pay for it."

"How is he?"

"Mind's going, I hear. It's a good thing we closed the office."

"How are you for money?"

"I'm just fine, Clyde. You don't have to provide financial support for everybody in the world."

"You're sure you're OK."

"You gave me that bond, and there's pension money. I'm just fine."

"Good."

His mother got up and made the tea. Later on they would walk up the main street to the Brockton Hotel, much improved from his days in town, and have their dinner. Then he would drive back to Toronto where Jane would be waiting for him in the hotel room. Or so he assumed, though always a suspicion lurked that she would have vanished as she had that night in Paris, and that this time she would not return.

Her Toronto tenants proved to be demanding, but they were responsible, and when their lease was done, the house was in good shape, and Jane put it on the market, at a price Clyde would have guessed was too high, but she sold it, quickly, and realized a substantial profit.

It was on a Friday night, the two of them lying a little breathless after making love, when she turned on the light, reached out and took a piece of paper from the table beside the bed. She handed it to Clyde.

"That was quite satisfactory," she said. "You do a lady very nicely. Here's the payment for your services."

It was a cheque for the amount that he had given her. Clyde had been wondering what to do about the interest on the money. What he had offered her was, in effect, a second mortgage, but he had never thought to exact that kind of rate. Still he had assumed that she was grownup enough to realize that he was significantly out of pocket, and if she wanted to be proud and independent after making her pile, she ought to offer at least bank interest or the rate of inflation, not low in recent years. Whether he accepted or not. He could certainly afford to do without the income, and had the investment gone sour, he was prepared to share the loss, but as he looked at the pretty, smiling face, how pleased with herself she looked, he wondered if years from now she would figure out she had taken money from her fancy-man without even noticing it.

"What shall I do with all that nice money I made?" she was saying. "Shall I buy another house?"

"You really want my advice?"

"Of course. What's an old man for if you can't get a little wisdom out of him?"

"If you're going to buy another house, buy it here in Ottawa where you're close by. You were lucky with this one, but at a distance too much can go wrong."

"You're being serious."

"Money is a serious matter."

"No it isn't. It's just a game."

Clyde chose to say nothing. She was after all very young and very pretty, and she was naked, and he was in her bed.

"Maybe I should just spend it on beautiful things."

"Why not?" he said. "It's all yours."

9 | Danny

Clyde hadn't expected to meet Danny in that kind of a bar. It was a watering hole for the suits as they were called now, the civil servants, lobbyists, businessmen who believed that they ran the affairs of the country, and perhaps did. Clyde had been walking back to the office after a meeting in the East Block – he went on foot more often these days, to get a little exercise – when he followed an impulse as he was passing the bar and strolled in. At this hour Jane would be panting and sweating through her workout at the gym. She'd suggested that he take it up, but the lifting and heaving and striding didn't appeal to him. He was largely fatalistic about aging, and travelling by shank's mare was his gesture toward staying in shape, that and regular golf in the good weather. The week before Clyde had taken a look at a cabin for sale out on one of the lakes. Yesterday he had decided to buy it, someplace to go on his own, away from the office, his apartment. Maybe he'd do some swimming in the summer.

Clyde had noticed Danny on the far side of the room sitting across from a plump smiling man with darkly tanned skin that gleamed as if he had rubbed it with olive oil. When he laughed he revealed tiny, very white teeth. Clyde ordered a Corona. The bright sunlight and the feeling of spring in the air made it seem like a good idea.

Danny saw him and waved. As Clyde was lifting the glass to his lips, Danny stood up, came toward him. The limp was growing more pronounced as Danny got older. It must be a strain on the hip joints the way he walked. Perhaps someday he'd be crippled. He looked as if he might be losing weight.

"How's it going, Clyde?"

"Fine, Danny. You?"

"Not bad at all. You still with that blonde girl?"

"That's right."

"So, where is she?"

"At the gym working out."

"Wants to keep her tight little butt."

"Yup."

"Marion wants to talk to you. Elaine and the girls visit all the time, but she's always at me about when Clyde's going to arrive. One of these days, I tell her. But when I saw you now, I said to myself, Well, God sent Clyde here just at the right time, you better speak to him."

"Tell her I'll come around soon."

"I already told her that."

"Say whatever you want."

"I'll say I saw you and you promised."

"Okay."

"You don't stop in at my little house either."

"I keep busy."

"Always welcome. If Hazel ever comes up here, you bring her round. I'd even cook dinner for the two of you. Just about my oldest friends, aren't you?"

"I guess that's so."

"I better get back to my date. You're looking pretty good, Clydie, but we're not kids any more are we?"

"Next thing you know, Danny, you'll be getting the pension."

"I don't know that I need it. Marion's going to look after me."

Danny limped back to the booth by the wall. As Clyde watched, a voice was speaking to him: there are no rules, it said. You couldn't predict how things would turn out. Clyde drank down his beer and hiked back to the office.

A couple of days later, when he left work, he walked across to Elgin and south under the highway to the little brick house where Marion had settled. He wasn't sure whether he'd find Danny there at this hour of the evening. When he knocked the door was answered by a tall, plain girl. He guessed she was one of the grand-daughters, introduced himself.

"Oh hi, I'm Cecily Haverman. Grandmother will be glad to see you, Mr Bryanton. She asks about you."

Clyde entered the house as Cecily went off to fetch her grandmother. He recognized furniture from the house she had shared with the Senator. Marion had kept more than she needed, and the front room was crowded, two Victorian upholstered chairs, each with a table beside it, a long serving table in front of the window, and two straight chairs tucked against the wall. Jammed in together like this, the furniture looked as if it was waiting for an auctioneer to dispose of it.

"I brought too much, didn't I Clyde?" Marion said, as she made her way past the oval table that overfilled the dining room. "I haven't learned the lesson of abnegation. Don't suppose I ever will."

Marion had a cane in her hand. Cecily was standing behind her grandmother, and there was some resemblance between the two, though Marion was handsome as she always had been and Cecily never would be.

"Thank you for coming over, dear," Marion was saying to the girl, dismissing her.

"Are you sure you'll be all right?"

"Danny's coming first thing in the morning to do the laundry and put out the garbage. I can manage quite well on my own till then. And I have Clyde here. Perhaps the two of us will get a little drunk and say things we shouldn't."

The girl looked at Clyde, as if hoping for reassurance that this wouldn't happen. Clyde just smiled at her.

Once she was out the door, Marion, who had taken her place in one of the upholstered chairs, sitting very upright as she always did, turned to him.

"Who is this man, Clyde?"

"What man?"

"The one who comes here, the skulker."

"I don't know about this Marion. You'll have to explain."

"Danny has instructions not to let him in again. But Danny's just a little fellow, not very strong."

Clyde looked at her, the eyes that were fixed on him, shining, intense, perhaps too much so. He wondered if this was some kind of senile delusion, men coming to persecute her. It troubled him to imagine that her brain had begun to feed on itself, the outside world irrelevant and lost.

"He had some story about a body in the trunk of a car. And he asks me about you."

"Start at the beginning, Marion. When did this happen?"

"You think I've lost my marbles, don't you Clyde?"

"What you're telling me isn't very clear."

"I suppose I sound like a madwoman. I didn't dare tell Cecily because I knew she'd think I was insane, but I thought I could tell you."

"When did this happen?"

"I *am* a little vague about time, Clyde. I know I'm getting very old, but whatever you may think I am not demented, not quite yet. I thought I could trust you to know that."

"You can, but you have to tell me all the details."

She stared at him, angrily, as if she might take up the cane and thrash him with it. Took a deep breath, sighed it slowly outward.

"This man came to the door. Danny didn't let him in at first, left him on the porch and came and told me his name. It meant nothing to me, but I said I was willing to speak to him. He sat there, in that chair, where you are, and at first he asked questions about James, not altogether unreasonable questions, but I told him I didn't catch his drift, what he was after. He said something about newspapers. I told him that James was long dead and the newspapers had no business with him now. He was not unpleasant, and when I said I was tired, he left. He asked about you. I think it was that day he asked about you."

"What did he look like?"

"Quite an ugly man, really. Face like raw beefsteak. Big teeth."

"Tom McKay. Would that be the name?"

Marion looked at him, suspiciously now.

"So you do know him."

"I know a man named Tom McKay who looks like that. He's not a friend, in fact he probably came looking for information that might be damaging to me."

"Why would he want that?"

"It involves a young woman."

She was quietly thumping the cane against the floor, slow repeated beats like a drummer keeping the rhythm of a dance.

"What men won't do for that. Well I'm past it all now."

"You said he came more than once."

"He came in the evening the second time. Danny wasn't here. No one was here. I was a fool to let him in. He'd been drinking, I suspect, and he was determined to discover whatever secrets he was hoping to dig up. A few years ago, I would have had him out of the house in no time at all, but I've lost that firmness, I find. Odd how these things depart. However I had still the sense to keep my lip buttoned. I gave him my name, rank, and serial number. Surprised I remembered it after all these years, but he seemed to miss the point. When he found I wouldn't answer his questions, he tried to frighten me."

"How did he do that?"

"I told you."

"Tell me again."

"A story about a body found in the trunk of a car. He said it was a friend of yours, and you must know something about it."

"Then what happened."

"I refused to say a word. He tried all kinds of tricks to rile me up, but I had made up my mind. Even if he raised his hand against me, I decided, I would not speak one word. Name, rank, and serial number. Nothing more."

"What happened?"

"He went away."

"Did he come again?"

"No, unless he turned up and Danny got rid of him. I told Danny I didn't want to see anyone who isn't family or a known friend. No salesmen, no charitable soliciting. We have raised the drawbridge."

"That's very wise."

"Now that I've told you all my troubles, would you like a drink? Robert brings me a bottle of whisky from time to time."

"I don't think so."

Name, rank, and serial number. He could imagine Marion reciting them. She was a fierce old woman.

"If this man comes back again, Marion, call the police. Don't open the door to him. He won't harm you in any bodily way, I'm certain of that. He's a well-known journalist with a reputation to consider. His only interest in you is that he wants to do me harm, and he's looking for stories that might be damaging. So it was very good of you to say nothing. I'm grateful. Now I'm going to call Robert, tell him the story, and have him phone the police and get them to warn him off. I could call, but it will be more effective coming from Robert. I'm sorry I appeared to distrust you at first, but I didn't understand."

"Old women do have delusions about threatening men, I suppose."

"When I phone Robert, do you want me to ask him to send one of the girls over to spend the night?"

"No. I think Cecily would faint if she had to confront the man."

"I doubt it. She reminds me of you a little."

"I was never that plain."

"No, I'm sure you weren't."

Clyde found the telephone and called Robert Haverman. Without going into too much detail about his connections with Tom McKay, he gave him the name of a reliable police inspector and suggested that he call and lodge a complaint. Use the Senator's name, he said. The policeman was old enough to remember the Senator. He also suggested that he follow up the call with a short note to McKay reporting that he had made the call and demanding that he keep away from Marion.

"Is he a dangerous man?" the serious voice on the other end of the phone said.

"All journalists are dangerous men," Clyde said. "He wants to do me harm, and he would not hesitate to involve anyone else's reputation."

"But Marion doesn't have anything to hide," he said.

"Of course she doesn't."

Clyde hung up the phone. He told Marion he'd be back on the weekend, walked from her house to Elgin street, flagged a cab, and gave him Danny's address. The pink flamingo stood guard on the front lawn. Danny had furnished the house, but it still looked a little as if he might be camping out, a leather recliner, a nondescript stuffed chair, a coffee table with newspapers piled on it, a couple of pin-ups of muscular young men tacked to the walls. Danny settled in the recliner. A glass of wine sat on the floor beside him.

"Surprised to see you drinking wine, Danny. Something left over from Sunday mass?"

"Nothing but the best, Clyde. I've come up in the world."

"I've just been talking to Marion."

"I told her you promised."

"She told me about Tom McKay coming round."

"I thought she would."

"Maybe you should stay through the evening for the next while."

"Cecily was there when I left. She seemed fine."

"Can I have a glass of that wine?"

"A little shaky?"

"Maybe."

Danny went to the kitchen and came back with a glass of wine.

"This McKay person is out to ditch some dirt, do I have that right?"

"I went off with his girlfriend. I guess he holds a grudge."

"I guess he does."

"He had some story about a body in a trunk?"

"I suppose he heard about your old friend Gerald."

"Jelly? What about him?"

"Clydie, you didn't hear? You read all the papers, don't you?"

"I guess I didn't read the right one."

"Well they found Mr Gerald Wendorf in the trunk of a car parked down by the bay in Hamilton, and Mr Gerald Wendorf was very dead from being shot."

"When was that?"

"A couple of weeks ago."

So Tom McKay had added things up and assumed that Clyde must have some connection with Jelly Wendorf, or he did some phoning around and picked up an old rumour. Well he could chase Jelly's corpse forever, and there was no harm to Clyde in it, but one thing could lead to another. He could only trust that the warning from Robert Haverman would keep him away from Marion. He could go around and see McKay, but from what Clyde had observed of the man, he suspected that a confrontation with Clyde would only excite and encourage him. It was probably what he was looking for.

Name, rank, and serial number.

"When did Marion start using a cane?"

"A few months ago. The doctor wants to operate on her hip, but they're afraid her heart isn't strong enough."

"I didn't know she had a bad heart."

"Neither did she. I guess she hadn't been to a doctor for years until she started in with that hip, and I said she better see someone, and when she wouldn't I told Elaine, and we got her to make an appointment."

"And he told her she had a bad hip and a bad heart."

"I know, Clydie, I should never have bothered her about it. I should have just got her a cane. Once you start doctoring, there's no end of it. "

"Well, there's one end of it."

"Don't talk about it. I hate it, sickness and death. She wants me to go to a doctor, says I'm too thin, but I'm not ready for it. I just want to wake up one morning and find I've gone in the night."

"How do you suppose you'll wake up if you died in the night?"

"In heaven, Clydie, in heaven. I go to mass, you know. I even confess sometimes."

"I'll bet they find that exciting."

"Don't be mean."

They sat in silence for a while. Clyde studied the hairless, muscular torso of one of the young men on the wall.

"So tell me again, what happens to my house if Marion dies."

"Nothing. You keep it as long as you live."

"They can't take it away from me."

"That's right. You have a life interest in it."

"And what happens when I die?"

"It goes back to the estate."

"Who's that?"

"Elaine and Anne and the university."

"They don't really need it, do they?"

"When you're dead you won't need it either."

"Still and all," he said, "Marion once said she'd fix it for me to inherit it properly."

The telephone rang, and Danny went into the kitchen to answer it. The conversation was short. Danny came back in the room, sat down on the recliner, lifted his crippled leg with one hand.

"You'll never guess who that was."

"Who?"

"That McKay person."

"What did he want?"

"Said he wanted to interview me. For a story he's working on."

Clyde looked at Danny, who met his look. Small, hooded eyes. Clyde didn't know what he might be thinking.

"I told him I was busy right now."

"So he'll call again."

"And I'll tell him what a wonderful person you are, Clydie."

Clyde drank up.

"Thanks for the wine, Danny."

"Say hello to Hazel when you're talking to her."

"I'm going down next week."

"Don't forget to invite her for dinner. I do a nice tuna casserole."

A few months later, a weekend in August: Clyde had driven to his new cabin with a canoe he'd just bought, things he planned to leave there, a few books, a radio, the cigar box of old photos. Jane was out of town on business. The cabin gave him a place to hide out; he liked being alone there in the woods. Clyde had planned to stay at the cottage all weekend, go back to town Monday, but Perry called to say that a young woman they were interviewing as a possible replacement for one of their consultants had asked to move up her appointment to an earlier hour. Perry had to drive his daughter Lucie to a day camp, and he wanted Clyde to be there to meet the woman. So Clyde packed up. When he got back to his apartment, he found a message from Danny telling him that Marion was in hospital.

In the morning, he met with the young woman, who looked starved and eager, curiously pouted lips, fishy, or as if perpetually ready to kiss. Clyde gave her coffee and began to ask her a few questions. She was very nervous, so he kept the questions simple. Her hand shook as she lifted the mug of coffee to her lips.

"You can relax, you know. I haven't bitten a young woman for weeks."

She turned her head, eyes flared, as if prepared to consider that as an insult or some kind of sexual innuendo. Maybe it was; he hadn't thought so. It was possible that he was out of touch, no longer knew what might be treated as amusing. It was a relief to both of them when Perry came in the door. The young woman leapt to her feet as if she might hurl herself into his arms, but she only put out her hand to have it shaken.

"Sorry to be late," he said. "Parenting duties."

They went through the interview, laboriously enough, the young woman almost as nervous with Perry as she was with Clyde. They thanked her, shook her hand, and she left the office.

"I don't think so," Perry said when she was gone.

"No, not that one. One wonders what she'll do with her life."

"Take a lot of Valium."

"How's Yvette?"

She was in her forties now, pregnant, and Perry worried that she was too old to be having another child.

"She's fine. Just don't ask about me."

"What about you?"

"Blood pressure." He pointed to the ceiling.

"Too high?"

"That's what they say."

"What do you do about it?"

"They'll try again in a couple of weeks. If it stays up, they'll put me on medication. I'm supposed to relax, take things easier, get more exercise."

"Want to take the afternoon off to play golf?"

"I have to pick up Lucie at the day camp."

"Tomorrow."

"How about you? How's your blood pressure?"

"Feels OK to me."

"You don't go to the doctor every year for a checkup?"

"You go to a doctor, they find things wrong with you, and you end up dying of them. Marion went to a doctor, and now she's in the hospital."

"I'm younger than you. Why am I the one with high blood pressure?"

"So do what the doctor tells you. Relax."

Perry nodded. "What were the figures like for last month?" he said.

"It's summer. Nothing happens. We broke even, well close to it, broke even if you ignore depreciation on the office equipment."

"Do we ignore depreciation?"

"This month we do. Let me know what time you want to go out tomorrow. I'll be glad to play with somebody I can beat. I was in a foursome last week with some young guy who was driving the ball two hundred and seventy five yards. Patted me on the back at the end."

Perry wasn't really listening. Clyde went to his own office and sat down with the draft of a lobbying campaign. He didn't think it was very good. In the evening, he thought, he'd visit Marion.

When he did, she was surrounded by family, and he wasn't sure she recognized him. He'd done his duty. After a few days in the hospital, she was moved to a nursing home, and over the months there was a long slow depletion. Danny called once to say that she'd asked for Clyde, but when he got there, driving through a January snowstorm, she had lapsed into vagueness and silence. If she had more secrets to tell him, they had slipped her mind.

A couple of months later she died, and the funeral, held at the Anglican cathedral, had a choir, organ, a string quartet playing as the mourners gathered. Clyde recalled the Senator's short bare ceremony. Elaine, he suspected, had chosen the more splendid, decorative approach. What was the point of being high church if you didn't have all the trimmings? Clyde knew he'd be called on in the next days and weeks to complete the winding up of the Senator's estate. He'd already received a call from the university, a dean trying not to appear crass, but wanting to know what they'd be getting. He suggested they be patient.

Clyde offered Danny a ride home from the cemetery. He parked in a lot near Danny's house and a short walk from a jeweller who was repairing Clyde's old wristwatch and had phoned to say it was ready. Danny turned and looked at him as he took out the keys.

"Marion always said you'd fix it about the house."

"Fix what?"

"So I don't have to give it back."

"You don't have to give it back. The house is yours, for the rest of your life."

"She said you'd know how to make it mine. She said she'd give it to me."

"The Senator's estate bought the house, Danny. It wasn't Marion's to give or not give."

"The Senator's estate is you, Clyde. I may be just a stupid little queer, but I'm not so stupid that I don't know that. They do what you tell them."

"There are laws. What happens is what the Senator said in his will."

"Who's going to know the difference."

"Who's going to know the difference when you're dead?"

"Why can't I make a will? Why can't it be my estate?"

"Because it doesn't work that way."

"You don't want it to work Clyde. The smart rich people like you do what they want, and the poor stupid little queers like me are left sucking hind tit. I suppose you want me to go back to giving blow jobs in the bus terminal."

"Nobody's talking about the bus terminal. The house is yours till you die."

"I looked after her. I talked to her and made her food. I was her only friend."

"Danny, they're grateful. There's a pension. You're not going to be in want."

Danny was getting out of the car. Clyde opened his door, stood up. His back was stiff.

"It's you who won't do it. Marion promised me. More than once."

"Then she didn't know what she was saying."

"Oh yes she did. She knew what she was saying. And she said a lot of things, Clyde Bryanton, that you wouldn't want me to repeat to the butcher boy."

"Don't threaten me, Danny."

"Why not?"

"Just don't."

"You wouldn't want to know all the things Marion told me."

"Marion was old and confused."

Danny had turned to walk away, looked back, screaming.

"Oh, of course she was. I'm a stupid little faggot and Marion was a crazy old woman, and you're the only one who can wipe his ass without getting his finger in the shit."

"That's enough Danny, goddamit. Just let it go." Clyde found he was shouting too.

"You're so perfect, Clydie. Well you can go fuck yourself. I want that house before I die, and she promised it. And you better fix it."

Clyde turned and walked away, fast, and kept walking. It was nearly closing by the time he got to the jewellers to pick up his watch. Back to the office, there was a pile of messages, one of them asking him to phone Jane at her apartment. It was too late to answer most of the others, and he didn't phone Jane until he got back to his own place. He was tempted to ignore her call and get quietly and thoroughly drunk, meet up with all the ghosts that attended him. But he dialled her number.

"How was the funeral?"

"Very formal. High church. Little boys hooting in the choir."

"I'm making fish soup," she said, "not exactly bouillabaise, but it looks OK and there's enough for two. You want to come over?"

Clyde agreed. When he arrived she was wearing an old-fashioned frilly apron over the track suit she wore to the gym.

"I know," she said, as he looked at the outfit, "it's ridiculous."

One of the photographs in his unopened, perhaps unopenable cigar box out at the cabin, was a discreetly posed nude of Jane at eighteen taken by a middle-aged professional photographer in his private studio. Brave girl she'd been. Still was.

Jane concentrated on stirring the soup, dropping in a handful of bread crumbs to thicken it. It smelled good. Clyde knew where she kept dishes, and he set the table, poured himself a glass of white wine from the bottle that stood open on the counter. Jane served the soup with thick slices of French bread, and they ate heartily.

"I started lifting weights today," she said.

"Why?"

"I think my arms look spindly and weak."

Jane wiped her bowl with a crust, ate the bread and took a drink from her wine glass.

"I've been thinking about a house," she said.
"The market's way down."
"To live in."
"You tired of the apartment?"
"It seems like time for something more permanent."
"Have you found someplace?"
"I haven't really started looking yet. I thought I'd talk to you first."
"You don't need my advice."
"I wasn't thinking of advice."

It had been a long day, Marion buried, Danny screeching at him. Clyde waited, didn't speak. He knew now what was coming, and he wondered what he was going to say. He wished this had happened tomorrow or next week. *You're so perfect, Clydie. Well you can go fuck yourself.* Jane drank a little more wine.

"Are you going to be chivalrous, or do I have to ask?"

He looked at her, so wide-blue-eyed, the tiny blonde hairs that grew in front of the ear, the delicate hollow of the cheek.

"You're suggesting we should live together," he said.

"I was hoping you'd suggest it."

Clyde didn't want to have this conversation. He was happy with things the way they were, but he knew he wasn't allowed to say that. He wished there was some way he could change the subject, lead her to bed, make love, laugh, and then go home. There are no rules. There is always another secret. If he said no to Jane now, it would be the beginning of the end, or so he suspected. He looked at her again, the soft flesh at the throat, the mole on her neck below the ear.

"Maybe I should think about it?" he said.

"That's an answer, Clyde."

"Is it?"

"Yes. If you have to think about it, it means you don't want to do it. This can't be a brand new idea to you, can it?"

"Why not?"

"Because you're not stupid."

"I wouldn't count on that."

"Oh cut it out. This is a decision. Yes or no. There's no place for cute little jokes."

"You're right. It comes down to something simple. I like having a place to go home to. I need a place of my own."

"Fuck and run."

"Put it that way if you like. I don't think that sums it up, by any means."

"I'm being unfair. So what? I offer to live with you, and you turn me down. It doesn't make me very happy."

Clyde sipped the wine, unable to think quite what else to do.

"I guess I know what your response would be if I said I wanted a kid."

A cold chill. That's what his response would be. Clifford and his girlfriend were talking about marriage. He could be a grandfather.

"Maybe I should go," he said.

"Take me to bed first," she said. "If that's all you're good for, I might as well get some while you're here."

In the event, he wasn't much good for that either, so he dressed and left, not sure whether the whole thing was at an end. By the fall Jane had taken a job with International Trade. The job was in Vancouver, and this time when they said goodbye, they knew it was finished between them. He dreamed about her, regretted the loss, called Vancouver in the middle of the night once or twice, but gradually he learned to be alone again.

Then suddenly it was a bright day in June, and Clyde stood in a small crowd under a maple tree in a backyard in Kingston to celebrate Clifford's marriage. A few feet away Noreen was leaning toward the man who was with her. Garth, his name was, and when Clyde was introduced, he found his hand being gently shaken by one that was bigger, stronger, more callused.

"Garth came to dig up the septic tank, and he just stayed," Noreen said. Garth said nothing much, smiled. He had thick hair, light brown shading into white, and beside Noreen, who was thinner than ever, elegant in a black pantsuit but the neck and face beginning to look a little stringy, a hint of crepe in the flesh under her chin, he looked huge and solid. Clyde was getting softer with age, Noreen getting harder.

A clergyman, some connection of Denise's family, married the two young people. They stood for the ceremony in temporary arbour of white ribbons set up in a corner of the yard, just in front of a bird bath and a bush covered with blossoms. Clifford's best man was someone he'd known in university, a man Clyde had never met before, Nathanael his name was, and he wore his hair shaved almost to the skull. Like so many young men these days, he did something with computers; you were never told just what, too old and stupid to understand. Clifford wore a dark suit that Clyde hadn't seen before, and with his swimmer's build, his hair cut short, he looked good. Denise wore a white gown with a lot of fabric sculpted around the shoulders and bust and hips. Clyde didn't think it was flattering to her, but she had presumably chosen it herself.

"What do you think of the wedding gown?" Noreen whispered to him just after the ceremony ended.

Clyde shrugged diplomatically.

"She looks like the Great White Whale waiting to be harpooned."

"Be good," Clyde said.

"I am being good, Joe. I didn't say it to anyone but you."

Clyde's mother was talking intently to Clifford and Denise, tiny and frail beside those two, so tall and young and full of health. She and Clyde had driven down from Ottawa this morning, had hotel rooms for tonight. A young man passed by with a tray of champagne, and Clyde took another glass. He saw Alan Simmons, Noreen's father, staring at Hazel as she chatted with her grandson. Alan looked alert, but behind the shining eyes he was addled. The evil chemistry of Alzheimer's had taken him away, and when Clyde spoke to him he was greeted with a smile, a nod, a friendly noise in the throat, but it was clear that the man had no idea who he was. His son John stood close beside him and held his hand, to reassure him and stop him from wandering off.

Clyde's mother made her way back across the smooth, trimmed lawn.

"What a handsome boy," she said.

"They seem fond of each other."

"She's very tall."

"Yes."

"Clifford and his Amazon," she said. "Did you know they're planning to live in the country and raise horses?"

"They didn't tell me."

"What is that you're drinking?"

"Champagne. Shall I get you some?"

"I could hold it in my hand, but I'm getting more allergic to alcohol. It makes me all buzzy and flushed."

"When did you decide that?"

"The last time Peggy gave me a glass of wine, and I tried to drink it."

Clifford and Denise were talking to Alan Simmons. He was smiling, and when Clifford put out his hand to shake, the man took it, but

John still held firmly to the other, the way you held the hand of a child crossing a busy street: all of life was perilous, incomprehensible fast traffic for the man now. What did he know of his own dementia? Did he see the man he once was vanishing into the irreparable reaches of incoherence? Did he long for the return of meaning? Clyde's mother read his mind.

"If that happens to me, Clyde, take me out and shoot me."

"It won't happen to you."

"Who's to know?"

Denise's father, Fred Symchuk, appeared beside them.

"Thank God for the weather," he said. "Denise and her mother wanted to have the ceremony out here, but all I could think was that it would rain, and there wouldn't be room for everyone in the house."

"It's a beautiful garden," Hazel Bryanton said.

"Cathleen's pride and joy."

Near where they stood was a bed of brilliant red poppies interspersed with dark blue bachelor's buttons, A bush of white roses was in bloom behind them. A cloud went over the sun, and everything was darkened for a moment, but then the sunlight came back.

"Do you suppose, Clyde," Fred Symchuk was saying, "that I should bring you in for a seminar with one of my classes? A voice from the real world."

"Ottawa isn't the real world, Fred. You know that."

The man taught something in the school of business. Clyde didn't know what.

"We do case studies, but it's pretty abstract."

"Once you've said 'You have to fly by the seat of your pants,' what is there left to say."

"But property. You know about property."

"I knew more when I was twenty-five."

"You've chosen the wrong man," Hazel said. "You don't get much out of Clyde, Mr Symchuk. I'm his mother, and he never tells me anything."

"Your parents are the last people you tell," Fred Symchuk said, and they all laughed. Clyde was looking at Clifford who had his arm around Denise as they talked to a group of people their own age. His son. He knew him and didn't know him at all. Fred Symchuk was leading Clyde's mother over to examine a bed of roses. As she walked away, he heard the voices of two young women as they walked past him.

"Our day will come, sweetie," one of them said. She had fine, sculpted features, dark hair, dark blue eyes.

"Do you think so?" the other said. She was taller and heavier, wearing an elegant pantsuit of pale silk.

"Things are changing."

"I'd like to get married."

"We will."

Perhaps it would come in his lifetime, certainly in theirs. Clyde found Angela Simmons standing in front of him. The red extruded eyes, as if someone was choking her to death, the skirt too tight and too short for a woman of whatever age she was.

"So," she said, "Clyde Bryanton. I hear your little popsie took off."

Clyde nodded.

"I guess they all do, sooner or later," he said.

"Nice wedding," she said. "Did you hear about Jerome?"

"No." He could hardly remember her son.

"He got married last fall. Nothing like this. I don't know why the silly girl wouldn't have an abortion. Come to that, I don't know why he got her pregnant. I thought we were past all that now. The modern world where sex is no longer a problem."

"Maybe it will always be a problem," he said, though he wasn't sure he believed any such thing.

"I married too young," she said. "Now Jerome has married too young."

"Were you pregnant?"

"Pregnant? I was a virgin, poor dumb little bunny."

She turned and walked away, her hips tilting awkwardly as her high heels caught in the earth of the lawn. Clyde stared after her, saw her husband, still holding the hand of his demented father, such sadness to it all, and just as he was thinking about that, he saw another brother-in-law, Michael Oster, at his elbow, hair a little thinner, the big shoulders slightly hunched.

"You talk to Alan?" he said.

"I tried."

"Do you think he recognizes us at all, some vague recall of faces he used to know?"

"I don't think so."

"I saw him staring at Noreen as if there was a glimmer. He knew she was someone he should remember. She was always his favourite."

"Was she?"
"Everyone in the family thought so."
"He was polite to me, but I thought I was resented. That would explain it."
"Martha's always been jealous of her. She was older, had to be responsible. Noreen was the baby, could get away with anything."
"I didn't have to deal with all that."
"The only son."
"Just me and Hazel."
"You missed your father."
"I thought I did. But I didn't know him, so I didn't know what to miss."
"What did he work at, before the army?"
"I guess he was unemployed for a while. Then he got a job handling freight for the railway. When he joined the army, his young brother took over the job."
"My parents were depression generation. Hell of a time."
"We were lucky."
"You like this girl he's marrying, young Clifford?"
"Sure. They seem to get along well."
"Can I ask you an indiscreet question?"
"Why not?"
"Did you ever get it on with Angela?"
"No, why?"
"She says you did. I didn't believe it."
"You were right."
"I think it's a relief for John to have his father like that. An excuse to escape from that crazy woman."

He smiled at Clyde and crossed the lawn to where his own formidable wife was bent toward a tall old man who was one of Denise's relatives, listening to him and nodding in agreement. Clyde picked another glass of champagne off a passing tray, looked around trying to calculate his own mood, the amount of alcohol in his system, to make sure he stopped before he started to feel clever. Clifford came to where Clyde was standing and put out his hand. Clyde, a little surprised, shook it.
"Thanks," Clifford said.
"For what?"
"I don't know. Whatever. Teaching me to play golf."
"You're very welcome, Clifford. I hope you make each other happy."

"I don't think Mom likes her much."

"The girl's stealing her son. No mother likes it. She'll get over it."

"You ever hear from Jane?"

"No."

"How come Perry isn't here?"

"The baby's sick. Gets sick a lot, I don't know why."

"Diplomatic sickness?"

"No. Some breathing problem. Gets a cold, it turns into asthma. Perry and Yvette are writing you a letter, he said, to send it with the present. Michael was asking me if I thought your grandfather recognizes any of us now."

"I used to think he knew me, but not anymore."

"And which of us is going to be chosen next?"

"Grandma Simmons is waving at me."

"Go do your duty."

It was growing late in the afternoon, the light was changing, and when Clyde looked up, he could see swallows flying rapidly through the air, hunting. He finished his champagne and went to where his mother was standing at the edge of the lawn. Denise had gone into the house to change, and Clifford came over to say goodbye to his grandmother. After the two of them left, Clyde drove his mother to the hotel on the waterfront where they were to stay. He had planned to have dinner with her there, but she insisted that she'd eaten enough at the reception. She would watch TV for a while then go to bed.

That evening, Clyde sat by the window of a bar on the top floor, looking our across the water, watching the lights reflected in the dark surface. He was lonely, and yet the loneliness was a kind of pleasure. His mother was, he supposed, asleep by now, two floors down, while Clifford and Denise were celebrating the promises they had made. Alan Simmons was being driven to Ottawa where sleep would come to him too. Was it possible that the deranged cells of his brain could still offer kind dreams?

When he drove his mother home to Brockton, he stayed for a couple of days, moved some furniture to the basement for her, and wondered as he did, when he'd begin to find such things beyond him. His golf clubs were in the trunk, and he drove down to the course where he'd spent so much time years before and played nine holes, joined up to make a threesome with a some American tourists who were passing through. He saw a married couple who looked familiar, but he could no longer put names to the faces. That night his mother invited Peggy Wilberforce over, and the three of them had dinner. His mother had sent him out to buy a bottle of wine, but she herself drank none of it. Peggy teased her a little about her drinking problem.

"You're right, Peggy," his mother had said. "I do have a problem with alcohol. One glass and I light up like a lamp."

And now it was the night before Danny's funeral, and as he lay alone in his cabin Clyde recalled that small, friendly dinner. He remembered so much, but could he make sense of it all? His mother had created a decent life for herself in the little house in Brockton. Up till now Clyde had done nothing to spoil it: a small achievement. He lay in bed and waited for the light to return, shivered with cold, even with extra covers piled on the bed, the wind loud in the trees of the hillside. In the summer when there were boats on the lake the cabin felt almost suburban. Now it was more like a lean-to hidden in the dark woods. Forest from here to the tree line, then tundra and ice the rest of the way to the pole.

He'd have to wake early in the morning to get to Ottawa in time, one stop to make on the way. The cold November night and the northwest wind made him feel more alone, as if he might die here, not to be found until spring. He lay solitary, what his mother had done for years, he supposed. The woman had such quiet force, what they used to call strength of character, but time was catching up with her. She was even ready to admit, now and then, that she felt a little tired.

It was early and still dark when Clyde left the cabin. The wind still blowing, and he could hear water slapping against the shore below him. He left the power turned on; Gordie Peters was coming to drain the pipes and the pump later in the week. Clyde took the extra key that was hung underneath the cottage. Didn't leave it there in the winters.

As he drove to town a few flakes of snow fell, vanished. The funeral was to be at eleven-thirty. He'd shower and dress before he met his mother at the airport.

First he would see Tom McKay. The man was a bit of a celebrity, as happened with some journalists who made everything they wrote personal, and it was well known that he always ate his breakfast in a diner not far from Parliament Hill. McKay wrote columns about the place, the sharp comments of his favourite waitress, condescending pieces of work, Clyde had always thought, and the waitress with her bits of folk wisdom was probably an invention, but the columns were popular.

They got quoted.

When Clyde walked into the diner, he saw the man sitting in a booth near the back, a plate of food in front of him. Clyde was glad to see that McKay was alone, though he'd decided that even if he wasn't, he'd interrupt. He walked back through the restaurant and sat down on the opposite side of the booth.

"Who invited you?"

Clyde didn't answer. He noticed that the skin at the ends of the man's mouth was cracked, sore-looking. The flushed skin of the face dimmed to a mauve pallor at the edges of the raw redness. A bit of egg clung to his lips, and he wiped it with a paper napkin.

"You got a letter," Clyde said.

"My readers write to me all the time."

"A letter from Danny O'Connell. He wrote to you, and then he did away with himself. He had cancer, they told him, and he didn't want to lie around waiting to go. He could be very determined, Danny."

"This would be your little fag friend."

"He was my friend. He was also a pain in the ass."

"You take it that way do you? Up the back."

"Cut the horseshit."

"None of my business how a man gets it off."

"Danny was mad at me. He had no right to be, but he was. A stupid business. What I want to say is that I don't know what Danny thought he knew about me or anybody else – maybe things he heard from a sick and muddled old woman – but whatever it was, either it's not true or I don't care."

The man thought about that.

"But you're still hoping I'll tell you what he said."

"You tell me, I deny it, so you can print it by saying I denied it. What do I get out of that? I've thought about it, and you can print whatever you want."

"You figure you've got nothing to lose."

"I've decided my secrets aren't worth telling."

"Not what I hear."

"You went around bullying an old woman hoping to get something on me. What did you find? Nothing."

"The man in the car trunk?"

"I ate in his restaurant."

"If there was nothing in the letter, you wouldn't be here."

"I could ignore it, wait and see if you had the guts to publish whatever Danny told you and then sue if it was lies, but that's not what I decided to do. I want to look you in the eye and say that I don't care what you do. I've been around the block a couple of times. I did what I did. Chances are I'll soon be a grandfather. I'm ready to take it easy, go south to play golf all winter."

"Hotshot golfer. But I beat you, didn't I?"

"Don't get above yourself. You beat me because I let you."

"So that's your story is it?"

"Yes. What's it matter? It was a long time ago."

McKay wiped his plate with a piece of toast, put it in his mouth, chewed a little and washed it down with coffee.

"So was she a terrific fuck?"

"Yes, of course."

"She was something special, that girl."

"But you couldn't get it up."

"She tell you that?"

"Not exactly."

Tom McKay drank more coffee. Clyde found himself imagining that Jane was on the other side of the restaurant, watching the two of them, laughing at them. She was in Vancouver, married to someone her own age.

"I'm going into hospital next week," Tom McKay said. "Bypass surgery. This was my last plate of bacon and eggs, and you spoiled it."

"Blame Danny. He sent you the letter. His funeral's this morning."

"Maybe you'll be lucky, and I'll die on the table."

"I wish you no evil. You haven't been listening to me. I've taken two days to think about it all, and I'll live with what happens."

"I could make this my last column. This is what life is like, two old farts fighting over a cute little piece of ass."

"I'm not fighting."

"You're here, sitting at my table, spoiling my breakfast."

"I'll leave. You can order another one. Eat it in peace."

Clyde stood up. He felt a little dizzy, hung onto the booth for half a second till his head cleared. He looked at the dark bulk of the man opposite him, turned and walked out. He'd drive to his apartment, make some toast and coffee, get cleaned up, then pick up his mother and they'd go and listen to the priests pray over the corpse.

Danny and the church: he was part of it or it was part of him. That first summer after Clyde and Hazel moved to Brockton, Danny would try to get Clyde to go into the church with him, told him about the confessional with Father Marcotte listening, waiting to hear every bad thing you'd done, how many Hail Marys you'd have to say. One day Danny got Clyde as far as the church door, urging him to come inside, daring him to enter the confessional. It gave Clyde a sick feeling, the strangeness and secrecy of the holy place, the priest waiting there, hidden. He had been to church with his grandmother once or twice when he was little, first all the singing and then being sent out to Sunday School. It was embarrassing to hear the loud unmusical voices, but there was no kneeling behind a curtain to babble your secrets to a listening ear. The thought of that gave him the same nauseating tingle as the dirty jokes he had to pretend to understand.

The summer sun was radiant that day as they stood at the church door, the cicadas loud, Danny urging him to open it, daring him, and at last Clyde drew the heavy door outward and looked, and there, caught in a beam of afternoon sunlight, was the naked man hanging on his cross. Clyde was shaken, he turned away from the injured, swooning figure. He closed his eyes, then opened them, ran as fast as he could, Danny behind him shouting.

Perhaps, you were born for it, religion, or you weren't. Danny, even when he was on the street, loved it all, and now the priests would have something to say for him, a form of words. Clyde, when his time came, would have to go down with nothing but some barren secular farewell. Clifford would do his best for him, he supposed. The wind chilled the skin of his face, and as he reached the car he remembered what he'd said to Tom McKay about retiring and going south for the winter. Maybe next year.